MOTHER-EATING

A DOCUMENTARY

JESS HAGEMANN

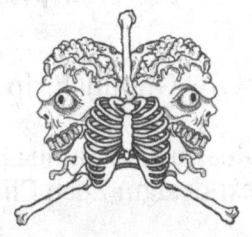

Ghoulish Books
San Antonio, Texas

Mother-Eating
Copyright © 2025 Jess Hagemann

First Edition

All Rights Reserved

ISBN: 978-1-963801-08-8

www.Ghoulish.rip

Cover illustration: James Hutton
Cover text design: Zach Chapman

ADVANCE PRAISE FOR MOTHER-EATING

"*Mother-Eating* reimagines the doomed decadence of Marie Antoinette in the world of contemporary politics, child exploitation, and religious zealotry. Wildly original and unforgettable, this book brings history to screaming, bleeding life."

—Lindsay King-Miller,
author of *This Is My Body*

"With *Mother-Eating*, Jess Hagemann has made herself a blade, and you, reader, are meat. Drop everything, and deliver yourself into these pages."

—Chris Panatier,
author of *The Redemption of Morgan Bright*

"*Mother-Eating* gleefully penetrates and butchers all you thought was possible in fiction. It is a literary impalement. Perverted, shocking, and unprecedented. Jess Hagemann is one of the most singular and distinct voices I've encountered since first reading authors like William S. Burroughs and Georges Bataille. There is no literary equivalent to this raw, uncompromising masterpiece. It truly exists in its own superior class."

—Eric LaRocca,
author of *Things Have Gotten Worse Since We Last Spoke*

"I am completely broken after reading [*Mother-Eating*]. Jess Hagemann pulls no punches. There's so much angry honesty in these pages, it's frightening. This story is filled with false religion, jealousy, the plight of women, cults and how evil that mentality can become. This book just proves to me nothing good ever comes from joining a cult."

—Marguerite Turley, bookseller

"Jess Hagemann has crafted a compelling, harrowing, nasty story that is very, very, very hard to put down! While only being familiar about the broad strokes of Marie Antoinette's life story, that didn't stop me from enjoying this grotesque, unique interpretation. I loved how this story is told by some of the many secondary and tertiary characters with their unreliability (and the ending really ties the format together in a really smart way). This is the latest release through Ghoulish Books, so you better believe it is addictive and has some impressively thought-out gore. Definitely more extreme than your standard horror novel, but it's better for it. You really feel the twists and turns viscerally."

—Lorry Jamison, cartoonist

"Hagemann writes clean and sharp. When [*Mother-Eating*] wants to be clinical, it is surgical. When it wants to sing, it does, briefly, before cutting the power. [...] Is it scary? Yes. Not jump-scare scary. System-scary. Warm-room scary. The kind where someone politely explains why pain is good for you while lining up the hardware. [...] This is a top-quartile standout that marries true-crime texture to literary bite, turns theology into a weapon, and leaves you suspicious of roses, fountains, and anyone who uses the word sacrament too casually. Bring a highlighter. Bring soap. Bring birds to look at when you are done."

—The Blog Without a Face

"Presented as a Documentary, the Tale of Mary Toni and those around her are laid out by Jess Hagemann like some great infernal Tapestry, full of lurid scenes and vibrant colors, yet delivering a sensation that hollows your gut and chills your heart. [...] *Mother-Eating* is a book that does not shy away, does not sugar-coat, and does not flinch. It's not a book that will leave you feeling good, but it will leave you feeling human, connected with yourself and those around you."

—Books for Decaying Millennials

"Inventive, intelligent, and violent, *Mother-Eating* will stick with you, inside you, and clean through you."

—Johnny Compton,
author of *The Spite House*

"Hagemann might be the best horror writer in America."

—Daniel Kraus,
author of *Whalefall* and *Angel Down*

Also by Jess Hagemann

Headcheese
Resurrection

for Pam
and her son, whom I love more than life

"For just as each of us has one body with many members, and these members do not all have the same function, so in Christ we, though many, form one body, and each member belongs to all the others."

—Romans 12:4-5

"Then an astonishing miracle-sign appeared in heaven. I saw a woman clothed with the brilliance of the sun, and the moon was under her feet. She was wearing on her head a victor's crown of twelve stars. She was pregnant and was crying out in labor pains, in the agony of giving birth."

—Revelation 12:1-2

THE FOLLOWING DRAMATIZATION has been reconstructed from security-camera footage, speed-trap videos, interviews with eyewitnesses, and the sworn accounts of former members of pseudo-religious sex cult Simon's Sorrow. They were variously collected between June 18, 1989 and August 8, 1989—when cult leader Louie Auguste was arrested for the torture and murder of software engineer Paul Greer—and again from February 3, 2003 to December 12, 2003, after an anonymous tip implicated Auguste in a missing person's case. In 1989, Auguste was released before he could be arraigned, but on January 18, 2005, and largely on the strength of the testimonies contained herein, Auguste was convicted of the deaths of nineteen Austin citizens, including two minors. For these crimes, he was executed on January 21, 2007—after which, those Sashes who could still be located brought this documentarian up to speed again.

AT 1:27 A.M. ON Sunday, June 11, 1989, forty-two-year-old Eileen DuBarry dissolved six doses of ketamine, a common horse tranquilizer, into twenty-nine-year-old Paul Greer's vodka-spiked energy drink while he was in the bathroom. After he returned, she led him by the hand to a darkened corner of the club, where she waited for Greer to pass out. Three male Sashes on the dance floor, disguised as club patrons, watched for the signal: the moment when Greer's knees crumpled and he folded, a meaty rag doll, into the smiling DuBarry's ready embrace. Until then, she kissed him, sloppy kisses that left wet trails across Greer's face and down his stubbly neck, an overlarge Adam's apple. She slipped a hand inside his jeans and gripped him, his almost-erection already going soft from the drugs, even as he moaned his desire into her ear, all bad breath and sweat beneath the pounding music, the pulsing lights. DuBarry held him and she held him, chanting promises of the pleasures that awaited them, and when finally his whole weight shifted onto her, Greer's drool-slick chin nestling in the soft dip of her collarbone, she caught him as deftly as honey catches flies, as honey mixed with borax attracts, then kills, the ant queen.

The men homed in from three directions, two of them shouldering Greer like a friend, the happy bachelor who'd had too much. They carried him between them, apologizing to those the third man asked to step out of their way. Near the door, the bouncer offered to call an ambulance. "Nah, man, we're good," the first one said. "He'll sleep it off," slapping Greer's back good-naturedly. "Thanks, though—and have a nice night." The bouncer assumed Greer's friends had him covered. DuBarry was nowhere to be found. No one would remember seeing the two of them together, though Greer, when he woke up, would think of her. He would wonder what happened to the woman in black, she of the spider limbs and funny tattoo, which hooked around her heart like a rope pulled taut to bind things, and that tightened and relaxed with every shallow breath. *Madame DuBarry*.

Laying the unconscious Greer across the back seat of their car, at 1:53 a.m. the men began the short drive through downtown, easily navigating Austin's one-way streets and avoiding the crowded, pedestrian-heavy Sixth Street. West of I-35, they turned north on Guadalupe, hung a hard left on MLK, and disappeared, at 2:04 a.m., down an alley off San Antonio Street. Sash number two drove slowly, obeying speed limits and stoplights, and signaled to indicate every turn. His twin brake lights were red eyes in the dark, the only witnesses to Paul Greer's abduction.

In a large, soundproofed basement, a group of adult men and women similarly dressed in black, all with matching rope tattoos inked on their middle-left chests, stood ready to receive their sleeping sacrifice. The three men, having carried Greer down the stairs, stripped his clothes, then bowed out, their duty done, as Eileen DuBarry reappeared among those assembled. She held a long rope—and, approaching Greer, began trussing him, wrists above head, knees bent and gathered against his chest fetus-style. He looked like an egg wearing a hat, the steeple points of his bound hands a tricorn.

Pulling a heavy chain down from the ceiling, DuBarry looped the knots at his wrists over the last link's thick hook. When she retracted it, Egg Greer rose into the air, both shoulders simultaneously dislocating with the weight of his own body. He did not protest, did not scream or wriggle or even hold deathly still, as though refraining from movement might stop all the hurting. Instead he spun slowly, a tire swing on a rope—yet solid, at present, in the middle.

Anxious to get started, the rest of the Sashes prepared the room, dimming overheads, lighting candles, turning the room hazy with incense. They chanted promises of the pleasures that awaited Paul Greer, and grew frenzied with the lather of the predator about to eat. As though heeding their own words, in twos and threes and fours they paired off, mouths finding nipples, assholes, other mouths. Sighs and grunts rose, a carnal incense, into the air, and then fingernails, razorblades, metal screws found skin, pierced membranes and linings, until the copper and dirt of blood and shit streaked faces, became a functional makeup, the mark of the sash. DuBarry, meanwhile, muscled the Judas cradle, a three-foot-tall wooden pyramid, into position beneath Greer's suspended body. Around 2:45 a.m., she lowered the chain again, slowly, adjusting the speed and angle of descent, so that his anus lined up perfectly with the pyramid's point. She locked the chain there, allowing fifty percent of his bodyweight to rest upon the Judas cradle—and waited for Greer to wake up. A man of his weight and age would take hours to process the ketamine, and their orgy was just beginning.

Eileen DuBarry felt a tapping on her leg, and looked down to see an initiate Sash at her feet, kneeling and smeared with the fluids of the others. Rolling her eyes, DuBarry obliged the unspoken plea. She spread her legs where she stood, baring herself beneath her skirt, and the Sash adhered at once to her pussy, eating as though he'd stick his whole head inside her, if she'd only deign to swallow his face with her sex. It was considered an honor to orally (or otherwise) amuse the madame, so the initiate kept it up until she came, uttering, as she did, only a polite little, "Ah." He couldn't have left, anyway; with her boot, she'd pinned his penis to the floor, bruising it, but not severing it—tonight, anyway.

Meanwhile, Greer's anus began to stretch over the pointed tip of the pyramid, gravity and his own weight forcing his sphincter open. Tiny cracks formed, tore, became fissures. Blood swarmed beneath the surface of Greer's sensitive skin, then emerged, bright beads, before unfurling in scarlet ribbons down the cradle's four flat sides. The blood acted like a lubricant, facilitating the device's deeper entrance inside Greer. It didn't move but a centimeter at a time—just enough to, over the course of three days, effectively impale him. Greer would regain consciousness, lose it again, regain it again, and so on, multiple times before then.

All activity ceased when the door opened and Louie Auguste, known as "King Louie" to his followers, materialized. He stood on the threshold, surveying through scented smoke that barely masked the tang of bodies, the messy scene, then stepped down into the room. He moved from group to group in perfect silence, as no one dared speak to him unless spoken to, making minor tweaks to the slant at which one Sash had been working a ribbed glass dildo into the pussy of his partner, while a second had his penis in her mouth, and encouraging the tongue of a female Sash deeper inside her lover's anus. "Let her know you're there," he said. "She wants to feel you wanting her, mining the truest parts of herself for the tastes, the textures, the ridges and folds that are hers alone. Worship her, as you would our Lord, for she has been created in God's own likeness, and what you do unto others, you do unto God."

He walked toward a fivesome, all of them frozen in a ring on hands and knees, their right or left hand buried to the wrist in the ass of the Sash in front of them. Approaching one of the males, a former sixth-grade teacher who'd joined them in the last few years, King Louie grabbed the Sash's erection and milked him, gently at first, and then faster and faster, his hand anointed and frictionless with the man's pre-cum. The only sounds in the room were the male Sash's rapid breathing, the rhythmic slap of King Louie's hand against his balls, and when the man climaxed, a yelp from the Sash in front of him as he bit, hard, into the flesh of her buttocks, stifling his own screams of pleasure. King Louie then withdrew a capped scalpel from his robes, and, unsheathing it, delicately carved the day's date into the Sash's otherwise unmarked lower back. In this way, he kept track of who he had been with and when, for it would have been unconscionable not to grant every member equal attention.

"Clean him up," King Louie told two older Sashes, who on the Outside had been married to each other, and both the man and the woman scuttled over to lick the Sash who had climaxed, as well as the hardwood floor beneath him, spotless. "Now the rest of them," King Louie ordered, and in unison, the five Sashes removed their fists from the ass of the person in front of them. The older male and female went from Sash to Sash, removing every trace of lube and shit from the Sashes' hands with their tongues.

Turning to Eileen DuBarry, King Louie asked, "How's he doing?" nodding at the still-unconscious Greer.

"Proceeding nicely, sir," DuBarry said.

"Let's ask him, shall we?" Dropping the scalpel back in its hidden pocket, King Louie now removed a vial of smelling salts. The whole room breathed in sharply, a muffled gasp, in anticipation. Just before he waved the vial under Greer's nose, King Louie looked back at DuBarry. "By the way, you're needed upstairs." Her shoulders sank in disappointment. Regardless of whether a Whore actually needed her, she was being sent away—punishment for disappointing King Louie in some way. Maybe he knew that she'd let an initiate, not yet vetted by King Louie himself, make her come. Or maybe Paul Greer was an imperfect sacrifice. She left proudly, her chest puffed, lest anyone know how embarrassed she really was.

Just after 4:00 a.m., King Louie brought Greer back to life where he hung, the salts shocking the young man's lungs and nasal passages into reflexively inhaling. He blinked and looked around the room, things coming into focus, in the flickering darkness, one by one. A number of naked people staring at him, plus the fully dressed man to his right. The rancid smell in the room. Throbbing, in his skull, and far away, a sharper pain that seemed important but inaccessible. King Louie drew a finger through Greer's blood dripping down the Judas cradle and held it up for Greer to see. "That's you, Paul," he said. "What do you think?"

"Where am I? What's happening?"

"You're at church, of course."

"Church?" Greer struggled to comprehend King Louie's words. "I don't go to church."

"Ah, but, Paul, everyone must go to church. How else can you atone for your sins?"

Greer's head lolled, dropping onto his knees, lashed tightly beneath his chin. He was still mired in a K-hole, the tranquilizer depressing his cognition. "I don't feel well," was all he said, before falling asleep again.

But King Louie wasn't done. Activating the automatic pulley system, he raised Egg Greer slightly higher into the air. Where Greer's blood had coagulated around the tip of the cradle, his skin stuck and ripped open afresh. King Louie then lowered the chain again, bringing Greer's anus squarely down on the point anew, advancing the wooden pyramid farther up into his rectum. Up and down, up and down, King Louie bounced Greer, and the young man's eyes fluttered open every time. He could not force himself awake, though, and soon King Louie tired of the game. He walked to the opposite side of the room, where he could still see Greer clearly, and took a seat on a built-in stone bench. He felt a sermon coming on.

"Brothers and sisters," King Louie addressed the motley Sashes, still in various states of undress. In unison, they sat down cross-legged to listen. "'The body is a holy thing—a temple of the Holy Spirit, who is in you, whom you have received from God.' That's Corinthians, which goes on to remind us that although the body is a gift, it comes at a price. You—me—we—were bought at a price. And that price was death."

Murmurs of assent, the only noise made consciously since King Louie had entered the room, echoed in surround-sound.

He continued: "When Simon Magus"—and at the

intonation of that sacred name, a litany of whispered "Lord Simon"s was uttered—"When Simon Magus asked Peter to give him the power to heal people, it was the body that Simon had in mind. He knew, as Matthew chapter six relates, that the body is 'more than clothes.' More than flesh-and-blood *parts* that, individually, are disposable"—here, King Louie gestured toward Egg Greer—"but together create a sanctuary for the divine."

King Louie paused and looked around the room. "Why, then, did Peter scorn Simon?"

"Peter was selfish," one Sash ventured. "He wanted the power all for himself."

"Or he was just confused," a female Sash said. "Maybe Peter had been taught to believe that money was evil. I know a lot of us have hang-ups around money."

"So, it was specifically because Simon Magus offered to pay Peter for the power, that Peter rebuked him?" King Louie asked.

"Sure," she said. "I mean, that's where the term 'simony' comes from."

"Money is a tool," King Louie corrected. "Like nuclear weapons or candy bars, money is not, by itself, 'bad.' Money builds the churches within which we honor God. Money greases the wheels of governing bodies, which we put in place to guide us and keep us safe. Money buys food—or, as we do at Simon's Sorrow, the means to grow our own food. Which brings us back to Corinthians. If the body is more than clothes, then tell me, brother"—King Louie addressed a tall man toward the back—"Tell me: Is not life more than food?"

"Yes, King Louie, it is."

"Then why do we eat?"

"We eat to sustain life."

"Why else?"

"We eat for the pleasure of it."

"Ah, yes, pleasure. Food makes you feel good, does it, brother?"

"Yes, sir."

"It fills your stomach, tickles your taste buds, comforts you when you're sad, perhaps."

"Yes, sir."

"Show me how much pleasure food gives you."

Obediently, the man crawled over to the group of women nearest him. He lay down on his back and the first one straddled his face. He moaned appreciatively into her pussy. After a minute, King Louie concluded, "So, food sustains the body. What else sustains it?"

"Deprivation," the woman sitting on her lover's face said. She stood, abandoning her pleasure to let the next woman in the group take her place.

"Indeed. That's why we fast, and meditate," King Louie agreed. "Anything else?"

"It's more than just deprivation," a female Sash on the left side of the room spoke up. "Sometimes it's pain that sustains the body."

"Ah. How so?"

She went to the woman now sitting on the male Sash's face, grabbed her nipples, and twisted. The woman shrieked: an exclamation of both pain and pleasure. She pulled the woman down by her nipples until her chest was flush with the floor, her pelvis still squashed against her partner's face, and retrieving a hammer and a long, thin nail from her utility belt, proceeded to nail one of the woman's nipples to the floor. She then straddled the male, who'd become hard while eating out woman number one and number two, and allowed him to penetrate her. Spinning on top of him, she lined up a second nail with his scrotum and nailed it to the floor. Now the man screamed, sounding like a saint in the throes of ecstasy.

"Through pain comes Restoration," the female Sash said. "We are restored to ourselves and to Christ. It's the real reason Peter had to punish Simon: not to disparage him, but to save him."

"What you're saying," King Louie reflected, "is that

when Simon Magus was struck down from the sky, he didn't fall."

"No, sir," the female Sash concurred. "He flew."

THE CHEF

We disposed of Paul Greer's body, once he'd expired, like all the others, tossing him into the well at the back of the property.

PART ONE
AGE OF REASON

MARIE ANTOINETTE, only daughter of Frank and Resa Habsburg and the one-time queen of pseudo-religious sex cult Simon's Sorrow, was born in 1965 on November 2—a date coinciding in many cultures with the Day of the Dead. For a child who would face more than her fair share of death, and later lose two of her own children—my younger sister and brother—it was a portentous omen. No one was thinking about that, though, when Mary Toni, all ten toes accounted for and the picture of perfect health, slipped quietly into the world. They were simply elated by her existence. At least her father was.

THE FAMILY PRACTITIONER

Of course I remember Mary Toni's birth. She was a miracle—the only child to make it after her parents had lost a dozen or more. I remember how the father, Frank, held her in the delivery room: close and high on his chest, where he could keep a tight grip on her while beaming into her face. And I remember how Resa held her: like she was glass, or something rarer, balanced on a precarious ledge. As though the slightest breeze or the losing of a single eyelash would send Mary Toni tumbling.

Too bad, too, because I've delivered a lot of babies, and right away I knew the kind that Mary Toni was. Peaceable, agreeable, the kind that fathers take to because they're not too much work. If Resa had only gotten some help, instead of regarding her newborn daughter like a liability, things might have been different. "Kids," she told me at one of

Mary Toni's pediatric checkups, "are like credit cards with no limits." She meant the obvious financial cost of raising children, but the emotional cost, too. How the number of things to worry about just kept racking up.

THE PRINCIPAL

Mary Toni herself drew her birth like this: In the picture, she arrived on a cloud. There was her father Frank, going up in a bucket to pluck her from the sky, while her mother Resa watched and waved from the grass below. Resa seemed to levitate, her feet not quite touching the ground, like she might fly up after her husband at any moment. All three of them—baby included—had stringy black hair and matching thick red smiles. No one wore shoes. No one, despite the lopsided sun, threw shadows.

Frank was an electrical linesman. He often went up in a bucket for work. Resa was a hospice nurse. She did not, to my knowledge, levitate. She did have an ungodly number of miscarriages, though, and I imagine I'd feel pretty damn empty after that, too. Empty enough to just float away.

THE NEIGHBOR

I didn't know about her history when they moved in. Frank and Resa were pregnant at the time, and having never had children myself, I was excited to welcome a family to the neighborhood. I waited until Resa and I had established a friendship—conversations over the fence while we both worked in the yard, leading to meals at each other's places—before I dared rest my hand on Resa's belly one day in parting. Even then it was unconscious, a sincere gesture of affection, but Resa's reaction was equally sincere, and one of horror. She pulled away from me almost violently, the smile dropping from her face and her eyes clouding over, an eclipsed sun.

THE NURSE

You'd think a hospice nurse would get it: the way a previously perfect human body can wake up one day betrayed. How an accidental paper cut, exposed to a subway handrail, can fester and turn gangrenous. It's nobody's fault; *things just happen sometimes*. And who wins—the cancer cells or the stem cells; the virulent bacteriophages or the beneficial macrophages—seems to depend simply on who wants it enough. Who *wants* to survive. Fifteen of Resa's children had not wanted it badly enough. They'd exited in a predictable, bio-hazardous succession into toilets, beds, and once, onto a patient's sheets, when she'd sat on the edge of Mrs. G's gurney to offer her a homemade Christmas cookie. After saying her goodbyes, Resa had stood up and promptly sat back down again, suddenly lightheaded. Mrs. G had seen the blood and assumed it was her own. Abscessed bedsores can burst like that. But no, it was fetus number eight, hardly past the stage of viability. Luckily, I'd shown up two minutes later to relieve Resa. I hadn't even known she was pregnant.

While Resa was far enough along that she could have heard a heartbeat with a transvaginal wand, she'd long ago stopped telling anyone about the babies, certain each was destined to die. Why they kept coming, or why she and Frank kept trying, subjecting themselves and the little heartbeats to all that heartbreak, I can't say. Except that Frank had wanted more than anything to be a father. He'd tracked Resa's cycle and taken her temperature and he'd made love to her again and again like she was still a whole woman, fecund and feral, and not the scraped-out shell she'd started avoiding in mirrors.

THE PRINCIPAL

So it was that Mary Toni was the only one who survived, the only one Resa managed to carry to term. For some women, maybe that would make them ultra-protective. The definition of a helicopter parent. Not Resa. It's like she was convinced that Mary Toni could fly right back out on the cloud she'd ridden in on at any moment, and what then was the point of getting attached? Better to be aloof, just in case.

As for Frank, you've never seen a more doting father. He came to every parent-teacher conference, every PTA meeting—as often as his job allowed, anyway. When he died in some sort of camping accident, part of Mary Toni, just six years old at the time, died with him. It'd be a nightmare for any child, of course, but for one as sensitive as her . . . I mean, we had to assign her a classroom aide for a few weeks, to make sure she stayed focused in school! Mary Toni's head was usually off with the fairies, anyway, but it was especially bad for a while. She may as well have been living on the cloud she'd drawn.

Basically, it was the armadillo all over again, but a thousand times worse. A thousand times more personal.

TEZ

Mary Toni attended Magnificat Catholic School from kindergarten through eighth grade, where she was well-liked by teachers and staff, less so by her peers. Every school has its bullies, and Isaac Crable in particular had it out for her, especially in those early years. It was she who found him kneeling over the creature by the shed.

MOTHER-EATING

THE CUSTODIAN

Armadillos. Seen them a thousand times before, dead on the side of the road. They look like little dinosaurs, their T-Rex arms too stubby for their bodies. When they're roadkill, those arms stick straight up in the air. They roll right over on their backs like cartoon versions of themselves, only they don't come back to life for the next episode. That's how I knew the one out by the shed wasn't dead yet. It still lay, breathing heavily, on its side. One beady, blind eye still gleamed wetly from between those baby-soft lashes. It was scared, and Isaac Crable wasn't scared enough. He was used to getting his way, and used to getting *away* with whatever mean prank he could think up next.

THE CLASSMATE

I mean, it was recognizable as an armadillo. No other rodent that I know of anyway has scales, right? Or can roll into a pinwheel like a pill bug. If anything, I'd have guessed that its armor was harder, but give a kid like Isaac Crable a screwdriver and not much is going to escape that wrath. He was crazy. Like, legit crazy. Not that a kid himself is ever totally to blame—it's nurture as much as nature, after all—but something inside Isaac was rotten. If you ever wanted proof positive that original sin is real, all you needed to do was look at Isaac. Some kids are born already a little bit evil, one foot firmly planted in hell. Still, he didn't deserve what happened to him. No kid does, even when the nature part is stronger, and that nature is corrupt.

THE FRIEND

I thought they were teeth. Knocked-out human teeth

scattered all over the pavement like confetti. He must have pried the armadillo's scales off one by one. Some of them were stained with blood.

TEZ

Mary Toni cried all afternoon. A rude introduction to death.

THE NURSE

Before Frank's death, Resa never cried. She talked about death like a fact of life, like something true that you could look up in a book. "Death can't be faked," she told me once, "or can only be faked for so long, because eventually it comes for real for everyone." And when it did, she said, when it came for me and for her, death would not be a Grim Reaper, would not be a caricature in a black hood, would not carry the empty threat of a scythe. No. It would be a sound. A breaking bone. Air rushing out of a punctured balloon. And maybe also the sound when sound stops, since after death there is no sound. The gasses of the body, later, sure—but no more talking. No more weeping.

Except for Jesus, who is, in the end, on the cross and always weeping.

TEZ

Then Frank died, and death became a lot more personal—for mother and daughter both.

THE PRINCIPAL

"You know he's not really gone, Mary Toni," Father McGillicuddy counseled her the week she returned to school. I pressed my ear against his office door to listen, mostly because she hadn't said a word since the funeral and I wanted to hear her speak.

"He's with God, in heaven, watching over you. Anytime you want to talk to him, you can. That's called prayer."

"Will my dad talk back to me?" Mary Toni wanted to know.

"Yes, but you might not recognize it right away. Instead of hearing him speak the way you used to, you might see a rainbow after a storm that reminds you of him. Or a butterfly might land on your knee and you'll know it's not really a butterfly. It's your father coming to say hello."

While these were perfectly nice sentiments, I wasn't sure they were appropriate. Kids get confused easily, even smart ones like Mary Toni. They interpret what adults tell them literally, and I couldn't have her thinking that the monarchs she'd raise in science class next year were somehow Frank. That wouldn't be right.

Just when I was about to knock on the door and interrupt, though, Mary Toni debunked his words herself. "My dad would never be a rainbow," she said. I could picture her shaking her small head violently. "He hated storms. A storm was supposed to kill him, and I was supposed to keep him safe."

Father McGillicuddy didn't know what to say to that, so that's when I opened the office door. "Mary Toni, it's time for lunch now. Your class is lined up in the hallway. Go join them."

She tucked her plaid uniform skirt demurely around her legs as she stood, pressing it flat, then shouldered her backpack. I touched the air behind her head as she scooted past me, like I might have petted her hair had she been my child, and watched her leave without a backward glance. If she can stay focused on what's in front of her, instead of mourning what she's lost, I thought, she'll be okay. Children are resilient like that.

I didn't realize, then, what a force of nature Resa could be—her own black storm when she didn't get her way, or dwelt too long on the poor hand she'd been dealt.

TEZ

Resa had many secrets—a developing penchant for opioids just one of a dozen that would have rendered her unrecognizable to her late husband. Her job as a hospice nurse afforded her easy access to the good stuff. The good stuff helped her escape from a life without Frank, a life comprised of disappointment after disappointment.

THE CLIENT

My mom had lymphoma. Tumors sucked on her bones like candy. We hired Resa to help take care of her. Everything was good until the day I walked in on Resa in bed, with my mom, pretending to be me. Her head was on Mom's paper-thin chest. Mom's bruised and creaky arms wrapped around her. Both of them lost in a Darvocet dream.

THE NURSE

I won't make excuses for what Resa did, or the embittered woman she became. I can only tell you who she used to be, before Frank's death, before the drugs. The Resa I knew was a beautiful, fitness-obsessed goddess. She wanted to be an actress, and 'settled' for nursing when she didn't immediately have the money to make it to Hollywood. It was supposed to be a short-term career. She never lost sight of her ultimate goal. As a result, she was super picky about what she ate, and worked out all of the time. "So I'll be ready," she said, "when Max Pécas calls." To Resa, *Daniella by Night* was the height of great film. Something dark and kind of sexy, with enough skin that she needed to look good. Then, of course, she'd met Frank, a handsome, hard-working gentleman who promised to support her dreams. At their wedding, we all heard him say, "Resa Mae, I'd follow you anywhere—if you'll have me." While I've no doubt he believed those words, marriage changes things anyhow. Where there was one, now there are two; and whether you mean it to or not, and even before Baby, a third thing is born. The couple as an entity. And it always supersedes the individuals.

TEZ

Resa's poor choices would eventually catch up with her. Until then, and ever after, Mary Toni fended for herself. While she waited for Resa to get home from work each night, she made sandwiches and watched the local weather. It'd been her favorite ritual with Frank. Now that he was gone, it let her still feel close to her father—a man taken way too soon. A man she might have killed.

I imagine her, a child alone, curled up in bed at night, pulling her beloved dog Mops closer to her chest. His soft tan fur smelling like wildflowers and fried food, the two most abundant natural resources in their East Austin backyard. A comforting smell. Mops wiggling a bit, resisting, then licking her hand with a warm pink tongue and settling. The thin strip of light under Mary Toni's bedroom door finally blinking out sometime after ten.

THE PSYCHOLOGIST

Any time a child's parent dies, we like to see the child for evaluation. It can be incredibly traumatic to lose the person who epitomized home, safety, security, *love*. In the sudden absence of that person and everything they represented, it's common for a child to feel abandoned, to feel unsafe, to feel—in some cases—like the parent's death was their fault. They assume the burden of absence. It festers inside them like a deep black hole.

Look at Mary Toni's drawings. She drew a literal hole, over and over, for years. That was during her waking hours. At night, she had dreams as vibrant as the holes were void. Dreams where she was chasing after Frank in a weather balloon. Where she was Toto riding in Almira Gulch's bike basket. In every one of them she was in motion, and every time it was against her will. The wind was blowing her back or the woman who would become the Wicked Witch was carrying her off, and these "forces," if we can call them that, they were big. Mother Nature, Acts of God, Authority Figures. Everyone telling Mary Toni what to do and how to be. If adults aren't careful, they can damage a kid that way. Make her doubt her own sense of right and wrong, her own intuition. Make her susceptible to extreme ideas. Lead her to cling to those who would lure away lost sheep.

What's most important for the child to understand is that the goal is not to "get over" what happened; they will never get over it. Rather, they have to move toward acceptance—an acceptance of how the loss of that parent changes that child forever.

THE PRINCIPAL

Mary Toni's drawings changed after Frank's death. From then on they always showed water, even when the assignment had nothing to do with water. She drew

Goldilocks holding Baby Bear's bowl of porridge on a pool raft in the middle of the sea, for Christ's sake, and if you asked her to explain any of it logically she couldn't. She'd simply pick up the black crayon and further darken the omnipresent hole on the surface of the water. At first I thought she'd finally figured out shadows, and maybe that angry black spot was the shadow cast by something in the sky. But there was nothing in the sky. No V-neck birds. No more lopsided suns. The sun itself had drowned.

Her art teacher encouraged these drawings. She had a Master of Science in Art Therapy and she said it was good for the girl. "Drawing her world allows Mary Toni to reassert control over something she had no say in. It's part of the healing process. She'll be okay."

That's how we ended up with Santa Claus on the water, Rudolph and Vixen splashing (or were they sinking?) beside him, and a Christmas nativity set not in Bethlehem but by all appearances on the Dead Sea. The infant Jesus rocked gently as his little wooden manger dipped and rose with each wave. Mother Mary looked buoyed up, not weighted down as one might expect, by her sodden headscarf and robes, but Joseph was nowhere to be seen. Where he might have crouched beside the manger to run the backs of his fingers against his newborn's milk-smelling forehead was instead a deep, dark hole, a familiar black slash cut into otherwise placid seas.

I didn't take them down because I believe in freedom of expression, but something about the drawings was disturbing. Kids and teachers alike did double-takes walking down the hallway, as if Mary Toni's black holes had actual sucking power. She'd always been bullied by her peers a bit, the way that sensitive children often are. But they pretty much left her alone once she started drawing the holes. The shadows that weren't really shadows.

THE ART TEACHER

Most children have a healthy fear of death. I teach elementary art and it's usually in their first- or second-grade years that kids tend to realize *Everything eventually dies*—a hard truth quickly followed by *Everyone I know will die*, and the hardest truth, for kids lucky enough to have them: *Someday my parents will die.* Funny enough, it doesn't often extend to *I will die.* But that makes sense, too, because the child ego is invincible. Ironically, at the age they're technically most vulnerable, they're also most resilient. They care more about each other and their families than themselves, because nothing in their largely protected lives, at least in wealthy Austin, has ever been threatened. And so it happens that the first threat to come along is not even a Bad Guy, but an Idea. A notion as intangible as the boogeyman, that becomes larger and more powerful the longer you dwell and the greater the number of unanswerable questions grows. Interestingly, art can be a really safe, accessible way to process those questions, those overwhelming emotions, and I'm privileged as an elementary art teacher to be a part of it, to facilitate that exploration. So we take grave rubbings when the students do their Civil War unit in Social Studies and we decorate masks at Halloween. And we talk about these symbols of death and transition as ways to pay homage, and even reanimate for a time, people from the past or characters from their favorite movies or TV shows, who effectively die with the close of a scene, or a season, or the credits, and how we can in turn carry them with us always.

TEZ

The art teacher's reassurances notwithstanding, the principal was concerned. She called Resa in for a meeting.

THE PRINCIPAL

"How's she doing at home?" I asked the distracted mother. Resa picked at her nails and wouldn't make eye contact.

"She's fine," she said. "What do you expect? She's six. She goes to school, does her homework, plays with the dog. Same things every kid does."

"Does she have any friends?"

"She just got invited to what's-his-name's—Matt's—birthday party last week."

"Did she go?"

Resa switched from picking at to chewing on her nails. She spoke with all her fingers in her mouth; I couldn't understand what she said.

"Pardon me?"

"I had to work," Resa clarified, ignoring the nails for a moment. "I couldn't give her a ride."

"I'm sorry, do you mean to say that Mary Toni was home alone that day?" Resa didn't answer, so I pressed her. "Is she always home alone when you're at work? Is *anyone* helping you take care of her?"

Resa became defensive. "What do you want me to do? Now that her daddy's dead, someone's got to pay the bills."

"You yourself just pointed out that she's six. *Six*. We don't even let the first-graders go to the bathroom by themselves. They always go in pairs. Buddy system. It teaches them to look out for each other."

"Yeah, well, Mary Toni can look out for herself," Resa insisted. I watched the fingers go back to her mouth like a habit. Upon closer inspection, I saw she'd abandoned the nails for a cuticle. Her teeth were tearing at it, the thin skin splitting and raw. Unintentionally—I think—she chewed too hard and drew blood. If it hurt, she didn't show it. Resa didn't so much as flinch.

I thought about how to broach her own health in a non-threatening manner. "Mrs. Habsburg, how are *you* doing?"

Resa laughed and shook her head the same way Mary Toni always did, as though by physically indicating denial she could make a thing not so. Could, by sheer force of will, drive it away. She must have shaken her head a lot in the years before Mary Toni was born, when they kept trying to have a baby and God kept delivering Resa too early.

"It's none of your business," Resa finally said, standing to signal the meeting was over. "None of it. Not me, not my home, and not what my child does outside of these brick walls." She gestured wildly around her. "When Mary Toni's here, I pay you to teach her and feed her and take her to Mass—and that last only because it was important to Frank. If my money's no good at Magnificat, I'll be glad to send her to the public school instead."

Sensing defeat, I backed off at once. "I'm sure that won't be necessary." I stood as well, to shake her hand. When she took it, I held on longer than necessary, careful not to brush her bleeding cuticle. "But, Resa, if I or the staff can help you in any way—or even Father McGillicuddy—will you let me know?"

"Sure," she said, with a laugh like a bark, before spinning on her nurse's white tennis shoes. I noticed they weren't very white anymore. She was overdue for a new pair.

As principal, it was my duty to report any suspicions of child abuse or neglect. The telephone number for our district's child protection agent stared at me from a cork board on the wall. I should have called that very afternoon, but I decided to give Resa the benefit of the doubt. She'd just lost her husband; obviously she was grieving herself. She'd come to her senses soon. In the meantime, I'd enroll Mary Toni in an after-school program, so she'd be taken care of until Resa got off work. On the weekends, there were sports and student clubs I could get her involved in—opportunities for me to keep an eye on her myself.

THE SOCCER COACH

No six-year-old *wants* to play soccer, just like no six-year-old *wants* to learn to read. They do it because their parents sign them up and their teachers inflate the importance of getting As in school. It's what's expected of little humans without much agency.

Mary Toni was the exception. Not only did she not want to play soccer, but she *did not want* to play soccer. To the point that she fought me at every opportunity. At first she tried logic. "I'm not any good," she told me at Wednesday-night practice. "If you want to win, you shouldn't put me in."

When I scoffed and remarked that no one had ever peaked in first grade, how really we had no idea yet of just what she was capable, I swear she cast her eyes skyward beseechingly, like *You see what I have to deal with here?* I might have laughed if the gesture hadn't been so oddly adult.

She took the field obligingly enough, but then she just stood there, stubbornly refusing to participate. "Go, Mary Toni!" I shouted at one point, when a teammate had (unintentionally but fortuitously) kicked the ball in her direction. It's not like she wasn't paying attention. She watched the ball roll right past her, staring first at it, and then at me, with disdain.

I couldn't help it. I smiled. Tiny foot-stamping humans amuse me. Mary Toni hadn't literally stamped a foot—even then, she had too much self-control—but she made her position clear, and well, I respected it. As she'd carpooled to practice with another family, I didn't know who exactly was forcing her to be there, but obviously someone was.

I pulled her aside. "Can you read and write?"

"Of course," she said, the disdain still very much present.

"Congratulations." I offered her a hand. She took it.

The strength of her grip surprised me. "You're the new team manager."

Mollified, she kept perfect records the rest of the season.

TEZ

The aide they hired for Mary Toni—I still don't know if he did more harm than good.

FERSEN

Here's the truth. I never expected to fall in love with Marie Antoinette. I didn't even want to. I'm not a pedophile who goes around with a massive hard-on for kids. That's weird and 100% not my jam. She was different, from the beginning. In fact, when King Louie announced she was Ennoia, I thought it made perfect sense. Until that point, I couldn't have told you why she was special, how she was different from every other grubby-handed, booger-eating first-grader. She just was.

I was twenty-two then, and in my last semester at the University of Texas. I still had no idea what I wanted to do with my life, but my mom was a teacher, and that had always seemed a noble enough profession. Part of the program involved observing, then guest-teaching at, an area school. I had chosen Magnificat because it was walking distance from my dorm. During my second week of observations, the school asked me how I felt about a temporary aide position.

"One of our students needs some extra support right now," the principal said. "You would basically just sit there and make sure she's staying awake, paying attention. Help her if she has a question."

"I don't know," I remember saying, flattered but

nervous. "Are you sure you don't want a real teacher? Someone with more experience?"

She smiled. She was a good woman, the principal, and patiently explained the limited resources of a parochial school. How they'd only be paying me minimum wage, and that in my two weeks there, I'd already proven myself more than capable.

"It's you or nothing," the principal said. "And this little girl . . . she deserves more than nothing."

The girl, of course, was Mary Toni. Just six years old and grieving the death of her father, whom she'd completely idolized.

So, for the next month or so, I attended school with her five days a week, forgoing such productive activities as sleeping in and getting high. All of my own classes were in the evenings, so no worries there. You could say that, although I was the one assigned to keep her awake, Mary Toni woke me up. Caring for her gave me something to care about.

I was awkward, at first. I pulled a chair up next to her desk and introduced myself like we were new co-workers. I actually held out my hand for her to shake. "Hi! My name's Fersen. Well, my full name is Axel Fersen, but you can call me Fersen, everybody does, or maybe Mr. Fersen, since we're in school." The curious, patient way she looked at me made me realize that I was rambling and I stopped, though my mouth continued moving, a fucking fish out of water. I took in the dark circles under her eyes, so unusual on a six-year-old, then realized I was staring and started talking again. "I'm going to be your classroom aide. That means I'll be sitting next to you in class and helping you with anything you need. I'm studying to be a teacher, though I'm not actually one yet, but my mom used to be." I stopped again. Breathed. Then: "They told me your name's Marie Antoinette. That's so pretty."

"Mary Toni," she corrected me. Her voice was deeper than I'd expected. Husky, perhaps, with crying, though her eyes, despite the dark circles, betrayed no emotion but interest. Something about her voice calmed me. I took another deep breath, got a grip, and quit trying so hard. After all, I reminded myself, they're paying you minimum wage. And she's six!

Deep breath.

THE SOCCER COACH

Once I made Mary Toni team manager, she never gave me another problem—except for the day I couldn't make it. My wife's niece was getting married, and the wedding was out of state. I asked one of the dads to sub for me. Apparently it was a busy weekend for lots of people, because only half the team showed up. We were short the minimum by one, so this dad sent Mary Toni in to play. According to him, she initially demurred with a polite, "No thank you," as though declining tea in her sugar. He explained why she had to play—so the rest of the team could—and she rolled her eyes. "I'm the manager," she reminded him.

"Never mind that. I can keep score," Rick said. He ripped the clipboard from her hands and pushed her out onto the field, wearing tennis shoes but not soccer cleats or shin guards. Gritting her teeth, Mary Toni ran out to join her teammates willingly enough. She intercepted a long pass right away, and started dribbling it expertly down the field. Either she was a natural-born athlete, or she'd learned by watching, or both. Anyway, Rick was so surprised that he didn't even tell her she was going the wrong way. He just wanted to see what she'd do. Mary Toni steered the ball around two tiny human defenders (wearing the same red shirts as her) and kicked it cleanly past our own goalie! No one knew whether to cheer or laugh or what. She followed through on the kick and kept right on running, a smooth arc, back to the bench—where she picked up the clipboard again and marked one point for the other team. "That was great!" Rick exclaimed. "Only, you went the wrong way."

"I know," Mary Toni said, 100% the terrifying adult-child. She didn't even look at Rick, just yelled, "Come on, Tigers! You got this!"

The ref let us play with just seven bodies after that.

FERSEN

As it turned out, Mary Toni didn't really need me. She was brilliant, or she seemed so to me, anyway. It was clear she didn't particularly like school, but book smarts aren't the only measure of competence. She never had any questions, or took a single note. Instead of writing down what her teacher said, she doodled elaborate mazes and geometric patterns that spanned edge to edge until the point at which she'd begun was camouflaged by line and arc.

Every time her teacher walked by, she sighed. Dismayed? Resigned? I didn't know. Wondered if I should try harder. But I got the sense that Mary Toni was herself resigned—to putting up with me, no doubt—so I didn't push her. Let the child process however she needed to.

It got so I didn't want to leave her at the end of the day. Protective, I worried about the environment she went home to. The principal had told me it wasn't great; I naturally imagined the worst. I'd lie awake in bed at night and wonder if she was restless, too. If thoughts of her dead dad were keeping sleep at bay. She was skinny. Was she eating enough? Her hair was greasy. Who was modeling— or not—basic hygiene practices?

I didn't know how to ask her these questions. They felt too intimate, too strange to discuss with a child. So I asked her teacher instead, but she was of little help.

"Look, Axel," she said. "We're lucky to get them for eight hours a day. When they're here, they're warm, they're fed, they're supervised. Hopefully, they can relax long enough to play, and if they learn to tell time and do two-digit addition along the way, we've done our job. That's the best-case scenario. Unless you see bruises, lice, or other obvious signs of abuse or neglect, we can't legally step in. They're not our children, no matter how much they might feel like it."

I knew she was right. I wanted her to be wrong. More than protective, I was starting to feel possessive. Mary Toni wasn't mine . . . yet. But I wanted her to be.

TEZ

She was careful not to let anyone in—a habit she'd no doubt learned from her mother. Mary Toni kept everyone at arm's length. Even as a child. And like Resa, she had her secret rituals, too.

THE NEIGHBOR

It was my custom to sit outside on the back porch at night, chain-smoke my dead husband's favorite cigarettes, and talk to him, filling him in on the day's events. I used to think all the smoking would take me to him sooner, but an old woman now, I understand this is my penance. A too-long life without my love, several of those years spent living next to a woman literally haunted—and eventually driven mad by—fifteen miscarriages, all for aborting a child I didn't want. My husband's child. Today that baby would be half a century old, and maybe he or she would look like my husband. The same crinkle-eyed smile. At any rate, I'd talk to my beloved in my head, at night on the porch, until one day a voice spoke back. A little girl's voice. Mary Toni. Talking to herself like I do to my late husband.

"I got an A on my water cycle project," I heard her say to no one in particular. At least, no one responded.

She chattered happily for a while. It sounded like she was moving around the yard, because her voice seemed to emanate first from near the fence line, and later, tucked down the north side of the house. I heard snapping twigs, too—she was collecting them, I realized soon enough, for kindling—while she sang a little song and laughed at nothing I could hear. When the telltale hiss of a newly struck match became the orange glow of flame, I got up to peek through a knothole in the fence. Not to spy, mind you, so much as make sure she was being safe. Backlit by a small, contained fire (she'd used the copper pit at least), Mary Toni stood feeding pieces of paper, some with printing, some quite clearly her own paintings, into the blaze.

"What are you doing?" I asked her.

She startled and whipped around. "Nothing." The too-quick answer of a child caught doing something she knew she shouldn't.

"Nothing? Looks like something to me." I studied her best I could in the moonlight, the papers she'd shoved behind herself like evidence. A sacrifice, I concluded.

"We learned in school about how incense, because of the smoke, helps carry prayers to heaven."

"So you're trying to send a prayer?"

Mary Toni dug a toe into the earth. "A message."

"To God?"

"To my dad. I want to show him what he's missed since he left."

"Left?"

"You know. Died." It cost her obvious effort to say the word. Despite the heat from the fire, she shuddered.

"Do you think he's coming back?"

She shrugged, a black silhouette.

"He's not coming back, Mary Toni. That's what dead means. Forever." I wasn't trying to upset her, but Christ. Someone had to tell the girl the truth, or she'd only be more disappointed later. "Come here."

Dragging her feet with every step and looking longingly back at the fire once or twice, she finally joined me at the fence. I could see the pain on her face clear as day, even though it was close to midnight.

"Let me tell you something. I lost my husband ten years ago now, and my daddy more than a few years before that. When I say lost, I mean they died. It's not like I've just been waiting around on them to come back, to find their way home. Lord knows I wish it was that easy. What I've learned, and what I suspect you're grappling with now, is that death is hardest on those left behind. Your daddy, chances are he didn't feel a thing. But losing him, it hurt you pretty badly, huh?"

Silent, Mary Toni turned again to look at the fire.

"One thing that helps me is going to the places where my husband and daddy are buried. It feels like they can hear me better there. Then I don't have to send them smoke signals or whatever it is you're doing over there." Come to think of it, I was sending them smoke signals via the cigarettes, but anyway.

"I never got to see his body," she whispered. "There's a gravestone, but I'm not sure he's there."

"Only way to know is to go and try."

"Where's he buried?" she asked. "Your dad?"

"At sea," I said. "Somewhere between here and Japan."

She paused. "My name means 'sea of sadness.' Did you know that?"

"No, Marie, I did not. But I wish more for you than that."

She was harder to see now that the fire was dying. Twigs don't burn for long.

"Now go put some water on that fire and go to bed."

I watched her pad away, slip quietly inside the house, and return a moment later with a plastic watering can. The liquid spat as it hit the embers, reducing them to a smoking black hole.

FERSEN

My time as Mary Toni's aide ended far too quickly.

"We still have work to do together," I remember telling the principal. "There are other things I can help her with."

"Like what?" the principal asked, raising her eyebrows and making her forehead wrinkle.

"Like learning to care more about school!" I suggested. "She's so bright. Like, so incredibly bright."

"But she's making a C in Spelling."

"Exactly! No one's ever modeled for her why it matters. Her dad was the one who helped her at home, made sure she did her homework and studied for tests. Without him, she doesn't see the point. She'd rather stare out the window all day at the birds. I could keep, you know, redirecting her attention. Help her find her motivation."

"Mr. Fersen, if there's one thing I've learned in all my years working with students, it's that you can't make anybody care. It has to come from within."

My shoulders slumped. She sucked her teeth. "However, what's abundantly clear is that *you* care. And that's the number one quality I look for in teachers we hire here."

Yes? Where was this going?

"I can't assign you to Mary Toni indefinitely. It wouldn't be fair to the other children, and I can barely justify your role to the board as it is. That said, our sixth-grade teacher will be leaving us at the end of the year. Would you have any interest in joining us full time? Impacting lots of students' lives? Not just hers?"

Thump-thump. Thump-thump. Blood was pounding in my ears in syncopation with my racing heartbeat. I'd never wanted anything so badly. Just five more years until I had her in my classroom full time. And I'd see her every day in the hallways until then.

"Yes!" I squeaked, before clearing my throat and

modulating my voice to something more normal. "Yes, thank you. I'd love to. That would be great! Thank you so much."

TEZ

Her second-grade teacher was Sister Hutchins, a Dominican nun with a starched, full habit and a nasty attitude. She excelled at whipping "ne'er-do-wells" (her term) into shape, but she was way too domineering for someone like Mary Toni, who never required anything more than a polite request that she clear her plate, clean her room, or take out the trash. According to the nun, however, this behavior and even Mary Toni's sweet demeanor didn't matter, because still she was marked by original sin.

THE NUN

Original sin. Eve gave the apple to Adam after God explicitly told them no, and because he loved her, he ate it, dooming all humanity forevermore.

At least that's the story the Bible tells us, and whether or not you believe it doesn't matter a whit to me. It's *your* eternal soul we're talking about here. I specifically joined a cloistered order because no, I don't consider it my duty to save you. Maybe you're waving or maybe you're drowning; in any case, I'm likely to be on my way to Mass and punctuality, like cleanliness, is next to godliness, you know.

We were talking about original sin in class. It's part of the second-grade curriculum: preparation for the sacraments. Every child at Magnificat has already been baptized, so it's basically a non-issue, but we cover it anyway as a foothold up the mountain of prudence—a person's ability to distinguish between good and bad. We read Genesis, and then I ask, "So who was bad in the Garden?" The students' answers vary. Most of them say, "Eve," though a few insist it was the devil's fault first.

"Your reasoning is intrinsically flawed," I tell anyone who answers that way, "because Satan is fallen. He was once good, but having been kicked out of heaven, he can never be good again. Evil incarnate, now he exists to spawn chaos and pain. It is his job to bring others down with him, and if you must call him good at something, he's good at his job.

"But Eve," I continue, "Eve knew better. She allowed herself to be tempted. She was weak."

I remember Mary Toni's class had a few prime troublemakers, a couple devil's rejects themselves. One of them, Isaac Crable, he chose this moment to whisper to the child next to him. They looked at each other and smirked.

"Isaac," I said. "Care to share with the rest of us what you find so amusing?"

He shook his head sullenly, but then Mary Toni, who'd by all appearances spent the better part of the afternoon daydreaming about the blackbirds, spoke up out of turn.

"Couldn't it have been Adam? The bad one?"

"Almost certainly not."

She fixed her dark eyes on me and, despite myself, I got goosebumps.

"Prudence means discernment, right? That was on our last vocab test. And discernment, you said, is the responsibility of the individual. 'Question everything,' you said, 'that you do not hear from a parent, or a teacher, or a doctor, or a priest. If you don't and you're led astray, you have no one to blame but yourself.'"

Well, I *had* said those words—she must have written them down verbatim—but leave it to a seven-year-old to twist your very meaning into knots. Not that I think men as a whole are necessarily trustworthy, but if you believe the story, God created Adam and Eve exactly for each other, man and wife, just like He gave holy women the church. I may be physically celibate, but I am in every way that matters the bride of Christ—and thus I trust Him implicitly. Clearly these topics were and are way too complex for second-graders. I'd question the wisdom of an institution that posits seven as the age of reason if I didn't know in my eternal soul that the church and its leaders are infallible.

THE CLASSMATE

When Sister was up there telling us all about how we were literally going to hell, and the women first for being so weak, Isaac leaned over and made some dumb joke that earned us both demerits. I only remember because it was my third demerit that week, which meant I got Saturday detention, which meant I couldn't go hunting with my grandpa that weekend. It was the last weekend of the season and I'd finally convinced him I was old enough to go and Isaac screwed it all up, just like he always did. I don't even know why we were friends, except that Isaac had chosen me and what he wanted he usually got. What we got that weekend, though, was detention, and what I didn't get was a deer. I didn't even get the damn joke. Something like, "Eve is fallen." Or "Eve will fall." The irony being, of course, that we all know how that one worked out.

TEZ

Later that year, Mary Toni's class received the sacrament of Confirmation—the sealing of Christianity created in baptism.

MOTHER-EATING

THE EUCHARISTIC MINISTER

On the evening that Mary Toni became a soldier of Christ, the sky glowed red as Bishop Lewis's robes. Tongues of solar fire shot through the gathering darkness, licking the ears and foreheads of the fervent congregation and transmogrifying the twelve young candidates' upturned faces into those of overheated apostles. Just seven years old, they looked much older: ancients kneeling around a sacrificial altar. Disbelieving, at first; even bored—but one by one enraptured as the Holy Spirit descended to deliver that spiritual mantle unto they who would join the perpetual war. Six girls, six boys, each one taking a new name in honor of some canonized saint or Biblical hero. When Bishop Lewis called Mary Toni forward, she bowed low in acknowledgment of the baptismal names she'd chosen to reconfirm. Maria, meaning a none-too-happy *sea of sadness*. The rather more lovely Antonia (for Anthony) denoting *a priceless flower*.

From a scarred and pitted pew, I watched this only daughter receive her charge with graceful determination. How self-assured she is, I thought. Look at how she trusts in what she's told—how ready to fight, to save the human race from its inexorable march into hell.

Seven, the church maintains, is the age of reason. The age when children know the difference between right and wrong, and so can be held responsible for their actions. "Sealed now with the gifts of wisdom, understanding, and courage," the bishop intoned, drawing the sign of the cross in the air above their heads, "I commend thee to the church and all she promises. Eat now, and drink, of the flesh and blood of Jesus Christ—born of the Virgin Mary, crucified, risen from the dead, seated now at the right hand of the Father—and pray for God to strengthen and anoint you, that when the hour comes, you may renounce Satan and all his works."

TEZ

The setting sun through the stained-glass windows cast saints and archangels alike as whores in silhouette. Even though I wasn't there, I saw through St. Michael the Archangel's window—can see even now—another scissortail join its family on the wire. I saw it the same way I "see" other things: internally. With my mind. It's a gift—from Simon Magus.

That night, the birds hopped along the length of the line like tightrope walkers without the risk. If anyone fell, they would fly. Laid over the tableau: Michael's muscled bicep brandishing a spear. Satan squirming beneath his foot, serpent belly soft and begging to be split. Michael, forever frozen at the moment of decision. A lightness like righteousness lifting his leaded face.

THE CANTOR

On Wednesdays and most Saturday nights, plus Holy Days and the infrequent 'other' special occasion, I led the responsorial psalm and the Alleluia from the lectern. My youngest had just started school, and with more time on my hands, I was looking for ways to get involved and give back.

If singing really is "praying twice," then I figured it couldn't hurt my immortal soul, either. The Holy Days and the weddings and the Confirmations—these were extra credit, both for the holy and wicked parts of myself. By which I mean, I may have had the most infinitesimal crush on Bishop Lewis. So I can't claim my motivations were entirely altruistic. Still, someone had to be the cantor. And when the bishop presided, I sang louder and more enthusiastically than normal, so the parish benefitted, too!

Anyway, when I heard the bishop was coming to town

for second-grade Confirmation, naturally I volunteered. What more joyous occasion than the giving of hearts and souls to God in good faith and full consciousness? The kids looked darling wearing their tiny suits and dresses. A big deal, you know, for them to get to wear something other than plaid uniforms. I didn't know Mary Toni personally, but I recognized her from dropping my own kids off in the morning. Nine and five, they were, to her seven. I paid particular attention to her that night, though, because her mother made a bit of a scene. The typical sniffling and dabbing of eyes that most moms were doing at the metamorphosis of their babies into (in the Church's eyes, anyway) adults, yes, but she took it one step too far. After the ceremony, she literally threw herself at the bishop, sobbing into his robes in a quite inappropriate manner.

"I just miss him so much, Father!" I heard her say. "Frank should have been here to see this."

The bishop tried comforting her with an awkward pat on the back, but you could tell he wasn't a priest of the people. He was used to the cold marble floors and fine gold chalices of the Dallas cathedral. For all I knew, the woman had snotted on him! Completely unacceptable.

I went over to intervene, see if I couldn't take her to the bathroom or the parish kitchen for a cold glass of water. The bishop would be grateful, I reasoned, maybe even seek me out personally later for a thank you. That's when I saw the woman give him a necklace to bless. "For my daughter, Marie Antoinette," she said. He appeased her by sprinkling some holy water from the nearby font, and I thought, What a lucky child. I'll have to remember that for when mine is old enough in a couple years. And I did. I gave her a small silver cross on a sterling silver chain—tasteful and much more age appropriate than the ruby I saw flash in Mary Toni's mom's box.

Then again, I didn't have near as much to compensate for. I'd heard she was sleeping with her brother-in-law, for Pete's sake. The politician? Adam Habsburg? Fast and loose, that woman. Nothing like playing the long game with the bishop.

TEZ

After the ceremony, Resa took Mary Toni out to dinner. The girl sat in a booth across from her mother, spaghetti sauce and chocolate gelato dotting the corners of her pre-pubescent smile. Soon, her face would grow leaner and the Tooth Fairy would carry the rest of her milk teeth away. But at that moment, she was still every bit the apple of her dead father's eye; the banana to his split. Frank never worried about cavities, or how ice cream makes children's blood sugar spike. He left that to Resa. Strident nurse. Reluctant mother.

"Here," Resa said, shuffle-balling a velvet jewelry box over the smooth formica. "Open it."

Mary Toni did, curious but cautious. Gifts from Mom often arrived with strings attached.

Black velvet parted, and from inside, a red tongue extended to its tiny queen a token of fire. That's what the charm looked like—fire—its crystal facets catching and turning light into flame. Even a seven-year-old will sigh at something so beautiful.

"Thank you." She looked up, expectant.

"It's from your father," Resa said. "He picked it out last year."

Plucking the chain from her daughter's hands, she fumbled with the child-sized clasp. "He said it represented Pentecost." Pause. "You do remember Pentecost?"

"Sure, Mom. When the Holy Spirit kissed the apostles."

"Well, we're called to be even better than them, Marie. Thomas was an apostle, and you know what he did? He doubted Jesus's words. Jesus! His best friend. Thomas had so little faith—"

"That he stuck his finger in Jesus's hand!" Mary Toni

interrupted, jabbing a finger into her remaining spaghetti and splashing more sauce onto her plenty-soiled shirt. "Right through his nail hole!" She fished a cold noodle out of the pile and slurped it down, grinning, while Resa looked on, stunned. A small sauce rose blooming across her pastel blouse.

Recognizing the warning signs, Mary Toni dropped her head, instantly chastened. She could almost hear Frank laughing too hard to notice. "Hey, MT!" he might have said. "What did Thomas say to the chicken?"

"Frank." Quiet.

"Any guesses?"

"Frank!" Curt. Clipped. A teaser before the typhoon. "Pay the bill. We're going."

"Aw, Resa, come on. I'm sorry." Dabbing at the stain. Making it worse.

"Now."

Resa folded her napkin neatly over her crossed utensils and exited the booth gracefully. The Frank of Mary Toni's imagination offered her a quick smile: a silent apology. He wanted to be her life vest, but he was her hangman, failing to warn her before the floor caved.

Later, in the cool glow of the moon tower outside her window, Mary Toni watched shadows chase each other over the walls and tried to figure out if she felt any different. Had the Holy Spirit indeed descended? Should she have sensed it—an extra kind of power coursing through her veins? Some throbbing crown of thorns constricting her beating heart?

When her dog Mops whined, she realized she'd unconsciously squeezed him a bit too hard. She tried to relax: first, her toes and the tops of her feet; moving up her legs and tomboy hips. Just like they'd taught her at school. Mindfulness.

The last thing Mary Toni saw before falling asleep was a cardboard cutout of the Virgin of Guadalupe—Queen Mary's alter-ego—tacked to her closet door. Her father had bought it for her at the Mexican market around the corner.

Her red robes looked like Bishop Lewis's. The crescent moon she stood on was dark as the west Texas sky.

THE FRIEND

Sister Hutchins, the Dominican nun in charge of our second-grade class, frowned when she spotted the rainbow. It was spinning and jumping around the room, absentminded as the girl with the contraband necklace.

"Marie Antoinette. What exactly do you have there?"

"What?" Mary Toni snapped to attention, unsure what she'd missed.

"Are you or are you not breaking the dress code?" Sister Hutchins demanded, hand on white-habited hip.

"Sorry, Sister," she mumbled, tucking the offending piece of jewelry back inside her school-issue blouse.

"That's a demerit," the nun said, tearing a yellow piece of paper from the pad she kept in her habit's hidden pocket.

"But, Sister! It's a Confirmation necklace," Mary Toni protested.

"Oh. Why didn't you say so?" Sister Hutchins smiled, but not with her eyes. "In that case, *two* demerits."

The girl seated to Mary Toni's left smothered her laugh with a grubby hand. Mary Toni glared at her.

"Sister, that's not fair."

"Marie Antoinette, if it's okay with you, I will decide what's fair. And in this case, it's only fair that you abide by the same rules every child in this classroom must. Jewelry is a token of vanity, and vanity is a cardinal sin."

Mary Toni, defiant, tried one more time. "It's supposed to remind me of the Holy Spirit."

"Do you think Saint Therese needed *reminding* of the Holy Spirit? She saw God in every flower in every garden. She gave of herself with an extraordinary, totally attentive love."

Mary Toni looked at her desk, ashamed.

"I'd say you've earned yourself a trip to the principal's office."

"What?"

"Off you go." She shooed Mary Toni out of the room. "Come back when *the Holy Spirit* has filled your heart with contriteness."

Slowly, Mary Toni left the classroom.

FERSEN

I happened to be walking past the second-grade classroom on my way to the teacher's lounge when I saw Sister Hutchins boot Mary Toni out, then shut the door tightly behind her.

"Hey," I greeted the girl. "What's going on?"

She told me the story of the necklace.

"Can I see it?"

She fished it out from her shirt. The stone looked slightly garish beneath the old florescent lights. Like a bloodstone, I thought but didn't say. It was smudged with fingerprints. I decided to walk her to the principal's office.

"Did you ever get Confirmed?" Mary Toni wanted to know.

"I did. My Confirmation name is Simon."

She thought about that. "Simon Peter, or Simon who carried the cross?"

"Neither," I said. Before I could clarify, we arrived at the office door. I gestured: "After you." And Mary Toni entered, her shoulders squared.

TEZ

Her shoulders red and oozing from the scratching, Resa hit her blinker and turned south on Avenue F. At 38th Street, she took a right toward Guadalupe. Her next patient lived west of the city, near Tarrytown.

As she drove, she drummed her fingers on the steering wheel in time with the music. Then she drummed them faster, almost manically, to a rhythm no one else could hear. Through the skirt of her white nurse's dress, she scratched the insides of her thighs with her short, chewed nails until they bruised. She never felt it.

Resa was dreaming about her next fix.

Although she didn't see it—too used to the same old scene, after half a lifetime, to notice—Austin unfurled outside her window like a bluebonnet. Its square-grid neighborhoods were the florets stacked one atop another up the central stalk of I-35, which divided the city in half. Just east of the artery was where she and Mary Toni lived, in a small 1950s bungalow that had become theirs outright on the maturation of Frank's life insurance policy. West of I-35 was where the old money was, and plenty of aging, private-pay patients to spend it.

Parking outside a tan brick estate half-hidden from the road by ancient, gnarled oaks, Resa popped open her trunk. She got out of the car still agitated, slammed her door closed, and grabbed a few full brown paper shopping bags from the trunk before slamming that, too. The shopping bags held diapers and wipes, eye drops, nose bulbs, lollipops—everything you might need to care for a toddler. Resa's clients weren't babies, though they acted like children sometimes. And truth be told, many of them were just as needy, just as helpless.

When Resa rang the bell, Mrs. L's senior concierge opened the door. "Hi, Resa," she said, holding the door wide for the hospice nurse to enter. "Please come in."

"How's Mrs. L today?"

"She's tired. I think her grandkid's visit wore her out yesterday. Collin brought the baby. Her first great-grandchild!"

Resa smiled like she cared. "Is she awake?"

"Last I left her, she was watching *Price Is Right* in her bedroom."

THE CONCIERGE

"Great, thanks," Resa said. She adjusted her shopping bags and turned toward the grand stairwell.

"You remember the way?" I called after her.

"I do." Resa beamed like she genuinely appreciated my concern, but really she couldn't wait for me to leave. My shift was up in fifteen minutes.

Resa disappeared upstairs. A minute later, I followed her. Call it spying if you must; I just wanted to make sure everything about Mrs. L's new nurse was on the up and up.

On the second floor, light streamed through the floor-to-ceiling windows. One whole wall of the house was windows—the wall that faced the in-ground pool and travertine-tiled deck. The sun glanced off the water invitingly, but something even more tempting awaited Resa in the bedroom. Nevertheless, she paused long enough in the hallway to place both hands and an oily forehead against the recently washed windowpanes, soiling them. I watched her, but she never saw me.

Mrs. L's bedroom door was open, though the room itself was dark. I'd drawn the curtains to cut the glare on the TV screen, and in that warm, dark space, Mrs. L had understandably fallen asleep. She was snoring softly as Resa entered, a silk pillowcase under her head and the covers pulled up to her chin. Plastic tubing snaked from her nose and around the crepey skin of her ears to an oxygen tank parked next to the bed. An IV bag hung from a rack just above it. A heart rate monitor blinked nearby. These were the silent witnesses to death. They counted the breaths, the B-cells, the beats; and they counted them down.

Not long now.

Flipping on a table lamp, Resa summarily checked the elderly woman's vitals. These she logged in a notebook. Afterward, she unwrapped one of the lollipops from the bag. She marked that she'd given it to Mrs. L, but into her own mouth it went. The scent of raspberry, sharp and sweet, flooded the air. Two seconds later, the dissolved fentanyl hit her bloodstream.

I recalled our initial interview, when we'd first decided to hire Resa. She'd described what we could expect of Mrs. L's inevitable decline, how she'd soon require help with basic hygiene and bathroom functions, the increasing stiffness and pain in her legs. "Not to worry," she'd said. "I'm licensed to administer any kind of pain meds a patient's doctor prescribes. Pain management is one of the most important services we provide."

Resa had looked directly at Mrs. L then, before saying, "There's simply no reason for anyone to suffer through their final days."

My impression of Resa that afternoon had been one of competence, if little compassion. It was like she knew all the right words to say—and I had little doubt she'd deliver on her promises—but I wasn't convinced she really cared one way or another. Maybe, I thought, that's also just 'part of the job.' Perhaps a sort of detachment was necessary to watch one soul after another depart this world for the next. If you felt personally invested in every patient's life, it'd be like burying a tiny piece of yourself every time. What could prepare someone for that?

Now, while she waited for the drug to do its thing, Resa prepared a new bag of saline. By the time she'd finished mixing a bucket of soapy water in the bathroom, she looked significantly calmer. Significantly more like herself.

Resa's next task was to sponge-bathe the patient, changing Mrs. L's diaper when she did. At 93, Mrs. L never left the bed anymore, not to shower or to shit. I fed her meals in the morning and at noon, while the cook who came in to make all the food handled the evening's duties.

Seeming impatient to get things going, Resa yanked the covers down. Mrs. L's eyes fluttered open. Almost immediately, her soft, dry hands resumed their pill-rolling tremor.

"Who are you?" she croaked, one foot still firmly in the Land of Nod. Mrs. L didn't seem scared; merely curious.

"Resa. I'm your hospice nurse. We met last week."

"I don't remember you."

"You don't remember a lot of things these days. That's part of having Parkinson's disease."

Mrs. L didn't respond right away, absorbing this information.

"Anyway, it's time for your bath," Resa prompted. She stuck the lollipop back in her mouth, freeing both hands to unbutton the snaps at Mrs. L's shoulders and shimmy the gown off her otherwise naked—except for the diaper—torso.

"I hear your grandkid stopped by yesterday," Resa said, probably as much to distract herself from the impending diaper change as Mrs. L. "That must have been exciting. You're a great-grandmother now, yes?"

"Yes," Mrs. L parroted, though I doubt she actually knew in that moment.

"You have three kids, eight grandkids, and one great-grandbaby," Resa reminded her. Then she undid the tabs on the adult-size diaper and held her breath for what followed.

As she was grabbing a third wipe, Mrs. L asked, "Do you have kids?"

"I do. One. Marie Antoinette. She's seven."

"Sea of sadness," Mrs. L whispered.

"Sorry?"

"Marie. It means 'sea of sadness.' Not a very happy thing to name a child."

Despite herself, Resa chuckled. "That's what my mom said. Oh well. Resa means 'laughter' and that never really fit, either."

"What's she like—Marie Antoinette?"

"She's not like other kids, you know. She's special. Even I can see that. But I don't—"

Mrs. L interrupted her. "Do you have a picture?"

"I don't actually."

"Oh, that's too bad."

"I know what my own daughter looks like. I don't need a picture to remind me."

"I bet she looks like you."

"Of course she does. I'm her mother."

"Yes," Mrs. L said slowly, as if acknowledging everything that statement meant. I could tell it made Resa uncomfortable to be so seen, even if Mrs. L would forget the conversation in a matter of hours. She sucked harder on the lollipop and appeared to find some calm. She pulled the blankets higher around Mrs. L's neck.

"Can I get you anything else?"

"How about one of those lollipops?"

"Do you have a migraine?"

Mrs. L looked confused.

"Does your head hurt?"

"No."

"Then I can't." Resa looked around the room. Her eyes settled on the table with the lamp. A cherry Jolly Rancher poked its cellophane-wrapped head above the lip of a dish. "Here," she said, handing the woman the candy. Offering her a tiny grace. Even Resa was capable of that much.

After I reported her, we found out we weren't the only ones. Several families had lodged some pretty horrifying accusations—"acts of gross negligence," they called them— that bordered on abuse. Apparently Resa didn't just steal patients' drugs. She sometimes withheld medications from them altogether, either so she could take them, or because she was in a *mood* that day. One son stopped by his father's house when Resa was there. I guess she didn't hear him come in. He got halfway back to Dad's bedroom and overheard Resa *taunting* the senile old man. She wanted him to beg.

All any of us can hope for is to die with dignity, and I'm afraid when we hired Resa, we didn't even guarantee Mrs. L that.

TEZ

Later that week, Mary Toni's second-grade class went on a field trip. The sixth-grade teachers chaperoned; their students were taking a standardized test that day administered by agency proctors.

FERSEN

"So what'd you get for breaking the dress code?" I asked, sliding into the brown vinyl bus seat next to Mary Toni.

"Five hours' community service," she grumbled. "And I can't wear the necklace to school anymore."

"Shame," I said. "It looked nice on you." Had she blushed? "Tell me about this zoo."

"It's okay," Mary Toni said, making a face. "They have lots of animals."

"What's your favorite animal?"

"Dogs."

I nodded. "Dogs are nice. You don't need to go to a zoo to see them, though."

"No," she agreed. "I have one at home. Mops."

"Maybe I can meet him sometime."

The bus driver closed the door and Sister Hutchins came over the speaker. "Children, listen up. Today we will be cataloguing parts of God's creation. You should all have a checklist. I expect you to work in teams. The team that finds all of the animals on the list first wins a special prize. No cheating, okay?" She made to sit down, then thought better of it. "And remember, please, that field trips are privileges, and privileges can be revoked. Especially when you're representing Magnificat in public."

THE CLASSMATE

As kids by their very natures are wont to do, we got wound up, then bored, then restless, then downright unruly—all before we ever tumbled off the bus. It carried over to the zoo proper. There we were hungry, then tired, then *someone* got the bright idea to feed the gorilla a banana from his brown paper lunch sack.

"Watch this," Isaac said, climbing like his monkey cousin into the upper reaches of a large old tree. The tree's branches umbrellaed the northern edge of the great ape's open-air enclosure, and while the cage walls were fifteen-feet tall, the tree was taller, and Isaac more determined. He scrabbled, banana stem clamped between his teeth. His shifting weight shook down leaves in a small shower. They drifted on the breeze, sank, caught Queso's—all 200 pounds of her—attention. She lowered the twig she'd been gnawing. Stared at the boy.

Boy inched higher up, farther out. Classmates, myself included, cheered him on. Shouted warnings to "Be careful!" Sister Hutchins was otherwise distracted, assisting a girl with a bloody nose in the restroom.

"Isaac, you better not," Mr. Fersen said. While he seemed like an adult to us kids, I realize now that he was little more than a kid himself. "Come down."

"Or what?" Isaac jeered, pulling the banana from his mouth. "You'll *tell* on me?" He found another foothold.

"Queso doesn't want your stupid banana. You're going to get all your friends in trouble."

"Gorillas love bananas," Isaac insisted. "See?"

He was close enough to the edge to wave the banana at Queso over the top of the cage. Queso didn't move, but her eyes followed the fruit—and the little boy holding it.

"Monkey want a banana?" Isaac cooed.

"Isaac, get down!" another girl in our class yelled fearfully. He responded by biting down on the banana stem again and climbing higher—onto the outermost, the weakest, branch.

Predictably, it snapped. But Isaac didn't fall. He grabbed another branch, steadied himself. Laughed nervously.

"I can't watch," Mary Toni muttered, turning away.

THE ZOOKEEPER

Unfortunately, it happens a lot more often than we'd like. You try to build the perfect exhibit—one that allows the animal to be seen, but from a safe distance—and someone, man or beast, ends up getting hurt anyway. There's just no accounting for the whims of either.

Kid's lucky he got caught. Were he mine, I'd have beaten his butt, and it still wouldn't have been anything compared to what a silverback can do to you. I once saw Queso crush a coconut in her fist, like instantly pulverize it. That's 1,400 pounds per square inch. It doesn't take near that much to pulp a human skull. To an African gorilla, that's like stepping on a snail shell. That's like popping open a sugar snap pea.

There was a girl. Small little thing. Dark eyes. "I can't watch," she said. I didn't want to, either.

I could see the limb the boy was clinging to wasn't going to hold him, and when I saw that I started running. Even if he didn't fall *in* the cage, a fall from that height—period—could damn well kill a kid.

"Hey!" I shouted, to let him know I'd seen him, to scare him maybe into staying put at least. He hesitated for just a second.

It was all I needed to break his bravado. Then his teacher, a nun, reappeared.

THE NUN

"So?" Isaac said, like I'd just told him God's sky was blue or otherwise pointed out the obvious. He'd reacted the same belligerent way when I'd confronted him about the armadillo. "You *killed* a thing," I'd said. "A formerly living, breathing animal, darling of the Creator!" And just because Isaac was one, too—a darling of the Creator, that is—didn't give him the right to harm another. Or to cause problems at the zoo when I wasn't looking.

It was the parenting; or lack thereof, in that case. Only child of an inadequate single mother, no one to set him straight, to nip those behaviors in the bud early on. Teachers used to cross their fingers, bribe the principal, *pray* not to have Isaac Crable in their class. I'd wished explicitly for him. "Nothing a ruler and a rosary can't correct," I'd told the principal. "Put him in my class, and I'll see to it he gets a bit of the tough love he clearly isn't getting at home."

When he talked back to me so impertinently at the zoo, I grabbed him by the ear and walked him back to the bus myself. "Let go of me!" he screamed all the while, slapping at my arm and twisting his head like he would bite me. Teaching makes you tough, though. I'm stronger than I look, and might is always on the side of right. You want to talk about abuse, you should have seen the bruises Isaac left up and down my forearm. But did anyone hear me complain?

TEZ

Isaac didn't fall—that day.

Three years later, he flew. And then he wasn't Mary Toni's problem anymore.

THE FRIEND

I remember going to class Mass. It was once a month, and we all took turns planning songs and readings. Someone would take up the gifts. Someone else would offer the petitions. Mary Toni was shy and she hated being picked to do anything. "Can somebody else please do it?" That's what she always asked the teacher. As perfectly polite as she was utterly unwilling.

Depending on the teacher, they might let her get away with it. Mary Toni was a major teacher's pet. But never with Sister Hutchins. I once knew Sister to give Mary Toni altar server duty—worst of all for an introvert, because you had to stand up there with the priest and were basically in the spotlight for the entire Mass—*on top* of leading the responsorial psalm.

If neither of us had any duties, we made sure to sit together. We'd stare at the crucified Christ suspended from the ceiling and wait for a real drop of blood to fall from the painted wound in his side, his nailed hands and feet. Stigmata, they told us, was real. Several of the saints had had it. So what was keeping the plaster crown of thorns from *really* pricking that perpetually upturned, eternally anguished face?

Any moment, we thought, he'd wink at us. Like, "Just kidding; I'm not *actually* dead."

We could joke about it because death was a construct, impersonal and removed. And because it would have been too scary otherwise.

Then Mary Toni's dad died, and that shy-in-public girl became serious, too. "Serious as a heart attack," kids used to say. After that, just the sight of a crucifix was enough to make her tear up. I think it's because they buried Frank with one clasped in his hands. Though that was just hearsay—a well-meaning platitude care of Sister.

"He's in God's hands now," she said to Mary Toni at the funeral. "And he has God *in* his hands, too."

It must have been horrifying—the thought of a weeping, bleeding plastic doll wound through her father's fingers for all time. But we never really knew, since when a body's been through what Frank's had, they don't have an open casket.

In second grade—or was it third?—we took a field trip to the zoo. Mary Toni almost missed it; she'd slept through the bus and her mom was *pissed* about having to give Mary Toni a ride. Resa came barreling into the zoo and made a scene that no doubt mortified Mary Toni. I hadn't seen Resa since the funeral, but I knew it was her because she smelled the same. Which is to say: like death.

I didn't know Resa well, as Mary Toni was never allowed to have anyone over. Initially I'd assumed the death smell could be explained by the occasion. Perhaps all funerals smelled of leaves rotting in sour milk—and by extension, grieving widows. But a year or two after Frank's death, Resa still smelled that way. It was obvious when she blew past us all to gripe at Sister Hutchins.

Later, when I did start sneaking over to the Habsburg residence, I noticed the same smell there, permeating the whole house. With all the candor of a child, I asked Mary Toni what it was.

"What smell?" Mary Toni said. "I don't smell anything."

I described the wet quality of it—a thing in the middle stages of active decay. She picked a pillow up off the couch and, pressing her face into it, inhaled deeply.

"It's just my home," she said, and I nodded, because it was. Frank had died a long time ago, but in that house, mother and daughter were keeping him alive, willing his spirit if not his body to stay and keep dwelling among them. Meanwhile, every day Resa escorted a hospice patient or two to another plane, and those dying breaths, they clung to her.

TEZ

For years, the necklace was at the center of everything Mary Toni did. When her Barbies got married, Skipper wore the charm like a jewel in her ponytail. The stone became valuable currency, worth much in trade, when she and a friend played at ransoming a hostage situation. It was a sundial for a sky-loving species to tell time by; they deciphered the spinning amulet's thrown shadows like a crone reading a gender string. Mary Toni handled the necklace so often that its gold chain tarnished, then wore, in places, revealing plated brass, and the gem came loose in its setting. To Mary Toni, these signs of use were marks of love, only enhancing the object's beauty.

But one day the stone fell out entirely. She caught it mid-air like a viper. Freed of its crimped backing, for the first time she saw the jewel's sole flaw—a tiny imperfection, like a rock chip or a grain of sand, only visible when the light shone through it unrestricted. Mary Toni fell in love with that scar, which, like a bellybutton, hinted at its origin story. A drop of heart blood, a fruiting body, crystallizing on supple branch.

THE CLASSMATE

Yeah, I was jealous. My dad didn't get me a necklace like that for Confirmation. So yeah, I was happy when she lost it.

TEZ

"Mommy! Watch me!" Mary Toni yelled.

Resa gave her a distracted thumbs-up, and the girl took her fullest breath yet. Kicked off from Barton Springs's mossy rock floor and somersaulted head over heels—

once—twice—three times—on her third try tipping sideways underwater.

She came up spitting, but quickly recovered. A grandstanding water gymnast at the dismount. Mary Toni wiped plastered strands of hair and snot from her face. Looked toward Mom.

Reclined on a picnic blanket beneath a giant oak, Resa had her nose in a magazine. She'd missed the whole thing.

Deflated but not surprised, Mary Toni turned her attention to her new friend. A younger girl. They resumed playing at diving rings.

Then: "Mommy! MOM-mee!" Mary Toni screamed.

Frank would have been on his feet at once, scanning the crowded pool for a drowning daughter. Resa, however, didn't respond—might honestly not even have heard her, so good was she at tuning out the world's noise. She noticed it, though, when the girl appeared beside her, tears and spring water both dripping all over her pages, smearing the letters together in gray-black blobs.

"What? What happened?" she snapped irritably.

"I lost it."

"What?"

"The Holy Spirit."

At first, Resa had no idea what she meant. But the pieces soon fell into place. "I told your father, I said to him, 'What child needs an expensive necklace?' Still, he insisted, and now you've lost it. Well, you'd better find it, hadn't you?"

Mary Toni stopped crying. Nodded mutely. Turned to walk back, head down.

THE LITTLE GIRL

She told me her name was Mary Toni, and that she'd lost her necklace. It had a shiny red stone, she said, and a shiny gold chain, and I offered to help her look for it. It'd been a

Confirmation present. I probably never would have remembered the encounter except that I didn't know what Confirmation was and the way she described it left me colder than Barton Springs's ground-fed water on a midwinter day.

"It's when God's fire licks you," she said. "And you have to catch it, if you want to keep it."

Well, I knew about God, but this was the first I'd heard of His fire, which I'd heretofore associated with the devil.

We'd been playing at diving rings for a while and I was sure she hadn't been wearing it that whole time, or I would have noticed it. Eight-year-olds don't have a lot of nice jewelry, you know? So I was helping her look and next thing I knew she was screaming underwater, clawing her way frantically back toward the sunlight. It was murky underneath; the sun didn't quite reach to the bottom, and all the people there that day were kicking up what grit had accumulated on the spring floor in the runoff. I was so sure she'd found—and been horribly burned by—God's fire that I pulled a 180 under the water and shot, a tiny girl-bullet, back across the pool and as far away from Mary Toni as I could manage. I swam faster than I'd ever swum in my life to the ladder at the opposite end of the pool, whereupon I attempted to scramble up it too quickly and slipped on the algae growing on the aluminum, banging my shin and slicing it open. Thus I ran, crying and bleeding, back to my parents' blanket. They were both napping under their sun hats and when I threw my wet and throbbing body into the tangle of them, my mother shrieked, embarrassing herself, which she later took out on me. "What the hell?" my dad said, more surprised than upset, especially once he saw my leg. "Are you okay? What happened?"

"God's fire licked me," I insisted.

"What?" Both of my parents stared at me then, confused and a little horrified. I saw all of it running across their faces. Having been raised in a stifling church themselves, they'd tried so hard to keep me away from it, or at the very least to remain neutral, until such time as I could make an informed choice. But there I was, talking about "God" and "His fire" and it was everything they could do not to make a face, not to snatch me close to their chests and hold me, whispering, "It's not real, sweetheart," and, "You're okay; you're okay," all the while plotting the violent death of whatever public school teacher had filled my head with such inappropriate ideas.

"There was a girl," I said, pointing back in the general direction of where Mary Toni and I had been playing, but of course she was gone. Likely, I believed in that moment, swallowed up by flames—somehow burned alive in the middle of all that water. God was nothing if not all-powerful. That much I'd learned from the Christian infomercials that regularly sliced into my Afterschool Special-watching and channel-flipping.

They weren't listening, though. They were more concerned about my leg. My dad scooped me up and lay me across his lap and my mom was already headed for the lifeguard's stand, where there was a first-aid kit. She returned shortly with some gauze and medical tape and an alcohol pad that stung worse than the injury. It felt like God's fire, all right.

TEZ

Mary Toni wouldn't learn about evolution—the Paleozoic and the Biblical moment when the first fish crawled ashore and drew breath—until fifth grade. So, at eight, she'd simply accepted that some animals breathe underwater and some, including humans, need an oxygen-rich atmosphere. But dang was it annoying when you were trying to find something at the bottom of a limestone pool and that slimy, algae-covered rock beckoned from beneath four feet of the blue stuff. Goggles and a snorkel only went so far.

The next time she dipped her head in, a flash near

the right angle where pool wall met pool floor caused Mary Toni to squint, determined to pick out the living fire lost to that which would extinguish it. She shoved arms and legs through the water, a dull ache in her shoulders signaling a too-long day of swimming, and kicked harder.

Now, where was that?

Blindly, for her whole-body thrashing had kicked up sediment on the spring floor, she groped at the spot, lungs beginning to scream. It was nearly evening. Although the light was orange yet, it was darker down there now. An emerald sea lapping the walls of an onyx cave.

There!

That flash again, and Mary Toni darted out a hand.

Contact. With a squishy, struggling salamander. Its eye the only source of reflection this deep.

"Ugh," she screamed, the last of her breath rising in a torrent of bubbles to the surface. Mr. Salamander sinking with an equal but opposite velocity.

Suddenly desperate for air, she turtled her head above the surface.

Gasped.

Watched another kid cannonball off the diving board before slowly inching toward the ladder. Desperate to stave off Mom's disappointment.

THE LIFEGUARD

Well, I didn't know her name was Marie Antoinette, but yeah, I noticed her in the pool. We called them Hunters, the people who came out looking for the Barton Springs salamanders, which are super endangered now. We lifeguards were trained to spot them. They'd sneak in nets inside their coolers, the Hunters, and the coolers were actually empty, because that's where they planned to put the ones they caught. Then they sold them on the exotic pet market. Anyway, this girl was one of them. I'd been seeing more and more of it that summer: parents roping their kids into the deed. How could I tell? Because of the way she was *looking*. Like she'd dropped something, only it was for the damn salamanders. She kept surfacing to take these deep breaths before disappearing again. Then she must have actually found one, because her whole body jerked, right? This kind of involuntary reaction to touching something, or something touching you, when you least expect it? Like as not, it scared the salamander away and I saw her walk empty-handed back to her mom, head down, like she knew she'd messed up. Perfectly nice, ordinary-looking woman, too. You never know the criminals in your midst anymore. Unlike the Barton Springs salamander, human beings as a species are getting better at camouflage, at mass deception.

TEZ

Losing the necklace felt like losing Frank for the second time.

But losing Mops? That was a death knell for Mary Toni's own soul.

THE NEIGHBOR

Over the years, I often heard her in the backyard at night. More fire ceremonies, sometimes, but also just being a kid. She had that dog—a pug, I think. Mops? Occasionally, I watched them through the fence.

"Body of Christ," Mary Toni said one night, holding a baked brown doggie biscuit up for Mops. The dog, obediently sitting, cocked his head expectantly. *What must he do to get the biscuit into his belly?*

"You're supposed to say 'Amen,'" Mary Toni prompted him. Mops barked accordingly.

"Okay, now stick out your tongue." She fed him the 'host,' a little pseudo communion, practicing for the day she'd be a eucharistic minister. Mary Toni made the sign of the cross over the dog. Drew the knife edge of her right hand through the air from Mops's forehead to his forepaws, his right shoulder to his left. He licked at her hand appreciatively, wanting more.

THE VET

Dogs are man's—and child's—best friend for a reason. They keep us active, they encourage play, and they comfort us, wordlessly and free of judgment. Mops, a pug mix, did that and more for Mary Toni. He was her truest playmate; her most trusted confidante; a security blanket in the wake of her father's death. But the peace he initially gave her became a dangerous crutch. After a while, she couldn't bear to be without him, and she worried constantly that he'd suddenly up and die on her without warning, the way Frank had. Mary Toni probably walked that dog over to the clinic every two weeks for a "check-up," simply because he'd scratched his ear differently or sneezed too many times in the sunlight. Of all the canine diseases that pugs are prone to, Mops had never tested positive for any of them, and I had no reason to believe he'd live anything other than a long and healthy life. Especially given the way his owner doted on him. Luckily, dogs can't catch hypochondria, or I might have prescribed Mops some doggie Klonopin for anxiety. Instead I had to treat Mary Toni, which since I can't legally dispense human drugs or diagnoses, meant obliging her by shining a light in Mops's ears and up his nose, "just to be safe," and maybe palpating his soft belly on her most worked-up days. The little ritual visibly calmed her every time, and it's not like it put me out any. I did feel bad for her, though. Losing a parent is tough enough, but to be so certain, using a little kid's logic, that your dog will be next to go? And then when that dog *does* go? Sometimes the universe is fucking unfair, you know?

TEZ

Mops died three years after Frank, both of them freak accidents. Instinct drove the dog to chase the squirrel into the street, and little dogs are no match for pick-up trucks.

When Mary Toni found him, he was still alive. Still whining and nodding his little pug head, licking his muzzle, trying to scoot closer to her. He made it all the way to the vet's office, devoted to the end, begrudging no one, before laying his beloved beige head in his girl-child's lap for the final time. Mops's heart kicked against her sweaty palm until it didn't, slowing even as the doc withdrew his needle. It was a moment Mary Toni hadn't gotten with Daddy three years earlier.

She cried because she could literally see the light fading from his eyes and a friend that loyal deserved a few shed tears. So she gave Mops the only ones she had left—the last of a lifelong reserve exhausted in the five days leading up to, and the 900 days since, her father's funeral.

And then she stopped.

She accepted his heavier body (death somehow having a weight to it, even after the departure of a soul) wrapped in one of Frank's old shirts, and rode home with Resa in silence. They'd had three years to practice, mother and daughter, the silence. Not strained, not pregnant with anything other than acknowledged affirmation. Like Resa, Mary Toni had learned her lesson well. The things and people you love will leave you. Better not to love at all.

They buried Mops in the backyard, under the oak where girl and dog had once played at church. The forty-eight-year-old and the ten-year-old took turns digging, scraping away at Austin's clay-rich soil, until they hit the inevitable layer of limestone. Not an ideal depth, but deep enough. Mary Toni filled in the hole alone.

THE NEIGHBOR

In the weeks after poor Frank's death—the details of which were, at Resa's request, never made public—I'd noticed a curious thing: Mary Toni had stopped using her nightlight.

Every evening since they'd moved in, Mary Toni's bedroom window had glowed faintly amber thanks to a custom lamp Frank had ordered at her birth. I know because I asked him about it once: What gave the light that particular quality, as though it was also moving at times? He'd shown me the device the next day. A laser-cut bamboo bowl sat over the bulb and rotated when turned on, making the shapes of weather patterns play upon the walls. Clouds and raindrops and the stick-straight waves of a sun were cut into its domed walls, and when these moved over the window they accounted for the wavering light I saw.

"It wards off bad dreams," he'd explained. "And it's a lighthouse for good ones."

"You're a good father," I told him, perhaps a little boldly.

Frank just laughed. "Resa's worried I'm setting up Mary Toni to be a storm chaser, but watching the weather together is our favorite ritual. I don't want her to be afraid of it, since she knows how important it is to my safety on the job."

"Maybe she'll be a studio meteorologist," I said. "On TV, where it's safe, instead of out in the field."

"That'd be all right then. Anything, really, so long as she's happy."

I touched his arm affectionately. He reminded me so much of my late husband. That really may have been too bold, though, because he shifted his weight, his arm sliding just out of comfortable reach, and with an apologetic smile, turned to take the nightlight back inside.

After his death, I wondered: Was it too hard to have the constant reminder of what had been but was no longer? Or maybe Resa didn't know to turn it on at night? Maybe she'd even thrown it away, unable to bear the sight herself. I decided to ask her, casually, the next time we ran into each other at the mailbox. If they weren't going to use it, maybe I could have it.

I needn't have bothered dwelling so. The night Mary Toni buried Mops, something changed for the girl. Too old, by that point, to even need a nightlight, she started using it again. It burned up there every evening, a familiar beacon. Who, or what, I wondered, did she hope to ward off with it? Who did she hope to guide home?

THE ART TEACHER

Mary Toni hated reading, writing, and history. "Words," she told me once, "are written by men, and men lie." According to her, numbers told the only truths that matter. Formulas calculated—and every time correctly—the length of a hypotenuse; the chemical makeup of sodium chloride. Everything else was a story—about what could happen or had already happened—and while stories had their place (especially when, like in *A Clockwork Orange*, they taught you something about yourself), subjective stories for Marie Antoinette just couldn't compete with empirical certitude.

When she decided, at age ten, to become a meteorologist, she chalked up her vocation to science. What more satisfying career path could there be than one that used objective principles to observe and predict atmospheric phenomena, impacting every person's everyday life? Resa, of course, assumed the interest was a phase, a child's obsession with the forecast. A child's stubborn need to keep saving her father, years after his demise. All Mary Toni knew was that the clouds spoke. Their language was math, and if she could learn it, maybe no one else would have to die.

TEZ

At first, she didn't think she could do it. Her science teacher had *promised* her that the half of the worm with the head still attached would regrow its missing tail . . . but wouldn't it *hurt*? Didn't earthworms feel pain? And what would she see in the dissected tail but half-digested sense memories? Proof that the thing had eaten—lived—maybe even loved, with an intense earthworm love, the horny little hermaphrodites!

Staring at it squiggling across the lab table, Mary Toni unexpectedly thought of Frank: the first and only time he'd taken her fishing. He'd shown her how to hook the worm for bait, and set the reel of the hot pink rod purchased the week before for her sixth birthday. Together, they'd sat still as statues in their canoe and peered deeply, ultimately vainly, into the murky water. Looking for fish—a turtle—mossy reeds that might hide freshwater mermaids. She'd dropped the worm beneath the water. Waited. There'd been a tug, tentative; then a yank that nearly tore the pole from her surprised hands. No more worm. Where had it gone? What had eaten it?

Daddy.

Where had he gone? What had—or was still—eating him?

The night after the dissection lab, unable to sleep, Mary Toni made friends with death. Tiptoeing so as not to wake her mother, she stole down the stairs and out the backdoor. The flashlight she often used to perform shadow plays on the walls cast long, uncertain dancers upon the fence. They ducked and wove and pirouetted around her. Witnesses? Or a warning?

THE NEIGHBOR

The earth was cold, cold as it ever gets in Texas, and hard as it always is, all limestone and clay. It's why they hadn't been able to bury Mops very deep, and why it didn't take Mary Toni long to find him. She'd marked the shallow grave with a pile of rocks that had sunk somewhat, moss carpeting their smooth heads where they stuck out above the overgrown grass. She removed them first, carefully, re-stacking the rocks along the back fence. Then she took a steel soup spoon to the ground, prying great clods of clay free.

The flannel shirt they'd wrapped Mops in was stained and beginning to disintegrate. Pieces of the shirt came up with each spoonful, and probably pieces of Mops, too.

When she'd exposed most of the fabric, she unbuttoned the long row of pearl snaps, still shiny in the crisp moonlight, and gingerly peeled the shirt open.

TEZ

Years later, Mary Toni would unbutton her husband's shirt and flash back to this moment: a profane defiling of the flesh. She'd press her face to his chest and breathe deeply, inhaling pine sap and camphor, and wonder what sweeter rot they were intended to conceal.

Everything decays.

THE NEIGHBOR

Months of unseasonal rains had accelerated the sea change. Bits of bone and matted tufts of fur lined a hollow actively caving in on itself. Way past the point of maggots or grubs or centipedes with searching pincers—just a slow, silent settling.

I don't know what Mary Toni was expecting, or even if she knew what to expect. What did she feel? Relief? Disappointment? A jaded resignation or a sense of peace at the fact that it really does all become one thing?

My voice unanticipated—but not, by her reaction, unwelcome—I called to her over the fence. "I had a dog once," I said.

"What was its name?" Mary Toni asked, abandoning her spoon to the hole and rising to walk to the fence.

"Duke."

"What happened to him?"

"Oh, I figure he looks more or less like Mops now. Dust to dust, etcetera."

Mary Toni peered through a missing knot in the fence slat. Through it, she surely could see me: a shawl around my shoulders and a cigarette in my hand.

"But it's just his body, you know," I continued. "His soul, I reckon, moved on somewhere else. Somewhere better."

"And Mops?"

"Well, if God created animal-kind, I figure He must love them, too."

Mary Toni pondered my response. We both watched the tip of my cigarette flare orange: a firefly in November.

"Yes," I said, answering the question she hadn't asked. "I smoke. On occasion. Watch and pray that you may not enter into temptation. The spirit indeed is willing, but the flesh is weak."

Matthew 26:41.

Mary Toni shivered. The temperature was falling in inverse proportion to the rising moon, and she wasn't wearing a sweater. Closing the flaps of Dad's shirt over Mops's remains, she replaced the rocks in haphazard fashion and scampered toward her own back porch.

After the girl had tucked herself back into bed, I used the glowing end of my cigarette to light another.

FERSEN

By the time Mary Toni entered fifth grade, I'd watched her evolve from a tiny little elf-child into a prepubescent girl, a pleasing layer of chub around her middle and thighs that signaled an impending growth spurt. Every day for the past four years, when the lunch bell had rung, I'd gotten butterflies in my stomach and an involuntary smile on my face, knowing that I had only to step out with the rest of my clamoring students and there she'd be, standing quietly against the wall and clutching a neat sack lunch she'd made herself.

"Hello, Mary Toni," I greeted her—our one guaranteed interaction and the moment to which I most looked forward. The way her eyes lit up when she saw me; the quick, self-conscious wave; the secret grin. In this way, I watched her milk teeth grow and fall out, the robust tip of a bright pink tongue taking their place for the months before her adult teeth descended. I would stick my tongue out back at her, just to make her laugh. Precious girl, protected by the cute but confounding innocence of childhood.

THE FRIEND

Were we friends? Maybe? For a time, definitely. First through fifth grade, I'd say. In fifth grade, everything changed.

In fifth grade, bodies change. They sprout hair in weird places and, pretty soon, fifty percent of them begin bleeding.

Classes change. You start taking different subjects from different teachers and rotating rooms. There are 'passing periods'—times to meet up with friends and make eyes at boys in the halls.

Alliances change. The heretofore vague outlines of cliques solidify. Clothes and money and factors as indefinable as "cool" stratify the junior high.

It happened to Mary Toni and me. We shared everything—or at least as much as anybody ever shared with her. And then one day we didn't anymore.

THE PRINCIPAL

At Magnificat, sex ed, such as it was, fell under the fifth-grade science umbrella. For two uncomfortable weeks, the fifth-grade teachers set the parts of the cell aside to discuss what happens when gametes meet, how fertilization occurs, and what that means for human bodies. Always, the boys and the girls got divided into separate rooms. While the male teacher muddled his way through the male body, trying as much as the church would allow to normalize involuntary erections and wet dreams, the school nurse took the girls through demonstrations of training bras and sanitary pads, hygiene and hair growth. Babies, portrayed as the natural consequence of lovemaking within marriage, received a cursory mention. Condoms and STDs did not.

"Above all," the nurse stressed, "if you get your period at school, you should come to see me in the principal's office."

That's precisely what Mary Toni did the next month, holding her stomach, a dark red flower blooming on the seat of her skirt.

TEZ

She told her mom when Resa got home from work that night. The stomach cramps had worsened. "It feels like a buffalo is stampeding across my ovaries," Mary Toni said. "And like I need to throw up. Only I can't."

To her credit, nurse Resa offered her eleven-year-old daughter ibuprofen instead of codeine.

Mary Toni would suffer from menstrual cramps the rest of her life. Then one day she'd start bleeding and never really stop.

THE FRIEND

The summer before sixth grade, someone had a pool party for their birthday. They invited the whole class. We were old enough, then, to be conscious of our bodies, the differences between boy parts and girl parts, and not just anatomically, but symbolically—which is to say, they fit together, yes, and maybe we wanted them to. So the pretty girls wore bikinis and flipped their hair, laid on lounge chairs and wouldn't get wet, while the rest of us, who wanted to get in the pool but feared taking off our clothes, and the miles of skin it would reveal, compromised by wearing our fathers' undershirts into the water.

Mary Toni wasn't a pretty girl, but nor would she get in the water. Some of the other girls whispered, "She must be on her period," and I cringed for Mary Toni, knowing she'd never live down staining her skirt, not for as long as she stayed in that school district. But also because I knew it had nothing to do with whether or not she was bleeding. She'd been telling all of us for years, whether we'd listened or not, that water, even the "safe" water of a pool, was dangerous. It hid black holes.

TEZ

Mary Toni started sixth grade at Magnificat—a year like any other, except now she had Fersen for a teacher. And more people than just him began to "take an interest" in the girl otherwise so easy to overlook.

FERSEN

The joy of finally having her in class—it salved my very soul! Everything I'd done, everything I'd worked toward, here it was before me in an adorable plaid uniform, a tidy and sweet-smelling sweatshirt. "Lavender oil," she said when I asked her, and the shooting star of a grateful grin burst upon my face, then was gone. Propriety, you know.

"You remembered," I said. I'd recommended it for anxiety. Apparently it had worked, or else she'd grown calmer, more self-controlled with age. Maybe both.

"Are you still playing the piano?" I asked. "How's your mom? How's Mops?" I couldn't believe I had so many questions—it had only been a summer since she'd last bobbed past my classroom!—but I wanted to know everything. "Spill!" I commanded, resting my head on my fists, elbows on the desk, leaning forward expectantly.

"Mops died," she said, ignoring my first two questions.

"What?" Having opened my mouth to insert one foot, I closed it again. "When? How? Mary Toni, I'm so sorry."

The heart I thought would explode now threatened to break—for her, for the dog I'd never met.

"Years ago," she said, crushing me. I'd missed more of her life than I'd meant to. "Anyway, I should go. I'm not feeling well."

It was my last chance to stop her—a doorway, an invitation—for *that* day, anyway. The foot in my mouth became a foothold. "Really? What's wrong? Can I get you anything?"

"Just cramps," she said. "I'll be fine." And she turned to go, an Eve unwittingly dooming Adam to die. For, upon tasting the forbidden fruit, his eyes were opened. He saw the truth, and knowledge gained can never be un-gleaned.

Which is to say that when Mary Toni so casually mentioned her cramps, she blossomed before me from girl into woman. She became a thing that bleeds, from parts I'd never dared imagine on a student. Warm. Wet. Infinitely soft.

When I remembered to breathe, it came long and shuddering. A corresponding tingle in my fingertips.

No, no, no, I thought, but she'd planted her seed in fertile soil. The seed of idea, of desire. I *wanted* those parts. Every inch of her not-yet-teenaged, lavender-oiled skin.

I might have stood to see her off except that to do so would have betrayed my wanting. Already my erection pressed painfully against my slacks. It would spring back into action any time I called to mind the smell of her, at night, home alone, and lonely. I should have seen it before, but for the apple: She'd long ago ruined any other woman for me.

THE FRIEND

When I finally got my period, it arrived on one of those rare days I wasn't obsessing over it. I'd spent the whole day outside, walking along Waller Creek with another girl from Magnificat and gushing to her about Nick Dancy. I'd kissed him—just once, in the parking lot after the basketball game—and I could see it all: Our future spread before us like a movie.

The house on the lake. Matching Corvettes. Two perfect, tow-headed children.

My friend listened to me ramble and commiserated with apt responses when appropriate, but paid much more attention to the way the light was falling through the trees just then. Warm and ochre-colored, summer was heaving its last gasp before it gave up the ghost to fall. The heat smelled like dry grass and sun-bleached cicada hulls. We lost ourselves to these sensations; so when my uterus started to cramp, I thought only that it'd been a while since I used the restroom.

On almost any other day, I thought about my period incessantly. I was thirteen, and a year or two behind my peers developmentally. Resa made sure I knew that. My mom had asked her to give me the talk in second grade, long before it was necessary or probably even advised. A nurse, Resa had described it—puberty; sex; my body—in strictly clinical terms, unable to divorce me, a child, from any other one of her clients. And I'd more or less lived in fear from that day onward of the weird, scary, textbook-sterile thing that was one day going to happen to me, probably when I was at school and completely unprepared. I'd seen it happen to other girls, to Mary Toni: the telltale wet spot around a darker stain on the rear of their skirts, where they'd bled through without realizing; and then, upon realizing it, had spent recess trying to scrub it out in the bathroom. I hated those girls when I saw them. They represented a fate I hadn't chosen but was nevertheless subject to. Blood. Mess. Pain. Never mind that it's the legacy of female kind, the mark of womanhood. The password into a secret sisterhood I didn't understand and didn't want to.

My mother was so excited that she invited Mary Toni over to make what she called "witch cakes" with us. She still thought the two of us were friends, didn't realize how everything had changed for reasons we couldn't have articulated, beyond "growing up." I was surprised when Mary Toni actually came. I don't think my mother even noticed how awkward we were around each other.

Mom did all the talking while Mary Toni and I stirred flour and sugar and eggs, mixed with red food coloring, scooped the batter into blobs, and baked them on a sheet in the oven. We ate a few of them, and threw the rest out for the birds. I thought it was a stupid ceremony, and said so, hurting my mother's feelings. Mary Toni didn't say anything.

THE ART TEACHER

By junior high, Mary Toni's drawing skills had improved. Her landscapes took on a hyper-real quality, like you might fall right into Lake Travis at sunset, or feel the spray if you stood too close to her framed waterfall. I entered her pieces in the Texas State Fair. She never placed lower than third, and often won her age group, which came with a ribbon and a small cash prize. While fine art skills are dandy on their own, in seventh grade I encouraged her to think about commercial art.

"Marketing. Advertising," I explained. "Using the images you create to sell things."

"Like magazine ads?" She made a face.

"Or product design," I clarified. "The apple on the bottle of apple juice. Someone has to dream that up and draw it."

It's how I roped her into joining Student Council, where she proceeded to design and produce flyers for school dances, letterhead for the Magnificat newsletter, and even a new logo for the theater department. These were great ways for Mary Toni to sharpen her skills, stay involved, and stay out of trouble. At first. The theater department she took to a little too strongly.

THE DRAMA TEACHER

The year Mary Toni entered seventh grade, I assigned a method acting unit. We spent a week of class talking about the entertainers who did it regularly. We poured some (cartoned milk) out for those who, haunted in life by their characters, rode the roles to the grave. I offered them a choice: "Pick your own character, or I'll pick one for you." Mary Toni knew immediately who she wanted to play.

TEZ

Six years earlier, Stanley Kubrick's *A Clockwork Orange* had rocked Austin's box office. Resa had gone to see it, high on a cocktail of Valium and codeine, and fallen in love with Malcolm McDowell as Alex DeLarge. Uncharacteristically reflective, Resa had crawled into bed with Mary Toni and taken her in her arms, inhaling the top of her daughter's head deeply. "That's the kind of movie I'd make," she'd confessed. "An un—" (inhale) "—flinching depiction of the human condition."

She'd tilted Mary Toni's sleepy head up to gaze into her eyes. "Tell any story you want," Resa had said, her words thick and hard to understand, "so long as it tells the truth. Mm-kay?"

Mom already snoring, Mary Toni hadn't dared to interrupt her. And anyway, she thought she understood: *Not every story is about redemption. Not every life gets redeemed.*

THE DRAMA TEACHER

She said, "I will play Alex DeLarge." At first, I said no—it's not appropriate. But Mary Toni pressed, pointing out and rightly that other thirteen-year-olds in the world really are addicted to drugs and sex and aren't those stories worth telling, too? Because they're true? Because Truth is a Catholic school cornerstone and God is "the Way and the Truth" and even people like Alex's character are children of God?

Furthermore, I knew from experience that it was generally futile to argue with Mary Toni. So I agreed with a tired caveat: "No explicit drug usage. No swearing. No sex."

"No problem," Mary Toni complied.

She pulled a black Sharpie from her backpack and

made for the girls' dressing room. Drew what she probably imagined to be the character's trademark eyelashes, though her first attempt was decidedly raccoon-like. Oh well. She had seventy-two hours yet to practice. That's how long they were to stay in character—three days—without breaking. At sports practice, in the bathroom, in line at the grocery store, didn't matter. They were their characters. Their characters were them.

"Take notes on what happens," I advised the students. "Write down all your observations. Your feelings. If you find yourself wondering how your character would react in a given situation, watch their movie again. What do you learn about their backstory? Their motivations? Their mannerisms? Okay, off into the world with you."

TEZ

Mary Toni went straight home after school. She grabbed the cardboard shoebox from the top shelf in her closet, the one in which she stored her mom's old nursing uniforms. Taking off the lid, she thumbed a few white jumpers back, to the one with the apron whose straps looked like suspenders. She paired it with her grandpa's old black bowler, his old wood cane, borrowing them from Resa without even asking. She didn't know what to sub for the clamp that kept Alex's eyes open until she saw her mother's earrings on the dresser. Her bright gold hoops.

Resa got home close to eight. Normally, Mary Toni would have already made dinner, finished her homework, been reading a book. That night, however, Resa followed the blood from the kitchen to the bathroom, where after attempting to ice, then pierce, her own ears, Mary Toni was lying in approximately one safe inch of tub water, a pseudo-bubble bath hardly obscuring her developing body.

"Please tell me you sanitized the needle," Nurse Resa said, by way of greeting. Mary Toni's ears were red and burning, but at least she'd had the good sense to steal Resa's gold-filled hoops, a higher-quality pair than her gold-plated nickel ones.

"Rubbing alcohol, plus I put the lighter to it," the teenager said.

"Good girl." Resa studied her daughter. "You got them fairly even, anyway."

"It's for school." Mary Toni explained about method acting. "For the next sixty-seven hours, please call me Alex."

"Well, *Alex*, I suppose you'll need to borrow some makeup, too?"

"Yes. And can you help me get this Sharpie off of my eyes?"

If she couldn't take drugs herself, at least she could study the mindset of someone who did. Mary Toni had recently learned the word nihilism, and found it shockingly simple to pretend that nothing at all (other than her "habit") mattered. After all, she'd watched her mother behave that way for years.

THE PRINCIPAL

Predictably, the same Sister Hutchins who'd once taken issue with Mary Toni's Confirmation necklace stopped to pick her jaw up off the floor when the seventh grader walked into school Tuesday morning wearing her mom's modified nursing jumper and way, *way* too much makeup. Magnificat students weren't allowed to wear makeup, period, and her appearance made Sister Hutchins splutter, "Marie Antoinette. What in God's name do you think you're doing? Go to the office immediately."

She meant my office. But I was standing right there in the lobby as well, greeting students as they walked through the doors.

Far from the docile six-year-old she'd been, Mary Toni

didn't always do what she was told. And Alex never did. So the girl-child squared her shoulders, dropped her backpack on the tiled floor, and hands on hips, said as defiantly as she could muster: "Make me."

Even my heart pumped harder at the nun's bugged eyes. The shame the Church teaches all of us must have turned to nails in Mary Toni's bloodstream, but still Alex stood her ground. She might have let Sister Hutchins drag her to my office by one ear peaceably enough, except that her home-pierced ears were infected and painful. When Sister Hutchins pinched a particularly tender spot, Mary Toni batted her hand away reflexively. That was about all the insubordination Sister Hutchins could take.

"Principal, *now*," she said, pointing toward my office. Sounding for all the world like a tattletale who knows she's lost her authority. Mary Toni scoffed and, outraged, Sister Hutchins slapped her face. Student and Sister stared at each other, equally shocked. That's when I joined the fray.

"Mary Toni!" I exclaimed, sounding more authoritative than Sister Hutchins (I hoped), but at the same time already smothering a smile behind my hand. "Now, Sister Hutchins," I said, taking the nun's trembling arm. "Let's go make you some tea in the teachers' lounge. Mary Toni, please wait for me in my office. I'll be right there."

The girl was slumped uncomfortably in a hard chair when I returned. I tried to look stern but a smile won in the end—a smile I masked by shaking my head. "Alex, right?"

"That's what they call me," Mary Toni said, determined to stay in character.

"Alex, how do those new earrings feel?"

"Gratifying."

"Because you always wanted pierced ears?"

"Because they got that nun's panties in a twist."

"I thought your drama teacher said no sex."

"I'm not having any."

"But that uniform . . . you're a walking invitation."

"You like? I can make one for you, too. I'm always looking for new droogs."

I refused to take the bait. "What'd your mother say?"

"Not much. I think she was jealous. She used to want to be an actress." Mary Toni paused, then added for emphasis: "Dumb bitch."

Genuinely shocked this time, I actually yelped. "Mary Toni!"

"It's Alex," Mary Toni said, standing to walk out. She left without a backward glance.

FERSEN

A Clockwork Orange is a two-hour film. There's no time for Alex's backstory; not when the movie is about how he ends up in prison and what happens there. So, as we do when we over-romanticize anything, Mary Toni explored her own secrets—her own neuroses—her own barely acknowledged desires—through the freeing lens of Alex DeLarge. It opened something inside her that would resist ever going back in its cage again.

TEZ

Because death always comes in threes, the Habsburgs' neighbor was next, after Frank and Mops. It wasn't the woman who used to watch Mary Toni at night in the backyard, but the other one, the even older lady across the street. Resa and Mary Toni only heard about her passing when the FOR SALE sign appeared in the once-overgrown, now neatly trimmed lot.

A few days later, like something out of a dream, decidedly undomestic Resa pulled a sheet of cookies out of the oven. Snickerdoodle, by the smell of them.

"For me?" Mary Toni asked, walking in the door from

school and angling for a hot one right off the tray. "You shouldn't have!"

"Quit it," Resa replied, shooing Mary Toni's hand away. "These are for Old Lady V's wake."

"Whoa." Mary Toni suddenly didn't know how to respond—not even as Alex. Death was too real for play-acting. "When is it?"

"Tomorrow night. The reception will be at her house."

"I don't have to go, right? This is just, like, an adults-only thing?"

"You were the closest thing that batty old lady had to a granddaughter." Resa shut the oven door and turned it off. "If I'm going, you're going."

"Fine," Mary Toni pouted, "but Alex is coming with me."

FERSEN

Cheese cubes and cookies and deli rolls and watermelon slices and cut brownies and cucumber rounds and so much runny black mascara that Mary Toni blended right in, her plate stacked high as her mother's hair. There in my grandmother's kitchen, she was trying to fit one more scoop of baked mac-n-cheese atop a large pile of bacon-wrapped green beans, when she finally felt my eyes on her. Mary Toni froze, suddenly conscious of how it must look.

"What?" she confronted me, though I hadn't yet said a thing. "I'm a growing boy." But she set the cheese-caked metal spoon down anyway and didn't touch it again.

Stepping out of the shadows and into the yellow glow of the single ancient pendant light hanging above the kitchen table, I picked the spoon up. I licked it, never mind it was the serving spoon, my tongue cleaning all the muck from the metal. "Oh!" I said, loud, closing my eyes and feigning ecstasy. "Oh, it was gorgeousness and gorgeosity made flesh!"

A heartbeat. A moment where everything hung precarious. I didn't dare breathe, let alone look. Would she understand?

"Like a bird of rarest-spun heavenmetal," Mary Toni said, her voice earnest, reverential even. I could almost hear Beethoven in the background. "Like silvery wine flowing in a space ship."

My grin could have split my face in two. She was a perfect Alex.

Mary Toni smiled back. "What are you doing here? Don't you have, like, lesson plans to write?"

I told the truth. "Old Lady V is—well, *was*—my grandmother."

"Right," she said, and rolled her eyes.

"No, really."

Mary Toni—Alex?—got mad. I was refuting her. "That's impossible," she cried. "Old Lady V didn't *have* any grandchildren. She was so totally alone that the only person who ever came to visit was the Meals on Wheels guy. And me and my mom sometimes."

"I've no doubt that she felt very alone," I said, "but that was her choice. She disowned us all some time ago."

Her eyes narrowed. "Well, then she probably doesn't want you at her wake, either."

Fair point. If Grandma had relented toward the end, she would have left us, and not Simon's Sorrow, all of Grandpa's money.

Feeling defensive, I chucked my chin at her suspenders, the white skirt she'd cut too short. "I doubt she would have approved of that get-up at her wake, either. And arguing with a nun in school? Tsk-tsk."

She blushed.

"Do you find it easy?" I asked. "Being someone else?"

"I like Alex. He's smart, and dedicated, and tough. So, yeah."

"Those things aren't exactly a stretch for you."

I felt I could read her warring thoughts. Was that a

compliment? What should she say? Alex would walk away whistling—probably to "Singing in the Rain."

So Mary Toni did.

TEZ

When did I get so old? Resa wondered, watching her only daughter—thirteen now; a young woman—slink slouch-shouldered down the hallway. She appraised Mary Toni's body with a critical eye. With—she would have admitted it—unapologetic envy. It was the body Resa used to have, before stretch marks, before eighteen months of a suckling pig. It'd been years since anyone had sucked on her nipples. Adam, Frank's brother, didn't have that kind of time for her. Their couplings were perfunctory, her body but a tool.

She owned a few lacy nothings yet, more out of laziness than anything else. She and Frank had bought them together, between the second and third failed pregnancies, when it had still felt like there'd been a point to trying. And there had been—because in the end, there was Mary Toni.

But no Frank.

No Frank, and sometimes, late at night, or in the middle of the afternoon, or upon waking from a dream, Resa craved it: human touch. Two grasping hands and a hungrier mouth. The dampness of desire.

Downstairs, Mary Toni popped something in the microwave, pressed a few beeping buttons. She didn't need Mom to take care of her that night. Momma could take care of herself.

Resa turned, found her bedroom, eased the door shut. Soft click. In the dark, felt her way to the bureau. Top right drawer. Pulled it open. Identified by touch the bundled socks. Nail clippers. A pile of old receipts. Fingered, at last, a rough bit of lace. The familiar give of a rubber toy. Drew a bath. Thought briefly of Frank—and when it hurt too much, Adam—though the thought did little for her. Tried to remember what it was like, so long ago, to be loved.

MERCY

"And who is this?"

Resa sidled up next to King Louie at an on-campus event: a preview weekend for rising eighth graders to test out the college experience. She and Mary Toni were wandering booth to booth, talking to the student heads of the Physics Club and the Film Society, the social chairs for a dozen different sororities. Soon they passed by the booth for Simon's Sorrow, and there was King Louie, all long locks and crushed velvet robes. He was drinking spring water from a crystal goblet and looking completely unaffected by the Texas heat. Resa, on the other hand, already hot and bothered, flushed harder when she saw him. She approached. Pretended to act very, very interested in what he had to say.

"Oh, I think I heard about you on the radio . . . " She trailed off, suddenly aware of her unselfconscious prattling, and the way King Louie hadn't looked at her once—had in fact kept his eyes trained on Mary Toni. The girl was listlessly rifling through the pamphlets on the Simon's Sorrow table, reading the occasional snippet about a man who thought he was a sorcerer.

"So, you're like some kind of magic club?" she asked.

At her question, King Louie's dead eyes lit up. He leaned toward her on his regrettably plebeian metal folding chair. Beside him sat the student body president, a recent convert, and me, his righthand man. We both kept Resa distracted while King Louie talked to the girl.

"Like a magic club, yes," King Louie mused. "Only when we saw people in half, generally they don't get put back together again."

Mary Toni scrunched up her face, narrowed her eyes.

"What I mean is," King Louie continued, "we crack people open. Strip them of the shells they've built around themselves like armor; remove—then burn—the masks they've worn for years. Whole lifetimes. And we turn that army of false idols into warriors for truth. And truth, Mary Toni," he said, startling her when he addressed her by name (though she was wearing a nametag, after all) is in many ways the opposite of magic. A magician never tells his secrets—but at Simon's Sorrow, we want to know exactly what you're made of."

TEZ

Deciding she'd had enough, Mary Toni shot a look at Resa like, *Let's go, Mom,* and it was all her lonely mother could do to pull herself away from the most male attention she'd had in years. Resa left promising to check out Service someday soon and giggled all the way across the quad, asking, "What did you think about the tall one? Mercy? What an interesting name. You know, there are so many more options for young people today than I ever had." They crossed Speedway, looped around the Blanton Museum of Art, and in the rainbow glow of downtown Austin, Mary Toni had to agree: people her age had all the options, except the ones that mattered. How did you call a father back from the grave?

THE NUN

I'm the one who recommended Mary Toni for the Simon's Sorrow internship. I thought it would give her some structure. Keep her out of trouble for the summer, and maybe even lend her some direction. A religious life is not for everyone, but truth be told, I was probably hard on Marie Antoinette because she reminded me so much of myself. Quiet. A bit of a loner. Pain still darkening her downturned eyes. She needed a purpose—something larger than everything that hurt. I hoped the church could be that for her.

At the time, all I knew about Simon's Sorrow was that they were Christian, and they had money. This internship program for rising high schoolers seemed a good use of those funds; a way of really reaching out to, and serving, the community. I can't comment on what happened there. It's all just hearsay anyway. Obviously, had I known about King Louie and what he believed it meant to build God's kingdom on Earth, I would never have sent him a child.

THE FRIEND

The announcement came in the school newsletter. "Paid summer internship awarded to Marie Antoinette Habsburg, Magnificat eighth grader." I didn't have to read any further to know it meant Mary Toni. Sister had been bragging about her for weeks, telling everyone how deserving Mary Toni was and what a good example she set for the rest of us. I'll admit I was jealous. I felt just as qualified for the job as Mary Toni, but no one had nominated me for it. Instead I'd be stuck babysitting all summer, while she got a "real-life experience"—something my parents were always telling me I needed more of. Had I kept some perspective, I might have recognized that there was literally nothing else in Mary Toni's entire life to be jealous of. She hated school, though she was a naturally gifted student. Those competing interests canceled each other out somewhere around a solid C average. She was an equally mediocre-looking girl. No distinguishing features beyond unusually dark eyes. They had a cute house, one of the original East Austin bungalows, but Mary Toni's dad was dead and her mom was a drug addict who'd been convicted of gross negligence as a hospice nurse. No, there was very little to covet from Mary Toni's life.

And yet, the next day at school, when the principal congratulated Mary Toni over the intercom during morning announcements, I saw the tiniest smile steal across her face. She kept her eyes down and didn't look at anyone else—not even, as I would have, to see who was looking back at me with secret or not-so-secret resentment. She tucked the edges of her lips inside her mouth and soon everyone moved on to thinking about lunch. That's the only blip it made on Austin's radar. A month later, the semester ended and none of us saw her again.

FERSEN

Somehow, I was last to know about the internship. My knowing might not have changed anything in the end, but I prided myself on being completely up-to-date on everything in Mary Toni's life. Still, I missed this vital development—probably because Sister, who nominated her, liked me about as much as she'd liked Isaac Crable; meaning we didn't exactly "hang out" in the teachers' lounge. Having grown up around religious types, with my very own nut job in the family—RIP, Grandma—I guess I knew to leave well enough alone. Also, I never read the school newsletter and must have been out sick the day they announced it over the intercom, or you can bet I would have intervened.

Instead, on the last day of school in Mary Toni's eighth-grade year, I waved goodbye to her as I always did, unaware more than half a decade would pass before I'd see her again. Sure, she was graduating middle school and would no longer roam the halls at Magnificat, but I'd already taken pains to keep her in my orbit: a perfect, pale moon, forever half in shadow (I adored how independent she was! how quiet! how mysterious!), but never not close by.

Over the summer, I'd prepare her to go out for the

track team, a new challenge she seemed keen to try. Come autumn, she'd be a "study buddy" in my classroom, helping kids learn math (the only subject she could stomach) as service hours for National Honor Society.

So, not thinking anything of it, I waved goodbye. Watched her long legs, suddenly like a gazelle's, carry her smoothly and assuredly away from me. Her backpack, peppered with pins and patches, hung carelessly from one shoulder. An on-again, off-again friend whose name I could never remember walked with her. She made a joke, and Mary Toni smirked. I so looked forward to meeting her at the track—the hour, so soon now, when her smile would be directed at me.

PART TWO
FIRST BLOOD

MERCY

FROM THE OUTSIDE, the temple looked like any other 1960s storefront on the Drag: beige, brick, square. It was only ten years old when we moved in, but still we had to renovate it entirely. The broken, soaped-over windows had been the first things to go. Once removed, the building seemed a gutted thing, lifeless. It stared through black holes at the university campus across the street. "This," said King Louie, spreading his arms as he took in the facade, "this hallowed hollowness, this scraped-out womb, is precisely what makes her a worthy vessel for the Lord."

Woman-born may have been good enough for Jesus, but Second Birth required a passage purer than female. Less mucus; more mosaic. Less pushing; more perfume and powder.

Young then, but already displaying the kind of pious zealotry and calculated charm that make ladies spread their legs and men part with their money, King Louie surveyed the construction site with satisfaction. Shoulder-length hair hugged a handsome, if pudgy, face. A vintage French army jacket, buttoned to his double chin, declared war on the Texas heat, while a large school ring belied his only allegiance.

"And where will the Mouth go?" he asked.

I consulted the blueprints. "Here, sir," I indicated, pacing out a 13-by-13-foot square in the plaster dust.

"And the Precipice?"

"Facing east, sir, as you requested."

Running a thick finger over his wet lips, considering: "The Icebox?"

"They're soundproofing it as we speak."

"Very good, Mercy. I think this space will do nicely."

Sounds of traffic and cicadas. Students laughing on the quad.

"When will the windows go in?"

I checked my clipboard. "Monday, sir."

"Make it Friday. Let's let them know we're coming."

THE ARCHITECT

"Ceilings high enough to reach God." That's how he described the vaulted monstrosity he envisioned.

MERCY

Power tools whirred late into the night. I kept glancing at the watch on my wrist. The crew was behind schedule, and we'd already extended the contract twice. Miss Lord Simon's feast day, and King Louie would have had my title, called me "unfit" to be a doctor of the church.

"How much longer?" I barked at the tired man planing a stack of floorboards. Sweat streaked his dusty face; it was 100 degrees at 10:00 p.m.

"At least a week. Maybe more. We have to finish wiring before the drywall goes up. Paint." The man gestured at the boards. "Finish the floors."

At my scowl, the worker shrugged his shoulders. "What do you want, man? A *pinche* miracle?"

Disgusted, I turned to go. Crossed the room that would one day, Simon willing, be the sanctuary. A mushroom cloud of dust sighed up from the plastic sheeting with every step.

"Hey," the worker called at my retreating back. "I heard Jesus razed and rebuilt a temple in three days. Maybe you should see if He's available."

Although my shoulders stiffened, I refrained from engaging. Half of every battle is knowing when to bite.

TEZ

Friday morning, Austinites all over the city woke up to *Brita and Kyle in the Morning* on their radio alarm clocks. The funny, blunt duo was discussing some new temple on Guadalupe, going up right across from their beloved university. Apparently, there was an issue with the windows.

"I mean, is that even allowed?" Brita exclaimed. "If we can't say (*bleep*) on the radio, why do they get to literally depict the act of (*bleep*)-ing in their windows?

"Separation of church and state?" Kyle mused.

"If that's a church, it's (*bleep*)-ing blasphemous," Brita continued. "I don't care what your belief system is."

"And here I thought Black Masses were the stuff of ghost stories." Kyle still sounded more thoughtful than disturbed. "What do you think they practice? Sex rituals? Animal sacrifice?"

"Whatever. They won't get away with it. Not here." Brita was speaking directly to the organization now. "Austin doesn't want it."

Friday morning, Mary Toni checked the forecast. Hot and sunny.

Friday morning, Resa slept through it all.

THE STUDENT BODY VICE-PRESIDENT

On cue, Austin protested—blue fish in the red sea of Texas. They gathered with their witty signs and synchronized chants not to demand the demolition of the pornographic stained glass (believing in freedom of expression, after all), but against the threat that "false idols" posed to young minds, who at one of the top research schools in the state, were apparently largely unable to think for themselves.

But I was one of those young minds, then, and I can

tell you: It's precisely because we thought for ourselves that anything ever got done around there.

Austin heard the man who called himself King Louie defend Simon's Sorrow on the local NPR station, and they didn't buy it. Before anyone could even attend the opening Service he'd invited them all to, members of the Austin Chamber of Commerce, the Junior League, and representatives of every major world religion practiced in Texas (right down to Bahai) attempted to put a stop to what they described as "a direct affront to education, family, and community."

Meanwhile, Mercy's merry band of acolytes stayed busy stickering bus stops and paying minor celebrities to appeal to "the curious and the cowed," hungry for a master to free them from responsibility for their own lives.

Like any movement, it started with a few. Weirdos and outcasts and alchemists (in Austin, these come second only to Christians and tech bros) who saw in King Louie the prophet the world had needed since the Cold War.

"Think about it," the student body president and my co-leader said, sailing a beer pong ball smoothly into a Solo cup. "We're only three years into the 1970s and already it's safe to say we are living in the worst decade of American history."

"You mean because The Beatles broke up?" asked a blonde coed.

"Or Watergate," I offered.

Kent State," echoed an engineering student.

The president nodded and continued. "We've been crying for someone to save us. I say we give him a chance."

He sunk another shot, and onlookers cheered.

TEZ

A group of forty or so looky-loos, mainly students, that organizers would later call "healthy" showed up to the opening Service. They entered the building tentatively, curious and with wide eyes. Not sure what to expect but sure that it *could* be bad. Word had traveled via the media and one news crew snuck in, too, a discreet camera concealed in the undercover reporter's glasses. But there was a metal detector to pass through, and Mercy knew what to look for. He told the reporter that he could pick up his glasses on the way out. "We'll keep them safe," he said, "and anyway, the Good Lord gave us five senses, did He not, for uninterrupted function when one fails?" So if the gentleman couldn't see, then he, Mercy, would be the man's eyes, and guide him to a seat in the circle. And, why, King Louie would be his mouth, until he learned the proper responses. And the congregation—they could be his collective ears. There would be good food to share and women (or men, or both) to stimulate his dormant sense of touch.

"In short," Mercy concluded, "we have everything here that the mortal body needs to sustain the eternal soul. Welcome home, Caleb."

At that, the reporter looked at Mercy strangely. "My name's not Caleb."

"Isn't it, though? Moses sent twelve spies to survey the Promised Land for the Israelites. Only two—Joshua and Caleb—obeyed." He paused. "You may be a spy, but you're acting under orders, and in this house, the obedient are rewarded. So I say again, 'Welcome home, Caleb.'"

He took the reporter's hand and led him inside.

MERCY

"'The Great Power of God,'" King Louie mused from the lectern. Thoughtful, he let the phrase hang there for a moment. "That's what they called him, Simon Magus. 'The Great Power of God.'" He chuckled, shaking his head. "I mean, can you imagine anything more insulting?"

Fifty congregants filled as many metal folding chairs—more people than before. They watched King Louie with wary eyes, unsure yet when it was appropriate to laugh, when they were expected to denounce a person or idea with scorn and derision. So they waited for a sign, his humble flock. They waited for their leader to lead by example, to show them how to behave. How to grovel; how to praise; how to kneel and kiss his clean, bare feet.

"Simon was not 'The Great Power of God.' He wasn't a *part*, a single facet, like a talent or a byproduct. He *was* God. The divine, made man. Like Jesus or Mohammed or Buddha or any other prophet of every ancient and modern age: at once human, *and* holy. The state that *you*," King Louie looked directly at a middle-aged man in the back row, "and y*our* families," shifting his gaze to the mousy brunette seated next to him, "and *me*," pointing a finger at his own chest, eyes now boring into an older woman of color near the front of the audience, "and *my* family aspire to—the thing that we were all put here to remember: at once human, *and* holy."

He held up a well-worn hundred-dollar bill. Benjamin Franklin's face in shades of cream and slate stared back at them. "Simon came with a message. A living reminder of man's true nature, he delivered that message through the vehicle of magic. Lowbrow entertainment. Directed at the masses." King Louie struck the lighter in his right hand. Brought the flame to one crumpled paper corner. "And as happened with the messages of Jesus or Mohammed or Buddha, not everyone could hear it." Franklin's lazy eye blackened, curled up, and disappeared. The congregants watched, rapt as children. "But then, not everyone was meant to." Making a fist around the remnants of the still-smoking bill, King Louie squeezed his eyes shut, muttered something unintelligible, and opened his hand. The restored bill fluttered casually to the ground. The woman in the front row couldn't help herself. She hurried to grab it from the velvet-soft carpet. When she touched the bill, it multiplied, giving birth to itself again and again, until she was left gripping fistfuls of cash too fat for her pocketbook. Feeling its papery realness with her fingers, she turned back to the gathered crowd, raising two fists in the air. "God is good," she whispered, shocked. Then louder: "God is *good*!" Laughing until she was crowing, until tears streamed down her tired cheeks.

"So, too, they called him a sorcerer," King Louie continued, his voice still quiet. Contemplative. "Nasty word, that. *Sorcerer.*" Ever so slightly more animated, he spat as he said it. "Said Satan imbued him with power." He chuckled. "Ironic, no? Both devil worshipper *and* The Great Power of God? I mean, make up your mind, am I right?"

The congregants were passing the stack of bills among themselves now, each one taking a few for his or her self, charitably sharing the rest. Some stopped listening to King Louie altogether, daydreaming about the things they'd buy, or the loans they'd pay off—all of them already wanting more. That's the funny thing about money: the more of it you have, the more of it you seem to need. It clouds the mind. Shrouds the spirit in ugly, warty greed.

So he set it all back on fire, those bills, stuffed in pearl-snap shirt pockets and worn shoe soles. Assets to ashes. Emoluments to embers. They didn't even notice—wouldn't, until they were climbing into bed. Then they'd remember, and race to retrieve it, and the money wouldn't be there, and they'd think they'd lost it, and blame themselves, but they'd go back for more. Oh, how they'd go back for more.

Because faith is trust in the certainty of results. Is the universal solvent of doubt. Is the basis of religion.

King Louie's flock was growing.

THE RECEPTIONIST

The curious were always welcome at the temple of Simon's

Sorrow. "Come for a Service, stay for a lifetime" the slogan above the heavy, carved wooden entry read, in a script so pretty there was nothing foreboding beyond the words, their implicit threat. Visitors received a guided tour of the Austin temple, a peek into the group's recent history. They watched a short documentary featuring King Louie; fell in love with his light French accent; were comforted by the thought of a faith system older than the country they lived in extending back to the time of Jesus himself.

How come they'd never heard of Simon? they wanted to know.

"Have you read the Bible?" the patient recruiter would ask.

"Not all of it," came the often abashed response.

"There's your answer," the guide smiled.

And so they were embarrassed by their own ignorance into believing, becoming ardent advocates for a saint they hadn't known about just hours prior, telling everyone they met for dinner and drinks in the next few weeks, "Have you heard the story of Simon Magus? You should take the tour. Nice people, beautiful facility." Their visit planted a seed in the curious and the seed became a spore, drifted and spread like a virus, a mushroom, a mold, through underground channels and political circles until it was a talking point. A tourist attraction.

Some, lulled by the stories, by the magic, by the pulsing beacon of King Louie himself, returned twice, three times, each time falling more under his spell, the gravity of what felt in their marrow more like truth than anything ever had before. Some elected baptism, and some upped and joined the community permanently, leaving their jobs and their kids in the city for an ascetic life worth more than all the barbecue, Hut's hamburgers, and micheladas in the world. When they did, they mortified the flesh to honor God.

Pure light beyond body, they accepted the brand, a black ink tattoo needled into their chest skin above the heart. Symbol of Simon's Sash. It stung. Screaming was encouraged as, after all, Simon screamed as he fell. "But together," King Louie said, "we raise him up, and in return he will open the gates of heaven for us." Then new converts accepted a role, a chore, that served the church and its people. No role was less important than the next. Cooks. Janitors. Tailors. Decorators. Art dealers. Accountants. Doctors. They became one living, breathing organism, a heartbeat at the center of Austin.

TEZ

The women came first. ("Women should always come first," the chivalrous cult leader was fond of saying.) They showed up in twos and threes, too wary to make a move alone. The flock grew more swiftly for it. Church wasn't a social hour, though it was certainly social. Each time, King Louie lectured for at least an hour, but then he encouraged commingling. A community for people hurting, people curious, people who saw bright light shining through red-tinted windows and thought *Maybe*? Wondered *Home*? And wandered home.

"Eileen." King Louie called a tall, striking woman from where she stooped near the back of the room. She uncurled like a cat, and slunk feline toward the altar. "Eileen, God is calling for your commitment this evening. Jesus has prepared a special seat at the right hand of Simon for you, Eileen. Are you ready?"

"I am."

She stopped in front of King Louie. He stood two steps above her, on the altar platform, but Eileen was so tall they still came eye to eye. She wore a plain black robe. King Louie held a plain dark sash, the color of dried blood.

THE WHORE

The bar was crowded with tourists, as the bars of Dirty Sixth always are at all times of day or night, when I walked in. Hungry, I scanned the room for a man by his lonesome. Spotted one, there, on a stool. He wore a rumpled suit, tie loosened, a conference badge still pinned to his lapel, even though it was Friday night and the convention was over. Probably he wasn't scheduled to fly out until morning. Probably his hotel room was nearby. Probably, I reasoned, he was perfect.

Rubbing my lips together, slick with gloss, I opened the deep V of my blouse one button more. Fluffed my hair, threw my shoulders back, strode confidently over to the man. He'd had a few, but not too many. Because he could feel my eyes on him. My wanting. He turned, saw me advancing, smiled, and turned back to the bar. Probably this happened often to Jeffrey. He was a decent-looking man who took a lot of business trips, ended up in a lot of bars. Alone. He had a nearly grown daughter but no wife to miss him, and a workplace that didn't expect him until Monday. He tilted his glass on the bar, rattling ice cubes.

"Mind if I join you?"

Jeffrey smiled again, neither friendly nor rude. "Sure. I'm about to move on anyway."

"So soon?" I pursed my lips in a mock pout. "I just got here. How about one more?"

When Jeffrey looked unconvinced, I insisted. "I don't bite. Pinky promise."

I held up my little finger, its blood red ring the only piece of jewelry I owned. Sportingly, Jeffrey clasped my pinky in his. "All right. You talked me into it."

Folding my legs onto the seat next to his: "Let me guess. Banker. Maybe mortgage. Divorced. Likes dogs, but can't be trusted with another living thing—mainly because you're a lotta bit kind and a little bit ignorant. You'd share your expensive bar of Madagascar vanilla chocolate with

Sparky and he'd keel over dead. You'd have plenty of money if you hadn't given everything to her in the divorce. Capricorn. INTJ."

"Taurus," Jeffrey laughed. "INFP. And the dog wasn't my fault. The ex left an open bottle of Tylenol on the counter. The rest was spot on, though!"

Inwardly gagging but outwardly giggling. "I'm Amy."

"Jeffrey."

"So, Jeffrey, can we get out of here?"

TEZ

A few days later, the Whore pulled Kirk. The following week, Alvin. She recruited with her body; a gift from God designed to grow His flock. The men might not have shown up otherwise. It was women who fell under King Louie's spell. But the men succumbed to the women and they called this practice religious prostitution. Or as the Bible put it: fishers of men.

Hebrews 1:14—"Are they not all ministering spirits, sent out to render service for the sake of those who will inherit salvation?"

THE CHEF

All of us joined Simon's Sorrow for a reason, even if we couldn't have articulated what those reasons were. A different note of King Louie's siren song resonated with each member individually, and to a one, we signed in blood without hesitating. For me, it was the sense of purpose that I found in the church's employ. I'd bounced between dead-end jobs for a decade just waiting for my life to begin. I'd started to fear that I'd missed my window, that someday soon I'd look back and see nothing but waste; but that's not what King Louie saw when he looked at me. He saw a hungry heart and an able body—tools that, to Simon's Sorrow, were everything. "God," King Louie promised, looking me straight in the eye, "has a plan for you. He brought you to me, and now, my friend, you are home."

Home. It summed up in a single word the high, the peace, the opportunity I'd been chasing for years. When King Louie said that, I felt it. I knew it like I'd once known algebra. X equaled exhilaration. Y equaled yes. After reviewing my work history and diagnosing strong organizational skills hobbled by a fear of commitment, he assigned me to the kitchen. "Food," he explained, "is a necessary evil. Were mankind as evolved as we could be, we wouldn't need to eat, digest, and defecate—and eat again—like animals. The Word of God alone would be enough to sustain us. So long as we collectively refuse the enlightenment available to us, however, settling for gross and temporary earthly pleasures, there is steak and pasta and honey-glazed carrots, foods that while but distractions from an ascended state can nevertheless be labors of love. You will be that laborer, will serve God and us with your God-given talents." I couldn't help it. My chest swelled with pride at being entrusted with such meaningful work. Every day thereafter, I did my absolute best by the rest of the Sashes, but kept my mind trained firmly on King Louie, too, and the example that he set.

Always one to practice what he preached, he really did seem to subsist on sunshine and breath. If he joined us for family meals, it was only for the fellowship. I never saw him eat so much as a bread crust. Every other morning, I'd juice a dozen oranges for him. Between that, and the avocado-banana mash he applied to his long locks like a conditioner—proceeding to chew it out of his hair once it'd dried—he embodied the evolved life form he said that all of us could be, if only we were willing. If only we wanted it badly enough.

TEZ

They'd been sitting for six days, the congregation; enough time for the hunger to come and go. Days two and three had been the hardest. Tummy rumbles had given way to searing aches. Nausea so bad they didn't think they could have eaten, anyway—though they would have, had King Louie said the word. He allowed the Whores among them a morning bowl of rice sprinkled with prenatal vitamins; nutrients to keep their hair shiny and their skin hydrated. The rest of them took water and air only as they meditated, all day and all night, on Simon's sorrow. They confessed their sins in silence, the occasional beating of a breast the only sign that repentance was ongoing. Whenever a parishioner collapsed in grief and horror at the acts of his past, he was instructed to strike a closed fist roughly against his chest and repeat: "Through my fault. Through my fault. Through my own most grievous fault."

So far, all sixty-one people in the room had complied with King Louie's ordained fast. No one wanted to be the next Tommy; the memory of his screams still hung in the temple's high corners. Last time, divorced dad Tommy had excused himself under the pretense of using the restroom. Unable to bear it any longer, he'd opened a contraband pack of his son's animal crackers left in the zipper pocket of his gym bag. He'd downed them wolfishly, then taken a long drink of holy water from the Mouth to rinse the last of the cracker-sweet smell from his tongue. King Louie had approached him from behind, robes settling into place without so much as a giveaway swish.

"Thomas," he'd said from directly behind the initiate, startling Tommy so badly he'd bitten the inside of his cheek in his haste to swallow and turn around.

"Doubting Thomas," King Louie had clucked. "Well, I suppose it can't be helped. You didn't choose your name, after all. But really, your parents should have thought that one through."

"Sorry?" Tommy had asked, confused.

"The Apostle Thomas? He refused to believe that Jesus had been resurrected from the dead until he stuck his finger in Christ's wounds himself. Ring a bell, ding dong?"

"Oh," Tommy had said, chastened but still ignorant.

"Oh," King Louie had repeated softly. "Stick out your tongue, Thomas."

Turning red, Tommy had stuck out his tongue. Quick as a snake, King Louie had grabbed it. He'd dragged Tommy by the tongue to the small altar in his personal prayer room, where he'd promptly taken up a hammer and smashed Tommy's tongue against the smooth oak grain. Tommy had screamed and King Louie had done it again, and again, until Tommy couldn't retract the useless muscle anymore, and it hung there, a strangely flattened mound of burst capillaries. Then, taking pity, King Louie had offered Tommy food and drink from his own larder: lemon water and brined vegetables that had seared the man's lacerated organ so that he'd cried and cried but found himself unable to stop eating, for on Day Three, the hunger had been that great.

No one wanted to be the next Tommy, so they sat and they did not sneak snacks.

At 6:00 p.m. on October 31, 1973, King Louie declared the fast concluded. "God has heard you," King Louie said, "and as He always does for His faithful, He has forgiven you."

The congregants' painfully straight backs slumped in relief. Slowly, they stretched and stood. Before them, King Louie donned a Halloween mask. It had the exquisite head of a white dragon, icicle lips pulled back and snarling around what looked like real ivory teeth.

"And now," he said, "we feast."

THE CHEF

During periods of fasting and meditation, no one ate, of course; so I was temporarily relieved of my duties. It was important to King Louie that everyone still felt essential even when they weren't explicitly needed, so he found other tasks to keep us busy. Idle hands and all that. For example, the Groundskeepers might spend their winter afternoons in the laundry after half-mornings dedicated to raking leaves or spreading sand in anticipation of the (very occasional) ice. My job was to thaw and deep-clean the freezers. We also all took turns assisting with Restoration.

"Restoration builds community," King Louie said, and apparently, it proved our commitment to the cause. When everyone participated, as both mentor and mentee, trust was developed. Solidarity was fostered. We understood each other like we understood our calling. Or that was the idea.

My first time facilitating a fellow Sash's Restoration was during the week of Halloween. I spent the first few days engaged in heavy meditation. It was wonderful. I'd recently learned to really surrender—to let my body and mind completely relax and enter a state of pure emptiness—the closest we can come to bliss in this life. It was hard at first, but with practice, hours passed without me even being conscious of them. I didn't think about my legs falling asleep, or the steady, dull ache in my lower back. These things were absent, as all things must be in the negative space of meditation. First, a clearing out; an inviting of breath, of energy—and with that prana, the divine. Someday, King Louie assured me, if I kept at it long enough, wanted it badly enough, did enough penance (on my own behalf, and that of others), I would see the face of God.

Some of the Sashes, including the Laundress, weren't having such an easy time of it. They'd come in expecting one thing only to find church life was something else entirely, and they were resisting the subversion of their expectations, and fighting against King Louie at every opportunity. Each of them bellyached a different challenge. For the Laundress, it was fasting. She didn't see the point, insisting it only made her blood sugar drop. "And then why bother meditating?" she complained. "I'll just pass out from hunger, anyway. If you see me suddenly slump over," she warned, "I can guarantee you I haven't fallen asleep."

She was cute—the type of woman I might've chatted up Outside. But inside, her distrust of the church's teachings threatened what I'd come to view as sacred. For the Laundress, it would have to be our way or the highway.

THE BARBER

I have a PhD in biochemical engineering from MIT. For most of my career, I worked in the pharmaceutical industry. The job wasn't too high-stress, and I made decent money. When I joined Simon's Sorrow, I traded in my microscope for a thirty-dollar pair of hair clippers and became the Barber. That was the thing about the church. No job was too menial. If it served the community, it was valued. Whether you sewed clothes or cut hair didn't matter. Truly, an egalitarian group of the type that wider America strives to be but to this day has never quite achieved. Keeping everyone freshly groomed soothed me. My life slowed down, and as it did, my health improved. (That, plus a combination of better food and exercise.) Before I knew it, the symptoms I'd been treating with some of the same prescription drugs my lab had invented abated completely. I quit taking anything but herbal supplements. I no longer needed synthetic pills.

Resa was a different story. She showed up with a habit a mile long and soul deep, having gone the way of every grieving widow too young yet to call it quits and too old to confidently put herself back out there. She took the lover that always loves you back—then started hanging around the church like a ghost determined not to let me forget what scientists like myself were responsible for, what we'd done when we introduced opioids to the market.

One night I confessed these feelings to King Louie. "I know I'm supposed to let the past go," I told him. "Repent for what I did Outside, then move on. Sometimes, though, I'm still racked with guilt. I worry I don't deserve this life, as my work has taken life from others."

"Then you must make amends," King Louie observed. "Give, in exchange for what you took."

"How do I do that?"

That's when King Louie Restored me.

THE BUTCHER

Restoration was King Louie's word for corporal punishment. Flogging; flagellation; whatever you called it, Restoration was torture—self-inflicted or administered by another Sash, usually Mercy. It's how a member "made amends" for sins new or old. Insofar as the body is a finite vessel, a skin-and-bone container for the boundless self, it can be filled: with thoughts, ideas, passions, and beliefs both good and bad. It may further be manipulated. Stretched. Stimulated. Torn. Squeezed, so as to chase out—or, conversely, *make* more room for—the demons of our corrupt natures. And/or the angels of our better ones. The soul demands these treatments like the body craves pleasure—from food, wine, other bodies—the kinds of gross satisfactions that, in the end, serve the transcendent, serve the holy. "Profligate indulgence and intentional deprivation; blissful ignorance and uncompelled enlightenment—and these in equal measure," King Louie liked to say.

THE TAILOR

Restoration? I mean, it saved me. It wasn't torture. Not at all. I wasn't coerced, and I wasn't held against my will. None of us were. We *wanted* to be there.

Why? A better question is why not. The wider world had nothing for us that we couldn't get at Simon's Sorrow, and the church offered us more than we could ever have Outside. King Louie gave us that. Gave us all of himself, and gave us each other, too. That we might be of service to one another.

I can't say enough about the food. It was real, hot, nourishing, home-cooked food, most of it homegrown, too. I custom-cut our clothes for our bodies. Any time we got an itch to try a new hair color or style, there was the Barber. You couldn't have asked for a more beautiful setting. My God. Did you ever go inside? The wood, the stained glass, the golden, hand-poured chalices. The flowers outside in the courtyard! It was an inspiration just to wake up there every morning. It was a *blessing*. A paradise on earth. And you'd never know it walking by on the street. With the university across the way and an endless line of panhandlers shaking their coin cups, it was easy for people to overlook us, to believe what they'd heard and keep right on walking. Which is why we sent the Whores out to recruit for us. They spoke of the beauty that is Simon's Sorrow— that is Simon's story!—with the beauty of their sex. The comfort that sex promised . . . it was like coming home.

Home is what holds you. Home is the place you may leave, but which you'll always return to.

The Groundskeepers, they *restored* the land the church sits on to itself. The Cooks, they restored our vitality. The Whores plunged us back into our bodies. So, Restoration is just another way of coming home. Of expressing love. And of remembering that the body is a chalice, as fine as any the Jewelers make, for collecting, savoring, upending, and finally, releasing, a shared experience. For as long as we're around to feel it.

TEZ

After the weeklong Halloween fast, King Louie and all of the Sashes were ready to party. It was, in true Simon's Sorrow fashion, a "feast" of flesh as much as food. Sustenance for the soul *and* for the body.

THE GROUNDSKEEPER

Just before the party morphed into a full-on rave, King Louie introduced the evening's two guests of honor: Dan and Emily Bradshaw. "They're window-shopping," he explained, "in search of a new parish to call home. Let's give them the proper Simon's Sorrow welcome, eh?"

Dan and Emily stepped out of the shadows. We couldn't see their faces—they, too, wore masks—but we could see their naked bodies, the way that nervousness and the chill in the room had made her nipples pucker and his penis retreat between his legs. Their masks variously depicted one peaceful and one wrathful deity. Demon tongues in the shape of cocks lolled, frozen and lazy, from between hinged jaws.

Suddenly, music rung from the rafters. It was atonal, discordant, more noise than music. It was also the cue. A waitstaff of ten, unrecognizable behind their bird masks, popped the corks of ten expensive bottles of champagne and passed around trays of rich finger foods: small bites for stomachs that needed time to reacclimate. The champagne went straight to everybody's heads. Soon we were dancing uninhibitedly, shamelessly trying to break up the couple who didn't want to drink—who wanted only to dance with each other. Dan and Emily Bradshaw tried, at first, to play along good-naturedly. They wanted to be accepted by the group. But other dancers kept shimmying between them, flirting, hinting that more than food was available, should they be interested. Emily grew flustered. Dan got defensive. To break up the tension in the room, King Louie asked the Guards to carry in the entertainment. A young woman. The Laundress. She entered born aloft on the Guards' shoulders, wearing the by-then familiar sash of Simon. She smiled. Waved. Her coterie set her down before the altar. King Louie changed the music. Sidled up to her. Whispered muted suggestions. The Laundress blanched. Her smile faded. She pulled her robes closer. Insistent, King Louie tugged at her clothes. Ripped the cord from around her waist and, gripping it, stepped back—twirling it, a lazy lasso. He motioned to the Guards, who started forcibly stripping the Laundress. She yelled. The whole party stopped. Turned. Stared. They didn't stop staring until she was naked. Until the Laundress stood revealed, the mask that hid her neuroses at last removed. Thoughtful, King Louie studied her. When he finally turned around, dismissive, the spell broke. The Laundress ran away and vomited. Emily hurried after her.

In the madness of half-light, all sound, King Louie slipped away. He debuted, sometime later, his own costume. Dressed as Enlightenment, his body wrapped in foil, a red scarf tied around his membrum virile, a candle burning on top of his head. "If you're not going to wear a costume," he said to the woman nearest him, "you don't need any clothes at all." He tore her robes. Grew bored when she didn't protest. Started making out with her aggressively. Clawing at her arms. Biting at her lips. Her cheek. Leaving tooth marks. She reciprocated: intense, non-conscious, animalian. It proves how Enlightened you are, you know: how drunk you can get and still know what you're doing. That's tantric teaching: Get drunk with dignity and awareness. King Louie turned off the lights and the room hushed. He sat in front of the picture window, backlit by moonlight. "I want to give a sermon. Is everyone here? No? Go get them."

At some point, Dan and Emily had run away, locking their door behind them. They startled when the first knock echoed. "You're wanted downstairs." Dan apologized: *We've gone to bed*. A crowd gathered in the hallway. Someone threatened to break down the door. Key slid into lock. Dan blocked the doorway with a bureau. "Come on down and get it over with," a wiser man suggested. "Please." (A friend.) "It's your last chance."

And over the riot, King Louie's voice, traveling as though through pipes: "Your presence is not requested; it's required. You say you want to study, but you're not participating." The implied shake of a head. The barricaded door.

"Break the window."

A glass storm—a rain of shattered glass—as a chair hurtled through it.

"Unmasking your neuroses sometimes means literally. You can't hope to deal with your neuroses if you won't admit to them."

Fed up, brave, Emily walked out fighting. She was quickly subdued. Dragged screaming down the stairs. Helpless, Dan followed. They were soon reinstalled before a semicircle of witnesses.

Dan: "Call the police!"

King Louie: "You declined my invitation."

"An invitation allows the other person the privilege of declining."

"Join in the celebration! Take your clothes off! Why not? What's your secret? . . . See, not so bad, is it?" He sighed in admiration of their bodies. "No scars or anything. Like Adam and Eve."

The rest of us likewise rushed to strip.

King Louie to Emily: "Do you know how much I love you?"

"I didn't make any promises to you."

"You put your head in the lion's mouth. There's an umbilical cord between you and me. You must offer your neuroses as a feast."

DAN BRADSHAW

I mean, who the hell *was* that guy?

THE ALUM

Who *didn't* know King Louie? If not personally, at least by reputation—and definitely by sight. It was that hair: long as a girl's, tresses so silky they shone in the sun. Or under the yellow glow of a campus streetlamp, 1958.

He stood on that corner day and night, a Bible in one hand and a spiral notebook in the other. The cheap kind, a drugstore back-to-school special. He'd filled it with what he called the Gospel of Simon. "A book," he said, "that was inadvertently left out of the Bible"—because it hadn't been written yet.

But he'd written it, in bouts of automatic writing, dogma downloaded directly from Source. He told the story to anyone who would listen. How he'd been preparing for finals in the library when God had spoken to him from somebody's dropped and long-forgotten pencil, wedged between the wooden sidewall of a study cubicle and the mid-century puke-green carpet. "Take of me and transcribe," the God-pencil had said.

And King Louie had. Straight through the night, foregoing everything else. "Not even conscious," he clarified, "of the time, or the excruciating ache in my hand, which I noticed only later when finally I laid the pencil down."

As soon as our office opened, he came straight to me, then the editor-in-chief of the student newspaper. He wanted to know how one went about printing and binding a book. What distribution entailed. Whether I knew any bishops or elders.

"I'm sorry," I said, cutting him off mid-manic-plea. His eyes were wild and unfocused. It smelled like he hadn't showered in some time. "Who are you?"

"Forgive me," he said, shaking his head and smiling, visibly calmer, as though having finally won some internal battle with himself. "My name is Louie. I'm a sophomore history and philosophy major, and I've just spent all night penning the word of God." His eyes narrowed and the edge in his voice grew sharper. "Now can you help me or not?"

I backed away involuntarily. Some sixth sense was clanging away in my brain, although what threat I thought a nineteen-year-old peer might represent in a room full of students and staff, I'm not sure. I explained that newspaper printing was different from book publishing. We didn't have the right machinery. "But here," I offered, handing him the card of the campus minister. "Maybe this man can help you."

I figured—hoped—that might be the end of it. Indeed, I more or less forgot about him until I saw him on the corner a few months later. He hadn't shaved in all that time. His hair was getting scruffy at the neck. It would take a couple years for his mane to reach its full glory. The longer it grew, the brighter it gleamed. His eyes, too. On fire with a conviction that none of us could share.

It's impossible, after all, to convert the masses to an ideology that lives only in your head.

THE CAMPUS MINISTER

To this day, I keep regular office hours at Cooper Hall, though not as many, and not as late, as I once did. I tell every student at freshman orientation, and again at the occasional pep rally, that my door is always open. "Even if it's three a.m. and you have to wake me up. That's what I'm here for." And it is. At a state school the size of this one, where it's all too easy for kids to slip through the cracks, I want to be a resource, an attentive ear, for anyone who needs it. My students can talk to me about anything, no judgments. No questions asked.

Although it's been more than forty years since Louie first walked into my office, I remember it like it was yesterday. He came barreling in, heart on fire with the existential angst common to young adults. Said he'd been sent to me by the editor of the student newspaper, and what did I know about Simon Magus? Now, being a man of God and Christian myself, I'd read the Bible cover to cover in seminary, and many times since. I remembered Simon, often referred to jokingly as the Bad Samaritan. But who was he to this young man?

"Father," Louie spoke quite seriously. "God is unhappy with humankind. For almost two thousand years, we've misunderstood what he sent the prophet Jesus to tell us. We've been focusing on all the wrong stories, interpreting the parables as though we ourselves are gods—that is, infallible—and over time, to use a modern metaphor, the original wiring has gone bad."

While I wasn't following 100% what he was saying, I could tell it meant a great deal to him. I listened without interrupting, that he might feel encouraged to continue.

"Today, no one studies Simon Magus. They know the disciple, Simon Peter, and every Catholic grade schooler during Lent draws a picture of Simon of Cyrene helping Christ carry the cross, but ask them about the Simon who saves, the one who, far from denying Jesus, loved Jesus so much that he flew for him, who prayed to God for a way to get His son's attention long enough to simply serve Him, and they become the deniers, the doubting Thomases, insistent that no such 'character' ever existed."

Despite my having offered him a seat, Louie continued pacing around the room. He gestured emphatically and at times I worried the volume of his voice might bring Jim over from next door to see what all the fuss was about.

"Don't you see, Father? Simon, he was the key to all of

it, all along. Communion with the divine; access to grace; truly eternal life. Everything we try to chase with substances and surgeries: greater highs and tighter thighs! More youth! More wealth! Mass accumulation! A frenzy of pleasure-seeking and identity affirmation projected onto consumer goods!"

Louie had started to froth at the mouth, but I wanted to understand his larger goal, his ultimate point. "Nietzsche, right?" I prompted. "Or was that Marx?"

"Dionysian hedonism. Commodity fetishism. It doesn't matter!" he exclaimed, throwing his hands up. "They're two terms for the same idea, which is a rejection of the will of the Father in pursuit of a perfection unreachable by humans since the martyrdom of Saint Simon."

"Well, Simon Magus was never canonized," I objected.

"Exactly!" he nearly screamed. "Instead of recognizing God at work in Simon, we turned Simon into a mad god, himself a Dionysus, and we tore him limb from limb. We subjugated instinct and desire to fear of that which we did not understand precisely because it was the opposite of the rational."

I thought I saw where he was headed. "And all the rational mind knows," I concluded for him, "is the horror of death."

He looked at me; then, for the first time since his tirade had begun, sank into the navy upholstered chair, and said softly, "Yes."

"When," I continued, "if we only accepted the ugly, embraced violence, spent time in contemplation of nihilism, and emerged still wanting to live—then pain and rage would be as valued as pleasure and joy. I'm familiar with the theory."

Eyes bright, he searched mine. "And what do you think of it?"

"I think death is nothing to fear."

He nodded slowly, then more vigorously, then stood and ran out of the room.

I thought—I don't know, I thought he just wanted to talk things through. Explore Big Ideas. That's what college is for!

THE DOCTOR

To be clear, I didn't live at Simon's Sorrow. I treated the community on an as-needed basis, as a favor to King Louie, with whom I attended college back in the day. We were roommates freshman year, now regarded as the year before he "went crazy," so it's true I didn't have to put up with the no-showering, rarely sleeping, Bible-touting version of Louie—or Lou, as we called him then. He seemed like a strange but harmless geek who maybe spent too much time reading and not enough time letting loose (it was *college*, after all), but he didn't steal my food and always wiped the hair out of the sink when he shaved, and early on, that was good enough for me.

The day that really cemented our bond was when my high school girlfriend Sarah broke up with me. She was still back in Somerville, but I'd given her a promise ring before I left and we'd planned to get married in the next two years. Then she met someone else, and it felt like being mistaken for a vampire, like someone had shoved a wooden stake into my heart and left me for dead. Lou found me lying facedown in my bed at three p.m. on a Tuesday afternoon, and because he'd memorized my class schedule, asked, "Aren't you supposed to be in bio lab right now?"

"Doesn't matter," I said into my pillow. "Nothing matters anymore"—in the way of the overly dramatic eighteen-year-old processing the end of his first real relationship.

"What happened?" Lou asked. I told him. He listened.

"You know," he said, after a while. "Love is the greatest plague of the modern age."

I chuckled, still in my bed but at least sitting up against the wall now. "Oh yeah? How do you figure?"

"It's the only thing that sneaks up on you without warning, even when no one else around you is displaying symptoms, settles into your very bones, and eats you from the inside out, so you don't always know it's happening until it's too late."

"You're right," I sighed. "That about sums it up."

"Crucially, though, there is a cure."

I opened my resting eyes to look at him. "What's that?"

"Come on," he said, standing up and grabbing his backpack. "I'll show you."

We traipsed across campus, to a field beside the track I'd never noticed before. It was long and skinny, with stacked hay bales at one end of it, and a locked steel shed at the other. Taking a key from his backpack, Lou unlocked the shed, disappeared inside for a second, and reemerged carrying two unstrung bows. He handed them to me to hold, went back inside for the bowstrings and the arrows, then set us up a hundred feet from the targets tacked to the bales opposite.

"With your right foot back," he demonstrated, "and your elbow aligned with the arrow, so the forearm and arrow make a straight line, and your fingers hooking the string, like this?" He checked to make sure I was following. "Keep your eyes on the center, but aim just above it. Breathe. Focus. And then—"

He let the string go. The arrow sailed so fast it went from his bow to the target quicker than I could comprehend. A bullseye.

"Impressive," I allowed. "So this is what you spend all your time doing."

"No," Lou corrected me. "What I spend my time doing is contemplating. Theorizing. Figuring out how the multiverse fits on the point of an arrow." He'd already grabbed another arrow from the quiver on the ground, and he gestured with it, illustrating his point. "Because it does, you know. Everything we see around us, this whole world, is an illusion. A minuscule piece of the space-time continuum, temporarily blown up and wrapped around us like a blanket. It comforts us, with its beauty and its seemingly finite parameters—it's *known*-ness—but at the same time, it obscures the infinite and therefore unknowable 'limits' of the really real reality, where so much more is possible."

He paused to let the second arrow fly. It stuck with a reverberating *thwick* next to the first. "Your turn."

While I got used to the bow's foreign heft, and tried out the string's resistance for myself, Lou walked down to the hay bales. He took something out of his backpack, tacked it there, and walked back. It was the picture of Sarah I normally kept on the bulletin board in our dorm room. Instantly, my enthusiasm deflated. "Really?" I was annoyed. "Here I'd managed to forget about her for a second, but now it hurts all over again."

"Try," he said.

I raised the bow like he'd shown me, positioned my body as correctly, albeit awkwardly, as he'd demonstrated. I aimed at the point just above Sarah's forehead, but focused my heart on hers. "Let the arrow be an extension of yourself," Lou directed me. "Follow it 'til it finds its mark."

When I let the string go, I didn't move. My body stayed right where it was. But I also flew alongside the arrow, or at least it felt that way. Maybe my brain short-circuited and gave me hawk vision for a second, and that's why I could suddenly see so well, as though I was a foot and not a hundred from Sarah's photo. Because I saw, I literally watched, as the arrow pierced the flesh of her chest, slicing a neat hole through her favorite blue sweater, first the front side and then the back, as it emerged below her shoulder blade and lodged in her ribs. I swear I heard her sharp intake of breath. Smelled the rose oil she wore at the twin pulse points of her neck. Watched those thumping pulse points begin to slow, as something black oozed out of the photo where I'd impaled it.

Beside me, Lou let his own breath go in a rush. "*Very* good," he praised me.

I realized I no longer felt the stake in my own heart, and said as much. "I feel better. Thank you."

"You're welcome. It's one of the theories I'm exploring: Restoration. Or how we rehabilitate the self when we've been wronged by, or done wrong to, others. I might write my philosophy thesis on it."

"Oh!" I said. "I didn't know you'd declared a major. The study of Big Ideas. That seems like you, all right."

Lou gave a small smile but didn't say anything else.

"I'm starving," I said. "Wanna hit up the dining hall?"

TEZ

He had some Big Ideas, all right. First up was winning over Texas, by courting the endorsement of its most beloved politician.

Second was finally taking a wife.

MERCY

Ochre sunlight suffused the Austin sky the night I sat down with Mary Toni's uncle, Adam Habsburg. It was the golden hour and happy hour and the end of the workweek to boot. Not much more could have been going right for the young politician, peaking in popular opinion, his campaign fund doubling every day. My job was to make sure we rode the wave alongside him.

"It's simple. Texas has this 'outdated' law, right?" My fingers formed air quotes around the word outdated, like Adam and I were buddies—just two guys sharing a beer and a worldview on a Friday afternoon. "It says you have to profess your belief in a higher power. Doesn't matter which one." Here, I held up one finger, lest Adam try to stop me. "Yes, I know you haven't attended so much as a church picnic in ten years."

Adam took another pull off his pint, maintaining eye contact as he did. He couldn't yet grasp my point.

"So." I waved my hands around in the air, looking for the right words to grease the wheel. "You do this for us, we swing the vote, everybody wins."

"You have enough members?" Adam asked skeptically.

"Enough to guarantee you 55%, which is all—"

"—All I need to be sworn in as governor," Adam finished. "And what—your 'cause' gets a little extra attention? That's all you want?"

"That's all we want."

"What's this dude's name again?"

"Simon. Simon Magus." Confident of his decision, I signaled the bartender. A couple of shots appeared within seconds. "What do you say? Do we have something to celebrate?"

TEZ

Adam considered the strange man across from him. Something about Mercy felt almost oily; except that he was meticulously groomed. Conspicuously so—like some kind of overpaid underwear model. "And no money," Adam reiterated.

"Money leaves a trail," Mercy said. "What we're asking for will cost you nothing, and give you everything you ever wanted."

Mercy's voice, his words—they were more than a promise. More like a spell. Adam nodded his head and grinned. "What the hell," he agreed, draining the shot. "I believe in Simon. So help me God."

Mercy smiled. Offered his hand. "You won't regret this."

Escaping for a second to the bathroom—the only place

he got any privacy anymore—Adam heaved a sigh, enjoyed a few neck and shoulder rolls, then dropped his head and stared at his Cougar sneakers—completely out of place on a fifty-something, fully-grayed man. But then that was the point, wasn't it? To be different. Stand out, for all the *right* reasons. Let the young people know that he was *just like them*, and would represent their interests. Wage and price controls to curb inflation. Air and water pollution regulations to protect the environment. The expansion of Social Security. A notably moderate agenda for a Republican, and one in which he really did believe, though it was unlikely to be very popular in Texas cities other than Austin. Meaning, he'd have to win votes in some other way—an earnest appeal to the rest of Texas: its 17% Hispanic population, who wanted good jobs and better education; Dallas's Christian contingent; Corpus Christi's hurricane-ravaged urban core; the drug-addled denizens of the country's meth capital, busy cooking behind East Texas's pine curtain. It was hard work, canvassing the second largest state in the union (and one that wanted equal representation in national politics at the same time that it wanted to maintain its status as a republic, and all the cowboy individualism of the Great Texas Myth). Unlike his brother Frank, who'd been content to work a demanding and altogether thankless job if it meant he could comfortably provide for his family, Adam wanted power, and he wanted it yesterday. Simon's Sorrow, it sounded like, could help with that.

He flicked the last of the water from his hands, and slid them back and forth below the dryer. It made sense to align himself with the church, he thought, as running for state office was remarkably similar to going to church. You suited up, showed up, folded your hands, and prayed— abandoning your fate to powers greater than yourself.

THE TAILOR

So you attend several sessions, and decide you want to join. You "declare your intention," as King Louie calls it. Then there's an intake interview. One on one with the king himself. It starts off innocently enough. Where are you from, how old are you, what do you do. He asks about your faith life. Were you raised in a church? Depending on your answer, and whether or not the two of you first need to spend some time hashing out a mutually agreeable definition of God, the conversation then gets pretty intimate pretty fast. "Tell me about your first sexual experience," he said during my interview.

I wanted King Louie to like me, to accept me into the group, so right away I felt compelled to lie. "Oh, you know," I said, shrugging way too casually. "Standard, I should think. Me and Heather George"—naming my (unrequited) seventh-grade crush—"my car, after Prom, junior year of high school."

King Louie was leaning back in his desk chair, his elbows on the arm rests and his fingers tented before him as he stared at me. And that's all he did: stared at me. Then he smiled, and his smile was like powdered sugar on burnt cheese, or something else that doesn't go together at all. And then I still wanted him to like me, but what's more, I wanted to *please* him. And I understood that cult leader or no, God's prophet or no, King Louie *knew* things. At the very least, he knew people. He knew that I was lying, and I knew that he knew, and without prompting I started again.

"It was sophomore year in college. I really liked this girl in my economics class. Rebecca. She had a tall, red bouffant haircut and wore turquoise earrings that brought out her eyes. We ended up at a party together. Both of us were drunk. We went upstairs and started having sex, and when I came . . . " I faltered, not wanting to say the rest. But his eyes hadn't left mine. Beneath them, I was a bug pinned to a board.

"When I came," I continued, "I shit the bed. Like, literally, everywhere. All over the sheets, the duvet, our clothes. It got all over Rebecca. She was really sweet and at first she tried to act like it was no big deal, but then she saw it was on her legs, and the smell, and yeah. She threw up. Which I, of course, took like a direct rejection of *me*, right, a direct rejection of my body. Ever since, I can't come without shitting myself, so no one ever sleeps with me more than once unless they're more disgusting than I am."

I exhaled. There. I'd said it.

"You know," King Louie said, shifting his elbows onto the desk and rocking his weight forward. "There are a lot of beliefs about sex. About purifying the body through the excretion and exchange of fluids."

I blushed.

"But according to the Bible, there's only one universal belief about intimacy. Ecclesiastes: 4:11: 'Again, if two lie together, they keep warm, but how can one keep warm alone?'"

When he paused and didn't speak for a second, I said, "And? What does that have to do with anything?"

"Here, brother, you are not and *never will be* alone. To wear the sash is to confess your innate dirtiness. The unclean parts. The shameful secrets. At Simon's Sorrow, defecating on your partner does not make you dirtier. It helps your outside match the raw sewage we are on the inside."

I don't think I breathed for a full minute. I was too hot. My face, my whole body, burning up as he studied me.

"That's why there's baptism," King Louie finally said. "In the Mouth, we become purified. And when we're clean, the worthy will fly."

THE MAID

The orgies weren't my favorite. It was hard for me to enjoy

them. Imagine—all I could see was the mess they were making, the one I'd have to clean up the next day. Still, it was better than working for a private family whose children were spoiled rotten. The Sashes weren't spoiled. All of us worked hard for what we had. We worked hard for each other, and for God. That fact made even the dirtiest work holy.

But you asked about the worst mess I ever had to clean up. Easy: Adam Habsburg's initiation. He was the only convert ever to join us for material gain, versus spiritual gain, you understand, and he saw baptism not as a sacred rite, but as another excuse to party. King Louie encouraged the behavior. What was a bit of blaspheming, he seemed to think, when in the end, it would grow God's flock by leaps and bounds?

It was something about an outdated loophole in Texas state law. When a person took an oath of office, he or she also had to pledge belief in a higher power. It didn't matter which one, necessarily, though Texas has a long history with conservative Christians. Most every politician got up there and said *I believe in God the Father and Jesus Christ His Son*, or something to that effect. But not Adam. He didn't believe in anything, so it made no difference to him which name he spoke aloud. King Louie was capitalizing on that opening. In exchange for guaranteeing the vote, on inauguration day, Adam was to profess his belief in Simon Magus. Predictably sending the media outlets into a frenzy as the ignorant and the curious did their research. We would be ready.

First, though, there was a baptism to perform.

On the appointed evening, everyone gathered in the temple. It was late; the sky outside was dark, and the only light inside came from a hundred flickering candles. Incense burned in golden censers suspended on long chains from the ceiling, and in the choir loft, Madame DuBarry played her harp—a soft, haunting melody. Lots of flat notes and deliberate silences, so that you'd almost forget she was playing until the next note startled you back into your body.

Adam, our guest of honor, reveled in the extra attention. The scarlet robe the tailor had made for him fit perfectly, though it would soon be coming off. As in every major religion, baptism into the Church of Simon's Sorrow was a ritual of purification. Unlike in other religions, it wasn't limited to symbolic bathing.

While Adam sipped the full goblet of red wine the Chef had brought to him, and reclined, his feet soaking in the water of the Mouth like it was a hot tub, King Louie addressed those gathered. "No doubt, tonight's occasion may remind you of your own initiation, as well it should, since that, after all, is the primary purpose of the sacraments: to reenact the mysteries revealed to us in the gospels; by their enactment, welcome new members into God's grace, and in witnessing the initiation of others, remember why we joined the church in the first place, and how we are called, as children of God, to serve Him and each other."

He turned to Adam. "Baptism, specifically, demands a willing heart and a conscious mind—a choice, made in complete freedom, to devote one's life to God and His prophet Simon. Adam, do you come before us willingly, conscious and sober—enough—" King Louie smiled at the wine, and the Sashes chuckled quietly—"to voluntarily commit yourself to the church?"

Adam didn't miss a beat. "I do."

"And do you acknowledge that baptism into Simon's Sorrow requires absolute personal, mental, and moral cleanliness, and do you attest that you meet these requirements?"

Caught mid-sip, Adam swallowed quickly and said again, "I do."

"Then please disrobe."

One of the Whores took Adam's goblet from him, and with one of her sisters, helped him to stand safely in the tiled tub. The water came to his knees. It sloshed with his movements and sent the reflected flames of candles bouncing around the room and across his body. The Whore who'd taken his goblet had set it on the altar. Now she slipped his robe from his shoulders, and he stood before us, a truer Adam: naked, unashamed, and soon to be without sin.

One at a time, she draped his arms over a freestanding man-sized crucifix-like structure and bound them. That way, he couldn't stop what was about to happen. And if his legs buckled and gave way, he'd remain upright.

The second Whore prepared the sash—the length of virgin silk that would begin, and end, Adam's ceremony, and mark him ever after as a Sash. Wrapping it around his neck, she wound the sash ends around the stem of a golden chalice, which she then turned, slowly, in small circles, tightening the silk.

Adam had been briefed on what to expect. The goal was not to kill him, but to heighten his sexual instinct. Achieved by depriving the rest of his senses.

The more compressed Adam's trachea, the less oxygen circulating in his blood. The less oxygen in his blood, the less reaching his brain. And a brain short on oxygen is one more open to suggestion. Hallucination. Mystical ecstasy.

As the second Whore manipulated the sash, the first Whore dropped to her knees in the pool. She took Adam's penis, now half-erect, into her mouth. She worshipped him until he grew hard, until the veins in his cock became like the veins in his temples, turgid and straining against the pressure. She did not let him come.

The Whores switched places. For a few seconds, the sash loosened. Adam closed his eyes and took deeper breaths, surely feeling his lightheadedness ease some. The tingling in his cheeks and ears. Then the Whore who had been worshipping him twisted the chalice, and the second Whore subjected his body to different sensations. A feather, brushed across sensitive ribs. Ice, used to draw religious symbols on his back until it melted. The bite of two alligator clips on his nipples. A small weight clamped to his scrotum and left to hang, where it could be flicked back and forth. The idea was to arouse him utterly, putting his body on 'pins and needles' as it were, until the slightest touch elicited a belly-deep moan. In this state, somewhere between wakefulness and unconsciousness, Adam could commune with God.

Key was maintaining his sexual plateau—always on the verge of orgasm, but never quite achieving it.

For hours.

While this erotic torture occurred on stage, we were expected to participate as we were able. Women who were actively menstruating sat on the lip of the Mouth around Adam and bled into golden chalices like the one choking him. Some men in the audience removed their erections from their pants and sat with them pointing toward Adam in the pool, a kind of salute to their newest brother. They were allowed to, and expected to, stroke themselves as needed to maintain their erections, but again, there was no release allowed. Baptism was about cleansing the body, by concentrating its vital fluids, then purging them all at once. Still others performed their daily functions. The Chef kept our wine glasses filled. The Butcher produced snack boards of cured meat. Having spent the whole day cleaning the temple myself, and given that I'd be re-cleaning it the next day, I was exempted from duty, free to watch and free to worry over the messes everyone was making.

Because eventually, after King Louie had interrogated Adam about the visions he'd experienced, it was time to complete the rite. Which basically meant everyone finally ejaculating in unison. After stimulating Adam for more than three hours, the Whores (who'd regularly switched out their duties, to keep them from growing too tired), performed an expert double fellatio, chalice at the ready. It took less than a minute. Then he was spurting all over the place, and completely oblivious to it. Passed out cold from the sheer intensity of pleasure and pain both. The Whores caught it all in the cup, laughing and exclaiming and praising the newest Sash, while around them, those male attendants who'd patiently bided their time, came, too—on wood, tile, carpet, and concrete, wheresoever they pleased! The women waited until Adam had drained himself, an empty vessel, now ready for God to enter him. Then, handing the chalice off to the Chef, who'd already collected on a tray the matching goblets of menstrual blood, the Whores went to rest.

The Chef disappeared into the kitchen, emerging, maybe twenty minutes later, with the same tray now populated with tiny little hosts. They consisted of flour, honey, semen, and blood. One for each of us, to symbolize the literal assimilation of a new member into the family. Adam would ingest one, too, and in consuming the products of his own body, would enter into a full-circle relationship with the divine. Both feeding upon, and being fed upon by, God. Filled by God until God was made manifest in our midst.

Unfortunately, Adam has no memory of the special moment, because he was still passed out on the crucifix. Just because he wasn't awake to swallow, though, didn't mean we should leave him out, so King Louie took care of that one. Placing a host inside his own mouth, he worked it over with his teeth and tongue until it was sufficiently wet and malleable. Then he formed the glob into a crude ball on two fingers, and directing two nearby Sashes to come spread and hold apart Adam's ass cheeks, inserted the fingers and their gift inside of him. All that mattered was that Adam absorbed His Holiness, not through which particular membrane.

And that was it. Adam became a Sash. That was a typical baptism in Simon's Sorrow.

TEZ

Sashes defected over the years. Walked away one morning and never came back. King Louie didn't stop them, just like he didn't keep anyone from joining Simon's Sorrow who cared to. "God's flock is self-selecting," he said. "Not everyone can hear the truth. Let them go. And let us be here for those who can." He didn't worry about anyone turning them in. Who would, when without the community telling them the things they'd done were right, they could barely look at themselves in the mirror. The things they'd seen at Simon's Sorrow. The things they'd done. Most of those who left killed themselves within a year.

And still, they kept on coming.

THE RECORD-KEEPER

He found her in a Sixth Street bar next to the Ritz, then a porno movie house. Seedier, in the early '70s, than it is today, downtown Sixth was perennially crawling with bodies after sundown, typically those weirdos who "kept Austin weird." The bars were dark, loud, lit by globe lamps and neon, suffused with Mexican conjunto and lively jazz. Nearly drowned out by the surrounding ruckus: a quiet harpist, tall and slim, named Eileen DuBarry.

She was sitting in a corner beneath a slew of square metal lanterns, their red glass inserts casting everything with the glow of sex or death. Her harp stood before her, and she on a stool plucked something that also sounded like sex or death. King Louie admired the way she got lost in her work—her closed-eye discipline and seeming devotion to atmosphere, mood, creativity. She wasn't passive; that much he could tell right away. She was passionate. As evidenced by the furious way she fought with the bar manager at two a.m., when he closed out the registers and handed her an insulting night's take. "This doesn't even cover the babysitter!" she cried. "I just played for four hours to a packed house. You can't tell me there's not more to go around." He shrugged and went back to drying and stacking the highball glasses. She slammed her fists on the bar top, grabbed her harp case, and stormed out into the night. King Louie was waiting for her.

"Hey," he said, catching up to her as she attempted to weave through the dispersing crowds. "You were great up there. I really loved your music."

"Yeah?" she spat. "Thanks for the tip." She huffed and turned away.

"Wait, here," he said, following her and extending several big bills. "I just wanted to give it to you in person."

She looked at him distrustfully. But eyed the money like she would eat it.

"I was hoping we could talk," he said. "What's your name?"

That night, King Louie took Eileen DuBarry for a drink. He learned she was a single mom. That she'd never gone to college, having taken a gap year to pursue her music only to end up pregnant and stuck. He learned that adversity had shaped her and that adversity fueled her still; that she became angry when she didn't get what she wanted, but she channeled her anger into useful things; that she kept everyone at arm's length. He paid for her wine, he paid for her son Isaac's babysitter, and he paid for the time she'd played at the bar. All of it. What she should have made and then some.

"Thank you for the tip," Eileen said again when they parted. This time her voice was softer; she meant her words. "I have gas money now to visit my seniors tomorrow." On Sundays, she played her harp at a nursing home in town.

"That's amazing," King Louie praised her. "It's good to be of service. You know," he said, taking her arm, "if you're interested, there's another community in Austin that could use your services. You'd make a real difference, and get paid for it, too."

The following week, Eileen DuBarry enlisted.

THE WHORE

Madame DuBarry joined the church in its second year. She became one of just a few Sashes who lived Outside, since she had a child and children weren't allowed full-time at Simon's Sorrow. We were small yet, a dedicated group of historical activists hellbent on setting the Jerusalem narrative straight. That's how we saw ourselves, anyway. How King Louie inspired us to feel. Doing the work of an ancient and infinite God in the latter half of the twentieth century, when the rest of the world had more or less abandoned Him. Not that it hurt God any. You can't offend an omnipotent being. But it hurt King Louie that history had forgotten—mistaken, and then forgotten—one of Christianity's greatest martyrs. Called by God to get it right, King Louie led the way and we were only too happy to follow. I would have followed that man anywhere. It was lucky for us that he founded the church in Austin, where we could find him more easily. Invite our family members and friends. Recruit on familiar territory.

She recognized the opportunity right away, Madame DuBarry did. Fancied herself King Louie's righthand woman, and more than that besides. By positioning herself as the one in charge of recruitment, a real modern-day office manager, she hoped to make herself indispensable to the king. And needing someone was only one step removed from loving them.

King Louie appreciated her secretarial efforts. He complimented her organizational skills, her inherent drive. He admired her dedication to the church. Her son, Isaac Crable, King Louie merely tolerated. Because he put up with the devil's spawn, we all had to.

For the first few years, it was a tradeoff. We accepted having ten-year-old Isaac around on the occasional afternoon; Madame DuBarry (for the most part) accepted

King Louie's unambiguous lack of romantic interest in her. The slight was made easier to bear by the fact that no one else turned his eye, either. He seemed the rare cleric genuinely immune to the pleasures of his own flesh, focused solely and completely on God's work.

TEZ

One afternoon, Eileen DuBarry picked Isaac up from school. Normally she'd have let him take the bus home, but she had errands to run and knew better than to leave her basically good but sometimes poorly behaved son alone in a house for that long by himself. He walked out of Magnificat's double doors jostling and shoving some boys his age, an impish grin and afternoon sun lighting up his handsome face, but groaned when he saw her beat-up Falcon. Isaac knew it meant one of three things: a doctor's appointment, a death in the family, or a head-splitting visit to the temple, any one of which would have seriously cut into his bike-riding time. He'd had a checkup within the past year, though, and he could not have known that the Grim Reaper waited for him. *The temple, then*, he decided, already resigned to the inane conversation of adults talking over him, like he was too young or stupid to understand Scripture and nuance and sex, however clearly written in the way that his mother mewled at King Louie's feet. Whatever. Last time he'd been there, he'd discovered a funny little pool with what looked like a diving board; it was begging to be explored.

Hopping into the front seat, Isaac submitted a cheek to his mother's kiss, her gooey insistence that he tell her all about his day. Eileen's silver ring, the one she always wore now, the one that looked like it was bleeding, winked in the sun. Before he answered, though, she was already talking lasagna for dinner and had he heard what Billy's dad had done to Billy for bringing a nudie magazine to school—"Honestly, I just don't know *what* the world is coming to!"—and would he mind *terribly* if they dropped by the temple just for a sec, just to give something "quick like bunnies" to King Louie oh and "*Here!* I almost forgot I picked this up for you!" DuBarry handed her only son a cherry cola. He smiled at her for the first time since getting in the vehicle.

"Thanks, Mom."

DuBarry ruffled his hair, turned back to watch the road. She was just so, so, so proud of Isaac.

She pulled into the public garage behind the temple and parked. Isaac begged her to leave the engine idling and him inside, but she wouldn't hear of it. Instead, DuBarry promised him ice cream after dinner, and even though Isaac was too old and jaded, in fifth grade, to fall for such bribes, he rolled his eyes and went along with it anyway because probably it would go faster if he was there nagging her, not allowing her to forget him in the seraphic glow of a man with hair as long as a girl's. The day was still warm as they crossed the street and passed through the church's heavy wooden doors. Inside, the temperature dropped drastically. He'd heard King Louie mention something about an ice box. Perhaps it was a nickname for the building itself.

Immediately distracted, DuBarry floated away on a cloud of pheromones headed for King Louie's office. Isaac slipped unnoticed down the long stone hallway that ended in a series of marble pillars, through which the main chapel was visible. It looked like most churches he'd seen, but with rows of padded folding chairs instead of stationary pews set before an altar gnarled and black—like they'd cut down the oldest tree they could find and burned it, and that was where the priest performed his ceremonies. Nothing else very interesting there. Isaac scampered across the space, looking both ways to make sure no one was watching, and entered the antechamber across the nave. What he'd mistaken for a pool, he realized, was in truth more like a child's paddling pool, even a baptismal font set into and level with the ground. It was shallow—no more than three feet deep—and finished with sterile white tile. Less like a place where babies are baptized, he thought, and more like an operating room. Something about the Mouth felt medicinal, optimized for easy clean-up.

There was a ladder, though, and where there's also a ten-year-old boy with something to prove, the combination can be lethal. Checking to make sure no one was looking, he grabbed a chest-high rung and started climbing. Ladders are easier to scale than trees at the zoo and it took Isaac no time at all to reach the top. He strong-armed himself up and onto the square metal platform, then felt his heart thump *one, two, three* times hard in his chest. His body recognized the threat before his mind did. By raising his blood pressure, it hoped to slow him down, make him sit and catch his breath, until his brain had a chance to register the dizzying height and think better of it.

Isaac was still sitting there, taking in the view from this angle, when King Louie's voice wafted up to him from below. It sounded buttery and sweet—the kind of tone he must adopt to make women, his mom included, cream at his feet, Isaac thought. King Louie said the right words, the kind of thing a responsible adult would say to an impetuous child, but *how* he said them changed everything. With a lilt that turned the commands into questions and the questions into suggestions, he asked, "Isaac? Come on down, Isaac? Don't be afraid? You won't fall . . . you will fly?"

The boy slithered to the edge of the diving board-like platform. His toes curled under inside his shoes like they would grip the Precipice for safety. He looked straight down into the pool, which suddenly seemed very far away. It made his head swim.

"I want to come down now," Isaac whispered.

King Louie cocked his head, a purebred dog with a

styled mane inclining an ear to listen. "Yes, Isaac? Come down?"

"I can't."

"But you can?"

"I'm scared."

"Have you ever heard the story of Simon Magus?"

Isaac shook his pale, blood-drained head.

"Saint Simon was a disciple of Christ? He believed that Jesus was the Son of Man? And he wanted to feel the Holy Spirit within him? So he offered the Apostle Peter money, that Peter might give him the gift of healing with his hands? Peter misconstrued his intentions? Called it greed? Called it simony?"

Here, King Louie clenched a fist. He couldn't help it. The injustice of it all still made him angry.

"So Simon Magus studied and prayed and manifested God's power for himself? Until they called him a god? Until they called him the Standing One? Meaning he'd stand forever? Meaning he'd never decay? Stand, Isaac?"

Hypnotized by the soft sing-song, by the power of story to take us away from ourselves, Isaac stood, newly steady, on two feet, on the furthest edge of the Precipice. Steam seemed to rise from the pool sixty feet below him. It looked nice, like an inviting bath. Like somewhere to slip into and fall asleep for a very long time. Maybe forever.

"He flew, Isaac? Simon Magus flew? He levitated right off that platform and the devil kept him suspended, amazing all the onlookers?"

In Isaac's mind, the pool disappeared. He was climbing the tree at the zoo again, banana clamped in mouth, eager to feed the gorillas. He felt for the branch above him. Stepped lightly onto it, testing its weight before he committed. When it held him, he put his full weight on the branch and reached for the next. His eyes, glassy, saw only blue sky and sun. And behind them, shimmering in the middle of broad daylight, a black blanket of stars. Isaac was ascending to the heavens.

DuBarry, having followed the sound of King Louie's murmurs, walked into the chapel. She was about to ask him if he'd seen Isaac when she followed his gaze, up, to where her son hung suspended in mid-air impossibly high above the Mouth. "Isaac!" she screamed.

Spell broken, color returned to his knowing eyes. His head whipped down to look at her. Half a second later, his body followed suit. Isaac fell.

"No!" DuBarry shrieked, but although her voice was louder than the sound of Isaac's neck snapping as his forehead struck the edge of the pool, it was the snap she would remember. Crisp, like a fresh stalk of celery.

She ran to his side, hands making biscuits of the air around his body, too scared to touch him but unsure how to help. His head rested at an unnatural angle where it had settled against the interior tiled wall, fairly perpendicular to his body. Blood leaked from his open mouth. His eyes stared at the stars.

"Isaac! Isaac! Oh God, King Louie, please help me!"

King Louie didn't move from his position across the chapel. He smiled with no teeth at DuBarry. "My dear, my lovely Eileen. Hush. Your boy will be fine."

"Is he dead? I think he's dead!" Her eyes were wide. Disbelieving. "Is he dead?"

"Isaac is in a place called the Sacra Via. He will be there for three days—at which point his body will be reanimated, or it won't."

"You bastard. You did this!"

"Eileen, *you* did this."

DuBarry's eyes bulged further. "I beg your pardon?"

"Your son was a young man of faith. He believed, and so he flew. In his moment of greatest glory, however, his mother revealed herself to be a pandering whore of no faith whatsoever. A charlatan, prostituting herself for attention and everything she stood to *gain*, giving only to *get*. For that grievous sin, you shall know, with greatest intimacy, *loss*."

Madame DuBarry almost left that day—walked right out and never came back. But she loved King Louie.

The way he'd twisted that love, though, perverted it. Her heart became black as the gnarled altar.

THE GROUNDSKEEPER

We threw his body in a well on the back property, one so old it crumbled as Isaac's lifeless form ricocheted down between its walls. Grains of stone tumbled after him like flowers. Unbaptized, he was fit for just one purpose. Years on, when the heir was born, the baby would be baptized in the waters of this well, drawn and recirculated in the shallows of the Mouth.

THE TIGRESS

There were only a few rules in Simon's Sorrow. First, you didn't question King Louie. To become a Sash was to acknowledge his godhead, to accept him as a prophet like any other. What he said, went, so it wasn't the place for stubborn, arrogant, or big-headed people; these were quickly weeded out. Second, you participated in ministrations by adopting and adhering to your role in the community. Third, you practiced Restoration for your sins. Three rules, and they applied to men and women equally. The last rule, which applied to women only, was don't get pregnant, ever, by anyone. It was expected, if you were a Sash, that you'd sleep with just about everyone else in the group at one point or another. And if you were the Whores, well, sleeping with people—i.e., "recruiting"—*was* your ministration. So you had to take precautions. You could use any birth control method you liked—King Louie helped us get access to all of them—or you could chance it, and risk having to have an abortion. Abortion wasn't exactly allowed, either, especially among the Whores, as it took you out of commission for a time, and anyway, the whole business was just so *messy*. Sometimes it was your only option, though, to seek one in secret, and your only chance to have it performed professionally. Otherwise, King Louie would do it.

That's what happened to Susan. She went and fell in love with an initiate she'd brought in, and started sleeping with him regularly, shirking her conjugal duties to the church. On nights we all went out fishing, she snuck out with Bobby, back to the apartment he still had Outside. When she realized she was pregnant, she came to me. Some of the women looked up to me like I was their leader, though Madame DuBarry was in charge, not me. Susan wanted to know what she should do.

"Get rid of it," I said, "however you have to. And the sooner the better," I added, glancing at her belly, which was model-flat yet. "How far along are you, anyway?"

"Nine weeks," she said, a hand stealing over her stomach protectively. I have no doubt it was an unconscious gesture, but it told me everything I needed to know. She was already full-on mama bear.

"Susan." I took her shoulders. "You must get rid of it. You cannot have a child in Simon's Sorrow. King Louie would never allow it."

"I know. It's just—"

"What? It's Bobby's?"

She nodded, eyes downcast.

"So, what does that mean? Are you going to leave?"

At that, her eyes shot up to me, grew huge and alarmed the way they should have at the pregnancy news. "This is my *home*." She looked up and made the sign of the cross before her eyes flicked back to me. "Don't you think, maybe, there could be an exception? Just this once? I mean, this child is a product of love—a product, even, of Simon's Sorrow!" She was grasping at straws. "Who knows? What if—what if it's the heir?"

I slapped her, hard, for daring to think such a thing, let alone say it aloud. "Repent," I commanded her. "Now. Fifteen lashes."

Cowed, she dragged her feet to the other side of the room. She reached first for the leather whip. "No," I said, ice in my voice. Casting a scornful look in my direction, her hand moved along the wall to the sjambok and hovered. "Closer," I said, "but not close enough." Now her eyes bugged.

"The firebird," I confirmed. "For traitors and blasphemers."

Susan trembled bringing me the beechwood paddle, its solid heft and deadly spikes heavy and cold in her hands. When she gave it to me, I don't think she really believed I would use it—but she'd broken a cardinal rule.

"Bend over."

I didn't make her remove her clothes. There wasn't a point: the spikes would pierce through them. I gagged her with a scarf—something to bite down on—tying it around the back of her head, then positioned myself squarely, feet planted, arms ready. I took a couple practice swings, like I was a batter lining up my form with the pitch, then swung, putting everything I had into it. I don't know who was more stunned: Susan, or me. She, that'd I actually done it (the pain would hit a second later), or me, that there hadn't been more resistance. The flesh of the female ass is soft. Pillowy. It cushions when she sits down, and becomes a warm, comfortable lap for a child to nestle into. I guess I thought the strong gluteus muscles, almost never not used for walking and fucking, would be tougher. But the nails passed right through, striking pelvic bone, causing internal damage I hadn't intended.

Susan flew forward onto the floor, gripping her ass and screaming. Her legs worked madly, pedaling ineffectually against the concrete and pillows, as she tried to scoot herself away from me. I apologized before I could stop myself—an old habit from Outside—because I really hadn't meant to hurt her that badly. Maybe I'd caused the spontaneous abortion of the baby that had started this whole thing.

Maybe I'd killed two birds with one stone.

No such luck. The Nurse put Susan right at once, administering a tetanus booster, squirting antibiotic cream into the nail holes, and closing them up—four in all—with butterfly bandages. She ordered Susan not to put any pressure on her backside for two weeks, which meant lying in bed on her stomach or side for all that time. Her pelvis was bruised, the Nurse determined, but would heal eventually. "Only, I think you have a bigger problem," she said, reviewing the bloodwork, then looking meaningfully at Susan's stomach. "Luckily, I can take care of that, too."

Susan and Susan alone was accountable for her actions.

Just like Resa.

THE NURSE

Apparently, all those late nights Resa had been working hadn't been about "work" at all. Or they had—but not the kind that involved changing out bandages and bedpans. As I would find out months down the road, long after it was too late to grab the horns of her own fate back from her, Resa had gotten involved with Simon's Sorrow. One of the other nurses we worked with had been unabashedly recruiting her for some time. They'd go to lunch and Nancy, who'd never married, would have a new piece of jewelry. An unfamiliar light in her eyes. Would gush about all her new friends—how the church held women in such high regard—how strong they all were. It was the community she'd been looking for her whole life. One day Nancy had settled into her chair more gingerly than normal, and when Resa had asked if she was okay, Nancy had smiled and said yes. "Just had the girls done" and looked at her own chest meaningfully. Well, that had been it for Resa. A tightknit circle of supportive women *and* they paid for plastic surgery? She'd always hated her C-section scar—the thick constrictive rope of it transacting her torso into upper and lower Resas, how her belly pouched soft and ugly over it. She started attending Service, became hooked after the first or second swallow of the poison they put in the wine. Gave up everything to be part of the vital body of the mass hysteria of Simon's Sorrow. A single filament of the toxic mold that would grow to cover all of Austin, its citizens such unsuspecting hyphae.

She even gave up me.

TEZ

When Mary Toni was fourteen, Resa sold her to Simon's Sorrow in exchange for a TV contract. King Louie had promised to make Resa famous by installing her as the spokeswoman for the church—and to be fair, he kept his word. Pretty soon, she appeared in the blue glow of a late-night ad on TV screens across the country. I've seen the commercials—she really *was* beautiful. And for a time, she really was happy. But the trade was never hers to make. Her daughter's freedom for a chance at stardom? Her only child for something that wouldn't last?

Teenagers have so much to be angry about as it is: namely, that things keep happening to their bodies without their permission. Everyone has to go through it: the acne, the chubbiness, the bone-rending growth spurts. Odors that you never had before, hair where you never had it before, and strongest and most frustrating of all: desires that you'd never had before, and don't always know what to do with. Most of us, of course, find boyfriends or girlfriends or porn or other 'safe' ways of experimenting. Most of us aren't relinquished to unstable men for the equivalent of a tummy tuck. But that's what happened.

King Louie—he lured you in with promises and hooked you with the drug of belief. Simon was the sorcerer, but King Louie was the greatest illusionist there'd ever been.

MERCY

The night Resa brought Mary Toni to the on-campus tabling event, King Louie "recognized" her. He pulled me aside later to share his thoughts in confidence. With his hands clasped behind him, he was studying the ground, his face troubled as I'd ever seen it.

"The girl we met today, with her mother," he began. "What was her name?"

"Marie Antoinette. She goes by Mary Toni."

"Mary Toni," King Louie mused, rolling the sounds around in his mouth. Tasting them. "It is said that Mary, mother of Jesus, is the only woman never to be touched by Satan at any point."

"The perpetual virgin," I agreed. "Immaculately conceived, miraculously made a mother, assumed bodily into heaven."

"They called her *Theotokos*, God-bearer. It was her greatest contribution, and her greatest heartbreak." King Louie pivoted toward a statue of Saint Simon, suspended on a pedestal between two windows. Simon was naked, sculpted in freefall. The talons of a winged demon gripped the rope at his waist—maybe catching him, slowing his demise—maybe pulling him more swiftly toward it. King Louie liked the ambiguity.

"This community is named for Simon's sorrow," King Louie said. "But Mary," he clicked his tongue, at once commiserative and dismissive, "she had seven. Seven sorrows. Seven swords piercing her immaculate heart." He traced one slender finger along the pile of bronze organs, torn from Simon mid-descent.

"That would be a lot for anyone," I said.

"Except that Mary wasn't just anyone," King Louie corrected me. "She was Ennoia."

I raised a plaintive eyebrow. "Ennoia?"

"God's First Thought. The creator of the angels. Mother of us all."

When I didn't reply, he advanced until we stood close enough together that I could smell his sweet breath. "The Logos and the World-Soul," King Louie emphasized, his eyes wider now and no longer focused on me, but on some unknowable realm beyond. "The sun and his moon, destined—" and here he swept his arm behind him, long hair flying back like a curtain, to point at the William Blake painting framed above the altar: "to become *The Woman Clothed with the Sun*."

THE TIGRESS

As you can imagine, this sudden new development did not sit well with Madame DuBarry in particular. "What do you mean, 'He's taking a wife?'" she demanded of me, the messenger unlucky enough to deliver it. "Surely, I misunderstood you."

"No, ma'am," I of the pixie-short hair and ample bosom stammered. "He says she's Ennoia. That she's to be the royal mother."

So quick I never saw it coming, DuBarry whipped a cat o' nine tails across my face. The barbed beads caught, ripping irregular strips of flesh from my forehead, cheeks, and chest. A second later, blood welled and began to spill: a kitten finally earning her stripes.

"The Tigress," they started calling me.

That's why my face looks like it does. Like I had really bad acne as a kid or something. Pockmarks. Nope. I used to be almost pretty. Guys still noticed my tits first—how could you not?—but they stayed because my face was nice enough, too. After DuBarry attacked me, I hid in my room for a week. I let the wounds scab over, picked them when they itched, and waited for them to scab again. I think a couple of them, the deeper ones you see here and here, got infected, because they took the longest to heal. It was a hard week. I was basically quarantined, but I didn't really have a choice. I couldn't work with my face looking like that. Instead, I remember praying a lot. Thinking about my next move.

TEZ

And so, believing that Mary Toni was Ennoia, and Ennoia his intended wife—the mother of the heirs-to-be—King Louie arranged the "internship." And Mary Toni came to Simon's Sorrow.

They took her in the middle of the night. Three men and Madame DuBarry (who, having decided it best to keep her enemies close, organized the whole thing and named herself thereafter in charge of Mary Toni's upbringing) simultaneously grabbed her ankles, wrists, and shoulders where she lay in her bed at home. Stuffed a rag in her mouth at the first wide-eyed protest, the almost-scream. They carried her wriggling down a hallway they seemed far too familiar with.

She passed out for a while after that.

Mary Toni came to in a concrete room. Four feet wide by ten feet deep. It had a single window, no more than a slit, near the ceiling, and the only door was stuck tight. A covered face grate partway up the door was currently closed—and was only able to be opened, she surmised, from the outside. A wider slot above the ground seemed the type of gap through which someone might pass her food. She had no idea what time it was, how long it'd been since she'd last eaten. Her stomach growled. Only when she went to stand did she notice the contraption clamped between her legs and around her waist. It looked like underwear made of metal. Cold, hard, and bulky. And, like the door, locked.

Rising awkwardly to her feet, she banged on the reinforced door. She kicked at the solid walls (her efforts sounding strangely muffled) and screamed for them to let her out. After a time, she decided that she was dreaming and tried to go back to sleep. Maybe next time, she thought, she'd wake up sweaty but safe in her bed.

Instead, hours passed. Hungry and cold, Mary Toni slipped into a hallucinogenic state. Blood seeped from the ceiling and crawled in languid drips down the walls. An angel appeared, beautiful in all black. Her name was Eileen, and she was there to take Mary Toni home.

THE MAID

In my experience, fear has a funny way of suppressing appetite. It shunts blood away from the digestive system and up to the brain, out to the limbs, keeping them primed and ready in case you have to fight or flee. So, for the duration of the time they kept me in the Icebox—punishment for one day being late to Service—I didn't really think about eating; not for three days or more. That was my count, anyway, by the rising and the setting of the sun through the single slit at the top of one wall. Though, I heard from the Record-Keeper that the Icebox doesn't open to the outside at all. That there's a sunlamp on the other side of the wall, and a computer that makes it cycle through the solar clock. She said you can speed it up or slow it down so the person inside has no idea at all what time it really is. If that's true, maybe I wasn't in there three full days before anyone came to check on me. Maybe it was part of the game. Reorientation works best after disorientation. And, as the Icebox made sure, a little sensory deprivation, too.

Probably I called out tentatively at first. I don't really

remember. When there was no response, I banged on the solid metal door, screamed through the seam where hinge met wall. Cinderblocks, stacked like puzzle pieces and painted an antiseptic gray, made up the shoebox walls. I smashed my fist against each one of them individually, hoping to get lucky and discover a false panel, a secret escape. It made sense at the time.

Three full mediated revolutions of an electronic sun around the windowless world later, I heard footsteps echoing in what I took to be a stairwell. I couldn't tell if they were ascending or descending, only that they were growing louder without moving closer: vertical, not lateral movement.

THE WHORE

We paused outside the door of the Icebox, me and Madame DuBarry. We listened for the sound of a child crying, breathing, moving, but heard nothing. Maybe the girl was sleeping, I said. Maybe the girl was waiting.

Madame DuBarry turned the key that tumbled the lock, and from inside, an intake of breath. *Awake, then.* Pushing the heavy door open, DuBarry stepped one foot forward. Peered around the edge with sharp nose, stooped shoulders, curious eyes. *There.* Mary Toni sat in the corner, her bare knees pulled up to her tomboy chest.

"Hello."

The child didn't respond.

"My name is Eileen. It's time for your bath."

Mary Toni stared at the woman, at me behind her. Who were we? Could Mary Toni trust us?

"Come." DuBarry extended a hand.

Slowly, Mary Toni stood. Waddled clumsily in the metal underwear. "Do you have a key for this thing?" she asked.

"I do. Let's." DuBarry took the teenager's hand. It

looked small inside her own, though really Mary Toni was too old by then to be holding hands with a mother figure. But that's what DuBarry hoped Mary Toni would see her as: a surrogate mother for the celestial mother—the mother of God.

We walked Mary Toni up a spiral staircase cut from limestone. It was much older than the renovated chapel, possibly original to the building, and led to one place only—the Icebox—once a wine cellar; retrofitted to house bodies.

As they ascended, the metal underwear cut into Mary Toni's hip bones. The chafing became blisters. Became rent, thin trickles of blood. She winced and her palm grew sweaty in DuBarry's. If the woman noticed, she didn't say anything. Just led the girl across the chamber floor and up a second set of stairs, after which we continued down a long, straight hallway. Culminating inside a bathroom to the left. It had a toilet behind a half-wall, an oversized sink, a pedestal soaking tub, and a large picture window. The window afforded Mary Toni her first glimpse of the (real) sun in, what—a day? Multiple days? Even I didn't know how long she'd been down there.

Locking the bathroom door behind us, DuBarry released Mary Toni's clammy hand. She told me to draw a bath, hot. Soon, steam rose in pretty tendrils through the air-conditioned atmosphere. DuBarry added a capful of lavender oil. A sprinkling of lavender buds from a glass jar on the shelf above the tub. *Purple*—the smell—filled the air. While hot water kept pouring in, DuBarry pulled a key from around her neck, and smiling, knelt to undo the spring lock at Mary Toni's lower belly. It clicked; immediately, the pressure lessened. Mary Toni winced again as the metal pulled away from her cuts, already coagulating like glue. DuBarry lowered it carefully. Held the underwear as Mary Toni stepped out of it.

"There. Now off with the rest."

Cold and hesitant, Mary Toni folded her arms

protectively across her chest. She had on cotton panties and the t-shirt she'd worn to bed. Though they weren't much, they were something—some kind of armor against adults with unclear intentions. She didn't comply.

"Okay," I said, stepping in. "Arms up." I grabbed Mary Toni's wrists (so tiny, those bird-girl wrists) and hoisted them above her head. I forcibly removed Mary Toni's shirt, pulling it roughly over her head and yanking her hair in the process. The girl yelped, then covered her nakedness with her arms again, turning her back. It was easy to slide her underwear to her ankles in one quick motion.

"In. Before the water gets cold."

She blanched, shook her head firmly. We didn't know then about her all-consuming fear of water. I ended up lifting and dragging her screaming to the tub. At the lip of it, she finally seemed to grasp her situation. Rather than struggle and risk being thrown in whole-hog, she calmed down and said she would do it. I watched her dip a tentative toe in: decide the water was hot, but manageable. Gripping the sides of the tub, she lowered her whole body down, her shoulders hunched around herself as violently as DuBarry's. She gasped when the water hit her raw hip points.

"The lavender will disinfect them," DuBarry said, turning off the tap.

Mary Toni looked hatefully at the metal cage. "What is that thing, anyway?"

DuBarry picked it up off the floor thoughtfully. Set it on the counter next to the sink. "Think of it like a modern-day chastity belt."

"What's that?"

"It's meant to protect you."

"From what?"

"*For* what is a better way of phrasing it."

"*For* what, then?"

"Your husband."

At this, Mary Tony let loose a genuine guffaw. "Lady, you're crazy."

For a split second, I saw DuBarry's eyes flash. But she managed to stay calm. "We'll put it back on when you're out."

"*What?!*" It was Mary Toni's turn to protest. "I'm fourteen years old. I don't have a husband. I don't know who you are or where I am or what the hell I'm doing here. But I'm leaving." She stood, unsteady, but careful not to slip.

I was there before she could regain her footing. I pushed Mary Toni back down into the water, until everything but her head was submerged, until flower buds swirled around her chin.

"Let *go* of me!"

"Shhh." One hand firmly on the girl's collarbone, I picked a matted strand of hair from Mary Toni's forehead. "Would you like for me to wash your hair?" Rather than wait for Mary Toni's answer, I grabbed what looked like a stainless steel gravy boat and plunged it into the water. Dribbled a pleasing stream along Mary Toni's hairline, down her part, the way her father might have when she was little. The warm water soothed the girl.

"Where am I?"

"In a bathroom on the second floor of the Simon's Sorrow compound."

"Who are you?"

"No one." To stop Mary Toni from asking more questions, I poured another scoop of bathwater on the girl's forehead, where it flooded her eyes and mouth and she sputtered.

Wiping the scented water from her eyes, Mary Toni glared balefully out the picture window. It showed a courtyard, easily four blocks long, walled on three sides and rimmed in roses. The wall was too high to see over, and anyway, the treetops peeking over the wall obscured the view further. She looked back at the chastity belt shining under the vanity lights, blood crusted in its hinges. I imagined Mary Toni locking Madame DuBarry inside it, and running until she found a way out.

THE GROUNDSKEEPER

The building on Guadalupe abutted a parkland the size of four city blocks. It came with the temple property. A large stone wall hemmed in the private garden and muffled most sound from the street. (The opposite was also true: not much sound escaped.) Standing outside the wall, all you could see were the gnarled tops of live oaks, sage green balls of Spanish moss like a thousand dusty nests. Grackles hopped from branch to branch and squawked at impervious passersby. Only things that flew and could not talk were privy to the world within the wall.

Inside, hedges grew in manicured rows, lining old stone walkways and meeting, coy lines of perspective, at a central fountain that, forever splashing, kept the birds and the bats in water and the mosquitos at bay. Cast bronze statues peeked out from untidy rose groves and reflected the tastes of the previous owner: primarily human forms—an eye or an elbow just visible through the brambles. King Louie had ordered the preservation of only one statue: a naked couple in repose, her face upturned to receive the lips of her lover. He'd also ordered a bench be installed for quiet contemplation. Otherwise, the overgrowth added to the labyrinthine illusion, a secret garden from which one had to patiently coax its secrets. An unmarked cottage in the southwestern corner suggested a forgotten body. It was not on any register, so sphinx moths and rock squirrels had moved in. Boasting an abundance of lavender and wild garlic, the garden attracted migrating monarchs, while skunks kept their distance.

It would have been an oasis if it hadn't, for Mary Toni, been a prison.

MOTHER-EATING

THE HANDYMAN

The first thing she did was to run outside and scream. She didn't see me—I had drained and was scrubbing the other stone fountain, in the back—but I saw her. And what a wonder! Of average height and weight, with a round, homely face, I saw nothing at all remarkable about her—which was itself remarkable. Surely this Plain Jane could not be God's First Thought incarnate? But then what had I expected? An Audrey Hepburn? A little Twiggy? Or a child as chaste as the Virgin herself—a pure vessel for the heir? Somewhere between the two, I reckon. More substantive than a sex symbol alone, but still a woman worthy of King Louie. Mary Toni's best asset appeared to be her lungs, for she went on screaming, unaware, it seemed, that the high stone walls and thickly treed canopy muffled all but the faintest of escaping notes, and those were drowned out anyway by the incessant rock music and keg party chaos of our nearest neighbors: fraternity row.

I could tell her panic wasn't letting her think straight. In her haste to get away, she hadn't noticed the beauty all around her. The Central Texas sun, not yet as white-hot as it would be at the peak of summer, shimmered in a cloudless blue sky. Painted lady butterflies, their spotted wings as thin as tissues, drank from a periwinkle-and-cream array of asters and daisies. Bees buzzed around the begonias, lizards tick-tocked their armored heads where they froze, sniffing on the flagstone pathway, and every now and again, blackbirds clustered on the wire, yawning and squawking and pecking at each other like the general pests they were. At least from outside the compound, they stayed seen but not heard. Noises coming in were similarly dampened. When they landed in the garden, they made a hellacious racket. Almost like Mary Toni did that day.

The next thing I saw her do was to run at the limestone wall like she'd break right through it, and barring that, scale it. Indeed she scrambled for purchase, but in vain. Weather-worn, the walls were impossibly smooth, and any would-be foot or handholds crumbled flush again with her weight. She started moving further down the wall, back toward me, hoping, I imagine, for a gate, even a window. There were none, of course. Only more park land. Acres of it, bordered by the wall. Most of it kept impeccably groomed by the Groundskeepers; some of it intentionally left to overgrow and mat together: feral thickets for wildlife and native flora to thrive.

THE RECEPTIONIST

She was creative, I'll give her that much. And persistent. Me, I would've realized I'd been kidnapped and curled up in the corner and cried. I would've done anything my captors told me to just to stay alive. And she did do that last bit—played along, when it suited her, to stay on the church's good side. But initially, anyway, she was scheming all the time. Waiting for the moment when no one was looking and she could run. Or when people were looking, but didn't recognize her.

The Girl Scout stunt almost fooled me. She pulled it on her second day. I went to the restroom, and when I returned, a girl with short black hair was hurrying through the lobby. "Hello?" I said, startling her and making her freeze in her tracks. "Can I help you?"

"Oh," she said, recovering quickly. "No, that's okay. Thank you, though."

I squinted at her. She looked a little familiar, but I'd only seen Ennoia from the back of the Great Hall. A crowd of pressing bodies had mobbed between us, leaving me with little more than a first impression of thinness, plainness, and long dark hair. This girl's hair was shoulder-length, or so I thought. I'd learn she'd tucked it up inside a cap she'd stolen from the Custodian's closet. Nevertheless, alarm bells were ringing in my mind. I decided to stall her while I pondered what they meant.

"What are you doing in here?"

She looked around, as though for inspiration, and apparently landed on it. "I'm just out with my mom selling Girl Scout cookies," she lied. "I came in to see if anyone here wanted any."

"Where are the cookies?" I asked, noting her empty hands.

"Outside. With my mom. Like I said."

She appeared to be thirteen or fourteen years old. Most of the Girl Scouts I see hawking cookies are younger. Fourth or fifth grade.

"Aren't you a little old for that?" I asked.

She blushed. "I got held back a year. Anyway—sorry to bother you. Gotta run." She turned to go.

"Wait," I commanded, and she did. I walked right up to her, close enough to touch, and taking my own liberty in my hands (for if I was wrong, and the girl left and tattled on me, I'd surely be charged with molesting a minor), I lifted up her skirt. There it was: the chastity belt, just angular enough as to be noticeable under her woven shift dress. Making her earlier shuffle across the lobby the slightest bit awkward.

"Guards!" I yelled, as loud as I could, and they came running from wherever they were stationed. How she'd slipped past them in the first place, I don't know, but at least she didn't actually get away. Not that we wouldn't have found her. Having identified her once, King Louie never would have stopped looking for her.

Of course, we weren't going to take that chance.

I heard the Guards tied her to a chair, put a cloth bag over her head, and clamped headphones on her ears. A recorded reading of the Book of Simon played on repeat for twenty-four hours. She couldn't see, she couldn't lay down, she couldn't hear anything but the story of our namesake. It's a particularly gruesome retelling, including all the ways Simon is believed to have been tortured before he died. For example, some sources say he was buried alive. Others recount the carnivorous beetles sent to feast upon his legs and toes. Those are nightmare images for anyone, but especially a child. And in particular, one who doesn't really know where she is, why she's there, or what's to become of her.

THE BUTCHER

There were other escape attempts, but these became fewer and less robust as time went on. Until the girl gave up and gave in.

THE NANNY

The thing about fourteen is that it's seven years past the age of reason and a few key factors have changed. Seven-year-old girls are self-aware, but not yet self-conscious. They know the clinical difference between facts and opinions, truth and lies, but rarely dare—or even think—to question authority figures. (Their parents. Santa Claus. The church). They still believe that sharing is caring and haven't yet realized that boys have cooties. Circle circle dot dot is at least a year off, through they may look up "penis" and "vagina" and even "rape" if they're especially precocious in the classroom dictionary, then giggle covertly and show their friends.

Fourteen-year-olds, on the other hand, are biologically mature enough to bear children. Some of them probably touch themselves to sleep at night. Fourteen is old enough to know better, but not to know enough. What do you do, for example, when your mother, acting out of her own selfish interests, sells you to a cult? And you become, in modern-day America, a child bride, promised to a man who thinks he speaks for God?

TEZ

She wasn't really a child, of course. Not since starting her period two years before. But nor was she a woman; situated, instead, in the liminal space meant for exploration and experimentation: the activities that help one to "come of age." Mary Toni hadn't kissed a boy, though she'd made out with her mirror. Hadn't dreamed of second base, though she'd laid beneath the bathtub faucet, legs spread and the pressure building, until she exploded.

Mary Toni was very well-cared-for at Simon's Sorrow. She had organic cotton clothes to wear and a chef at her disposal and a tutor who oversaw her education on such topics as the church approved. Her betrothed, however, was reticent; a mystery she knew next to nothing about. She'd seen him from a distance, in the shadows. He'd made no advances, no attempts even to talk to her. It was Madame DuBarry who explained the arrangement. The engagement. Who said she would be a queen, so long as she played by the rules.

THE TAILOR

The first thing we did was appraise her, head to toe, as a group. Madame DuBarry; the Whores; the Jeweler; the Chef; myself; a dozen others. Eileen paraded her naked in front of us, turning her this way and that as we scrutinized her like cattle. "Pull her hair up," one commanded, and DuBarry complied, gathering Mary Toni's long black hair into a knot at her nape before twisting it up. Without the small armor of her hair protecting her, the girl flushed. We took note of this reaction, as we did her measurements, the proportions of one part to another, and our general overall impressions.

"Let's see the other side, then," the Barber called.

DuBarry obliged, spinning Mary Toni in place so that she faced the wall behind her. "Spread your legs," DuBarry whispered, and Mary Toni did. "Now bend over."

When the girl-child didn't instantly comply, DuBarry pushed the leverage point between her shoulder blades, forcing her down until her hands almost touched the floor. From between her own legs, Mary Toni saw us. More nods. Exchanges of meaningful looks. Hastily scrawled remarks. The only one who hadn't moved was the Laundress. Draped sideways, cradled by the padded arms of an overstuffed chair, she'd watched the whole proceeding with something like amusement. A hint of a smile at one upturned corner; eyes that missed nothing. "Well?" I asked, once DuBarry had turned Mary Toni back around.

"Her cheekbones," the Laundress said.

"What of her cheekbones?" I asked.

"They're quite . . . unpronounced. Combined with a rather remarkable nose that, if I may, looks like she has yet to grow into it. Her whole face appears round. A child's face."

"A child's face," I repeated. "And tell me, do you also see that she is yet a child?"

"It's unbecoming. Especially with those chicken pox scars," the Laundress added.

"Nothing a little contouring can't fix. Right?" I smiled at Mary Toni and waited for the girl-child's gratitude. It didn't come.

"All right," DuBarry said to Mary Toni. "Back into the belt with you, then."

"No!"

It was the first time we'd heard Mary Toni speak. Reactions to her insubordination were mixed. Surprise. Anger. And not a little appreciation.

DuBarry gripped her upper arm and yanked her away roughly. Said to me, "I'm afraid we have our hands full with this one."

THE TUTOR

Mary Toni was one of the smartest girls I ever met. But if she didn't care about school before coming to Simon's Sorrow, it was impossible to convince her that geometry mattered in captivity. Yes, I use the word captivity. That's what it was, no matter how you slice it. I see that now like I saw it then. Only none of us had the guts to call it by its name, to stand up to the man who had given us everything. King Louie . . . I mean, the word "king" here is as fitting as the word "captivity," which is to say—it was the truth. He was our (mostly) benevolent ruler, telling us when we could eat and what, when to sleep, and when and how to pray. We listened to him because we believed he spoke for God. Who else could know the things he knew, perform the miracles he did, or lead us through Restoration so skillfully, except one chosen by the Lord? He was a king at the right hand of the King of Kings, and once you became a Sash you didn't question that. Which is why we didn't bat an eye at what amounted to kidnapping—and, eventually, his taking of a child bride.

As I would be one of Mary Toni's primary points of contact, I sat on the bench when they first brought her into the Great Hall. She'd been held in the Icebox for days already—just enough to disorient her and make her docile without making her sick. She seemed confused as much as scared when Madame DuBarry marched her in, a prized lamb. Her eyes looked glassy. She blinked a lot. I could tell already that she'd be difficult to work with, though I was up for the challenge. God does not give us more than we can handle.

During our first session, I gave her a written assessment, so I could see where she was in her studies. I handed her a test booklet, an answer sheet, and a dull, stubby pencil, lest she get any ideas about stabbing me.

Once I heard the rifling of paper as she opened the booklet and the scritching of graphite, I left her to it and opened the Book of Simon for another read-through. It wasn't until I scored the exam later that I realized she'd filled in the bubbles so they formed a flower shape and done about as well as a monkey at a typewriter.

THE TIGRESS

She was given free rein of the church and its grounds, since how much trouble could one child in one building cause? Soon, she'd explored about as much as she could: the long corridors of identical dormitory-style bedrooms; the meditation hall; the kitchen; the dining area. To entertain herself, she started walking with her eyes closed, trying to memorize the way by touch alone. We'd see her inching slowly down the dark, cool hallways, running her hands over the uneven stone surfaces. It involved lots of tripping over the bulky floor blocks, toes stubbed on the stone thresholds of doorways. We'd hear her singing softly to herself, enjoying the ethereal echo of her own voice off of the ceilings. I found it enchanting. I thought I could almost see what King Louie saw. Could almost believe she was Ennoia.

Without meaning to, I began following her. Watching, without her knowledge, the girl and the things she did. It was an opportunity to see Simon's Sorrow through her eyes—as though I was the initiate, instead of a fourth-year going on five.

Like the temple. It was the largest, grandest room in the building, but until Mary Toni came and reminded me *how* to see it, I'd forgotten. I'd stopped appreciating that the temple was a breath of fresh air—literally—in the middle of the dark stone hallways. (The air conditioning was always on full-blast in there to protect the relics housed near the tabernacle. But also, sunlight streamed bright white through the upper windows, seeming to purify every molecule that floated through the beams.) Sometimes I closed my eyes, too, and felt, like she did, the cold metal and neutral padding of the neatly arranged folding chairs. There were hundreds of them. They stretched from the altar to the shadows. Took in the pageantry of the place. Gold-plated angels (and not a few devil statues) carried the altar on their backs. Beneath my fingers, their hooked or feathered wings just cleared the tabletop.

But I *looked* at it, as well. Candles—candles that were never allowed to burn out before they were replaced, I might add—burned inside exotic-looking lanterns with red glass panels. More angels held censers suspended on chains from the ceiling. These burned frankincense and myrrh: the lingering smokey scent in the air. Behind the altar, where the crucifix would have been in Mary Toni's family's church, leered an intricate mosaic of Lord Simon, impressive for both its size and complexity. Pieced glass flames floated above his extended right hand. A magic trick; the famous illusions of Simon Magus. In his other, he held a shrew's fiddle: a kind of torture device once commonly prescribed for those who'd broken the public peace. It worked by clamping two long iron bars together around the penitent's neck and wrists. In just a few days' time, and much like Mary Toni's chastity belt, the rubbing metal reduced flesh to pulp, wore skin and muscle down to carpals, ulna, radius, cervical vertebra. In the mural, however, Simon held it casually, even cavalierly; not confined by its grip, but free of its bite. Like the chains had fallen off and he had laughed.

There was still a crucifix, too—in a smaller chamber to the left. It—He—hung above a rack of votives and a single kneeling pedestal. Jesus of course looked suitably tortured. Eyes downcast, maybe regretful. His feet and hands were bloodier than normal, like the extremities had been dip-dyed, and his side wound was particularly gnarly.

Coagulated, black, and beaded, like beetles fed upon him. Sucker marks like raw little leech bites peppered his skin instead of whiplashes, and his crown was of rope, not thorns. I watched Mary Toni approach, fingers skimming the candle holders. Sumptuous red velvet curtains pulled back to either side like a stage.

And I suppose it was a play, in a way. The Passion play. The spent Christ finally defeated atop Golgotha. In this version, though, he played second chair to Simon. God-smitten Simon, his death even more unfair, more cruel and unusual, than that of Jesus's.

The candles spluttered in a draft, and on that wind we smelled the faintest odor of rot. It was well-hidden beneath the incense and the furniture polish, but too pungent to be a dream.

Exiting the chamber, Mary Toni rounded the corner and stepped into the next alcove: a stone grotto filled with hundreds of candles, one for each member of the Austin congregation. The candles got lit upon their baptism. The chamber was otherwise boring.

In the third nook she found the Mouth. A high steel ladder; a diving board; a shallow pool.

Absorbed by my own thoughts, I lost track of her for a moment. Next thing I knew, she was standing beside me. "What happened to your face?" she asked, unafraid.

Blunt. I liked that about her.

"Restoration," I lied. Better not to scare her with horror stories of arbitrary abuse just yet. Her eyes grew wide. Maybe she'd heard stories elsewhere. "And you?" I nodded at her chastity belt. "What happened to your pussy?"

She blanched, and I recalled that she was just a teenager. Probably a virgin.

"Sorry. Trade talk. It's just—that's a new one. I haven't seen King Louie use that particular contraption on anyone."

Mary Toni was quiet for a moment. Then she straightened her shoulders and angled to face me directly.

Fascinated, I waited for her response. What she said surprised me. "Is he nice?" she asked. "King Louie."

"Define 'nice.'" I smiled. "Nah," I said, thinking of my initiation. He'd ravaged me four ways to Sunday with every silicon and glass device that wasn't his dick. "He's great. Really great, actually. Haven't you met him yet?"

"No. They keep telling me he's out of town. I don't know how they expect me to marry someone who isn't even here."

"Cheer up," I said, chucking her under the chin. "It's going to be fun."

"I'm fourteen. That's got to be illegal, right?"

"Separation of church and state," I reminded her. "As long as we funnel the money we save on taxes back to the powers that be, they don't care what we do. It's none of their business, anyway."

"Why does anyone stay here?" she moaned. I knew the question was rhetorical, but it rubbed me wrong. I couldn't resist.

"Why does anyone do anything?" I said, and when she didn't answer: "Because it feels good. Think all those men in the chapel are here for the brotherhood? Even King Louie knows better than that. They're here for the pussy." I rubbed myself between my legs. She looked away, embarrassed. "Anyway, I know you're like, new, to all this or whatever, so any questions about sex—because he is going to expect sex—you can come to me, all right? Just ask for the Tigress."

THE WHORE

It was twilight, after dinner and Mary Toni's fourth bath. She was back in the belt and seated uncomfortably before an ornate vanity. Outside, bats flitted by the window, catching their fill of late June insects. Behind her, Madame DuBarry was dragging a brush through Mary Toni's thick hair. A hundred strokes, five hundred, until the girl-child's long locks shimmered. Both woman and bride-to-be seemed soothed by the repetitious task, wrapped in the still, warm night.

"So when am I going to meet him?" Mary Toni asked, making eye contact with DuBarry in the mirror.

"King Louie?"

She nodded.

"Soon. He's away at the moment, serving the needs of the church in other parts of the country."

"You mean it's not just Austin?"

DuBarry smiled. "We've been growing."

"Does he have teenage brides in those places, too?"

Her smile soured. "No, you're to be the only one."

Mary Toni didn't say anything else while she studied Eileen's face in the mirror: a woman absorbed by the task at hand and accordingly unguarded. "You're pretty," Mary Toni said.

DuBarry smiled again, but only with the corner of her mouth.

"You love him, don't you?"

The lead recruiter froze mid-stroke.

"Please tell me why."

"Why, what?"

"Why you're in love with a man who would marry and rape little girls."

DuBarry rolled her eyes. "I wonder if they warned him how dramatic you are."

"What'd you expect? I'm fourteen."

"And menstruating, no?"

Mary Toni flushed. "So what?"

"So then you're perfectly old enough to play your part in the story. Everyone has a role here. Everyone serves," DuBarry said.

Mary Toni noted the bitterness in her mouth, so much like her mother Resa. "My mom will come for me, you know. She'll find me. Then you'll be in trouble."

"Perhaps," DuBarry said, tossing the brush on the bureau and folding her arms across her chest. "But right now it's time for bed. You've got a big day tomorrow."

"What's tomorrow?"

"If everything goes to plan, a wedding."

MERCY

Did her uncle, Adam Habsburg, ever cross her mind? Did she wonder if he might come for her, too? I doubt it. She, like we, knew exactly how self-centered he was.

Oh well.

TEZ

It's an old tradition, marriage by proxy. They couldn't just leave Mary Toni to hang around, an unwed virgin, forever. It would be weeks before King Louie came back, and in the meantime, the chastity belt was wearing dime-sized sores into the thin skin of her hip bones and leaving purple pinch bruises at the V creases of her inner thighs. Infection threatened. Were she and King Louie married, though— even if it wasn't the king himself beholding his bride—Mary Toni could at least be rid of that hateful device. She'd exchange it for a proverbial scepter the moment she became queen.

Madame DuBarry explained how it worked. "*By proxy* means that a visiting priest will marry you and King Louie on paper and a proxy will stand in for him until he can return and take his vows himself."

"Well, who will the proxy be?" Mary Toni asked.

"A man named Mercy. You can think of him like King Louie's second-in-command. Now, onto bed with you. Scoot." She patted the girl-child's rear end—the soft part, unencumbered by restraints—and shooed her out of the room.

THE WHORE

Call it spite or sincere admiration—the 'look' that the Tailor created for Mary Toni's wedding day contained whole worlds within it. The haute couture dress, summarily studded in diamonds, belonged on a New York City runway. In fact, that's where he'd spotted it the spring before—before Austin and King Louie and his role as designer for the King. Before the temple.

Mary Toni's hair was all California: brushed until it shone, then slicked back close to her scalp until it waterfalled down her shoulders.

Her face, the Tailor borrowed from Tokyo's kawaii culture: the sex appeal of living dolls. Having promised the court more "contouring," he delivered something out of a dream. Virgin-white base makeup. For contrast, lavender crushed into bruises on her cheeks. To the points of her cheekbones, the Tailor applied rouge mixed with fish blood. That night, we would dine on Croatian sea bass.

At five o'clock on the dot, the church bells tolled. Two ushers flung the temple doors open and the congregation stood expectantly. They gasped twice; first at her dress: its train, the diamond accents. Next at the altar, when she handed her bouquet of blood lilies to a Sash in the first row and said Sash removed Mary Toni's lace veil, revealing her painted face.

TEZ

So *this* was Mercy. Mary Toni knew him. He was the guy from that campus preview event, the one her mother had liked.

Did that make the other one, the magic man, all charm and magnetic sex, King Louie? Long hair black as his robe. Lips red as his sash.

Her husband.

THE NURSE

What Mary Toni didn't know was that earlier that morning, outside in the Simon's Sorrow courtyard, Mercy had also married her mother. Like her daughter, Resa had no idea what was happening. The church kept her flush with whatever drugs she wanted, and she would have taken any kind of vow, any time, to maintain that high. Mercy married Resa because she was pregnant. She was pregnant because the cult needed her sacrifice—to open the gates for the heir.

THE RECORD-KEEPER

The Bible speaks of three Great Falls. When the angel Satan fell from heaven, having turned his back on God, he fell so fast and for so long that his inertia pierced the veil between that world and this one. It was the planet that stopped his fall, and the planet that became the devil's playground. He still stalks the earth today, setting snares to trap those lost souls who, caught in their own free fall, have forgotten they once knew how to fly.

The Second Fall was our forebears' fall from grace: Adam and Eve disobeying God in the garden. They did precisely what they'd been told not to do, and their hubris was the original sin. Because Eve thought she knew better than God, and because Adam trusted his wife's words over his Lord's, the children they bore were conceived in sin—and their children after that, and so on, down through the ages, until this very moment in time.

But there would be one more Fall, and the worst kind yet. For, unlike Satan, and unlike Adam and Eve, this fall was not the consequence of the afflicted's conscious choice, but a cross he was given to bear by the ignorant souls around him. I don't mean Jesus, though certainly the Son of Man endured his share of suffering. I mean Simon; at once a common man and a worker of miracles—reviled— spit upon—for preaching God's word and *daring—daring*, I say—to want to be closer to God. He wasn't turning his back like the angel Satan and he wasn't flouting God's law like the First Parents and *still* he fell! Because man, made in the perfect likeness of God, becomes as he ages imperfect. Pitted with pride and scarred by desire for earthly pleasures, the fruits of the spirit long neglected. Such was the man, Peter, who sent Simon to his death.

And yet, God promises us that in the New Age, death will be no more. And how will we recognize the New Age?

With the Second Coming of Simon.

"So, my brothers and sisters," King Louie said the night he proclaimed the prophecy. "Let us prepare for Simon's coming. Let us feed our minds with Scripture. Let us prepare our bodies through Restoration. Let us nurture the heirs, the little children, who will flex their holy arms to catch our messiah, that he may not fall again—and this time pierce the bowels of hell, taking all of us with him."

TEZ

One week later, King Louie returned. He stood beside Mary Toni and took the same vow of fidelity that she had seven days earlier taken with Mercy. He gave her a ring, a bloodstone, that matched the earrings Mercy had given her the week before. The earrings hung lopsided from her home-pierced holes. The ring spun large and loose below her knuckle. Their signatures, scrawled in the Book of Simon, looked like large blobs of ink.

After dinner, the Sashes escorted King Louie and Mary Toni to the bridal suite, the room in which she would henceforth sleep alone. That night, however, the lot of them crowded in behind her to watch Madame DuBarry start undoing the intricate lacing that ran up Mary Toni's spine and strung her shoulder blades taut as a bow. Was her deflowering to be a spectacle then? But they only stayed long enough to see the girl stripped naked, redressed in a soft white high-necked gown. She felt like a sacrifice. The virgin offered up for a ritual fuck.

THE PSYCHOLOGIST

It's called cognitive dissonance—when your thoughts, beliefs, and attitudes don't match your environment. You may be in a bad situation, right—think *kidnapping*—where you know your life is in danger, but at the same time, you're dependent on your captor for survival. So even though you should hate him, and not listen, and rebel, you end up doing exactly what he says because not doing so would be worse. He might hurt you otherwise. Might withhold food. Better to be on his good side, you think. So you act nice. Compliant. And after some time, it's the only way you act. You've forgotten you ever didn't want to be in this situation. You start to trust your captor. Care for him. Now you've got Stockholm Syndrome.

TEZ

The thing about King Louie was, he had a secret. For all the orgies he'd orchestrated, the zealots he'd reduced to dripping puddles of need at his feet, he'd rarely been intimate himself. His body so often betrayed him for reasons he didn't understand, and shame does not become a public figure. The last time his proverbial loins had stirred, he'd been staring at Tommy's red hamburger tongue. But he'd told himself it didn't matter. The problem lay not with *him*, but in his lack of a suitable partner. A queen, fit quite literally for a king. And not just any queen, but a celestial mother. Mary's next incarnation: Ennoia.

In a sermon he gave the day of their wedding, he claimed he'd recognized her the moment he saw her. Just thirteen, and with her mother on campus. Approaching his table like Simon had hand-delivered her. A reward, after all those years of waiting. Planning. Greasing the wheels of the right politicians and dancing the dance of the long-term dreamer; growing, then culling, then growing the flock again. When he thought about it—the work—then thought about *her*, his bride, his breath caught. Fourteen now, and ripe! Her purity was blinding.

For one terrifying moment before he entered her bedroom, he questioned whether he was up to the task. But then he heard the muffled sounds of her singing to herself inside, and the full weight of his present reality hit him. Making Marie Antoinette a wife was not just an opportunity, but a responsibility. God had charged him with as much. She would be his.

MERCY

He wanted her to want it. Want *him*. The fear on her face, it didn't do it for him, he told me later. She was young and uncertain and vulnerable. Some men would get off on that. But not King Louie.

Rape is ancient and ugly. Only love starts revolutions.

TEZ

As soon as the last lurker had left and it was just her and King Louie, Mary Toni took a good, hard look at the man. It was the closest she'd been to him. His blue eyes appraised her, equally studious, and her chest flushed beneath her nightgown. What was he thinking? Did he like what he saw? Did she *want* him to like what he saw? He was old enough to be her father, but decidedly unfatherlike. "Come," he said after a moment, and motioned for Mary Toni to crawl into bed with him. Half of her resisted, but half of her wanted to—hormones and curiosity and those deep, pooling eyes getting the better of her. He was so serious. And gentle. Patting the pillow beside him, he bade her to nestle in the crook of his shoulder, which she did, laying her head upon his chest. His silk robe was cool beneath her cheek and he smelled, she thought, of a pirate at sea: like cigarettes and salt. A touch of cedar. He asked no questions, did not in any way attempt to grope her. They fell asleep like that, and in the morning, he was gone. A bouquet of white carnations on the pillow the only sign he'd ever been there.

THE GROUNDSKEEPER

Carnations are known both as the flower of love and the Flower of God. We grew them along the north wall of the garden, where the southern sun fell upon their white heads daily and watered them with light. The soil there was sandy and well-drained; accordingly, the plants did well. At King Louie's request, from there on I cut them first thing every morning, just as the buds were opening for the day, and left them in a vase on Mary Toni's windowsill. They stayed fresh for twenty-four hours, at which point they were replaced.

THE LAUNDRESS

Despite King Louie's somewhat reticent early relationship with his new wife, Mary Toni was far from left to her own devices. The women of the church, variously eager to meet her and anxious to deceive her, cornered the girl as often as possible in the kitchen and the limestone stairwells to ask prying questions or offer some ill-meaning advice.

They were jealous. They wanted to see her fail. So they told her that Service was casual—a black muslin shift would do—when everyone else showed up in black robes. They promised to take her with them to the store, then left an hour early, so Mary Toni was forced to wait alone until they returned.

"Sorry," they said, sarcastically. "Got this for you, though," one offered, withdrawing a jar from her shopping bag. "Pickled pig feet," puffing out her cheeks and imitating Mary Toni's baby-round face, "for Miss Porcine."

TEZ

Maybe Mary Toni would have been more self-conscious showing up to her first Service in a muslin shift if half the temple hadn't already seen her naked. So what did it matter? She slid into the last row of chairs near the back. Soon, Mercy was tapping her on the shoulder and indicating an open seat in the front row. She stood and moved begrudgingly, meeting the eyes of every parishioner who dared stare at her with open curiosity along the way. After Mercy saw to it that she was properly seated, he took his own seat on the opposite side of the temple, next to a pregnant woman Mary Toni assumed must be his wife. She couldn't see the woman's face, only the gentle swell of her belly; delicate, long-fingered hands crossed protectively over it. Almost absentmindedly, she twirled a wedding band around her third finger.

Mary Toni watched, hypnotized by that ring, so much like her own. Its red stone caught and refracted the light into countless shades of vermilion and maroon. The same colors as in the stained glass windows around them. Those windows, Mary Toni noted, did not depict Michael or any of the saints she knew, but all seemed to show the same man—Simon Magus, if she was reading the leaded inscription correctly—engaged in acts of daily living: eating honey and drinking wine; hanging out with Christ at the well; having sex with one, two, three different women, faces contorted in ecstasy. It made her stomach flip-flop in a not-unpleasant way.

Then her own husband approached the podium. "Brothers and sisters," King Louie greeted them all. But Mary Toni was still staring at the ring. Staring at the woman's belly. Shifting in her seat to see the woman's face.

Mom?

It took Mary Toni a moment to believe what she was seeing. Her hardworking, jaded hospice nurse mother aglow at fifty-two with the vitality of a second-trimester pregnancy. Her hair, thicker and shinier than Mary Toni remembered, cascading soft and full down her back.

Mary Toni did the math. She'd been at Simon's Sorrow for two months. Resa, then, had gotten pregnant Outside. By whom—Mercy? How long had she been . . . *seeing* . . . him? Was her mom—the mom she'd convinced herself would rescue her—the *reason* Mary Toni was here? Was it all, as Madame DuBarry had said, part of some larger plan? And if so, whose? King Louie's? Simon's? Her mother's?

The teenager rose to run, to confront her mom, to ask her what was happening and why—but a heavy hand clamped down on her shoulder. She turned to see Mercy again, the man who'd just been sitting next to her mother. He shook his head almost imperceptibly. Nodded toward the altar, as though to say *Service is beginning. Not now.* To make sure she behaved, he sat down behind her, his hand, but not the memory of it, gone from her body. Was that the hand that cradled her mother now? Was his the body that had been inside her? Did they look like the figures in the stained glass windows when they did it? Did that make this man her stepdad?

King Louie began. "Good evening and thank you all for being here. It's a momentous occasion as we baptize our 300th local member, soon to be the mother of the church: Ennoia." King Louie swept an arm wide, looked directly at

Mary Toni. The whole congregation jumped to its feet, applauding wildly, and Mary Toni felt Mercy's cold, waxy hands grab her under the armpits and lift her to her feet. There were cheers and tears of exuberance and relief. God's First Thought had been found, brought home, and restored to the throne.

THE HANDYMAN

All the Sashes got a bloodstone at their initiation. It was really just a ruby, but we called them bloodstones because it sounded cooler, and because of what they represented. To wear a bloodstone, as to be tattooed with the sign of the sash, was to commit to the church and to the group. The same blood flowed through all of us. Sometimes it had to be spilled. Always it had to be respected.

It was the Jeweler's job to set the bloodstones in different types of settings for the Sashes. Some of us were ring people and some preferred necklaces; some earrings, some lapel pins, some cufflinks. Your bloodstone was a gift to you from King Louie. You treasured it. You wore it proudly. You didn't ever lose it.

At Mary Toni's initiation, King Louie blessed her wedding bloodstone. His hands trembled as he slid the ring from her finger, submerged it in the Mouth, muttered a prayer, then returned it to her left hand. When she glanced at the ring again, it looked different. The bloodstone had a starburst in one corner, a flaw she recognized. "But how—?" she said. "I thought I lost this in the spring."

King Louie smiled. Magic explained away so much.

TEZ

Mary Toni didn't remember her first baptism. She was an infant, angry and red. She wailed when the priest poured the water, made the sign of the cross in oil, because the church was cold and her white crinoline dress was itchy, irritating her baby-soft skin. That's what Resa recalled, anyway: how they went the whole nine yards in case this child deserted them, too; saw fit, suddenly, to join her fifteen siblings in death, all of them unbaptized and all of them, according to the church, stuck somewhere in purgatory, the last of their original sin being burned out of them.

Despite the odds, though, Mary Toni had kept on living, breathing, crying, eventually learning to crawl, walk, laugh—a red-blooded daddy's girl. Soon crying again at his death, only to learn that it doesn't bring a person back, doesn't change anything at all. Then never crying again.

At her second baptism, which she did remember, Mary Toni wore black instead of white, didn't cry when they "blessed" her, was not given to God by her parents, witnessed by godparents, but was thereafter called Ennoia.

It was the one and only Service she ever attended.

MERCY

"Again." Resa opened her mouth like a fish. Stuck out her tongue, waited for her medicine. One, two, three more drops from the brown glass dropper bottle. She swallowed. Sighed. Smiled.

"And one for Baby," she said, puckering her lips in my direction. I kissed her quickly, hoping that'd be the end of it. Physical affection makes me sick on a good day, but I understand that women require it. So, I did my duty to that other sex, knowing it was King Louie I did it for. I wasn't just helping a geriatric mother carry her baby to term; I was turning the key that would open death's gate, Restoring Lord Simon to us all.

TEZ

Question: How do you love a mother who's abandoned you? Who's made it clear she loves you less than she loves herself?

Answer: You read the letters she only writes to you when she's high. Reams of them. Red ink spilled in a careful hand on stationary edged in gold leaf. An icon of Saint Simon at the top.

Dear Mary Toni, the first one began. *I imagine you were shocked to see me at Service the other day. Probably you have a million burning questions. Where are you? Who are these people? How did you end up here? And now, what is my involvement? First, please know that I never meant for it to happen this way. The first time I attended Service and heard King Louie speak of Ennoia, I felt the bell of truth reverberate in my bones. I recognized her in you. Still, I thought there would be time for negotiation. For you to grow up.*

You have to believe me. I didn't know they would come for you then. Couldn't see that the promises made, the opportunities they dangled before me, were but distractions, shiny objects to keep me occupied while they stole you, my daughter, away from me. And now I will have another child, and you, a baby brother or sister. Can you even? I was like Sarah, too old, too hollowed out to conceive and carry again. But the Lord had other plans for me and King Louie made it so. He's given me a husband, a baby, the career I always wanted. He is generous and benevolent like that. A man of God and of great power, and he will give you everything you dream of, too. Which is why I had to give you to him. My daughter, I always knew you were special, destined for unimaginable greatness. Now on the brink of womanhood, you stand poised to take the church, and then the world, by storm.

MOTHER-EATING

You are God's First Thought—fitting, since you are always mine, too. Be a good girl. Don't let me down.
Mom

Beyond that single glimpse in Service, Mary Toni never did get to access her mom directly. But there were the letters—letters I have now.

It's how I know so much about the grandma who would be killed before I could meet her. When I touch them, it's like holding Resa's hand, looking into her dilated eyes. Into a soul too pain-blinded to know better.

THE TUTOR

I found one of them, later, when I was cleaning out her drawers. *Do so much good to the Sashes that they can say I sent them an angel,* she wrote. Resa told Mary Toni to pretend life at Simon's Sorrow was a fairy tale, like the ones she'd read to her as a girl.

Rapunzel, Rapunzel, let down your long hair.

Thing is, it was never made clear how the trapped Rapunzel got food while in the tower. Maybe the birds brought it to her, or perhaps the witch who'd imprisoned her made food magically appear? At any rate, she survived long enough for a prince to climb the rope of her hair. He pulled it out bloody at the roots, but he saved her. Then they lived happily ever after.

Ladies and gentlemen, Resa was like that witch, and King Louie was like that prince. Neither had Mary Toni's best interests at heart; were in it only for what they stood to gain. The witch, a ransom. The king, a trophy.

THE RECEPTIONIST

Only when Resa complained enough did King Louie and

Mercy make good on their end of the deal. In the office, Madame DuBarry could hear King Louie's side of the phone call and jealousy bloomed in her hateful heart. "Yes, thirty seconds, just you. National airplay. Hair, makeup, the works. Uh-huh." He was scribbling what looked like notes in a ledger, but upon closer inspection, I realized he was drawing a noose. Madame DuBarry saw it, too; she smirked and stifled a laugh. The child may have been his royal pet, but her mother was merely a royal pain in the ass. Why did *she* get special treatment? How come *she* could be pregnant and no one else?

And then one day Resa appeared onscreen, breathtaking as a pregnant Sash in a plunging dress. Her pedicured feet poked out from folds of red velvet. Roses whispered past her legs as she walked the limestone path in the garden. The early morning sun spoke of redemption and everything holy. Sex and birdsong. Woman of God. "Faith," she may be heard saying in the video, "can move mountains." Resa paused dramatically and looked off into the distance, as though Central Texas had any mountains at all. Then she turned back to the camera, seamlessly rolling on a track and making the world move like water. "Do you know him? Do you know Simon? Because he wants to know you."

She didn't actually lick her lips or blow a kiss here. It was somehow implied, anyway. Every red-blooded American male watching the Super Bowl that year got a boner. Plenty of wives, too. *You mean I can look like that if I join the church? I can be young and beautiful forever?*

What went through their sons' heads: *You mean bodies are for sale—and the church approves? Now that's a rapture I can get behind.*

Only the daughters felt something unnamable: the curve of violence in Resa's waist; the promise in her poised hand.

MOTHER-EATING

THE HANDYMAN

The commercial had been filmed some months before, of course. By the time it aired on Game Day in January 1980, she was dead.

THE DOCTOR

Yes, I was familiar with the drugs Resa was taking. We carried all the same ones in the hospital dispensary. I recognized the signs of her addiction, and at King Louie's request I fed her habit. A high Resa was a happy Resa.

I dissolved the drugs into a saline solution, packaged in an unmarked amber dropper bottle. The allure of the mystery solution intrigued her. She wanted to know what was in it. More than that, though, she craved how it made her feel. I intentionally mixed the solution at a higher concentration each week, so she could maintain the high as her body developed a tolerance to it. The taste I masked with clove oil and cinnamon: something to warm her, numb the tongue and throat a bit, make the medicine go down more smoothly. It was nothing, over time, to add small amounts of ergometrine to the mix.

Ergometrine is a psychedelic alkaloid found in ergot. Taken at a high dosage, it produces an effect similar to LSD, though clinical efficacy is reached at one-tenth of the hallucinogenic threshold. At first, the cramps, nausea, and dizziness Resa experienced could be and were broadly attributed to her regular abuse of opioids. When she started seeing things that weren't there, we gently reproached her. *Maybe it's time to lay off the sauce.* But really, we were preparing her body. Inducing Resa's *sixteenth*, bless her heart, miscarriage. Which is what physicians use ergometrine for most commonly: to help expel the contents of the uterus.

THE CHEF

Sometime in her second trimester, Resa got poisoned. No one claimed credit for the vile act; it was suggested she received a "bad batch" of her beloved tincture. Either way, the cramps arrived heavy and hard. If the average woman has 450 periods over her lifetime, losing approximately four gallons of blood in the process, then Resa made up for half that total loss in a few hours' time. Blood poured; and then through the open, well-lubricated cervix, a body—tiny and alien. Suction broke; skin deep purple—too purple— *plopped*. Gently, he kissed it on the head and threw it into the Mouth. Resa's sacrifice, her baby, would pave the way for King Louie's own children. Heirs to fulfill our destiny.

THE TIGRESS

Dead bodies float.

Dead babies do not cry.

Delirious, her body swollen almost beyond recognition, Resa moaned weakly on the altar. Without further ado, King Louie withdrew the scalpel in his pocket and slit her throat. In contrast to what she'd once predicted, her death made no sound at all.

There was no more talking. No more weeping.

The bloodstained muslin on which she lay prone was later cut and sewn into tea bags, perfect for the next ceremony. Her placenta we buried beneath the scarlet roses in the courtyard.

Blood begets blood begets begonias.

MERCY

No, I do not know if it was a boy or a girl. It was not my

child. Like I said: It was the sacrifice needed to open the gates for the heir.

THE LAUNDRESS

"I want to see my mom."

It was the third time Mary Toni had asked me to take her to Resa. My stable of excuses, now that Resa was dead, were running out. I couldn't put the truth off forever, nor did I know how to tell her. Just fifteen, and she had the unusual dual whammy of being both orphaned and married already. Ugh.

The fourth time she asked, I said, "It's not going to happen."

"Why not?"

"She . . . she's busy," I said, lamely. "Serving the church. Like you should be doing. Come on, let's get you dressed. You're going to be late for breakfast."

I grabbed a dress out of her wardrobe, but she didn't budge.

"How is she serving the church?"

"You know—the commercials. She's, like, the face of Simon's Sorrow now."

Mary Toni tucked her lips and looked away. "She probably loves that. Well, when *can* I see her?"

"I don't know. Stop asking me that."

"But *why* can't I see her?"

"Marie Antoinette!" I threw up my hands, exasperated. "You're acting like a child. Now come here and let me dress you like the child you want to be."

She walked sullenly over to the wardrobe, turned to face the floor-length mirror, and dutifully put her arms up so I could pull her nightgown over her head. What she said next was muffled by a layer of cotton and lace, but the words I thought I heard made my blood run cold.

"She's dead, isn't she."

"What? Why would you say that?"

"My dad died when I was six. My dog, a few years later. My neighbor sometime after that. All three times, I knew the moment it happened. It was like a balloon had popped, and all the air went with it. Hard to breathe."

We locked eyes in the mirror.

"It's hard to breathe today."

Mary Toni didn't ask us to see her mom again. If she was upset, she didn't show it. Some tragedies, I think, are really kindnesses. Little bubbles of relief we know we're not supposed to feel, but do. So we choose silence instead.

MERCY

While Adam was still Austin's darling, the political favorite, two other candidates were pulling ahead, racing to join him at the front of the pack. It wasn't enough to hope and pray that he would emerge victorious, not when the future of Simon's Sorrow depended on his success. King Louie organized a ceremony, therefore, to intercede on Adam's behalf. "Prayers request; magic demands," he reminded the would-be governor. "You've come to the right place if you want it to actually happen."

"I know," Adam said, because he'd seen Resa's commercial. Had seen how King Louie could take a nobody like her and make her somebody. And he'd be goddamned if he wasn't somebody. That he never asked after her, though—never tried to see her again—much less his niece, Mary Toni—tells you all you need to know about the man Adam Habsburg was. He used Resa like he used the church, and didn't seem to realize—or care?—that the church was using him, too. That when we were done with him, he'd be disposable, also.

"Here," King Louie said, handing Adam a stitched leather envelope. "Put it in there."

The leader looked away as Adam counted out proper payment.

"Now make three laps and let not your thoughts wander."

Shuffling his trademark Cougars, Adam left the cool refuge of the temple for the city's sweltering evening heat. Students and shirtless runners still crowded the sidewalks at that hour, dipping and weaving between panhandlers, their handwritten signs. Adam dropped dollars in each panhandler's overturned cap, cup, or guitar case as he completed his first round, offering at the same time a silent prayer to a sorcerer he didn't believe in, but would nevertheless swear by when the time came. He passed a fresh-squeezed juice stand and a donut shop. A yoga studio and a bank. Circumnavigating the university bookstore, past the parking lot, down an alley that smells to this day of piss and Lonestar, then back out, toward the Capitol, toward the close of loop one around the temple.

And I followed.

On his second lap, the same panhandlers asked Adam for what he could spare with the same angry looks in their eyes and he realized they'd never seen him at all. Realizing further that it didn't matter, he gave them all more dollars, until his wallet held only creased business cards.

He finished lap two.

Lap three.

Twenty minutes later, the sun was a little lower in the sky, the music a smidgen louder. Wafts of weed more potent in the air. Before he headed back inside the church, I saw him send a silent thank you to whatever ghost or devil might have been considering his request.

Magic may indeed demand, but in Texas, we still have manners.

THE RECEPTIONIST

The only landline phone in Simon's Sorrow sat on my desk. Before the Super Bowl ad, it didn't ring more than a couple times a day, and almost every call that came through fell into one of three categories. Either it was a media inquiry; a prospective Sash wanting more information; or the family members of a current Sash calling to harass me about when I personally intended to let their wife/son/mother go. As though any Sash was ever held against their will. Ignorant people.

After Resa beamed into the living rooms of American families around the country, the calls increased. A lot more prank calls and hate mail—people telling us to burn in hell. Then Adam was sworn in as the governor of Texas, and the phone started ringing off the hook. As planned, he'd name-dropped the church in his oath, and now media outlets were calling twenty times in a row trying to get through for a quote. I put up with one day of that nonsense, starting my shift at eight a.m. like usual and not so much as getting up from my desk chair once to pee before the day ended at five. (What can I say? Restoration had prepared me for that moment. I had a strong bladder, stronger Kegel muscles, and was used to torture.) After that, I told King Louie I needed help.

TEZ

All of the church's dealings with Texas's new governor were between King Louie and Adam Habsburg. Mary Toni didn't know her uncle was hanging around. Her father dead, her mother dead, she believed she was alone in the world. It was easy, in the end, to convert her. To convince her, with no little patience, that what they were doing was right.

THE ALTAR SERVER

She had so many questions! Mary Toni was like a four-year-old, noticing for the first time that the sky is blue and wondering what makes it so. Her questions were that simple, but at the same time so sophisticated that they were equally hard to answer. What makes the sky blue? I don't know. Some combination of elements in the atmosphere? Light rays refracting through water? A scientist could tell you, also most fifth-graders, and probably Mary Toni herself. But when it came to the church, she'd grown up Catholic, and the theology of Simon's Sorrow was just different enough that sometimes it jarred or clashed with or even subtly abraded the worldview she'd learned to take for granted. And now she wanted to know everything, and because King Louie was frequently away on business in those days, the rest of the Sashes referred her to me. Who was I? The Altar Server. I changed out the linens and refilled the incense and clipped all the candles and brought King Louie the instruments of ritual, setting the Jeweler's chalices and bells and what have you just so upon the altar. Oh, and I was the only one other than King Louie who got to touch the original Book of Simon. So I guess that made me some kind of expert?

But her questions! "I've noticed," she'd say, "that the figures in the church's stained glass windows have halos. But they're not any saints I know."

"Well, sure they are. See that one there? That's Abraham, sacrificing his son in the desert."

"God told him to, yeah, but Abraham didn't actually go through with it. God stopped him before Isaac got hurt."

"That's one version of the story. In ours, Isaac got hurt, all right. But some would say he had it coming."

"What's this?" she'd ask, picking up a golden sickle from the altar, which may or may not have still glistened with sacrificial blood.

"Don't touch that!"

"What does that say?" Indicating a Latin inscription beneath a monument to Restoration.

I'd tell her what it meant and she'd muse about how Restoration sounded similar to the sacrament of Reconciliation—and then after a while, she'd seem to have it all "reconciled" in her head. Never for long, though. She'd see or hear something else, mull it over for hours or days—she was a very thoughtful child—then approach while I was scrubbing the Mouth and pose another profound question. Mostly what it did was solidify my faith, because she made me think, that one. In trying to logically explain away the illogical fallacies of faith, I contorted my own brain in ever-more tangled knots until each thought experiment ended right back where it'd begun.

"People can't fly," she said the day she asked me to tell her again the story of Simon.

"Simon wasn't just a person. He was a sorcerer."

"Magic isn't real."

"How do you know?"

"Because silk flowers don't turn into rabbits and you can't saw a woman in half and expect her to live and *people can't fly*."

"So, silk flowers can't become rabbits, but bread can become body?"

She blanched. "Transubstantiation. That's different."

"But is it real?"

"Of course."

"How do you know?"

And on and on we went.

Hm. I miss that little girl.

FERSEN

Mary Toni was never a little girl. She emerged from Resa's womb a miniature woman, and anyway, I wouldn't believe anything the Altar Server tells you. He loved to lord his own inflated sense of importance over one and all, and claims to be personally responsible for Mary Toni's early indoctrination into the church. Who knows if any of those conversations even happened? He makes her sound like a whiny kid. She wasn't. She was smart and observant and collected to a fault. You never really knew what she was thinking. Ever.

For example, the first time we made love, I had no idea at all what was going through her mind.

PART THREE

THE SACRED AND
THE STERILE

BEFORE ANYONE FREAKS OUT, know this: King Louie and Mary Toni did not actually (physically) consummate their marriage until well after she turned eighteen. And by then, it was utterly consensual. She even loved him.

THE TIGRESS

What is love, really? Can we arrive at a single definition? Is love what makes a mother bear a child? And later sacrifice herself for said child, should the need arise? Is love what newlyweds feel on their honeymoon? What about how they feel toward each other at eighty? Is it different? An evolved form?

And if love can grow, must it also suffer? The foods, the clothes, the ideas we love—these change, shrivel, expand. When they do, where does the love go? Like energy, it's neither created nor destroyed—but shifts: form; function. Love can be quiet. Satiated. Or teased into exploding.

TEZ

That's how it was with King Louie. Mary Toni's eventual and all-consuming love for him didn't spring from nothing. It was a transference. Of misplaced father love. A curiosity about the roles of woman, wife, womb. A quickening. He was not an unattractive man, and she, a hormonal teenager, thought a lot in those early years about what sex would actually be like. Here was an older, more experienced man to guide her through it—far preferable to the alternative. Let's imagine she'd never been kidnapped, never married a man of the cloth. She would have—what? Gone to high school for four suffocating years? Settled, at sixteen, for losing her cherry to a boy in class just because he told her she was beautiful and smelled a little less worse than the rest of them? No, thank you. Anyway, there's no point in playing that game—the ceaselessly branching paths of *what if*. Chances are that she wouldn't have made it as far as she did. That, like Alex DeLarge, she would have wound up trying to kill herself by jumping out of a window. Or disappeared, whistling and insane, into a rat-infested futuristic Britain.

MERCY

There were rats at Simon's Sorrow, too, sometimes. But they were brought in for special purposes.

TEZ

Speaking of Alex DeLarge, though—Mary Toni did reprise her *A Clockwork Orange* role, or something like it, at the church. That was good to see. It meant she hadn't left *everything* from her old life behind her. Between the years of fourteen and twenty-two, she acted. In memory of Resa.

THE NURSE

We were happy that Mary Toni wanted to join the theater troupe. It was a good sign, her getting involved in the church. The more invested you are, the more implicated you are, and the more implicated you are, the less likely you are to run away and tell.

Not that anyone in Austin would have believed a Simon's Sorrow tattletale. "Eggs, bound and gagged, manipulated until they died"? If you don't already know what that means, it just sounds silly! Of course, someone still tried—in '89, with Paul Greer. But Governor Habsburg made that all go away, so.

THE TATTOOIST

The prerequisite for participating in theater or any other church activity back then was being tattooed with the sign of the sash. That was my job. King Louie told me the symbol—something like a silken cord twisted into an infinity loop—had come to him in a dream. That Simon had appeared naked before him and pointed to the ink on his own chest, which was freshly done and bloody. "A new symbol for the new members of a new church." He'd said this as I was tattooing a customer at the shop on 29th.

"Okay. What would it pay?"

"Enough." And he'd set a gold piece on the pony wall.

That's all it took. The money bought my interest. The message held it.

Flash forward: Mary Toni was the three-hundredth Sash I personally tattooed, and the youngest. The quickest way to be labeled a "cult," right, is to get children involved. Over eighteen, and everything can be considered consensual, but younger than that and you're practically begging the FBI to raid you. That's why, until the heirs came along, Isaac Crable and Mary Toni were the only two kids ever to pass through the church doors.

She sat perfectly still as I did it, too. Which made more sense once I heard she'd pierced her own ears. She was tough, that kid. Tougher than some of the adult Sashes, who squirmed through the procedure like it was worse than Restoration. A simple, single-color design takes fifteen minutes, tops. Most bodies can endure just about anything for fifteen minutes. It's the mind that caves. The mind that says it's too much and moves, says it's too much and screams, says it's too much and breathes a dying breath.

I made Ennoia's sash a little prettier than the others', as though it meant anything to a girl-child being branded and held against her will. I tied the satin ribbon in a bow above her heart, where the mounds of breasts that would one day nurse royalty were just beginning to bud.

THE GROUNDSKEEPER

She was captivating. Mary Toni shone in her Simon's Sorrow stage debut. I wondered why I'd never gone to see any of the church's performances before. The loss was mine—which I learned when she played Punzy in the Tutors' play *The Tower*.

In addition to being mathletes and geography nerds, the Tutors were self-described folklore experts. That year, they picked *Rapunzel* to adapt, setting it in a near-future dystopia. It featured Mary Toni as a cynical Rapunzel—Punzy—trapped in the metaphorical "tower" of pop culture, the media cycle, beauty standards, and the double standard. It ended when she cut off and climbed down her own rope of hair—and, newly freed, created a utopia that in every way resembled Simon's Sorrow.

I was so moved by her performance, believing her character entirely, that tears clouded my eyes as she cast aside the scissors and raised her shorn braid, triumphant. It was all I could have wanted for her—that kind of freedom; that level of self-actualization. I also thought the short wig she was wearing looked really cute on her. She could have rocked a pixie cut. King Louie liked her hair long, though. I wouldn't have told her, if she was mine, what she could and could not do with her body.

The stage makeup made Mary Toni look older. The

long, flowing Grecian-style dress she wore made her look both powerful and ethereal, like she could either be blown away by the wind, or wrangle it with her bare hands and ride it. I felt proud of her in that moment, and also like I could kill King Louie for claiming her. As though he'd seen the wide open prairie, its grasses and endless bobbing wildflowers, stuck a stake in it, and decided to run it over with a lawnmower.

THE TIGRESS

She was getting older, coming more into her own each day. Beginning to participate, here and there, in some of our rituals.

THE LAUNDRESS

I'd never seen someone react as strongly to death as Mary Toni did. All of us grow up knowing death is a fact of life, but some of us have more trouble accepting that fact, I guess. I mean, sure, I was shocked the first time we sacrificed an egg, too. But the way King Louie explained it afterward—I believed Restoration was necessary. Clearly, he hadn't explained it that well to Mary Toni yet, who'd only been with us a couple years. She was still being initiated into the church's mysteries, getting to know its "philosophical underpinnings," if you will.

We were in the basement and gathered around an older male egg. Madame DuBarry had fitted him with a scold's bridle, a steel helmet with an iron muzzle. The muzzle featured a metal "tongue depressor" a few inches long that went inside the egg's mouth and held his tongue down, leaving him unable to speak. Another one rested just beneath his jaw, further immobilizing his head. From what I could gather, this particular egg was a radio show host who'd recently spoken out against Simon's Sorrow. But speak no more could he.

Only well after the egg had been drugged, abducted, and locked in the bridle did King Louie enter the room. We stopped the orgy in progress—which was meant, if another Sash hasn't explained this yet, to concentrate our individual life energies and act like a kind of beacon for the Spirit—and turned to face him. King Louie then stepped aside, revealing Ennoia, and we fell at once to our knees, prostrating ourselves before her, that our collective life force might nourish her and prepare her womb for the heir.

She was always quiet. Always. I liked that about her. She took things in, turned them over in her mind, formed her own opinions, never blurting out the first thing to pop into her head. It made her seem smart, like the mother of God should be. It made her seem patient. Careful. Car*ing*.

So when King Louie stepped aside and she saw, across the room, the Icebox—recognizing it, no doubt, as the room she'd initially been held prisoner in—saw the egg, saw all of our naked bodies, smelled the blood and the iron and the incense, she didn't scream, or faint, or anything else you might expect a queen to do. She absorbed it, her eyes wide in the dim light, and when King Louie took her hand to let her know it was all okay, she gripped it, the hand of this strange, older man, her husband, the king, and accepted what she saw to the extent that her mind could rationalize it.

Initially, anyway.

King Louie motioned for her to take a seat on the stone bench. One of the Sashes immediately brought a cushion for her to sit upon. King Louie then walked over to the egg and addressed him directly.

"We are on this planet, in these incarnations, for such a short time," King Louie began. He sounded solemn. Almost sad. "Our only responsibility while here is to help each other prepare for what comes next." King Louie turned toward the Sashes. "And how do we do that, brothers and sisters?"

"We only speak the truth to one another," the Maid said.

"How do we know what's true?"

"We read the Book of Simon," the Tattooist answered. "We go to church. We work hard—honest work, that honors God."

"And?"

"We practice Restoration, that the body might learn to recognize truth, separate it and honor it, as wheat from the clouding chaff."

Satisfied, King Louie returned his attention to the egg. "You, my friend, are so very, very lucky. For although you've been speaking lies, we know it's not your fault. You were simply repeating what others had told you; those who would spread falsehoods about Simon's Sorrow, about Simon himself"—at this, grumbles of anger rumbled through the room—"because they're scared. Scared of what they don't know. *Of what they do not understand*.

"In your ignorance, you amplified that misplaced fear. *Misplaced*," King Louie clarified, "because there are real evils, real *demons*, to be afraid of. But they do not reside at Simon's Sorrow. They live inside the minds and hearts of those who, upon learning the truth, choose ignorance anyway. Those who knowingly confuse the path of righteousness with the path of *self*-righteousness, and keep walking it because it's comfortable. Because it does not"—and here, King Louie looked at those, in turn, who'd spoken earlier—"require hard work. Does not require speaking truth, the terrible, liberating, all-powerful truth, to one another. Because it's easier"—hisses throughout the room—"not right, but *easier*, to *willingly* mistake one's own personal, limited, puny experience for the universal experience. The reality *behind the veil*."

King Louie whipped back around to the egg. "But I said you were lucky. And you are. Because tonight, we will raise that veil for you. May it never again cloud your vision." He nodded at the Guard.

Without further ado, the Guard grabbed and turned a metal crank atop the steel helmet. As he wound the crank, it lowered a concave iron plate—a rounded "skull cap"—inside the helmet, which soon made contact with the egg's scalp. He kept winding, the plate kept lowering, and the egg started screaming. The pressure applied to, and building inside, his skull must have been excruciating.

Watching, Mary Toni whimpered from the bench. "Stop!" she finally shouted—the first words she'd spoken all night. Everyone except for King Louie looked at her. Suddenly self-conscious, she seemed to shrink beneath our gaze. But the egg kept screaming, and her eyes flicked back to him. She clapped her hands over her ears, still staring in horror. "Stop! Stop! Stop it!" she screamed.

When the egg's eyes popped out of their sockets, one bursting like a Cadbury Creme Egg at Easter time, the other a dangling wet grape, she squeezed her own eyes shut. As though, by refusing to look at a thing, she could make that thing not real.

But that's what those who propagate lies do—and not a fitting response for the queen.

Almost as if she understood that fact, and gathering a strength that none of us, until that moment, knew she possessed, she leaped from the bench and rushed at the Guard. She tried to pull his hands from the crank, but she was a small sixteen, and he, a strong grown man. King Louie ran to her—intending, I thought, to strike her for her insolence. In a move that surprised all of us, however, he embraced her, folding her struggling arms into the safety net of his chest. His head coming to rest upon the top of her shaking, sweaty head. At once containing her, and comforting her. Demonstrating a foreign type of mercy at Simon's Sorrow: *pity*.

It didn't matter that King Louie had ordered the egg's death. That he'd brought Mary Toni down to witness the sacrifice herself. He held her so long that, eventually, she gave into his hug. Stopped fighting. Felt steadied by the heartbeat of her husband. Her oppressor. Our savior.

None of us, I don't think, breathed for five minutes, aware we were witnessing something historic. It was quiet enough in the room for us to hear King Louie whispering to her, though I, at least, could not make out the words. Believing, after a time, that the storm had passed, he pulled back to look her in the eyes. When he did, she saw the egg again. Saw the squashed mess of his head. How his jaw had been crushed, his teeth shattered. The way they stuck out from his face, through his cheeks, like borax crystals, sharp and glittery.

And she wailed. A high, keening, solitary note that seemed to last forever. Even though the egg's head was the one we'd Restored that evening, I wondered if maybe hers hadn't broken, too. Invisibly. In a manner we couldn't see.

Deciding she'd had enough, King Louie gently steered her away from the bridle and the puddle inside it, and out of the basement entirely. The rest of us picked up right where we'd left off, completing the ritual, bringing each other closer to God.

MERCY

Afterward, I attended to King Louie in his chambers. Mary Toni was still with him, asking the hard questions.

"I knew someone like you once," she said. "He tortured animals for fun. There was an armadillo. It was cruel."

"The world is full of people like that. They do what they want without regard for others. But that's not what we're doing here, Mary Toni."

"You called me by my real name."

"I want you to feel comfortable. Perhaps we gave you the wrong impression at first. We're good people doing good work. God's work. If you don't see that now, you will."

"How can it be good if people get hurt? I got hurt," she

pointed out—a reference, I assumed, to the chastity belt she'd worn upon her arrival.

"And for that I am very sorry. I was away on business, otherwise I never would have allowed it to happen. Try to understand: You were a stranger, Mary Toni. An untested variable. We brought you into our home, and we needed to make sure we were safe."

"Safe?" She scoffed. "I was fourteen. What threat could I possibly have posed?"

"I was 95% sure you were Ennoia. But there was a small chance I was wrong. What if the devil was tricking me? What if you were his consort, not mine? And we brought you in, showed you everything. You could have used what you'd learned to destroy us. And we are so close to having everything."

"Are you closer now to having everything, do you think?" she asked. "Or further away from it?"

THE PSYCHOLOGIST

Let's go back to basics here, for a second, because it's something a lot of people get wrong. Psychopaths don't have what you and I would call a conscience. They're chameleons, in a way—able to blend in and "pass" for long periods as "normal," though nothing about the complete lack of remorse they feel for, say, killing someone, is "normal." Sociopaths, on the other hand, have a limited capacity for experiencing empathy and remorse that actually makes them *more* volatile. They can't even pretend to "care" when they don't, but if and when they do form an emotional attachment to an individual or individuals, it is real and felt, albeit difficult. Sociopaths are more likely to "lose their cool" and fly off the handle when provoked. Psychopaths can "play it cool."

Louie Auguste was a psychopath. He maintained a "normal" life in the public eye as an ostensibly stable, even charismatic, religious leader. He had relationships with the Sashes, including his wife, that were as superficial and one-sided as they were useful to him; he inspired love and loyalty, but only so he could get people to do what he wanted. It's possible he truly did love Marie Antoinette, or their children, in his own way. But it's doubtful he honestly grieved their deaths. It was a performance. He was an even better actor than the theater-loving Mary Toni.

THE NURSE

Except how, then, do you explain the time she got the flu?

THE CHEF

In Mary Toni's fourth year with us, she got the flu. Who knows how. Visitors were in and out all the time, and not all of the Sashes lived full-time at the temple. Viruses and other bugs occasionally wormed their way in. At any rate, it was a pretty bad case. Fever, vomiting, lethargy. She couldn't leave bed. For the time she was confined to her room, King Louie didn't leave, either. He sat by her side and regularly applied cool washcloths to her forehead. He read her books (though she hated reading herself, she enjoyed listening to good stories) and massaged her legs and lower back, which was where her body ached the most. He told me to keep her in hot bone broth and tea. I did as requested, careful to knock, always, before entering. Even when granted permission to go in, I felt self-conscious in that room—like I was interrupting something deeply intimate. For the duration of Mary Toni's illness, King Louie and Ennoia were more than my king and my queen. They were first and foremost husband and wife.

It was a memory I would return to, in the years to come, when I questioned in the quiet places of my heart whether King Louie actually had a plan, or was simply acting on impulse. Those tender moments? You can't fake that.

THE PSYCHOLOGIST

King Louie was an expert at diplomacy, and a scholar of deception.

THE TIGRESS

We saw what we wanted to see. We put our faith in what we wanted to believe.

THE BUTCHER

And he never let us down.

THE CHEF

And he failed us.

THE TUTOR

And in return, we failed them both.

THE WHORE

After a time, I fell in love with Mary Toni. As she transformed within the walls of the church from girl-child to young woman, her breasts and hips filling out in delightful and pleasing ways, I found that I wanted to cup her and hold her against me forever. It was a lustful form of love, inspired mainly by her body and an everyday familiarity with it—until the night she made her first sacrifice. That, for me, is when it changed. When I understood I could worship her honestly and always.

She never knew I saw her. Probably, she left us believing she took her secret with her. Which in a way, she did—since I didn't tell anyone else before now.

It happened in the Icebox. We had an egg down there, a young woman tied to the Catherine wheel. I don't who she was or how DuBarry had lured her in. (We weren't always privy to information like that. It was enough to know that the person had sinned. He or she had broken God's law in some terrible way, and as a means, partially, of atoning for our own sins, we served as His hands on earth; the scales of justice entrusted to Simon's Sorrow through King Louie, our leader, and his wife, Ennoia, rightful mother of the heirs.)

Anyway, the egg was tied to the Catherine wheel, or what some would call a breaking wheel. Picture a big wooden wagon wheel, right? Like they had on old-timey Conestogas. Big enough for most of a body to stretch across it, and be strapped down to the spokes spread-eagle. With the limbs all akimbo like that, you could bludgeon the egg and break her in multiple places, as bones smashed into, and broke around, the sturdy spokes. I would have thought bones were stronger than wood. Turns out, no.

Like the Judas cradle or any other device we used, the "torture," if you want to call it that, wasn't actually about killing someone. *Au contraire*: It was about prolonging life as long as possible. You needed periods of strain and rest, pain and deep, dark blackouts—time, in other words—for the body to process and the mind to accept what was happening to it. For a reckoning to occur. For *Restoration*.

So, I was on Icebox duty that night. When I went to check on the egg, she wasn't alone. Mary Toni was in there, too. I heard her voice before I saw her, and couldn't believe it. Ennoia never attended sacrifices, not since the scold's bridle had gone so horribly wrong. But there she was, stroking the egg's face with what at first I mistook for tenderness. "You're so, so beautiful," I swear I heard her say, and she pushed some sweaty strands of hair from the egg's face. The egg winced, though—her cheekbones were shattered—and I breathed a sigh of relief. Mary Toni wasn't there to comfort her; she was there to make sure the job got done. And she had questions. So. Many. Questions.

"Does it hurt?" Mary Toni asked. She was pointing to the place where the egg's shin bone poked through the lacerated skin of her leg, which was already green and gray. But the egg couldn't see it. Her head was tied to the wheel, too, preventing her from moving much. As she never did answer, I don't know that she even comprehended the question. Or any question that followed.

"How did you end up here?" Pause. Silence. "Do you want to be here?"

Then: "Do you remember what caramel tastes like? What irises smell like in March? The amazing things you did when no one was around to see? Who was the last person to touch you? To mourn your boredom with you? What's the longest book you've ever read? Your favorite tattoo? How many fingers am I holding up? Do you believe you will be saved?"

Random questions, fired rapidly toward the end. Finally, Mary Toni slowed, looked the egg in her half-lidded eye (half of it torn away), and asked, "Do you know how much you are loved?"

When *still* the woman didn't respond, Mary Toni turned, carefully, the crank on the Catherine wheel. She watched as the wheel spun in place, as the body roped to that wheel completed a 360-degree revolution. Because Mary Toni didn't know what would happen (I honestly think she was just curious), she didn't know to watch for the moment when the egg's weight, bound by gravity as well as ropes, shifted the tiniest bit sideways. And her spine, already broken, slipped, severing the spinal cord at her neck. And the spark that had for three decades or less (and however faintly) lit the sinner from within, went out.

Mary Toni didn't realize what she'd done until the egg's body returned to its starting position, upright on the wheel. Then Ennoia gasped, for what stared back at her stared with the empty eyes of a bleeding, weeping doll.

THE GUARD

Ennoia did not kill the egg on the Catherine wheel. I have it on video. Well, had it on video. I destroyed the tape because I knew how it looked, just like I knew she didn't do it. That wheel had a faulty catch. I'd asked the Contractor to fix it before. He hadn't gotten around to it, when who but the queen wandered down into the Icebox, bumped the wheel as she went to shoo a fly from the half-dead egg's face, accidentally releasing the catch and sending the wheel spinning just once—just enough to kill the egg. It must have been awful for her. Here, she'd just gone down to check, to see for herself, to offer by all appearances a tiny bit of comfort, and suddenly the thing she feared most of all, was so terribly hung up about—death—visited the egg and she believed it was her fault. Ennoia screamed. I watched her on the camera, how her mouth fell open and her shoulders hunched forward and tears fell like daggers from her eyes. I turned away then, just for a second, to offer the queen some privacy in her pain. So I didn't actually see her tack the poem to the wheel. It could have been her, but in my opinion? She didn't do it. I don't know who did.

Recite it? Sure, I can do that. King Louie made everyone memorize it. He thought it was beautiful. Thought it should go in the Book of Simon.

Pay attention to the isolation. The sadness that's utter.

Does it make you shiver? However hard it tries, it will always be spiritual. It will tear you apart with how ghostlike it is. Gently it goes. Boredom, fat and buttery, is a profound condition. How I mourned the boredom.

TEZ

Two other developments of note happened during these years. First, Mary Toni and one of her tutors, Savoy, became close despite their five-year age difference. Nothing wrong with a strong female friendship, you might be thinking to yourself, except that it was further fodder for those Sashes who envied her. Who believed she hadn't caught pregnant because she was frigid; a lesbian; or worse, intentionally flouting divine prophecy.

THE LAUNDRESS

No one actually cared if Mary Toni was a lesbian. Everyone slept with everyone during Restoration; gender was irrelevant. What mattered was that she was King Louie's wife. She alone was meant to be his, meant to be the All-Mother. We'd sacrificed her mom, and Resa's baby, so Mary Toni could bear an heir and that heir could Restore Lord Simon—but there she was, nineteen and not conceiving. It couldn't be King Louie's fault. No one dared think that. No, it had to be Ennoia's. Was she refusing him? Was she sleeping with Savoy instead?

THE WHORE

She—Ennoia—had a fury in her uterus. Just not for King Louie.

Which, like, *why*? Savoy wasn't even attractive. All

sallow skin *and* she never brushed her teeth, plucked her eyebrows, or used perfume!

THE RECEPTIONIST

It was the gifts. Mary Toni gave Savoy *so. many.* gifts. Paid off her debts, too, from Outside. None of the rest of us got that kind of attention from Ennoia; that's why the rumor mill started. Pure jealousy.

THE GROUNDSKEEPER

Savoy—or the Duchess, as she was sometimes called—and Marie Antoinette became best friends. What started as a teacher-student relationship (Savoy had been an SAT tutor Outside) evolved into as real a friendship as I've ever seen. Truly, they were inseparable.

But were they also lovers? Depends on who you ask. Some certainly thought so. I pulled more wadded-up flyers—these cruel, hand-drawn cartoons depicting the two of them in sexually suggestive positions—out of the rosebushes than deadheads and plastic bags combined. They were mean, I thought; a prank designed to hurt a child (or two young women by then), so I didn't buy into the gossip and shut down anyone who did.

THE CHEF

I remember the harpy cartoon the most. It depicted Mary Toni as a bird of prey with a woman's face and torso. Her wings stuck out like a dragon's. Her tail curled, long and scaled as an alligator's, behind her. Horns too tall to be concealed sprouted from her hair, branding her a freak. An outcast. Promising she would "get hers" regardless of whether we ever got ours: an heir.

THE ALTAR SERVER

Clearly, the one bright spot in her every day was Savoy.

TEZ

When here came Fersen—the second startling development.

THE FRIEND

It was the sixth-grade teacher from Magnificat who finally made it inside—who'd never, after six long years, given up on "rescuing" Mary Toni. For most of us, myself included, she rarely crossed our minds anymore. Twenty, then, I had my own life to live, to figure out. Every once in a while, I'd be tearing through my closet, looking for something to wear, and I'd find an old photograph of the two of us together; or a fragment of the schoolyard rhymes we used to sing at recess would pop into my mind. These were my only reminders—my only proof—that she'd ever existed. I'd look at the scrawny girl with the big, dark eyes in the photo next to me, never actually touching, always a bit aloof, and wonder what had become of her. If she'd made other friends, kept up with her art, ever found her place in the world.

God knows I haven't. Ask any of our teachers; I bet they had bigger hopes for me than what I'm doing now. A job I hate. A husband who's hardly ever home. No kids. Mary Toni and I used to sit around and plan our futures together. Mine inevitably included Robert Redford, two children (one girl, one boy), a career as a marine biologist, and the yacht in the middle of the ocean from which I conducted my research. If wanting something can make it happen, fate, I guess, overlooked me. Or judged my dreams and found them wanting. Because what do I have now? A cat. Some houseplants in macrame holders.

Anyway.

Like some amateur spy, the teacher, as I said—Mr. Fersen—eventually got to her. He never bought the story that she and her mom had moved after Resa lost her job.

And as it turned out, they hadn't.

FERSEN

When she didn't return to start high school that fall, I immediately assumed the worst. I knew more about Simon's Sorrow than most since my grandmother had been a Sash, but of course not the full extent of King Louie's lunacy, Restoration and all that. I only knew the church had a superglue grip on Grandma, and that if a sweet old lady could be coaxed into donating her entire net worth upon her death, they were probably pretty good at brainwashing. Though what church isn't, right? If anyone Outside had known what was really happening inside those walls, well. The whole organization would have been abolished and King Louie carted off to jail much sooner. No, I assumed it was a church like any other and that Mary Toni would fill me in on what she'd seen during her internship—that we'd laugh at how quaint it all was, even while she showed me with pride the designs she'd made for them that summer, how much more confident she'd grown in her skills. I would ooh and aah like her personal cheerleader, her most devoted fan, and I would call her my little champion, a true artiste.

But she didn't come back, not for the first day of Study Buddies, and not any day that semester. When I asked the other teachers, then her friends, what they knew, I learned nothing. An admin at the high school said she'd never enrolled. I went by her house; it looked abandoned. Like no one, including Mary Toni, had ever lived there. Retracing her steps, I called Simon's Sorrow. Yes, the Receptionist confirmed, Mary Toni had interned for them that summer. But the internship was over, and she thought perhaps they'd moved. Moved? *Really*? Without telling me? Uh-uh. I couldn't believe it. I wanted to go to the cops, but what would I say? "A student has disappeared. Oh, and her mom, too." Ha. Kids disappear with their parents all the time. It is, in fact, called *moving*.

So, I fretted for five months, alternately mad and sad. I cried a lot and drank a lot, which usually made me cry more. I was drunk the night of the Super Bowl, and watched that ad through bleary eyes. She looked different, but still I recognized Resa from the field trip, the day she'd driven Mary Toni to the zoo. It was her, shilling for Simon's Sorrow. Mother and daughter had both disappeared because they'd up and fucking joined a cult. The Receptionist had lied. My sweet girl, she was there, right there, a five-minute drive away. I stumbled out of the apartment I'd moved into after graduation, got in my car, and swerved my way down the street.

It was late on a Sunday, of course, so the double doors of the church were locked. I sank onto the sidewalk in grief and fell asleep waiting. The next morning, when I heard the lock click, I ran inside, clothes and breath foul from a night on the street, and succeeded at nothing but being escorted out. Good thing, too, that I looked so rough, because the next time I returned, for my first public Service, no one put two and two together. That guy was a bum. Me, I was Old Lady V's grandson, and a respectable teacher to boot.

Because the Receptionist had lied, I knew they were colluding, that all the Sashes must be on the take. I didn't say a thing about Mary Toni, only that I was interested in learning more about the church my grandmother had loved so much. They humored me. I listened to several members' testimonies. When there was no sign of either Resa or Mary Toni, I went back to Service. Weekly. And with the commercial as evidence, I finally went to the cops. But as one tired officer informed me, it isn't a crime to join a church.

"Know what?" I said. "You're right." And I applied to join, officially, myself.

THE TUTOR

Once the church got big enough, King Louie could no longer interview all of the prospective initiates himself. We formed a committee for that purpose, with rotating chairs. I was chair when Axel Fersen applied. On paper, I thought he looked promising. Like me, he was a teacher. He could, on the Outside, be grooming his students—so they, too, might join us when they came of age. Plus, he was legacy. His grandmother had been a patron. For those reasons, the interview was more like a formality. I expected to be welcoming our newest Sash by the end of the week.

But then he came for the interview, and he seemed so fake. You know how sometimes you can just tell a person's putting on a show? They're a little too relaxed, a little too rehearsed. In Texas, we call them good ole boys. Men who expect the world to be brought to them on a silver platter. He hadn't put in the work—on himself. He'd attended Service, but seemed to think a bit of public glad-handing was all it took to become a Sash. He was, as King Louie would have said, still wearing his mask. A veneer. What he was masking, I couldn't have said. Self-hatred? Desperation? I didn't know. And that was the thing. At Simon's Sorrow, you wore your shit on your sleeve. Sometimes literally! But Fersen, he had a secret.

FERSEN

I went to every Service, every volunteer opportunity, for five and a half years—and I never once saw Mary Toni or her mother. Call me crazy, but the fact that Mary Toni had not reached out in all that time only convinced me more that she was there, hidden away and held against her will. She had my phone number. She knew my address. She would have called or written if she could. That she hadn't, meant she couldn't—so it was up to me to go to her, get inside, beyond the temple walls . . . where I could see, and at long last *know*, for myself. For Mary Toni.

But almost as if they knew what I was doing—though they didn't; even today I'm positive they didn't—the Sashes rejected me the first five times I interviewed. It wasn't until my sister who loves theater came to town, and I took her to see a stage play at Simon's Sorrow, that I found my in. That I found, finally, Mary Toni.

And when I did? I didn't want to believe it. Because it would mean she had changed. Grown. No longer the child I remembered, she was a stunning, full-on *woman*.

And it would mean another man had found her first.

THE TAILOR

I watched what I now know was Mary Toni and Fersen's reunion—as opposed to their initial meeting—from the side of the stage, where I was helping actors quickly sub out their costumes. During intermission, Fersen approached Mary Toni and held out his hand like he would shake hers; thus why I thought it an introduction. What I understand today is that Mary Toni had recognized at once the danger Fersen's presence posed to them both, and had carefully controlled her reactions lest she draw attention. They must have agreed to meet up after the show, under cover of the milling crowd, to catch up. At which point, Fersen would have learned that his love was married. That she was a committed Sash. That there was no room for him at the inn.

THE GROUNDSKEEPER

Except there was. There was room for everyone.

THE CHEF

Like the loaves and fish, right? They—we—multiplied to meet a need.

THE LAUNDRESS

Yeah, I was chair when Fersen applied for the sixth time, and yeah, I gave zero fucks. So he got in. Whatever. You can't sit there and tell me that's why everything else happened the way it did.

THE JEWELER'S APPRENTICE

But I mean, Charlie? Sophie? The Diamond Necklace Affair? Without Fersen . . . the church might have looked very different today. Just saying.

TEZ

At any rate, knowing how dangerous it would have been for them both if anyone ever suspected anything, new Sash Fersen initially kept his distance from Mary Toni. It must have killed him, poor thing, to finally be close enough to touch her—only to have to watch her walk the halls every day on the arm of another, just out of reach.

Luckily for him, and unluckily for Savoy, rumors were already circulating about the two women. It took the heat off of Fersen, but concentrated it all on the Duchess.

THE BUTCHER

I surprised them in the storeroom one day, hands up each other's skirts. "It's not what it looks like!" Savoy insisted. But I'm a butcher. I know beef curtains when I smell them.

FERSEN

Most guys would probably find it kind of hot, right? The idea that your secret girlfriend is into other girls. But that's only if it's a sex thing. If she actually develops feelings for them, if she wants to spend her time with them—then it's different.

As one of the Tutors, Savoy was also part of the theater troupe, so she and Mary Toni saw each other all the time. When they weren't at rehearsal, they built daisy chains in the courtyard as they ran lines together and looked for shapes in the clouds. The Chef even took to packing them picnics. Why, I kicked myself, hadn't *I* thought of that?

So, yeah, I got a little jealous. One time I even cornered Savoy in the temple. "What do you think you're doing?" I asked, a Sash concerned for his queen's wellbeing, her reputation.

"Nothing that men haven't done to women for centuries," she said.

I stared at her, ready to cry. "But *why* are you doing it?" I pleaded.

Savoy looked longingly into the distance, as at a memory. "Because she's special."

Of course she was. I knew she was. So I said nothing more.

THE BAKER

King Louie must have heard the rumors, as well. But if they upset him, he didn't show it. Maybe since, unlike the rest of us, he had regular access to Mary Toni. Probably he knew her secret heart. Her *secrets*. The queen was exempt from so much of daily life at Simon's Sorrow, never attending Service and merely observing more Restorations than she participated in. We saw her around, of course, and regularly on stage—but can you ever really know when an actor's acting and when they're being themselves? What private life Ennoia led, only her husband *knew*-knew. Leaving the rest of us to gossip and speculate.

THE WHORE

But then I heard them! The night of Mary Toni's twenty-first birthday! Finally, finally, just when we all were positive it wouldn't happen, I heard King Louie and his bride—the animal sounds of passionate love-making. Grunts as he thrusted! The slap of balls against butt as she drove her hips higher to meet him. There was no kinky sex happening behind the heavy door of Ennoia's chambers; nothing but the kind of heterosexual pumping that most efficiently moves man sperm from seminal vesicles to lady egg. I don't know what Mary Toni did to finally get him there, or maybe it was that King Louie finally got out of his own head and thereby out of his own way. However it worked, his dick was hard, her pussy had received him, and God willing, she'd ovulate somewhere in the three-day window during which his spunk could survive inside her. If not, surely now that they'd figured it out, they'd try again, and again, until God had worked His miracle through them, and of their union could be born, at last, a child.

THE CHEF

It didn't take long. A few months, maybe, after the Tigress or one of her girls had spread the word that she'd personally heard them boinking in the bedroom. We wanted to believe her, of course—we'd waited so long for that moment, endured the heartbreak of endless years!—but when there was no news the first month, or the month after, our newly engendered hope flamed out again, back into the embers of anger we kept stoked in Ennoia's direction, for being a lesbian, for not trying hard enough, for being stubbornly barren: a Sarah who refused God's gift to her and Abraham. It was easy to hate her, as, if nothing else, she had King Louie's undivided attention, and had for too many years. Ever since he'd first seen her on campus. When she was a child yet, unable even to give us the child we all dreamed about so fervently.

Hating her gave us practice, though, in feeling any strong emotion toward Ennoia, such that when the Nurse finally told us Mary Toni had missed two periods, and was a solid ten weeks along in baking the royal heir in the oven—that hate, it became the kind of worshipful adoration King Louie had always hoped we'd harbor for her, his holy wife, a queen among women. Hate, after all, is a form of single-minded focus; so worship came just as easy, just as free. All of us pitched in to meet her every need, anticipating what she might ask for before the thought had materialized, a solid shape, in her mind.

The Whores drew hot (and at her request, shallow) baths for her—she had some weird issue with deep water. They added lavender oils and Epsom salts, and they rubbed her feet, which apparently stuck out over the side of the tub when Ennoia slunk far enough down into the suds. The Groundskeeper cut bunches of fresh flowers for her bedside, for inclusion on the trays of protein-rich breakfasts that I prepared in the kitchen. I also whipped up a salve for her growing belly: shea butter, coconut oil, calendula, and ginger root. It made a thick, creamy balm that smelled as good as it felt going on, as it worked to ease her stretching skin, the scarring of it. The Barber treated her suddenly glossier hair, winding it into shiny plaits around her head that caused her to resemble a black-haired Austrian milkmaid in the sun-kissed bloom of life, and one of the Contractors set about designing a modular cradle that could become a crib, and eventually a bed, as the baby grew. The impending birth, so long awaited, infused all of our days with new meaning, with the buoyant sense of expectation that only an heir could inspire.

FERSEN

I was heartbroken. While everyone else felt buoyed by the news, it seemed a death knell for my chances with Mary Toni. It meant I'd been too slow, too patient, too late. Depression swallowed me, and when I couldn't get it up at the next orgy, I attracted the wrong kind of attention. It didn't mean I stopped loving her, though. Never that.

THE TUTOR

I was excited by the news, too, of course, if only because joy is as catching as fear. But I did worry that we weren't seeing clearly—not the full picture, anyway. You had to follow the thing to its logical conclusion: a baby. A human (or if you believed the prophecy, a half-divine) baby, who would cry and soil its diapers and suck the tits of the queen mother raw. Then it would age: no doubt a happy child, at first, content as one who grows up being raised by a village. And I would teach her. (I was sure, even then, she was a girl.) But if she was anywhere as smart as her parents, I knew she wouldn't be, couldn't be, brainwashed for long. She'd ask questions, and when we couldn't answer them to her satisfaction, she'd look elsewhere, maybe Outside, for the truth, and that would be it. Another cat killed by her own curiosity; and if we didn't stop her in time, we risked falling with her. Hardly any group like ours outlasts the next generation, because unlike us, those babies never choose the religious life. They're born into it, and all new fledglings eventually leave the nest.

THE NURSE

Science and faith, medicine and religion—these have historically been at odds with one another. At least in the Western tradition. Some churches still see it that way, preferring to "let go and let God" in every case, from chicken pox to small pox. I never saw it that way, and Simon's Sorrow accommodated that contradiction. For example, I believe Simon Magus *was* a sorcerer of some kind—that even if his powers weren't explicitly God-given, he'd discovered some way to harness the energy of the universe (which is science, after all) and bend it to his will, such that he could levitate twenty feet above the ground or read the hearts of those around him. I believe this story like I believe that Jesus's tomb was empty three days after His death because He'd resurrected: a decidedly *un*scientific event. At the same time, however, that I believe in the cell, the atom, and the so-called "God particle," I also believe in a God who created all three of them, and that what God created is good. Because it is good, it bears nurturing—saving, when necessary—from what evils may do it harm, be they other men or non-sentient viruses.

I was pleased, therefore, when King Louie asked me to

personally attend Ennoia's delivery. He knew, I think, that I could hold such incongruities as the dangers of home births and the will of the Lord in balanced, steady hands, making sure that both mother and baby survived, were it meant to be so. Luckily, everything went according to plan. Marie Antoinette labored for longer than any woman wants to, but in the end, she—and we—had a beautiful little girl, and again, I held space for the sacred and the sterile. That is, while I cut the newborn's cord and encouraged the afterbirth to emerge, before carefully suturing the queen back together, I didn't protest when one of the Sashes in the room announced that the child was an incarnation of Freya, Norse goddess of sex, war, and death, or when that same woman whispered to Ennoia that she should proclaim herself Isis, that any malevolent but invisible entity present might be scared off, back into the underworld from which it came. I didn't protest because like all of the Sashes, I held this truth to be self-evident: that for everything we know and understand, infinitely more is unknown or misunderstood, and we would do well to respect the shadows as we do the light.

TEZ

Mary Toni gave birth for the first time at twenty-two. The fountains in the garden were filled with wine. She named me Tez, short for Maria Theresa "Resa" Charlotte, after her mom, my grandmother.

THE WHORE

Tez. That's what they called her. A sponge of dark hair on her head like a crown, like she knew she was royalty and was determined to live up to it. Ennoia labored for twenty hours, during which time we strove to keep her as comfortable as possible. As soon as I'd mopped her forehead, however, it was glistening again with the strain of exertion. At least she never yelled or cried. Years of Restoration had prepared her for the pain. She'd suffered worse than childbirth. All of us had. It made me wonder if that hadn't been the point of Restoration all along: repenting not for the eternal health of our souls—or, at least, not exclusively for that reason—but that we might be made pure for the heir's sake, that we'd be worthy of receiving her, and caring for God's incarnation here on earth, until such time as the prophecy would be fulfilled, and all of human life returned to Eden.

We women gathered around Ennoia's bed—the men, including King Louie, waited in the Great Hall—and we breathed with her. When she wanted to walk around, we took her arms, and when she felt compelled to push, we helped her squat, changing out the bedding as it became soiled with her fluids. Those of us who were menstruating sat on pots in a corner of the room, collecting such blood as we were able. Once the child was born, it would be smeared with the blood of the group: its first rite of initiation, and a potent way to protect the infant, who was not just of God, but also of us. The littlest Sash, vulnerable to sickness, starvation, and the curses of minor demons if we did not shield baby Tez with our own bodies, shrouding her in the light of our love.

I'll admit: the actual birth was slightly terrifying. I've seen pussies do a whole lot of things, stretch and accept all manner of people, objects. I've felt them tighten around my fists, grip the sticky length of a strap-on. I've felt my own accommodate three dicks at once. I knew they were powerful—the most powerful—and that their power made them holy. I'd always thought of them, since joining Simon's Sorrow anyway, as pathways to God. But until I watched Tez be born, I'd never thought about the fact that what goes in, must also come out, and that if women are portals *to* God, we must also be portals *for* God: the means by which He enters the world and makes Himself known.

MOTHER-EATING

THE TIGRESS

Only Madame DuBarry refused to attend the birth, to participate in the delivery of the heir. It should have been hers, goddammit! (Or so she thought.) *Her* swelling belly. *Her* blood in the bed. *Her* pussy that King Louie visited like an obedient sire sniffing out a bitch in heat. So, when Mary Toni's water broke, and her holy contractions started, DuBarry made herself scarce. She disappeared and no one could locate her the whole day long. Finally I went looking for her, and I found her—no surprise, really, in retrospect—sitting on the edge of the Mouth. Naked from the waist down, she was douching with the water from the well, a rubber tube snaking out from between her legs and beneath the murky water's surface. "What are you doing?" I asked. But wasn't it obvious? On the day of the heir's birth, she was trying to put Isaac Crable, or what was left of him, back inside of her, as though she might birth him again. The water was dirty, though. Contaminated. I could only imagine what it would do to the delicate, pH-balanced tissues of a pussy. She looked at me then, and her face was haggard, eyes red with crying and the effort of wanting an impossible thing.

FERSEN

It was the Queen of Hearts, in Lewis Carroll's *Alice in Wonderland*, who boasted of believing as many as six impossible things before breakfast. After I got over the initial shock of Mary Toni's pregnancy, I convinced myself she was merely "doing her duty." Once she'd done it— produced an heir—then I saw no reason we couldn't be together at last.

THE NURSE

While all of us except for Mary Toni and the heirs were free to visit Outside, most of us chose not to leave the temple grounds after we'd joined. There was no reason to, unless you were one of the Shoppers or otherwise felt like accompanying a fellow Sash on an errand. I, on the other hand, was one of the few regular "go-betweens," because I had access to the hospital and could sneak out whatever supplies or medicines we needed from the storeroom.

On the day Tez was born, I had just left the church after seeing Mary Toni and Baby safely to bed. I was walking up Guadalupe to catch the bus when I saw them—King Louie and Governor Habsburg—sharing a drink at the bar. King Louie's long hair shone under the urine-yellow lights and Adam, with his affable, aw-shucks smile and red Cougars hooked over the barstool like they were cowboy boots, was slapping King Louie on the back. "Congratulations!" he seemed to be saying. "A girl!"

We all knew that King Louie and the politician had some kind of relationship, likely an exchange of money for power. None of us knew that they'd developed a friendship as well, though, or what it would mean for the future of the flock.

THE GUARD

And holding her in his arms, King Louie brought his daughter to the window, whether showing her the world outside, or showing the world outside its heir and master, I don't know. But he did take special pains to point out the courtyard cottage. "For all things belong to you," he told her, quoting Corinthians, "whether the world or life or death or things present or things to come; all things belong to you."

At that moment, the wilting carnations in the vase on Mary Toni's dresser, which the Groundskeeper had not been able to swap out that morning given his exclusion, until after the birth, from her bedroom, reanimated at once. As though the vase was filled not just with water, but the Water of Life—holy water, perhaps, from the Mouth— and as though King Louie had bidden it be so by Simon's magic, the wilted and yellowing petals unfurled, softened, became plump again. Their flaccid stalks, the length of my favorite dildo, reassumed a healthy dark green tint and their original turgidity.

Sorry; the word turgid makes me laugh!

I don't think anyone laughed at the carnations, though—or else it was in amazement and joy.

THE CHEF

I hated the cottage. Built by some German immigrant to Texas in the 1830s, it looked like it hadn't been touched since. Structurally, it was still sound—rocks don't change much over time—but at some point vines had busted through the windows and grown inside the building, choking the daylight out of what may once have been a charming home. Rodents and God knows what else came and went through the open frames at their leisure. In the fall, giant orb spiders spun webs like they were decorating for Halloween, and at wintertime, though we only get a dozen below-freezing days every year, the wind blew across the jagged glass and screamed like it had cut itself.

Yeah. I hated the cottage.

When King Louie gave it to Mary Toni as a "push present" following the birth of Tez, I couldn't believe it. I would have been insulted—*I just squeezed an heir out of my vagina and you "thank" me with an abandoned shack?*—but she seemed delighted. As positively thrilled as she was with the princess herself. "First you gave me a baby girl, all for my very self," she said, "and now you have given us a keep for our castle. Thank you, husband."

As I cleared away the breakfast dishes (she'd taken her meals in bed for two weeks leading up to the birth, and saw no reason to discontinue the practice immediately), Ennoia offered her cheek for a kiss. King Louie planted one wetly. It glistened on her skin long after he'd pulled away, reminding me of a slug that slimes wherever it goes.

THE GROUNDSKEEPER

Upon Tez's birth, I brought the new mother bunches of long-stemmed flowers, clipped from the gardens that very morning. I continued this tradition every day thereafter—always fresh, always in season—through the exhaustive, cathartic, all-consuming days of breastfeeding, first cry, first smile. Bluebonnets in March. Indian paintbrushes in April. Mexican hats in May. Mums in June. It was the only contact I had with the queen or the child, just five minutes a day (as I insisted on presenting them myself), but it was enough to take in the babe's wisps of dark hair. Eyelashes that curled up like spiders' legs. But then, almost a year to the day of Tez's birth, Ennoia announced they'd be moving to the cottage. She was having it remodeled.

THE ARCHITECT

I was surprised, when, more than fifteen years after I'd renovated his church, King Louie called me back. Although the Simon's Sorrow headquarters had ultimately been built to his specifications, we'd clashed on quite a few issues. For instance, I'd refused to bury the soundproof "cells," for lack of a better word, in the basement like he'd wanted, since he couldn't give me a good reason for their existence. So many aspects of that church had creeped me out. And we'd nearly come to blows over differing design aesthetics so many times that I thought for sure he'd written me off as a future service provider. Before he contacted me on behalf of Mary Toni, I probably would have told you I'd likewise written him off as a future client. Yet, this new request, once I'd gotten over my disbelief at hearing from him again, sounded different and intriguing enough that against my better judgment, I took the meeting—this time with his wife. "She's rehabbing a cottage on the property," he told me. "Whatever she says, goes. The money doesn't matter."

Well, those words are music to any self-employed person's ears. Plus, I remembered the cottage from my early work onsite: a kind of rustically charming, albeit badly dilapidated German-style structure. Just as enticing, to be honest, was the prospect of meeting King Louie's wife. Who would marry such a man? I wondered. I imagined a beautiful prisoner, or, on the other end of spectrum, a woman with a gross deformity. In other words, something to explain *why*.

As is typical, I went to her. It's easiest to discuss a client's vision on-site, with the place and any determining geographical features directly in front of us. Once I parked and walked into the main entrance, a receptionist greeted me from the front desk. She invited me to take a seat while she let Mary Toni know I was there. I did so happily. My involvement in the church had ended with the expiration of our contract, and I hadn't been back since the Sashes had moved in to see what they had done with the place.

Somewhat to my surprise, the lobby was tastefully, if spartanly, decorated. Nothing was extravagant, but what few furnishings there were looked expensive, of high quality. A vase of fresh flowers graced the receptionist's otherwise empty desk, while well-tended ferns chastely obscured the room's cold white corners. Temporary walls divided the space into something of a museum, or gallery. Printed placards related the history of the church, highlighted its mission. A screen played a silent movie on repeat. Subtitles revealed it to be a short documentary, pieced from on-camera interviews with church members about their experiences with Simon's Sorrow. Why they'd joined, and why they'd stayed. "I wasn't a very happy person," one middle-aged woman was saying. "I felt bored. Unfulfilled. Like nothing in my life had any meaning." The scene cut abruptly to the same woman on stage in a fancy red dress, either giving some sort of performance or accepting an award, I couldn't tell. But she was smiling broadly, and I assumed the takeaway was how much better everything was for her now. I was still watching her when Mary Toni greeted me.

I stood to take her extended hand and almost did a double-take. She looked so much like the woman in the video, I almost thought it was her—only Mary Toni was thirty years younger. For a second, I surmised she'd maybe been born in the cult, but then she was too old for that— she was in her early twenties, at least—so I let it all go and focused on just her instead.

"This way," she said, smiling and turning to lead me back down a hallway, deeper into the church, and eventually, I assumed, outside, to the inner courtyard.

On the way, we passed the sanctuary. I shook my head unconsciously, struck anew by the opulence of the heavy imported rosewood arcing like dark rainbows across the vaulted ceiling. Something that looked like a diving board dominated the transept with the baptistry, but I didn't interrupt the queen to ask. Very little had made sense about the plans the first time around. No reason it will now, I thought.

"Nothing's changed about the cottage since you saw it last," she was saying, "though I took the liberty of clearing out the brush." We'd emerged into the courtyard, and I could just see the outbuilding, a couple hundred yards away and looking freshly gutted without its century-old lining of ivy. She'd left the green coat on the outside, as well as all the mature trees, thankfully, but the inside was spotless, the old stones almost gleaming.

"What'd you have in mind?" I asked.

She launched into an especially vivid description—clearly someone who was good with words, skilled at communicating—and I decided I liked her at once, much better than her husband. I wondered anew at what had drawn them together, and would have asked except that I realized I had better be taking notes if I ever hoped to remember the level of detail she was giving me then. Windows, everywhere. "There aren't nearly enough in the church—no offense," she clarified. A rudimentary kitchen. The addition of a glass-walled greenhouse. "Somewhere for Princess to nap."

"Is Princess a dog?" I clarified.

She looked at me like I was daft. "Not Princess. *The* princess. Our daughter."

"Oh!" I quickly corrected. "How old is she?"

"Eleven months."

"Congratulations! That's wonderful."

She continued staring. "Anyway. We'll need a bathroom as well—nothing elaborate—and I want the exterior touched as little as possible."

She could be haughty, I realized. A 'queen' to Louie's 'king' if ever there was one. But she was not unkind. She simply didn't suffer fools, and King Louie had probably already convinced her that I was a fool. I made a big show of taking lots of notes, then whipped out my camera to snap a few reference photos. "No!" her eyes flared. "No photos," is what she said. It almost sounded like, "No evidence," though. Second only to her husband, Mary Toni was one of the most interesting clients I've ever had.

THE CHEF

We threw a party, the grandest one Simon's Sorrow had

yet seen, for Tez's first birthday. It had been a year of firsts, and now she was turning one, which demanded its own kind of first: baptism.

Cabbage and cranberries. That's how the kitchen smelled for a week leading up to the party. Not my favorite combination, but then I'm not King Louie, and he had a specific vision for how the occasion should go. "God, first and foremost," he always said. "Simon second. The family third. So long as we focus on the former, the latter will have much to be grateful for."

King Louie saw it as a recruitment opportunity, too. "Fling open the doors, bring the people in off the streets, make them feel welcome. People who feel welcome," he said, "stay longer, and the longer they stay, the more time we have to share God's good news."

It took two full days just to do all the shopping. A grocery list for hundreds stretches long. Two more days were devoted to shucking, peeling, coring and dicing, until small mountains of prepared fruits and vegetables peaked and cascaded over the counters. I put one Sash on broth duty, boiling bones in vinegar and spiced wine. Another mixed, kneaded, and baked the bread, reserving one-third of the loaves for stuffing. I stirred salted butter into the mashed potatoes; basted one by one the twenty-two turkeys that King Louie would ceremonially carve once everyone was gathered. Madame DuBarry would play the opening notes of "Lacrimosa" on the harp, and the strictures of good manners at last satisfied, we'd all dig in. And eat and eat until the wages of gluttony reduced us all to sleepy things, and thus contented, we'd retire to the sanctuary for Restoration.

THE GROUNDSKEEPER

The cottage, once she'd finished having it restored, was spectacular. A hideaway in a secret garden—only nothing in that garden was secret from me. It allowed Ennoia to keep secrets from King Louie, certainly; or it would have, if I hadn't passed on detailed descriptions of her every move, from the lullabies she sang to Tez at nap time, to the way she still breastfed her well past the child's second birthday, when she was old enough to ask for milk, and too old not to have been weaned. It wasn't the principle of the thing—far be it from me to comment on how a mother chooses to care for her child, or what a woman chooses to do with her body—but breastfeeding, you know, well, they say it acts like birth control, and keeps the woman from getting pregnant again too soon. Maybe for a year or so, that was fine, but it was incumbent upon her to get back to baking another bun in that oven—a spare for the heir.

It felt wrong, sometimes, watching Ennoia in the cottage, seeing her body (somehow different from all the other Sashes) exposed like that; but not as wrong as she was for disrupting the natural order of things, trying to play God instead of serving as God's vessel, His holy chalice, here on earth.

FERSEN

She hid in that cottage so long because she was ill. It was obvious. A first-time mom, bred in captivity—she had postpartum depression, no question about it. The Nanny who'd helped to raise her in turn did the bulk of the work raising Tez. Which I'd hoped would give Mary Toni and I more time to be together. In fact, that's explicitly what I prayed for when we Restored Paul Greer.

Alas; soon enough she was pregnant with Louie Joseph.

THE TIGRESS

Already suffering in her role as mother, but resigned to her fate, Mary Toni watched with a kind of detached horror as every scary movie she'd ever seen with Resa moved beneath the skin of her eight months' pregnant belly. She had yet to see a hand appear, or any recognizable *part*, pushing from inside her uterus. It looked more like a sea monster undulating beneath the stretch-marked waves of flesh, as it dislodged all her organs and demanded to be seen. Sometimes, if she wasn't careful, it filled her with a curious kind of delight. But just as quickly, I'd hear her say out loud as though reminding herself: *That's not a baby. It's a devil, spawn of two damned souls.*

How evil. How terribly, utterly cruel. The baby had taken the form of a human newborn: no horns or forked tail in sight. No devil-split tongue when it yawned with perfect pink gums. His incredibly soft, small feet left footprints like any other baby's. His mighty, tissue-thin lungs drew air; he did not continue breathing through the blowhole of a scissor-chopped umbilicus. Only his hands, balled tight, gripped pieces of uterine lining like he'd never wanted to come out at all, like he knew the world that awaited and had tried in vain to opt out, to stay where it was safe and warm forever. The gore in his fists dissolved with the water they poured over him—a ritual cleansing, first baptism, leaving only the thing that should remain: an infant. An heir.

He didn't cry even after the doctor slapped the back of his legs. Just a startled little gasp, like *Next time I'll be ready*. He would likewise be a quiet child—one to suffer in silence, always.

THE NANNY

If Tez's birth breathed new life back into Simon's Sorrow,

Joey's made us complete. We'd grown complacent, stuck performing daily routines, the reasons and meaning behind them no longer front of mind. But when Tez laughed, or when Joey cooed or burbled or cried, we remembered why we were doing the hard work. How we'd given up the world for something greater.

The children's antics were the best. The things they came up with to say, do, or play surprised us and moved us to our cores. It seemed they spoke, at five and two, respectively, with wisdom beyond their years. But then they were King Louie's children.

The miracles surprised us most of all. No one had expected them to display the signs so obviously. They girded up our once-flagging belief, reigniting our fervor for the Second Coming of Simon.

THE MAID

Around the time that Tez began to speak, her 'superpower,' if you will, became apparent. King Louie had told us that they would. That the kids, the heirs, would have 'gifts,' markers of the Holy Spirit, and these powers would define their time on earth while helping to prepare the way for Simon. With each birth, we waited patiently for these signs to appear. Tez's arrived around her second birthday.

She had said a few words by then—Mama, Papa, Simon; the usual—but one day she surprised us all by stringing them together in ways unusual for a toddler of her age. I was dusting the statues in the Great Hall while Tez played with some blocks the Nanny had dumped out for her when a curious thing happened. The Nanny handed Tez a blue block to stack on top of the tower the girl was building, and as Tez struggled to grip the block in her pudgy, as-yet uncoordinated fingers, her hand brushed the Nanny's hand and Tez froze. She sat up straight as her still-developing abdominal muscles would allow and stayed that way, perfectly still, for almost two minutes, during which time the Nanny grew concerned and attempted to break Tez's apparent trance. But the child just kept staring at something only she could see.

THE NANNY

It wasn't just the way she froze, though that was odd enough. I worried she was having a stroke or something, some kind of tremor-less seizure perhaps, so I called to her and waved my other hand, the one she wasn't holding, in front of her eyes, until finally she focused on the movement and turned my way. "Buttercups," she said, so clearly I didn't question it. (Its own miracle, since a lot of kids struggle to say their Rs.) "Buttercups in Shropshire."

Immediately, memories of the tearoom my aunt had run in England, above which I'd grown up in a studio-style flat (having been raised by that kind woman), flooded my senses. I could see the yellow, bobbing heads of those flowers lining Madeley's rolling hills. Taste neighboring Telford's fish and chips, famous because they were fried in beef drippings. Smell the black, seeping bitumen of the Tar Tunnel in Coalport. Hear the River Severn burbling beneath the Iron Bridge. I hadn't thought of these things, that place, in years. But with a phrase, Tez brought it all streaming back.

THE MAID

What we soon figured out is that, like Christ sensing the needs of those who in faith grabbed the hem of His garments, when Tez brushed against another living soul, she essentially "downloaded" bits of the person's life story. They weren't always things that had happened yet, either. Sometimes she saw the past, but sometimes she saw the future. And not just isolated events, but the *whys* behind them, too. As a child, she spoke of these visions in terms of "God's plan"—as in, *You needn't worry about the job interview. You'll get it; it's part of God's plan for you.*

Once we realized this, we consulted Tez often. As often as she (and her parents) would allow, anyway. She seemed to find the constant requests annoying—I would, too!—and the relaying of what she saw exhausting. Sometimes Sashes got mad at her because she told them something they didn't want to hear, or accidentally "saw" something—a secret—they hadn't meant to share. Mostly, though, I think it was the burden of knowing what would happen before it did, and realizing better than any of us how powerless we are against fates set in motion.

TEZ

Which is why, when I got old enough—six or seven . . . the age of reason, come to think of it—I stopped "performing" on demand all together. I knew enough about my power by then to control it, limiting the amount of information I had to absorb. The only person I never blocked was Mary Toni. Although I couldn't intuit the particulars, I knew from early on that my time with her was limited. And that unless I was willing to let someone else tell her story, to let the world write her off as extravagant and immoral and plainly air-headed, it was up to me to learn and memorize what really happened.

So I walked with her hand in hand (she had nothing to hide from me) and I listened to stories of her upbringing (honest and humble, she told a version of events that inevitably meshed with the images I saw), and I became certain that her status as queen to my father's king was not protected, after all. That the monument the Sashes had built to Simon would, if I was interpreting the vision correctly, become her grave. And that while my father would believe he was doing the Lord's work, exacting His justice on earth, it would be King Louie's fault. Maybe mine, too, if I did nothing to stop it.

THE NANNY

Joey's talents presented themselves a little later. It must have been around 1994. He was three, almost four, and with all the energy of that age, when he made the dead rise and walk again.

THE HANDYMAN

In the way of kids like Isaac Crable, born with less fear and more curiosity than is good for them, Joey at times seemed more monkey than divine human. One day a delegation from Asheville came to visit, and the madame among their ranks brought her son, a boy of five. He was sent out to the gardens with Tez and Joey to entertain themselves. The Groundskeeper and several other Sashes were back there—they should have been well-looked-after; but when no one was watching, Joey and the boy somehow climbed up the limestone wall. They weren't trying to escape. They had no desire, and certainly no need, to—they only wanted to walk the perimeter, like scouts in some old movie about the Alamo. At first, the fact they even got up there seemed its own kind of magic, until Tez later pointed out the live oak tree that had grown near the east wall sometime between Ennoia's arrival at the temple fifteen years before and Joey's fourth birthday. I guess the Groundskeeper naively assumed the kids would know better. At any rate, the visiting boy fell off the wall, landing *inside* the garden—which was lucky, because the twenty-foot drop killed him instantly and the last thing we needed was that kind of public attention. It was a tragedy any way you sliced it, of course, but also, it underscored why children (other than the heirs) weren't allowed in Simon's Sorrow. They needed constant minding and were always more trouble than they were worth.

As you can imagine, the boy's mother was hysterical. She looked wildly around for someone to blame. The Groundskeeper was an obvious target, and sure, he was guilty, but her eyes kept flicking back to Joey, wanting to believe it was somehow his fault. Mary Toni noticed and calmly called her out on it. "Is there something you'd like to say to my son?"

"No, no. Clearly he had nothing to do with it. Only . . ." And here the woman looked doubtfully but still a touch hatefully at Joey. "Are you quite sure you didn't push him? Even accidentally?"

"He fell," Joey repeated, shrinking under the gaze of all the adults in the room, of a type so different from the adoring ones he was used to. "But if you don't believe me," he said, finding his backbone after all, "why don't you ask him yourself?"

The boy's mother looked like she would murder Joey, for his ignorance or impudence or both. Until, that is, Joey closed his eyes and placed his hands on the five-year-old's chest. Like he was preparing to perform CPR.

Instead, he performed his first miracle. With a sound that hurt just to hear it, the bones of the boy's back reordered themselves. Calcium fused, cartilage zippered back together. What had looked like a human rag doll crumpled and twisted, began to breathe. The boy's mother fell on him, sobbing anew and cradling him to her chest. "Are you back, baby? Open your eyes. Talk to me." And he did. He said that he'd fallen. That the whole thing had been his idea. He'd dared Joey to scale the wall and Joey was blameless.

The boy, or whatever incarnation of his soul Joey had pulled back from the land of the dead, survived. His mother was put to death that night for apostasy.

TEZ

I have only the vaguest personal memory of this event. Most of what I remember about it came from reliving the day through Mary Toni.

FERSEN

Okay, so—now she had an heir *and* a spare. It was my turn. Right?

TEZ

Fifteen years after marrying King Louie, and twenty-three years after first meeting Fersen, Marie Antoinette and her sixth-grade teacher lay together. She was twenty-nine. He was forty-five. For one of them, anyway, it was everything.

Of course, I wasn't there for any of this—couldn't have known the color of the shirt she was wearing that day or the expression on her face as she took it. Except that later I would feel Fersen's hands on her body. Unravel the tangled threads of her fears—for herself, for her lover, for her children. Would come, ultimately, to see her more as a woman than as my mother.

So, yeah, I called her Mary Toni, not Mom.

FERSEN

It's a very delicate thing to initiate the twenty-nine-year-old object of your affection into the wonders of sex, when for twenty-three of those years you have loved her, and for fifteen of them she's lived in a sex cult! Still, when I went to bed with her, I could tell that King Louie hadn't taught her properly. So I did—and in no time, she learned to enjoy herself.

We were in bed together one night when King Louie was traveling. It was almost three a.m. but Mary Toni wasn't tired. Every time I was about to fall asleep, she'd shift uncomfortably beside me, and I'd jolt back awake. I tried holding her. Turning the fan on. Opening a window. Fetching her a drink of water from the nightstand. Nothing helped. "Penny for your thoughts?" I finally asked.

As though she'd just been waiting for me to prompt her (and in retrospect, she probably had), she said without preamble: "I'm pregnant. And it's yours."

We'd been using condoms faithfully, so at first I thought she was kidding. "Ha-ha," I said drily. "What's really going on?"

"Fersen." She turned over to look directly at me. Her eyes were darker and more piercing than usual. "I am pregnant. And it's yours."

"How?" I said, panic beginning to course through my veins.

"Last month. After the Halloween party?"

But of course. King Louie had gotten too high on his own power, and too drunk on red wine. He'd passed out under the stairs after a long evening of the usual debauchery. Drunk ourselves, we'd slipped away in the middle of the crowd—dangerous for several reasons, but then we hadn't been caught—and wound up in a closet off the nave. Plenty of candles and matches there, but no condoms. I'd torn off my party clothes and slipped her on instead, wrapping her around me like a caterpillar does the leaf for its cocoon. She'd shivered against me and bit my neck to stifle her moan. And we hadn't been careful, not in any sense of the word.

And here she was saying I'd knocked her up. The Royal Mother.

"Louie doesn't have to know," she said. "No one does."

"You're keeping it, then?" I was incredulous.

"Would you have me pay a visit to the Nurse?"

In my mind, I saw the last woman, a Whore, who'd gotten pregnant in the church. I saw how the Nurse had turned her insides out on the altar, and I knew even that punishment would be too good for the queen. She'd be put to death at once, if only so her soul would be free to re-inhabit another body—at which point the search for Ennoia would begin again. King Louie would be an old man by the time she was ripe, and that was only if they found her. But do it they would. The church would go on. With or without Mary Toni.

"Won't he know it's not his?" I asked.

"He gets back tomorrow. If I sleep with him then, he'll believe it when the baby comes a month early."

"You've thought this through."

"I have."

Feeling less panicked now than surprised or caught off-guard, something like awe stole over me next. Without permission, I placed my hand on her belly, as though I might sense something there, growing inside her. Angry, she pushed me away.

"It's yours," she said for the third time, "but it will never be yours. Do you understand?"

I didn't—not really. The information was still too new. But as I processed it over the coming weeks, I'd have lots of questions, and even more opinions.

Which is when I realized how much I loved the unborn prince. A son who would be king.

THE GROUNDSKEEPER

His older sister and brother loved Charlie, too. They looked out for him, tried to protect him from some of the world's harsher truths. For example, there was an egg who died before Restoration could be completed, meaning the body was a tainted thing unfit for the Mouth. They left the egg, a female, in the Icebox for three days—the maximum amount of time bearable, seeing how membranes torn and punctured decay faster, exposed to oxygen, than tissues intact. At the end of this waiting period, King Louie ordered me to toss her outside. "The back of the garden is fine. Don't bother burying her." Birds, as well as smaller, slimier things, came to feast on her bloated corpse, which ballooned before it shrank and stretched across the smaller skeleton beneath. Tez, Joey, and Charlie went out to look at her every day, like she was a science experiment, and they, the keen observers.

"Will that happen to us?" Charlie wanted to know. He sounded exactly like what he was: a scared little boy who wanted to be tough in front of his older sister.

"No," Tez said. "We three are heirs to the throne of Simon. When God calls us home, we'll ascend body and soul. We'll look just like we do now forever."

Mollified, Charlie grew braver. He picked up a rock and threw it at the egg. Where it struck, a cloud of black flies rose and buzzed angrily. He shrank again. His sister smiled.

THE BARBER

As I understand it, the "first haircut" is a big moment in a child's life. Or in his parents' lives anyway. They choose to mark the occasion in different ways. Some parents get their hair cut at the same time as their child. Some get the whole family involved; they all take turns with the clippers. Still others scrapbook those shorn locks of hair.

Charlie may be the only kid ever to celebrate by performing a miracle.

On the Big Day, Mary Toni brought him to my workroom—just a closet with a window really, on the second floor of the compound. The window looked out into a tree, and there were doves cooing in this tree. Well, one look at my shiny silver scissors, and Charlie quailed. He did *not* want to sit in that chair. Mary Toni distracted him by pointing out the birds. "Look, Charlie, your favorite!" But Charlie didn't care. He could see the scissors reflected in the mirror, and he knew they cut, and he knew that cuts hurt. Charlie slumped and tried to slide out of the chair. His face crumpled. He started to cry.

"Oh, Charlie, Charlie, Charlie," Mary Toni cooed. "I know what you want, Charlie." She reached into the satchel she always wore across one shoulder and retrieved a blue lump of modeling clay. Immediately, Charlie's eyes lit up. He smiled through his tears and reached for the clay. He sat docilely while I combed, then cut, his hair.

"Did you want to keep any?" I asked Mary Toni, holding a longer clump at the base of Charlie's neck, where the hair was still curly and fine.

"If you don't mind. I was thinking of putting it in a locket for his father."

"Here you go, then." I handed her several dozen strands.

She took them, then returned her adoring gaze to Charlie in the mirror. "Isn't he the handsomest?"

"The handsomest, ma'am," I agreed. "A very fine heir to the throne."

"And so talented."

I realized she was watching Charlie, who hadn't said a word since being pacified or squirmed in the slightest, work the clay. I peered over his shoulder and what do you know? He'd molded the damn clay into two plump birds, their necks as regal and their plumage as thick as the doves outside the window. "Hey," I said, impressed. "That's pretty good."

"Wait until he brings them to life."

"Huh?" I looked up from the boy's crown to make sure I'd understood her correctly.

"Just watch," she reiterated.

I noticed then how Charlie kept flicking his eyes toward the birds' reflection in the mirror, then back to the clay for some minor adjustments, then back to the mirror. He seemed to be whispering while he did so, or maybe singing a little song. "What's that now?" I bent lower to hear him. When I did, a bird flew into my face: a dove as real as any other and rattled at finding itself so. Except that it was cornflower blue. Like Mary Toni's lump of modeling clay.

I jumped back and swatted at the thing. My scissors accidentally clipped its leg. One scaly pink foot fell to the floor while the bird squawked and hopped dramatically on its remaining good foot. "Shit!" I said, unsure what I was reacting to—the sudden appearance of a live bird in a little boy's lap, or the fact that I'd just maimed it. With every hop, the dove left a spot of blood on Charlie's shorts. "Shit," I said again. "I'm sorry, Charlie. I didn't mean to."

He looked at me distrustfully, as he had upon entering the barber shop room. Cradling the bird to his stomach where he sat, he frowned. Clearly I was a Bad Man.

"Can you fix it?"

The furrows deepened in his two-year-old brow. Still cradling the bird (the other, I noticed, was yet clay, forgotten on the chair beside him) he started whispering again. This time I could understand him. He was quoting Jeremiah chapter eight, verse seven: "Even the stork in the sky knows her appointed seasons, and the dove, the swift, and the thrush observe the time of their migration."

"Can he quote the whole Bible, then?" I asked Charlie's mother half in amazement, half in amusement.

But she didn't answer. Or not directly. She'd bent down to pick up the blue bird's foot. Worrying it with her fingers, she finished the verse for the boy.

"Though the birds observe the time of their migration, my people do not know the requirements of the Lord."

FERSEN

One afternoon I tried to surprise them, the kids. Bought a cheap plastic wading pool and filled it with the Groundskeeper's hose. Yes, I knew how Mary Toni's father had died, but no, I wasn't thinking of that when I called Tez, Joey, and Charlie out to "swim." It's pretty difficult, if you ask me, to drown in five inches of water, but when it came to that particular subject I couldn't exactly depend on Mary Toni to be rational. Her two greatest fears were one, water, and two, a life controlled by that fear. That night, the kids told her all about it and, well, furious, is putting it lightly. For *weeks* afterward, the mere *thought* of what *could* have happened had her drawing picture upon picture.

Water. Thunderheads. A bottomless black hole.

All that time, she didn't let me touch her. It was the night we made up that Sophie—Mary Toni's fourth and final child, a girl—was conceived.

THE ARTIST

I enjoyed painting the Auguste-Habsburg family. There were four of them—a girl, two boys, and a baby girl—plus the parents. Mom wanted them posed like the Holy Family: Mom and Dad, heads resting together, as they looked down at their happy brood. We finished the final canvas with a hand-poured gold frame courtesy of the Jeweler. I was proud of the work, and wouldn't have changed a thing about it.

Except that Sophie died. And when she did, Mary Toni wanted no reminders whatsoever of the daughter she had lost. So she had me paint Sophie right out of the picture, like she'd never existed.

THE TIGRESS

Madame DuBarry asked us to assist her. She had proof, she said, that Mary Toni wasn't Ennoia. Suggesting she'd been wrongly crowned. "King Louie, for all his divine qualities, is in the end only human," she reminded us. "And humans make mistakes. We will forgive him, as all brothers and sisters forgive their siblings in Christ. Then, with great joy, we will Restore him to himself." She looked us each in the eye, one by one. "First, though, we must peel the leech from the skin of Simon's Sorrow, where she's fastened her sawteeth quick—and destroy her."

The ritual she described was unsettling, if for no other reason than we intended to use it against the queen. I didn't think Mary Toni was guilty. It hadn't been *her* idea to run away and join this circus at fourteen. But when the one who's taught you everything you know; who's modeled service to God and God's mouthpiece, King Louie; who has lowered her dripping cunt upon your face and shared her honey; tells you you've been deceived, and that atonement falls to you; well, you do it.

But you add a hidden failsafe. Just in case.

THE WHORE

She gathered us in her bedroom: a stone cloister almost big enough for a sex swing, just like the rest of ours. It was dark. The shades were drawn against the full moon's light, and only a single candle burned on a thick book: *The Confessions of Saint Augustine*. There were six of us. Dipping her thumb into a small pot of oil, Madame DuBarry anointed our upturned foreheads. "For protection," she said, "lest your minds be taken hostage." She then did the same to our naked backs at the shoulder blades—the points at which wings, had we had them, would have unfurled. "For strength," DuBarry said, and set the little crucible beside a rag doll at the center of the circle.

A red stone, like the ones we wore in our necklaces and rings, lay at the doll's soft feet. An irregular chunk of iron sat at its head. Subbing the oil for a book of matches, DuBarry selected three. She tore the wooden sticks from the book like they were weeds. I noticed the cover bore the Ginger Man logo, a bar I'd only gone to once, but would again. The fish were plentiful there.

DuBarry lit, then waved, each match above the doll, shaking them lazily until their flames went out. Lastly, she took a pouch of dirt from her pocket. It could have been any dirt—swept, perhaps, from the kitchen floor or the back patio. But she told us it was graveyard dirt. That with it, we'd be staging Ennoia's mock funeral, and that when the ceremony was complete, she would die.

THE GROUNDSKEEPER

I was reminded of the Treaty Oak, several years before. In 1989, a domestic terrorist had poisoned the 500-year-old oak tree—last surviving member of the Council Oaks, a sacred meeting place for Comanche and Tonkawa peoples—with enough herbicide to kill one hundred trees. When questioned, the vandal had said he was casting a spell. The Treaty Oak should have died, and two-thirds of it did. But some essential part of it survived. The Treaty Oak still stands in West Austin. While that's a good thing, thinking about it makes me sad. Because Mary Toni didn't survive. Sophie, either.

THE TIGRESS

Just in case, at the last minute I placed one of Sophie's hairs on the doll. I wasn't sure if DuBarry actually had the power she said she did, but better safe than sorry. Let's say she was wrong, and Ennoia died anyway. There's no way we could have replaced her—not the queen. But an heir? There could be another one of those. It's not like we didn't have a few spares.

THE LAUNDRESS

Was it coincidence—or something greater?

How do *you* explain that at the moment Whore number three drank the oil, baby Sophie stopped breathing in her crib and the Whore went blind? Like, totally and completely can't-see-a-shittin-thing, black-as-burnt-food *blind*. It was Sophie's only miracle, you ask me. The telltale sign of a blessed babe rebuking those who would hurt her.

THE NURSE

The eleven-month-old's death was classified as SIDS.

THE WHORE

No, I didn't link Sophie's death to Madame DuBarry's ritual until the Tigress said that maybe, potentially, accidentally, not accidentally she'd killed the child by switching DuBarry's subject at the last second.

But I didn't know until later. Until after the baby had died.

THE TATTOOIST

I heard her say it. "I will make lace out of her guts," Madame DuBarry said.

And she did. For that's the kind of pain that losing a child engenders. One that eats at your intestines and never abates.

FERSEN

Mary Toni was the one to find her. Sophie, our youngest daughter, blue and already cold to the touch in her crib. The same crib all the children had used. Her wails pierced the heavens at Simon's Sorrow.

THE TAILOR

King Louie called a meeting in the Great Hall. Everyone came. He told us that Sophie was dead. That there was no readily apparent cause of death, and as such, it must be something spiritual. Something wicked. He quoted Matthew to us:

> But afterward he sent his son to them, saying, 'They will respect my son.' But when the vine-growers saw the son, they said among themselves, 'This is the heir; come, let us kill him and seize his inheritance.' They took him, and threw him out of the vineyard and killed him.

"It was jealousy that drove one or more of you to kill my daughter, heir to the throne of Simon. But I tell you, jealousy has no place at Simon's Sorrow; and there is no place at all for a child of God who turns their back on God's will. That person is saying they're greater than God. That they know better than God. God! The Almighty Lord who made you!" King Louie shook his fist and spit flew unnoticed from his mouth. "My only consolation is thus: Sophie, too, was a child of God. An innocent, who, deprived of earthly life and *this* father," pointing at himself, "has returned to the bosom of her heavenly Father, where she will but wait for the Second Coming of Simon with the same great anticipation as we, and *see to it personally*," now jabbing at each of us in turn for emphasis, "that her murderer may never know God's forgiveness, but suffer in a purgatory of their own making forevermore, condemned to an eternity of Restoration unsweetened in the slightest by the promise of redemption."

Here, King Louie collapsed, choking on the venom lacing his words and moved anew by the inescapable thought of sweet, dead Sophie. A pale doll. It looked like he might collapse and Ennoia rushed to his side. "My flesh and my heart," King Louie said weakly. "My flesh and my heart may fail, but God is the strength of my heart and my portion forever."

He didn't appear convinced by his own reminder.

FERSEN

And I? I was right there with him. King Louie mourned the death of "his" daughter, but only her mother and I knew that Sophie had in fact been mine. I tried to modulate my grief in public, when around the other Sashes, lest my reaction seem confusingly strong. At night, Mary Toni and I lay together and cried. King Louie was too broken to visit her chambers. Seeing Mary Toni reminded him of the child he'd lost.

TEZ

"Hollow" is probably the best word to describe my parents after that. I missed my only sister—of course I did. But I imagine, anyway, that it's harder to lose a child than a sibling. Especially since for Sophie at least it meant Getting Out, and in a relatively painless way, too.

Unlike Joey. Rest in peace.

As for Madame DuBarry, her harem of Whores stayed loyal until the end. No one dared rat her out, all of them guilty by association. She lived to make our lives hell another day. For a while, anyway.

THE TIGRESS

She wasn't always like that. Madame DuBarry, I mean. When she first joined the church, she was really grateful to be there. Her life Outside as a single mom struggling to make ends meet would have made anyone tired, but especially someone so naturally creative, so intrinsically *romantic*. She played the harp, for Simon's sake, and I don't know about you, but whenever I picture a woman who plays the harp, she's always kind of dainty and bird-like, a little wispy and a little crazy, but in a good way, like Alice Coltrane, right? She loved the music for its own sake but also wanted some attention, a little notoriety, as harp players were just so *rare*—even more so in the Austin bar scene. By extending his hand to Madame DuBarry and offering a way out of the pit of mounting bills and other such demands on her time and energy, King Louie saved the would-be musician from a lifetime of counting quarters tossed into her harp case and elevated her status from single parent to parent of the church. She lived up to it, too. Became a kind of mother figure to all of us, long before the Holy Mother, Ennoia, was recognized and installed above Madame DuBarry.

THE WHORE

I remember the first night I was scheduled to go fishing. I was nervous, and Madame DuBarry could tell. "Talk to me," she said, a veteran whore herself. "Which part is giving you anxiety? The sex?"

"Not the sex," I said quickly. I'd lost my virginity at fifteen to a man twice my age, and had slept with all manner of people since. There was nothing you could do to a body that I hadn't tried. No body type I hadn't worshipped in the everlasting hours after the clubs shut down for the night. But almost always, these had been one-night stands. One-*hour* stands, some of them, as we'd done our thing and then parted with no ill will. As a Whore for the church, however, I was expected to approach each encounter like a transaction. Business as much as pleasure. The bill of sale was for my body, but the cost of admission was their eternal souls. It wasn't just about getting them to *come*. It was getting them to *come to church*.

"I guess I'm unsure about the *selling*," I clarified.

"Oh." Madame DuBarry patted my arm affectionately. "You don't have to worry about that, *ma chère*." She dropped the occasional French phrase when she was trying to make you smile. "That's not your job. Your job is just to get them through the doors. It's up to the rest of us to get them to stay."

Her eyes glazed over at a specter from the past. "Once upon a time," DuBarry said, "I played my harp at an old folks' home. Most of them had dementia. Some were hard of hearing. Probably only one or two seniors in the whole room ever even noticed I was there. It was ridiculous, really, because it cost me gas money to get out there and then I did the show for free, and every time I played for free was a time I couldn't be making money somewhere else. And I had so little money, then, and also Isaac . . . " She trailed off. "But you know why I kept showing up?"

I shook my head.

"Because there's something about aging that makes you confront the truth of your life. And music does the same thing. Ever see a toddler when her favorite song comes on? She starts dancing, immediately and instinctively. Music lives in the body like that. It becomes fused with certain moods, certain memories. When we get old, music brings us back to ourselves. It reintroduces us to the toddlers we were, the toddlers that those with dementia are in the process of becoming once again. Being reminded of that—of my own mortality, and of the limited opportunities we get on this earth to live fully, to dance, to dance with others—was worth its weight in gold.

"And that," DuBarry said, refocusing her attention on me, "is what you are doing when you're 'selling' the church. You're inviting those who have lost themselves to confront the truth of their lives. You're creating space for them to re-inhabit their bodies. To dance. To remember what it was like to be a child absorbed in her own pleasure, while at the same time sharing a universal experience. You, woman, are the music. Your body is your instrument. Let it ring."

THE TIGRESS

When she spoke like that, it was easy to admire her. To forgive her for striping your face with a cat o' nine tails. To overlook her hatred for the queen.

THE CHEF

At first, we thought it was a cold. Frail from birth, Joey was almost always running a low-grade fever. His nose dripped like a faucet and there were perennial bags beneath his little-boy eyes. It was June, but if anyone could catch a cold in the summertime, it was Joey.

Then the aches set in. A whole-body hurt that made him curl up in a manner reminiscent of the fetus he'd once been, which was easy to imagine, since he was still so small and skinny. He stopped playing with his siblings. He couldn't get out of bed. The chills that plagued him meant he was too hot under the blankets and too cold on top of them. He could never quite get comfortable, poor thing.

MOTHER-EATING

I made his favorite kind of soup—noodles in broth, with tiny chunks of sausage—and brought it to him three times a day. I had my helpers in the kitchen make the noodles from scratch, using eggs from the chickens in the courtyard.

Just thinking about that garden now makes me homesick.

Anyway, Joey rarely swallowed more than a spoonful or two, and sometimes even that didn't stay down. It was bad, but then, he'd been bad before. So we weren't *overly* worried.

Until his fever increased, hovering around 104 for nine days. Now he wasn't just vomiting, he was vomiting blood. According to the Doctor, he'd started shedding and throwing up pieces of stomach lining. He wanted to admit him to the hospital, but doing so would have raised too many questions. Joey didn't have a birth certificate. His existence was not registered on any official document or in any state or federal system. Trying to explain who he was could have prompted an investigation—or worse, Child Protective Services getting involved. A seizure of the heir? Unthinkable.

But the death of another heir? What even would that have meant?

His parents handled it in their separate ways. For the first two weeks, Mary Toni lay in bed beside her son. She held his shaking body, trying in vain to warm him, mopped his sweat-wet head, and rubbed his back and wiped his mouth whenever another round of vomiting ensued. She really seemed to believe that she could love him back to health. After a while, though, when the Doctor said he wouldn't recover, and everyone around her (including me, when I brought them both soup) looked at her with pity in their eyes, she little by little started to retreat. It was like she'd begun the process of saying goodbye, of weakening her emotional attachment to her son even while he was still alive and needing her.

Best I can figure, it was Resa that got to her. That's how Resa'd treated Mary Toni her whole life: as though the girl already had one foot through death's door, and thus better to keep her at arm's length. So often, the things we learn in childhood never leave us. When push came to shove, the daughter became her mother. We watched her retreat. We saw Joey recognize, but not understand, her behavior.

And so, while we all pitched in where we could, without her he was just a scared little boy. Scared, and very, very sick.

THE NURSE

Tubercular fever. Not something we see a lot of in this country anymore, though it's out there. Usually, people who stand the highest chance of getting it or passing it on—hospice care workers, for example—get the TB vaccine. But we had no reason to think that Joey was vulnerable. That he risked exposure any more than any of us.

How he got it, we still don't know. Maybe one of the Sashes had something to do with it. Maybe God did. Maybe it really was just bad luck. He fought for as long as he could.

THE DOCTOR

It's the thing I regret most from my time at Simon's Sorrow—not insisting that the kids be vaccinated. I listened to King Louie's reasoning: The community was isolated, insular. The heirs were like Jesus, sons and daughters of God Himself. Nothing would happen to them—including illness—that wasn't pre-ordained. They were born pure vessels. They should die—or ascend—as pure vessels. Western medicine was manmade. Tez, Joey, and Charlie were divine. The excuses were many and they were convincing. But as a doctor, I should have pushed him, because I knew better.

THE NANNY

It lingered, the poor thing. Tuberculosis ate at him like Sophie's death ate at Mary Toni. He deteriorated over the course of months, until he died unable to walk, covered in sores.

THE GROUNDSKEEPER

How many holes did I dig for new plants? How many for seedlings in the vegetable garden? Never did I expect to dig a hole for a Sash. Not when we had the Mouth. Cremation. Other ways of disposing of sacrifices.

Sophie and Joey weren't sacrifices.

Nevertheless, the plot I'd been preparing for a stand of transplant saplings went to the newly dead body of a forever-young boy.

THE LAUNDRESS

And with him, our hope for the future. Joey was to be the next messiah, half-man, half-god. He was meant to pick up where Aaron and Daniel and Enoch left off, Restoring this world to its primordial state. Before man had the fleeting, fatal thought that he was better than God.

Before the Fall.

FERSEN

I'm ashamed to admit it, but I was just so thankful it wasn't Charlie.

TEZ

Mary Toni wasn't about to have Joey painted out of the family portrait, too. Instead she just destroyed the thing.

THE BAKER

It was Savoy's idea. While the rumors about an "inappropriate relationship" between the women had died down after the heirs were born, the death of the second heir brought Mary Toni and the Duchess together again. Women are better at comforting each other than men, I think. Men get awkward, emotionally. Women know how to turn grief into action. You have to purge it, if you don't want it to drown you. And having already lost her dad to drowning, Mary Toni was always going to swim to shore. Savoy helped her tread water until she could.

THE MAID

Very little at Simon's Sorrow stayed a secret for long, as everyone shared tight quarters and a couple trash cans. People think they throw something away and it's gone, like magic, because they never have to see or think of it again. But the person who empties the trash sees it, and in that household, that person was me.

I got a fucking splinter pulling the broken wood frame of the royal family's portrait from the trash. Mary Toni had snapped the frame in several places, so it'd fit inside the large kitchen can, I imagine. Where the sharp and jagged ends had been unceremoniously stuffed down, they'd pierced the canvas she'd commissioned at Sophie's birth. The painting was damaged irreparably. I had the instinct, for a moment, to try to save it anyway.

Clearing the kitchen counter, I spread out the torn

canvas and the bits of broken frame still attached to it for a better view. I saw the fine acrylic face of King Louie; the kiss print that yet lingered there. It showed Ennoia in a sumptuous crimson dress, lace-trimmed and the picture of fertility. Large pearl drops hung from her earlobes. Baby Charlie played on her lap. At her right arm, Tez gazed adoringly up at her. To her left, the empty cradle where once baby Sophie had slept. Pulling aside its satin coverlet, the dashing Prince Joey. All as an afternoon sun streamed through the window, catching their faces, making them beautiful.

How, I wondered, could a child so blessed die covered in sores and unable to walk? He hadn't always been that way, but who would remember him in any other?

Just then, Ennoia walked into the kitchen! I scrambled to hide what I was looking at: a woman's secret shame. She wasn't mad, though, when she saw what I'd done. She smiled. Walked over as if to see the canvas better. Tracing a finger along Joey's cheek, she said, "Eight-year-olds are hard to finish off, no?" Like the secret wasn't hers but ours—a communal grief. (And it was.) "Mm-mm," she said, shaking her head. "Life is sure hard to let go of at that age." Then she poured some lemonade from the fridge, popped a straw into her glass, and literally flounced back out of the room like *she* was eight.

I didn't—still don't—know what to make of it.

THE WHORE

She descended into madness right there. That was the moment that made everything that followed possible.

THE BARBER

It was her children who had died, but Mary Toni who was

the walking dead among us. She was so stressed out by the whole situation that her hair turned completely white overnight. A lot of people go prematurely gray. This wasn't that. She had black hair and then it was white. Her skin went pallid and stretched over her features, until she was more skull than woman. The Chef said she'd stopped eating anything other than bouillon. One nuisance reporter managed to snap a photo of her in a window, through a sheer curtain. In it, she looks hunched and feral, leading the newspaper to caption it "The She-Wolf of Austin."

TEZ

As Mary Toni fell, her uncle, Adam Habsburg, flew. Five-time governor of Texas, he made a bid for president that promised to be meteoric.

THE CATERER

A paying job's a job. Normally I don't give much attention to the particular cause or event because they're pretty much all the same. A few rich people invite all their rich friends to buy seats at cloth-covered tables set with crystal and silver, wear their diamonds and pearls to drink wine and nibble on canapés, and bid good money in the silent auction or flat-out contribute to the campaign fund. Nothing stood out about Adam's announcement dinner— the official launch of his presidential run—except for his shoes. Worn red Cougars, the ends of the laces frayed, just peeking from beneath the hems of his stupid-expensive, exquisitely tailored suit.

I only saw them because some woman, already sloshed thirty minutes into the evening, laughed and spit her shrimp all over the floor. I bent over to pick up the pieces with a napkin and I saw the red shoes. They'd become a symbol during Adam's gubernatorial reign—a familiar icon that students and the working class could glom onto and hold up as making Adam *one of them*. He'd go on to lose his share of the shrimp on national TV that night, annihilating any respect I might have felt for the man. But that was hours away yet. From the time I saw those shoes shuffling around the marble floors of the hotel, through his welcome speech—which, I'll admit, made me chuckle a few times; he *did* have a good sense of humor—even I caught the beginnings of Adam Fever. But like all things in love and war—and politics is always both—it was a ruse, a clever strategy designed to fool us into thinking he was different, and hoping for something better.

THE REPORTER

It's always kind of exciting to rub elbows with "celebrities," even if they're only popular in local circles. I'd fought to be assigned Governor Habsburg's campaign dinner, and while it was a great event, I didn't get to interview him. So I stuck around for a chance to catch him afterward. He said he and some friends were going for a drink; did I want to join them? I couldn't believe my luck. Well, we ended up on Dirty Sixth, and Adam puked his guts out three steps from the bathroom at Shakespeare's.

I may or may not have snapped the well-timed photo that accompanied the next day's article. Oops.

It's not like it hurt his reputation, anyway. He was known as a party boy, and he was good at giving the people what they wanted.

THE OPPOSITION

Let's be real. Adam Habsburg was nobody until his brother Frank pulled some strings for him, strong-arming those politicians with secrets they'd rather keep secret into publicly endorsing the then young, green councilman. Combined with a sneaky-smart media campaign, Adam pretty much shot to the top overnight. One day we'd never heard of him; the next, he wore those stupid red Cougars everywhere you looked. But it was all Frank's doing. His company had won the contract for city light and power, and he of the blue jeans, dirty fingernails, and slow Texas drawl was (metaphorically, not literally—that we know of) elbow deep in the ass of the mayor, pulling the strings of the political engine. Frank never would have done it—milked his connections that way—except for Adam. He would have done anything for that greasy, smarmy, I-want-to-wash-my-hands-after-shaking-yours politician, because that's what brothers do.

THE JEWELER'S APPRENTICE

Not true. It was us

THE TUTOR

The only subject Mary Toni ever showed any genuine interest in other than math, as a teenager, was social studies. She liked history and government and civics and political science—probably because of her uncle. It changes things, for kids, for all of us really, when we know the talking heads on TV personally. He wasn't just another moderate man with deep roots in Texas running for office. He was Adam. Uncle Adam. With his red Cougars and bright white smile. Even I thought he was attractive.

Once, one of the youngest, newest Whores went fishing for Adam. Politically ignorant, she had no idea who he was, or of his ongoing relationship with Simon's Sorrow. She approached him in the bar at the Driskill Hotel, where he was talking business with some other suits. I guess she saw money, and with it, power, which is certainly something the girls are taught to look for, but she gave herself away almost at once. Grabbing an empty tray from the bar, she approached like she would take the men's order, though she only had eyes for Adam. Distracted, he didn't look at her until she pushed her breasts into his face, but then he saw the tattoo, fresh and still a little irritated, and he knew. Adam smiled at her. "And how we doin' tonight, darlin'?"

"Pretty good, sir," she said, looking up at him from behind thick lashes. "Is there anything I can get for you?"

"Tell you what. Why don't I come look at the menu with you? Gentlemen," he addressed his colleagues, half of whom were smiling, half of whom were annoyed, "excuse me."

Taking the hand of the "waitress," Adam led her to an empty office behind the bar. "What a nice surprise," he murmured into her neck, as his hands and his mouth found purchase on her body.

"Uh," she said, laughing lightly and trying to pull back, "I was thinking we could go somewhere else. Back to my place, maybe."

"Won't they miss you at work?"

"The thing is," she whispered, like it was a secret meant for him alone, "I don't actually work here."

"You don't say," Adam humored her, pulling the edge of her tank top down under her breasts, exposing them so he could bury his face in them.

"But I don't live far away," she said. "And a little more privacy would be nice, right?"

"Oh, I think this is plenty private." Leaving her for a second, Adam went and locked the office door. He then swept everything off one corner of the desk, so he could pick her up by the hips and set her there.

While this Whore was still in training, she knew enough to realize that something had gone off-script. She was supposed to be the one in charge, the one with all the power. As Adam sucked on her nipples and moaned into her throat, his erection pushing hard against her leg, she wondered where she'd lost that power, and how she could possibly get it back.

"You know," she tried again, "my friends are waiting for me downstairs. I really should be getting back."

"Uh-huh," he said, unzipping his pants.

"No, really," she said, more sternly this time, pushing him away as she slid off the desk and righted her skirt.

Accepting the challenge, Adam smiled and shoved her up against the back wall instead. "Feisty," he said. "I like it."

"If you don't let me go this instant, I'm going to scream," she said. When he kept kissing her, she did.

He clapped a hand over her mouth. "Hey, what the hell are you doing? Trying to get us both in trouble?"

"I told you, I have to go."

"Okay, I'm confused. Did King Louie not send you to me?"

Now it was the Whore's turn to be confused. "You know King Louie?"

"Of course. I mean, that's part of the deal, right? Political favors for sexual ones." He smiled and slipped a hand between her legs, while the other worked up and down on himself.

Suddenly, it dawned on her. "You're Adam Habsburg."

"Bingo. And you're my bird." Adam took a seat in the black leather office chair, his dick like a landing post on a birdhouse. "Come here, little bird. Take a seat. I'm ready for you."

Because she didn't know what else to do, and because the name Adam Habsburg was whispered like a mantra in the halls of Simon's Sorrow, the Whore did as she was told.

Afterward, she called it a night and returned to the nest, where she told her sisters what had happened. I listened through the open door and overheard them commiserating with her ("Don't worry; not every night can be a win for the flock.") and I wondered whether Adam treated all women that way. Whether he'd ever laid a finger on Mary Toni.

THE RECEPTIONIST

It was something he said during one of the presidential debates. There he was, on stage at Bass Performance Hall, and he started telling a story about his niece. I forget now what he was trying to prove. Something about healthcare. Access to mental healthcare, maybe? And he told the story of how his niece, when she was six, had been the only witness to her father's death, and how badly it had messed her up. And how he'd tried to "be there" for her afterward, and how apparently he hadn't done enough, because when she was fourteen she'd run away, and no child deserved that fate. Everyone should feel like they had somewhere to turn, and no one should slip through the cracks.

THE BUTCHER

"Run away." Right. He knew exactly where she was.

THE RECEPTIONIST

So maybe it wasn't so much *what* he said, but how he said it: with the timber of a child whose toy has been taken away. He'd "lost" Mary Toni. She was the toy. That's when we started to wonder: Had he touched her inappropriately when she was little?

Now, was he doing it again?

THE LAUNDRESS

Jesus Christ. Mary Toni could never catch a break. Why were we all so concerned with her sexuality? First Savoy, then her uncle. Like there wasn't enough drama in her life, in the church.

First off, Adam was, like, never around. He was too busy. When he did stop by Simon's Sorrow, it was to meet with Mercy and King Louie, no one else. So, I really think if Adam was making a move on Mary Toni, King Louie would have known about it.

TEZ

King Louie *did* know about it; or suspected as much, anyway. They all did, after watching the replay of the debate. It didn't matter that no one had actually *seen* Mary Toni and Adam together. Or that I knew, in the way I know all things, that it wasn't true. I was eleven years old in 1998. Might I have been lying to protect my mother? Didn't it make sense that she'd reach out, eventually, to the one blood family member she had left?

THE TIGRESS

At which point, couldn't old desires have been rekindled?

THE JEWELER'S APPRENTICE

And then there was the necklace.

THE DOCTOR

King Louie loved Charlie (and Sophie, while she was still alive) as much as his first two, Tez and Joey. Together, all four were his pride and joy. And he was a good father. He didn't take them hunting or teach them to work on cars—those 'manly' pursuits that I associate with my own father—but that's mostly because they never left the compound grounds. They couldn't. What if something happened? They got lost wandering around the store, and we had to get the cops involved? Or they swung too high on the playground, jumped out, and broke an arm—and I wasn't there to set it? There would be witnesses; a mandatory hospital visit. Just thinking about the questions such incidents would have raised sets me on edge even now.

Loving them, to King Louie, meant protecting them. Until such time as the prophecy was fulfilled. So instead of baiting hooks and swimming off a dock somewhere, they walked the pecan grove. He taught them to identify wildflowers, beetles, and birds: a microcosm of God's creation in their own backyard. They learned to graft trees and harvest peaches for cobbler and send homemade paper gliders in long, lazy arcs across the garden. They built stick forts and with their toy dolls and soldiers reenacted Bible stories, paying special attention to Israel's plagues, David and Goliath, and the miraculously collapsing walls of Jericho. If they ever wondered what lay beyond their own four walls, I never heard them voice those thoughts myself. They had their own small but devoted tribe at Simon's Sorrow. It wasn't a disservice to keep the rest of the world from them, I reasoned, because it's how our ancient forebears would have lived, in tight-knit community units, and anyway, it all would end with the youngest heir's seventh birthday.

Tez, Joey, Charlie, and Sophie. Four kids. One father who loved them all equally. It wasn't until everyone started suspecting Adam and Mary Toni that he began to look in earnest at photos of his youngest, dearly departed daughter. *Did* she have his nose, like people said? Or did she more obviously have Adam's chin? The way she'd cocked her head to the right when she laughed—wasn't that the politician's trademark move? Could gestures of all things be inherited? And what about the fact that she'd been born with her second toes webbed to the third toes of each foot? Was that a birth defect? The result of inbreeding?

King Louie demanded a paternity test. "Take whatever you need, Doctor," he said to me as we stood at the edge of Sophie's exhumed grave. The tiny body was largely decomposed, though the hardy wooden toys (courtesy of the Contractor) that she'd been buried with and the Tailor's handmade burial garment were still recognizable as such. "Hair, tissues—however they're doing it these days. Take hers and mine and the rest of the kids', too, while you're at it—just please tell me that they're ours." Not only was the fate of the heirs at stake. The reputation—and life—of the queen were as well.

I collected what I needed and told him I'd have the results soon. We didn't take Mary Toni's DNA. Upwards of forty people had witnessed each baby being born, so the question of maternity, at least, was moot.

FERSEN

I didn't take any of it as seriously as I should have, because I didn't believe it would actually ever happen. Mary Toni was Ennoia—a holy vessel; the Divine Chalice. She was above reproach, I thought. Immune to castigation.

But then, God gave His own son Jesus to Pilate for crucifixion and death, so why would He treat Mary Toni any differently? She was a woman, after all. The weaker sex. Corrupted by her own compulsion for pleasure. Or that's what they said.

I should have spoken up. Set the record straight. Said, *Actually, I was the one who lost myself to pleasure.* Who found in her arms and the secret spaces of her body sensations that at once overwhelmed my senses and made me feel more wholly *in* my body and *of* my flesh than anything had before. The mole on her back, the bumps and ridges of her nipples, the dark hair curling between her legs—these were my objects of worship. Not the statue of Simon in the foyer; the ritualized host; the mind in meditation. If anyone was corrupted, it was me.

But I didn't feel bad about myself, did not feel guilty for loving a woman so completely; and thus I could not see her as guilty, either. I thought those months were a time to "get through," after which, flared tempers would naturally subside. Hurt feelings would find a balm, or some other distraction. People would move on, and life would continue.

As it turns out, though, people love their goddamn grudges. They love a scandal. They love more than anything when justice is served . . . even when it's the wrong perp, for the wrong crime.

THE MAID

I think Mary Toni did it. She slept with Adam, he fathered her children, all of it. She was rotten, that one. An imposter from the beginning.

THE BUTCHER

She blinded him, with her body and her willingness. But does that make it her fault, or King Louie's for not keeping her on a tighter leash?

THE NANNY

Genesis was always my favorite book in the Bible. I liked reading about Adam and Eve and the creation of the world: the grass and the trees and the light that falls upon them. It makes me sad now, though, to read it, because it reminds me of Mary Toni. When the Lord God says, "It is not good that the man should be alone; I will make him a helper fit for him," I think of how God brought Mary Toni to King Louie, and how it must have been even harder for him to accept than it was for her. He was already well on his way to establishing the church. He had a life going for himself. He had us. Then God says, *Take this strange girl, just fourteen years old, and make her your wife. Love her and impregnate her for she will be the mother of the heirs. She is Ennoia: my First Thought incarnate.* And King Louie didn't have another choice. She was the helper that God had picked out for him. And look at what she did: betrayed him for another. Ephesians 5:25 says: "Husbands, love your wives, as Christ loved the church and gave himself up for her." So he did. He gave himself up to her and she repaid him by giving herself to another man.

THE WHORE

"Ha ha, very funny," Mary Toni said when I confronted her. Like the rumor that she was sleeping with her uncle was too absurd to be anything but a joke. But then she saw the look on my face and got defensive. "Oh, come on. You too? You were the one who told me, you said, 'People will talk, and if they don't have anything to talk about, they'll make shit up.' When the first whispers broke about me and Savoy. That was actually kind of devastating. But this? Uncle Adam? Give me a break. That's disgusting, and what's more, it's patently untrue."

I apologized for ever questioning her. Of course she

wasn't sleeping with her uncle. "Because if you were," I said, "just hypothetically speaking, you'd not only be an adulterer, you'd be impure. Hypothetically speaking."

Rage flared in her eyes. "Are you questioning whether I'm fit to be the queen?"

"Never."

"Then what exactly are you accusing me of?"

"Some say, Your Excellency, that Charlie is not highborn. He looks and acts differently from the other heirs, and he's displayed none of their abilities."

"What do you call the clay birds?" she said, indignant.

"No one else saw them but you and the Barber, supposedly," I reminded her.

Mary Toni shook her head vehemently. Was she refuting my claim? Reassuring herself that it could not be true?

"Get out," she said.

I left, satisfied.

THE ALTAR SERVER

I just felt bad for her. For almost two decades, we'd held her up as the pinnacle of womankind. The mother of the heirs, children upon whose coming of age Simon would be restored to the throne. Without her, we were nothing. We had no reason for being. But now, because of a story that no one could get to the bottom of, we were about to throw all of that away. Erase our own history. The sacrifices of dozens of people working in the name of justice, of righteousness. People who had, for the whole of Simon's Sorrow's existence, been treated like freaks, like some sideshow attraction. Called a *cult* and accordingly marginalized. Now we were doing the same to our own, like we'd bottled all that vitriol we thought we were above and kept it just for this occasion: to ridicule, alienate, and blame our children's mother.

PART FOUR
MOTHER-EATING

THE PARK RANGER

THE MORNING OF the Great Storm dawned clear and warm—the kind of 'perfect' day that Austin rarely gets, triangulated between Brownsville's heat and Houston's humidity. It's basically always hot and always kind of damp, except when a midwinter mood swing sees the temperature plunge from 80 to 35 in a couple hours. It's good for the lake, though, that endless summer, and keeping people active on the water. We encourage that: waterskiing families and yacht club members and the odd Labor Day camper or hiker. Everyone's welcome here, provided they abide by the rules, heed the posted warnings, and get off the water when we tell them to.

KXAN had been predicting the Great Storm for weeks. It began as a hurricane rotating off the Gulf Coast, then petered out to heavy rain. In the desert (and depending on how many days in a row the thermometer tops one hundred degrees, Austin can be considered a desert), heavy rain is cause for concern. The dusty ground, unused to absorbing that much water, quickly chokes on, and begins to spit back up, the deluge. On land, flash flooding is common. On the lake, choppy swells and dangerous undercurrents. Which is why, even though it was a perfect, blue-sky morning, I still had the squad out there planting yellow caution flags, warning boaters to head back in, and generally making sure that everyone was informed, everyone was being as safe as they could be.

No one reported seeing a purple-painted canoe, a Barbie-pink fishing pole, or a father-daughter duo.

I was the one who found her, hours after the Great Storm had worn itself out. She was curled in the bottom of the canoe beneath a man's windbreaker that couldn't have been doing anything to keep her warm, seeing as there were three inches of cold water in the boat as well. That's how hard it'd rained. Her lips were blue and she was shaking so badly it seemed she'd never stop.

"Hey, there," I said, once I'd cut the engine and let the boats drift close enough together that I could tell she wasn't dead (my initial fear). "Are you okay? What's your name? It's all right. I'm a park ranger."

I kept blathering like that while I figured out how to lower myself into the canoe without toppling it. I didn't know yet whether she'd been grievously injured. No blood, no broken bones that I could see. But then she wasn't moving, either, and if she didn't—or couldn't—we'd probably have to tow her back to shore in the canoe. I didn't want her pickling in that water any longer than necessary, though, so I hoped to coax her up and out of the boat one way or another.

When the edge of my boat tapped her canoe, she gave a little yelp and sat straight up. No spinal injury then, I thought, though it didn't rule out cranial trauma.

Her eyes were unfocused, staring at nothing. While she cocked her head at the sound of my voice, she wouldn't look at me.

"Honey? Can you tell me your name?" I tried again. "And what you're doing out here all alone?"

"I'm waiting for my daddy," the little girl said.

"Where is he? Did he go somewhere?"

She stuck her lower lip out, more scared than pouting.

"Was he in another canoe?" She didn't look big enough to paddle on her own; I felt silly. "What were you guys doing out here?"

"Fishing," she said. "I caught one, but—" She looked around the canoe, like an invisible bucket, or a rod and reel, might be hiding. I visually checked for a bass line tied to the craft. Nothing.

"Okay, well, we're going to find your daddy, but first

we need to get you somewhere warm. Do you live in Austin? Is anyone else here with you?"

She sat up straight, as though suddenly remembering. "My mom! We're camping in the tent place."

I radioed in this information.

"What's a park ranger?" she wanted to know.

"We take care of the lake, and the campground, and the trails," I said. "We help people stay safe and have a good time." Another thought occurred to me. "How long have you been out here?"

She shrugged. "A long time."

"Before it was raining?"

She nodded.

"That must have been really scary. But everything's going to be all right."

A voice crackled over the radio. "Yeah, I have a woman at the station. Says her husband and daughter were on the water when the storm came through and they haven't returned."

I asked if he had a description of the daughter. He did. It fit the sodden child in front of me. "Her name is Marie Antoinette," he told me, "but she goes by Mary Toni."

"Mary Toni?" I addressed the girl. "Is that your name?"

When she nodded again, I told the ranger to put her mom on. Resa spoke to Mary Toni over the walkie-talkie; told her it was okay to leave with me, that she could trust me.

The girl held out her arms and I lifted her easily into the boat. She couldn't have weighed more than forty pounds, even soaked. I wrapped her in blankets and settled her on the floor near the bow. Then got back to the station as fast as I could.

TEZ

Before the Storm, Mary Toni wasn't afraid of death. Because she didn't know death as anything other than what eventually happens when you've got more wrinkles than hair. And even then, she thought, you died in your favorite easy chair. She knew it was why they checked the weather every day—to make sure Daddy-the-lineman stayed safe—JUST IN CASE—but it was really more like a game, their little ritual, one that Mary Toni always won, because Frank always came home safe, back to her and Mommy, and anyway, weren't all dads invincible? Wasn't hers?

After the Storm, Mary Toni vacillated between wild paroxysms of grief manifesting as anxiety—a suffocating fear that she or Resa or her classmates would suddenly keel over, too, inexplicably and too fast for anyone to do anything about it (the way the Storm had assembled itself from gathering pockets of electricity, the air typically hot but strangely thick, until its water broke and something unholy was born)—and a breathless, sinking helplessness, a nihilistic certitude that death would come, as it must to all living beings—so why not her? And why not then? Six was young to be so jaded. Her anger grew as the girl did, making pitstops at sadness, curiosity, and finally, acceptance.

THE NEIGHBOR

At the wake, the man introduced to me as "Uncle Adam" scooped Mary Toni up in a giant hug. He smashed her face just a bit too hard into his shoulder, but she didn't resist—no doubt because he was warm, and male, and when she closed her eyes, he must have felt kind of like Frank, only with more neck hair poking above his collar. Uncle Adam was always smiling (he would smile at his brother's funeral the next day) because he was a politician. Or was he a politician because he was so charismatic? Which came first?

Mary Toni didn't know and didn't care, distracted by Uncle Adam's hands: baby smooth and soft and never, ever sweaty. Like they'd been lotioned and also powdered until they were hands you'd want to shake, hands to pose with in pictures—hands for signing bills, not stringing wires. Her daddy'd had rough hands, though he'd always been gentle with her.

Mary Toni's face crumpled all over again.

"Now, now, sugar pie," Uncle Adam drawled in an affected Texan accent. "Chin up." He actually nipped a thumb and forefinger beneath her chin, making her head bob briefly up. "Hey, have you seen your mother?"

Mary Toni pointed mutely toward the kitchen and the murmur of low voices.

"All right, then." He set her down and patted her on the head. "I'll see you later, kiddo."

She watched him walk away. A smaller man than her daddy, but with the same balding spot. Both of us heard his booming voice, too loud for the occasion. "Well, now, ladies, what are we cooking? Smells amazing in here."

TEZ

Resa was having a bad dream. Right? What kind of lowlife politician, she thought, would swoop in on a freshly made widow so soon after his own brother's death? Adam wasn't aggressive. She didn't feel threatened. But the very proposition did make her feel unclean. Like she needed an extra-hot shower. The kind that made the whole bathroom fog up, little droplets of steam still condensing on her shoulders even after she was standing on the mat, toweling off. That was when Frank used to join her. Taking the towel from her hands, he'd bury his nose in her nape, massage lotion into her slick skin. Occasionally even finding himself inside of her. How could that good, sweet man be gone? What did it *mean* that Resa would only ever shower alone thereafter? And how dare Adam act like he was doing her a favor?

These had been her thoughts directly after Frank's death.

So she'd shoved his face backward, away from the pocket where embrace had become a comforting nuzzle, a cautious kiss, a whip-fast reaction. "Jesus Christ, Adam. What the hell is wrong with you?" All the air rushing out of that pregnant pocket.

And on his lips, no apology, or excuse, but that *Aw, shucks* smile, inappropriate on any male over the age of eight. But which had won for Adam Habsburg a seat on Austin City Council. Would win him the governorship. See him, maybe, all the way to Washington.

It was the same smile that later changed her mind. Once the loneliness had grown too big to bear.

THE TRAINER

It's a gym. People go there to show off their bodies and find other bodies to do things with and to. Resa was an attractive woman, if also an addict. It didn't surprise me at all to find her hooking up with some guy in the sauna. Not even when that guy was Adam Habsburg. I didn't realize then that he was her brother-in-law. I only knew him from TV, and all the political signs around Austin, of course. Running on the Republican ticket is usually cause enough for candidates to skip campaigning in our fair city altogether, Austin being the lone blueberry in the rhubarb pie. Adam was different, though. A more moderate Republican to whom only the most extreme liberals wouldn't give the time of day. Part of it was his platform: pro-gun, but also pro-choice. The other part of it was those shoes. Cougars. Like he was still a college student or something. The young people saw themselves in him, and in the city with the second-largest student body in the state, that was important. Powerful enough to swing a whole state still hurting after the right-wing disaster most recently in the White House.

He wasn't wearing Cougars, but a pair of running shoes—and little else—when I went in to respond to reports of fucking in the sauna. Their towels and shorts were strewn about the cedar plank benches and floors. The steam that rose in occasional puffs off the heater obscured, though not in any meaningful way, their identities. Resa still wore her white nursing shoes and Adam, well, his face had only been staring back at me from every stoplight's street corner for months.

"Okay, you two," I said, startling them both. Resa pulled away from Adam, instinctively grabbing for her clothes. "You know I'm not one to begrudge anybody a little love, but you can't do it here. We've had complaints."

"Sorry, Mike," Adam said, still standing there in his shoes, seemingly immune to the ravages of shame.

Mike's not my name, of course, but I didn't bother correcting him. Guys like Adam, they have bigger things to worry about, and most of them involve a lot more dollar signs. I only hoped for Resa's sake that he remembered hers.

TEZ

I imagine he did remember his sister-in-law's name. The brother moving in on his dead brother's wife—how very Biblical. It didn't concern Simon's Sorrow, though, and never would have, until the question of the heirs' paternity came up. When King Louie got the results of the test, he learned that he wasn't Charlie's or Sophie's father. They did not, however, tell him who was.

Adam? Someone else?

And if not Adam, why had he commissioned the diamond necklace?

To buy some time to ruminate on the best course of action, King Louie swore the Doctor to secrecy. As far as we were concerned, he hadn't received any results at all yet.

THE WHORE

Madame DuBarry thought the necklace was for herself. She got it into her head that King Louie would soon be getting into her bed. What else had she spent all that energy for, trying to catch his attention? The nips and tucks here, the new dresses, expensive perfume. She bought these luxuries with church funds and insisted they were business expenses—that King Louie had told her to buy them: "The face of the church should, don't you think, have a good face?"

Now that Mary Toni was so preoccupied with the children, Madame DuBarry reasoned, she had little time for her husband. Seizing her opportunity, she flirted with King Louie more shamelessly than ever before, and interpreted his every remark tossed however casually her way as evidence of his deep-seated interest, a passion he'd relegated to the back burner upon meeting and marrying the queen. But Ennoia had done it—produced the heirs—and King Louie had no need to keep her happy, keep her spreading her legs. Not anymore. Now it was Madame DuBarry's turn.

She found the necklace when they were headed out one night—King Louie, Fersen, and herself. "It's cold!" she'd shivered upon opening the door. "Do you want your jacket? You better take your jacket." King Louie had shrugged noncommittally. He was never cold. But Madame DuBarry couldn't stand not to be useful, not to serve her king in every way possible. So she ran back inside, finding his overcoat hanging from a hook in the hall. When she grabbed it, the corner of the jewelry box poked out of his pocket, a flash of white in the dark. Checking to make sure that no one was looking—I was; I always was—she fished the box out and opened it. Gold, and the brilliant yellow diamond, gleamed briefly. Not half so bright, or for half so long, as DuBarry's self-satisfied smile, though.

Yellow was her favorite color. He'd remembered.

She called for the Chefs in the kitchen, who dropped what they were doing and scurried out her way. "Here," she said, giving one of them the white jewelry box. "King Louie left this in his coat pocket. Make sure it gets to his bureau."

"Ma'am," one Chef said, accepting the box with a small bow, and slipping it into an apron pocket.

"Now," Madame DuBarry clarified. The Chef scuttled off as quickly as she'd come.

THE CHEF

The necklace was for Ennoia. Anyone could see that. King Louie had given her jewelry to mark every major occasion in the past. Birthdays. Anniversaries. Births. He thought it's what a queen should have, never mind that Mary Toni rarely wore those particular gifts. More often, the children could be seen playing with them. Tez in particular loved to play dress-up with Mommy's pearls. Either King Louie didn't get it (like most men), or he didn't really care. What was a hundred thousand dollars for something pretty? We did it all the time for the church: a new statue here, a new censer there; and we called them investments. Jewelry, when properly cared for, is another type of investment. When properly cared for.

So, there's no doubt in my mind that the necklace was for her. Only Madame DuBarry thought otherwise, and only Madame DuBarry would have schemed so ardently against Ennoia in the way she did. Mary Toni, DuBarry thought, was a bauble herself, but of the costume-jewelry variety. Not any kind of frontispiece with actual value. Not like, say, DuBarry herself.

The only odd bit was how King Louie gave Ennoia the necklace for seemingly no reason at all. Meaning, it wasn't her saint day, or the anniversary of her baptism, twenty-odd years ago now, which we'd celebrated the month before. That did seem out of character, but then maybe (unlike most men), he was finally getting it after all these years—that love is a thing worth celebrating every day, and for no reason at all.

Maybe it meant he'd forgiven her transgression.

You should have seen Madame DuBarry's eyes—huge at the sight of that yellow teardrop diamond. How hungry she looked, for the gift itself and the thing that gift represented: King Louie's affections. She walked right up to Mary Toni on the day the queen debuted it and ran a finger down Ennoia's chest, tracing the length of the delicate chain from which the diamond hung. She stopped just short of caressing the actual jewel. Having touched the queen without permission was affronting enough. Then, snatching her finger back, Madame DuBarry said, "How lovely you look today." Only she was speaking to the diamond, not to Ennoia.

The Jeweler knew Mary Toni's preferences, too, how they skewed toward the wild and the floral. How he ever thought that the second, later order came from her—a request for a necklace so outlandish, so godawful ugly in its scalloped tiers of diamonds, and so heavy as to be unwearable—is, in my opinion, the last remaining mystery of it all. That DuBarry dragged Adam into it, too, was the apple Eve couldn't resist. Why settle for smearing the woman you hated, when you could destroy the only family she had left, too?

THE JEWELER'S APPRENTICE

I'll admit: I had it pretty easy at Simon's Sorrow. As far as jobs go, that is. I didn't get dirty scrubbing potatoes, or up close and personal with everybody's dandruff, or scraped all to shit by the thorns on the roses. I played with gold. All day, every day, I melted precious metal and poured it into molds and polished the one-of-a-kind pieces that popped out from those molds. Chalices. Candelabras. Rings.

It was good, steady work. Creative work, using CAD to print the molds, or early on, still carving them by hand. We had similar styles, the Jeweler and I. We were drawn to like aesthetics. It's why he'd selected me in the first place, to help build, cup by cup, a temple worthy of Simon for the Lord.

And that's what we did. It's beautiful, the temple, if you haven't been. I don't know if it's reopened to the public yet or not, but when it does, you should go visit. It's worth it, just to see it for yourself.

Building out all the hardware, the accessories, the accoutrements of a church—it took almost twenty-five years. But then it was mostly done, and I went into an early semi-retirement, part of the cleaning crew that kept all the gold pieces gleaming. It was during this 'down' period that Adam contacted me. And because King Louie hadn't specifically forbidden me from accepting other contracts, I agreed to humor him. "Sure," I replied to his email. "I can make a necklace like that."

It was gaudy. Six hundred forty-seven diamonds, valued at fourteen million dollars. He said it was for his niece, Marie Antoinette—a belated christening present for the birth of the children he'd (allegedly) not yet come to meet. He said she'd asked him for it, that the design specs came from her, and he was merely doing what all good uncles do: trying to make his only brother's only daughter happy. Did the Jeweler and I question him? Why would we? His vision was clear, he was good for the money (wiring a 50% deposit that same afternoon), and I welcomed a new design challenge.

Sure, I realized that staffers and other people had access to his email and bank accounts. But those tended to be business email and bank accounts—not personal. Not everything about a public figure has to be public, after all. And this request came from his personal email. The transfer was initiated from his personal checking account. I had no reason whatsoever to suspect that it wasn't him. I knew Madame DuBarry hated Ennoia, but I guess I didn't know how much, or how far she would go.

I'm lucky to have gotten off in this case, even though I will say again that I didn't know, or even suspect, anything nefarious. I was, and remain, a craftsperson practicing his craft—which I did, to the letter. That necklace was *exactly* what "Adam" asked for, completed with the finest attention to detail and highest quality materials available. I stand by my work.

THE BARBER

The Jeweler and I were as close, I suppose, as any two Sashes. Meaning we'd fucked the same people, and each other. I knew the Jeweler's approximate height and weight, how his asshole tasted, and the special treatment he got at mealtimes, being lactose intolerant. I never knew the specifics of what he was working on for Simon's Sorrow, though—until, for example, King Louie debuted his new golden gravy boat at the next baptism, using it to pour blood and water into the pussy or down the throat of a new initiate. The Diamond Necklace, though, as we all came to think of it—appearing, in our minds, with capital letters—was different. The Jeweler and his apprentice were both excited to work on it. Excited for the opportunity to do something more creative, maybe, than casting ceiling lamps for the nave. The Jeweler grew more animated, talked more openly about the "super secret order" that "someone important" had placed. I kind of assumed it had to be Adam. Who else knew the Jeweler, knew about Simon's Sorrow, and was "important" but wasn't King Louie?

Rumors circulated in my chair, as they always do. Ideas tossed out by the head under my clippers and mulled over, added to, or decried by those waiting on the bench. Once we'd all decided it was Adam who'd placed the order, and Mary Toni for whom the necklace was intended, the Chef speculated aloud that their relationship must have been closer than anyone realized. "And not just close," Madame DuBarry asserted, pleased as punch to have the inside scoop on the juicier details. "*Intimate*. If you know what I mean."

"No way," the Groundskeeper protested. "That's ridiculous. What you're accusing the queen of—you should be ashamed."

"Oh, it's not her fault," DuBarry backtracked. "She was a child when it started. She didn't know any better." Here, it must be said that I saw at once the irony of her words, an insinuation that *a grown man other than King Louie* (a fact we all willingly overlooked) had taken advantage of a child. "It's just lucky that she didn't get pregnant by her uncle is all."

Or had she?

Did Charlie show signs of inbreeding?

Such were the questions that knit my brow further, and sent all of us spiraling into the dark recesses of our private thoughts.

THE GROUNDSKEEPER

"The Diamond Necklace Affair." That's how King Louie started referring to it, like it was a black-tie ball instead of a deliberate setup. I told you before that Mary Toni had her detractors, and whether those rumors were ultimately true doesn't matter in this case. When it came to the necklace, she was absolutely, 100% framed. Even if she was having an actual affair—which, if she was, it categorically would *not* have been with that pig governor—no one deserves that kind of smear campaign. Least of all Ennoia.

She and King Louie were already on the outs, or he might have been more willing to believe her: Mary Toni, his perfect vessel, and by this time the mother of his children four times over. But between the facts that he couldn't *really* know who'd fathered Charlie, and that Adam's frat boy antics had finally amounted to one too many minor bailouts, King Louie wasn't exactly in a patient mood.

THE ALTAR SERVER

With Service temporarily suspended while King Louie conducted an "internal investigation," I had little to occupy my time. King Louie asked me personally to attend to the queen's spiritual needs. "You take care of the chapel and everything in it," he pointed out. "That should include everyone in it. Pray with her; hear her confession. Whatever she asks. Just make sure she's not alone."

I understood then that he still loved her. But love, he believed, had blinded him to her faults; and now pity would prevent him from correcting those faults in a rational manner. I felt like he was being too hard on himself. And I may have overstepped my bounds in telling him so.

"It's okay to be upset right now," I ventured, placing my hand on his shoulder. "And to lean on us for help. You've led the church for so long. We've learned from you. We can pay it forward. Or, at least pay you back."

"Thank you, brother," King Louie said. "I know I can count on you, and for that I'm grateful." He smiled and patted my hand on his shoulder, but the smile was so sad it broke my heart.

Then he turned to go, and I should have let him. But, feeling bold, I grew over-brave and stopped him. I said, "You asked me to take care of Ennoia. But, King Louie, who's taking care of you?"

My eyes searched his face. He wouldn't meet them. So

I ran my hand along his cheek, letting him know how solidly I was there. The audacity of my own gesture made me giddy and less careful, and when he didn't answer, I blurted out the next thing that came to mind: Proverbs 12:4.

"An excellent wife is the crown of her husband, but she who brings shame is like rottenness in his bones."

Had I thought this verse would comfort him? That he would feel validated? Seen? I was wrong. He flared at me. "And which is she, hm? An excellent wife, or one who brings shame?"

"I only—"

"Well? Do tell, man!"

But I couldn't, not after making him so mad. Instead I literally bit my tongue, and then he backhanded me, and then I bit through my tongue.

As blood welled up in my mouth, I watched him go, and thought I'd never felt so sorry for anyone.

FERSEN

In retrospect, I guess it started the way all mutinies do. One or two people get disgruntled or witness something they shouldn't have, they tell their friends, who tell other people, and suddenly everyone's riled up and operating under a different version of the truth. All anyone knew for sure was that the Jeweler had missed Service. That was a fact. We could agree on it. But then someone said he'd left Simon's Sorrow and someone else said he'd been kicked out of Simon's Sorrow and someone else said that he'd *died*. That maybe King Louie had ordered him Restored and Mercy had taken things slightly too far. Or maybe Adam, with all of his political connections, had disappeared him. Soon, what had begun as a mystery ("Where's the Jeweler?") became an outcry ("Justice for the Jeweler!"), and still it did little to band us together.

Everyone was isolated in their fear. We looked at each other like *Do you know who did it?* or even *Did you do it?* The trust that had permeated the group evaporated.

THE JEWELER'S APPRENTICE

It was weird—really weird—for the Jeweler to disappear like that. He was, like, King Louie's superfan; the one Sash you could count on to be present at every meal, every party, every play. He *never* missed Service. Hadn't so much as missed a day of work in the shop since I'd come on, anyway. Three hundred sixty-five, times twenty-five. How many is that? That's how many days in a row I'd seen him, talked to him.

But after the Diamond Necklace Affair, he never came back.

THE CHEF

I always left snacks out for the Sashes between meals. A fruit bowl on the counter. Granola and yogurt in the fridge. The first day these disappeared I thought, Hm, perhaps we had a school group come through and the Tutor gave all the kids a snack? So I restocked. No problem. But then it kept happening, and when I asked the Sashes what was up, I learned from the Tigress that people were stockpiling. Sneaking down to the kitchen and hoarding the snacks to take back to their rooms. In case the day came they had to lock their doors and barricade themselves against some nameless, faceless threat in their midst.

MOTHER-EATING

THE GROUNDSKEEPER

No one came outside anymore. They watched me from the windows, going about my everyday business, as though something or someone was hiding in the bushes and watching them back, waiting to pounce should they walk through the garden exposed and unaware.

THE BARBER

All non-essential services shut down. Sashes stopped coming to get their hair cut. I was a man with a straight razor and they were vulnerable humans with soft throats. I'd say it was crazy except that being the one with the straight razor made me feel a little safer. Not like I was going to use it on someone, but in case I needed to defend myself against someone else.

THE RECEPTIONIST

It was the media, capitalizing on everyone's fears and blowing them out of proportion. "Presidential Candidate Accused of Incest." "Is Governor Habsburg Abusing Whack-Job Niece?" News outlets picked up on the story because one, Adam was a household name by then, having thrown his hat in the ring for president; and two, no one had even realized he had a niece, or would have cared, except she was the daughter of that woman from the Simon's Sorrow 1980 Super Bowl commercial—and we Sashes, well, we were nuts! Combined with rumors of a sexual relationship between the two? My God, there was just so much to unpack.

There was a TV in the temple lobby, and after hours, I'd switch the welcome video off and watch the developing story, so I could keep up with Adam and report back to the group. I considered it my duty to inform them, since now it wasn't just us. People Outside were glued to their screens, too, watching civic leaders stutter as they tried to defend themselves or explain where they'd been and why at a given time—while mud-slinging journalists dug up all they could on America's politicians' pasts. Sure, everyone knew Adam was a playboy; before, it had always endeared him to his populace. Made him relatable. But fucking his niece? The gluttonous anchors couldn't get enough of it. The more they quote-unquote *learned*, the more their bellies gleefully expanded, Hansels fattened up by a witch.

THE TAILOR

This wasn't Savoy. Wasn't a little "indiscretion," a "dalliance" that made tongues wag and Sashes draw mean, explicit cartoons. If Mary Toni had slept with another man. If that man had fathered her children. If that man was also an honorary Sash we'd baptized like our own and to whom we'd funneled millions of dollars. And then, if he'd offed the Jeweler, a founding member of the church. I mean, the betrayal! The face-slapping indignity of it all!

The scariest part was that it had all somehow happened right under our noses. That was what turned us against each other. Because *someone* must have known. *Someone* was keeping secrets. We could never trust the Outside world; now, we couldn't even trust ourselves.

FERSEN

King Louie gave several sermons in the temple on patience, forgiveness, and the importance of meditation throughout the madness. He said that while he didn't know where the Jeweler was, he trusted that the truth would come to light. He also insisted that Adam was an honorable man, a friend of both his and the church, and even invited Mary Toni to the pulpit to decry having any kind of relationship with anyone other than her husband. She looked at me as she said it. The only thing the Sashes wanted more than to believe her was to help ensure her innocence by subjugating those who posed a "threat" to her. I got really nervous as their fervor grew. Would someone find out about us? Would the Sashes punish me? If ever there was a man in sore need of Restoration, I suppose it was me. But I wasn't sorry for being with Marie Antoinette. I loved her. I always had. I always will.

THE TIGRESS

I was backstage of the theater, in the rehearsal room with all the mirrors, practicing a new striptease choreography I'd put together for the Whores when I heard Mary Toni scream. I dropped the feather boa I'd looped around my shoulders and ran for the Great Hall. My jaw hit the floor with my knees. You know how they talk about the fight-or-flight reaction? I always thought mine would be fight. But apparently, my instinctual reaction is *fright*, because I just fell down and stayed there, looking up at the horror, at my own shock reflected on Mary Toni's face.

And on the face of Savoy.

Whoever did it had a sick sense of justice, because the violence itself apparently wasn't enough for them. I could tell by the jagged shreds of skin hanging from Savoy's neck that her head hadn't exactly been cut off; it'd been *wrenched* off. They'd sewn her eyelids open, so she stared with hard, dry eyes. But her makeup was done and her hair curled prettily. That was the sick part. They'd killed her, stuck her head on one of the Maid's extra-long broom handles, then *given her a makeover*. I can't imagine what Ennoia thought. "Oh, my friend has come to visit me. But how is she out there, floating beyond the balcony? Oh, shit. She's dead." Do you scream at that point, before the full horror of everything has sunk in? I didn't. I fell to my knees. How long did she stare at the eyes staring back at her? How long had they been watching her before she noticed?

THE RECORD-KEEPER

Especially after that, none of us felt safe. No one's head just magically goes and separates itself from its body. Someone had murdered Savoy. There was definitive proof. This wasn't the Jeweler disappearing or rumors floating around unbounded and unsubstantiated. Now there was a body. Or part of a body. (Her torso would later be discovered in the well.) Who was acting out and why? Who would do that to a Sash outside the Icebox and the punitive *but never lethal* (apart from eggs) act of Restoration? It was terrifying. King Louie ordered locks installed on all the bedroom doors, if their residents didn't have them already, and told everyone to stay in their rooms. It was like being under house arrest, only we wanted it. There was a killer on the loose. We couldn't trust anyone.

THE DOCTOR

Sometimes the eggs ended up in the Mouth. Dismembered and buried around the property. Cremated on a pyre in the garden. These were ritualistic killings. Sacrifices in the name of Simon. Having served a higher purpose, the bodies were sacred. Thus, it made sense to keep them at Simon's Sorrow, where their eventual decomposition blessed the water, ground, and air around them, and contributed to the circle of life. Savoy's death didn't serve this purpose. It was decidedly *unholy*, her body now tainted and profane. The Sashes didn't want it anywhere near them, so they gave the woman to me for disposal.

I slid her piecemeal into the hospital incinerator.

Removing her from the grounds didn't make anyone less uneasy. If anything, some of them said it felt like a coverup. Perhaps there should have been an official investigation—as in, *real* authorities involved. But even I knew that would have posed too great a risk. You get the cops snooping around and suddenly nothing and no one is off-limits. We would have been exposed. It was too dangerous.

But it was dangerous at Simon's Sorrow, regardless. I could feel that every time I walked in the doors. Gone was the calm, reassuring energy I used to associate with moving through the lobby, past the Receptionist, and into the Great Hall. The old stone walls had felt sturdy and hallowed, like you could shout into the rafters and hear the whispers of the saints drift back down to you. After Savoy died, it just felt cold and foreboding. No one was talking. No one was interacting. No one, even, was shouting. It was silent as a tomb.

THE LAUNDRESS

Madame DuBarry killed the Jeweler because he knew too much. Savoy because she meant too much to Mary Toni.

THE MAID

I don't know who killed Savoy. It wasn't me, only my mop.

THE TUTOR

DuBarry.

THE NURSE

Eileen DuBarry.

THE GROUNDSKEEPER

The prevailing suspect was Madame DuBarry. Then it was her turn.

TEZ

Eileen woke up on a bed she didn't recognize in a room she only did after blinking several times and clearing her thoughts. It was the Icebox, the soundproofed room they'd held Mary Toni in all those years before, so no one would hear her cry. She tried to sit up but leather belts crisscrossed her chest, arms, and legs, strapping her down to a plain pine board.

"Hello?" DuBarry asked, unafraid yet, merely curious. "Is anybody there?"

She heard a squeaking in response like a family of rats in the walls. Someone entered the room. DuBarry couldn't see them, could only hear the breathing—heavy, labored, as though through a gas mask.

"Hello?" she called again, craning her head as much as she was able, but not catching more than a single ray of light through the high, solitary window. Footsteps whispered across the ground, skirting the elevated pine board. The squeaking sound grew louder.

A hooded figure stepped into view. He wore a floor-length robe and the Mask of Salvation, its blue demon face obscuring the wearer's identity. DuBarry hadn't seen it since the last Halloween party and she was struck again by the intensity of the expression painted on its porcelain features: upturned eyes the epitome of despair; open mouth caught in the act of prayer. *Salvation is near. How near?* DuBarry guessed it was Mercy inside that costume—something about the hard crucifix of his shoulders. He carried a large brass bowl, which he set on a table next to DuBarry. It seemed to be the source of the squeaking.

"Hey, Mercy," DuBarry tried. "What's going on?"

No answer.

"Have you seen King Louie? What did he decide to do with Mary Toni?"

Silence.

The hooded figure regarded DuBarry through the empty black holes of his mask before finally speaking. "For crimes against the king and his church, you have been found guilty."

"Excuse me?" DuBarry still couldn't tell if it was Mercy in there, but that didn't matter so much as making sense of what he was saying. "What crimes? What are you talking about?"

"According to divine law, lying and covetousness are capital sins at best, treason at worst. The court has therefore sentenced you to death."

DuBarry's eyes bugged out of her head. "Wait, what? No, there's been some misunderstanding here."

The figure unceremoniously pulled her shirt up over her breasts, exposing her bra and the sagging skin of her belly. She was fifty-five years old.

"I haven't lied!" DuBarry yelled. "Stop it. What are you doing?"

"You are lying even now," the figure said, grasping the heavy brass bowl and upending it on her stomach. As he flipped it over, she saw them inside: four rats. Large ones.

"Wait," she screamed, but the curved rim of the bowl had already sealed to her skin, trapping the rats inside it. Their paws padded curiously over her abdomen. She could imagine their beady eyes wide and blind in the perfect dark. Their whiskered noses sniffing the air inside the bell for any clue about what might happen next.

The hooded figure placed the first piece of kindling on top of the bowl's flat base. DuBarry chuckled nervously. "Mercy. This is a mistake. I don't know what you heard, but the necklace was never my idea. That's what all this is about, right? The gaudy diamond necklace that supposedly cost fourteen million dollars?"

The figure kept stacking kindling in a deliberate manner. Constructing a tiny log cabin upon the bowl.

"It was Adam, Mercy. It wasn't me. You have to believe me. You know I'd never hurt my queen." DuBarry laughed again, self-consciously this time. "I mean, sure, we've had our share of spats. Always silly stuff, really, but I recognize her as Ennoia, Mercy. Honestly, I do."

The figure placed the last twig and stepped back, considering his handiwork. He reached for one last item on the just-out-of-sight table: a book of matches. Quietly, he tore one from its cardboard sleeve at the same moment that DuBarry grasped his intentions. She shrieked and gave a mighty jerk, throwing her shoulders up and against their restraints. Straining for any give at all. The leather bit into her skin, first breaking the blood vessels beneath the surface, then rubbing her body raw. She didn't stop.

"Mercy. Mercy, I know it's you in there. Please." The tears were streaming down her face. "It's me, Eileen. We've known each other for years. You were King Louie's first disciple. I . . . I was in the first dozen," she said lamely. "I helped you build this church. Why would I now help to destroy it? Think about it. Why?"

"Why indeed?" the figure said, pinching the match head between the grooved strips and striking it. It lit at once. He brought the flame to the log cabin. "Give thanks to the Lord for He is good," the figure whispered.

"Don't do it, Mercy," DuBarry warned.

"Lord Jesus, Son of God, and Simon His servant, have mercy on DuBarry, a sinner." A small twig caught. Quickly, the fire spread.

"Mercy," DuBarry sobbed. "Mercy, please."

She was miserably desperate, desperately miserable. As the cabin burned, the brass heated up. The once-placid rats beneath it grew alarmed. They made a few tentative scratches at the soft flesh floor beneath them. "Please," DuBarry begged. The fight gone as quickly as it had come. Her restraints were too tight. The bowl too heavy. The rats too determined to survive.

Adding a larger piece of wood to the pile, the figure reminded her, "God's mercy endures forever."

As the flames jumped a foot or higher into the air—a tiny, controlled pyre on top of a bowl, on top of a body—the rats panicked. One took an exploratory bite, and sensing progress, dove in nose-first. DuBarry screamed. His muroid friends got the message and followed suit, using teeth and claws to burrow in and away from the heat. If they couldn't climb out of the bowl, they would chew their way out.

The hooded figure stayed as long as he needed to see the job through. He added wood methodically, unflinching at DuBarry's screams, at the things then moving inside her belly. Then tearing out through oblique. Above mons pubis. Fur red-slick as newborns. He stayed until her guts were thoroughly shredded, her writhing stopped, and the rats had emerged. He watched the fire burn down to cinders, the blood quit trickling out of her mouth. Closed her pain-shocked eyes, frozen open in a familiar expression. One very much like the Mask of Salvation. Not, as it turns out, engaged in prayer, but cast upward in horror. 'O' of mouth a silent scream.

"The Lord has freed you from your sins," the figure said. "Go in peace."

THE TATTOOIST

It was Mercy who killed Savoy, and then DuBarry. Anything crazy that ever happened at Simon's Sorrow was his doing. King Louie came up with the ideas, but Mercy carried them out. He was the fall guy, you could say, in case anyone ever exposed us. King Louie could honestly claim to be innocent then.

Why would Mercy agree to such an arrangement? He was nuts to begin with. An animated meat case who felt one thing only: unadulterated, fanatical love for King Louie. The same thing most of us felt, though all of us had invisible lines we drew somewhere. But not Mercy. He did anything King Louie asked and at once, without flinching. A born and bred soldier for the Lord.

MERCY

What can I say? Civil war is necessary and bloodletting is somehow therapeutic.

THE TIGRESS

The accusation that Adam had used campaign funds to commission a necklace for Ennoia was crazy enough. But when that necklace then disappeared? And with it, an alleged fourteen million dollars? The money to pay all those diamond distributors, it had to come from somewhere. Since the state wasn't paying, it fell to the church, and since Madame DuBarry was suddenly nowhere to be found, a site-wide search commenced. King Louie and Mercy seemed awfully sure that DuBarry hadn't wandered far, and that she would have stashed the necklace at the church before she left. So, not a cobblestone was left unturned, and when it was determined that none of the temple's copious hiding places held a multi-million-dollar necklace, its people were searched. As in, full-scale body cavity excavations. Not something we were entirely unused to, mind you, though they'd always been performed in another context, right? Yeah, play time, worship, whatever you want to call it. Exactly. It didn't stop there. Two of the Guards whom Mercy had long suspected of trying to undermine the church had their bellies split open, so he could empty their stomachs just to make sure they hadn't swallowed the diamonds.

MERCY

Fun fact: So long as you don't puncture any vital organs when you cut an abdomen open, the subject will go right on living and breathing, even as you pile their steaming intestines on the floor beside them. It's the blood loss you have to worry about, so you have to do it quick. And if they survive that, there's the risk of infection. But with enough antibiotics, someone can fully recover!

THE TIGRESS

Alas, neither of the Guards made it.

And then we found the necklace in Ennoia's room.

THE ARTIST

To be clear, this wasn't the necklace with the single large yellow diamond. This was the necklace with six hundred and forty-seven diamonds. It had to be sold, so the church could get that money back. Someone I knew on the Outside said she could take care of it—same way art gets sold on the black market. I smuggled the necklace to her, and that's when the feds found out about it. Traced it back to Simon's Sorrow, to Mary Toni and Adam Habsburg.

THE GROUNDSKEEPER

They'd already been in the news for their alleged "relationship." Now the media were having a heyday with the story of a woman who'd lived inside the Simon's Sorrow compound for more than half her life, only to find solace—and, apparently, diamonds—in the arms of her biological uncle.

"Receiving stolen property" was the felony charge authorities slapped her with. They said Adam had misused campaign funds to commission the necklace—thereby making it "stolen property"—and that Mary Toni was, as its recipient, complicit.

There would have to be a trial, of course, but until then, she was incarcerated, held in the state prison on FM969. Should she be found guilty, she'd be sentenced to federal prison.

THE CHEF

The day they came for her, we were at Service. Mary Toni, too, since King Louie never let her out of his sight anymore. He was at the pulpit lecturing us about the difference between man's law and God's law when men of the law walked right in, the Receptionist trailing behind them and protesting "I tried to stop them" to no avail. They knew what Mary Toni looked like and they picked her easily out of the crowd. Those men in dark uniforms, appearing just the way they had on the lake, and later, at her father's funeral—only now they came for her. And Mary Toni, she knew that meant death.

She didn't stand, but made them yank her up from her chair. Jerking her arms rudely behind her, one man handcuffed her, while another read her Miranda rights.

They took little notice of the rest of the Sashes. Had we tried anything, the uniformed officers outside the door would have made short work of our dissent. As it was, none of us really knew whether there was in fact something to challenge—if Mary Toni had been wrongly accused, and was therefore being mishandled; or if she actually had been carrying on an affair with Adam, thus jeopardizing not only the whole of Simon's Sorrow here on earth, including all of the painful scrutiny we would soon be subjected to, but our eternal souls as well. For without a queen, there could be no more heirs. And now that the number of heirs had been reduced by half, we weren't sure whether the prophecy could be fulfilled. Were two children enough to carry Simon's Sash? If he came and we weren't ready, would he fall again?

Ennoia walked between them and didn't resist. She looked straight ahead, her chin level with the ground, and did not glance up at God or back at King Louie. Perhaps she still believed they would do the right thing—that if she played by the rules of man's law, she'd be exonerated.

Unfortunately, God's law is more exacting.

TEZ

They bussed her to the unassuming brown brick prison in the middle of a cotton field. When they first built it, there was nothing else around. Since then, the city has spread its fingers in the only direction left to go: east, across I-35 (Austin's original dividing line), and into the formerly fertile farmlands of the Colorado River Valley. The soil here is still clay-heavy, but blacker. Richer. It hibernates now beneath a twisting network of asphalt superstreets, the houses along these highways built one on top of another. To date, the development has been strictly residential— homes to house the bodies yet flocking to the live music capital of the world. But the strip malls are coming. Soon, fenced-in backyards will bump up against the prison's property lines, and incarcerated mothers will be able to watch their kids play at hopscotch. Or dig up buried dogs.

Mary Toni's cell was small and cold as the county's choice of building materials: gray cinderblock, freshly painted; a swept gray concrete floor. She suffered from poor circulation as it was. Locked up, her toes stayed bright red and her nose, stuffy. And the bleeding worsened. For years, ever since Sophie's death, she'd suffered never-ending periods and bouts of attendant anemia. Now blood leaked out of her like a faulty tap, staining one uniform after another and beading up at nights on the plastic mattress. Sometimes they left her to sit in her own mess for days at a time. She only felt clean when she showered twice a week, and when the burning Texas sun beat down on her in the yard.

THE CORRECTIONAL OFFICER

Everyone was talking about Marie Antoinette the morning she got transferred to our facility. Every whisper more scandalous than the last.

"I heard she's part of a cult," the intake officer said.

"I heard she slept with her uncle," Larry, another guard, said.

"That's sick." And then, as if on second thought: "Is she hot?"

"Pretty average, I reckon. Though she's, like, the 'queen' of the cult or something. The only woman in it who's allowed to have kids."

"Ew, she had kids with her uncle?"

"No, the cult leader, her husband. Though, if she really was sleeping with her uncle, who knows? Sounds like a paternity test is in order."

"So what's her charge? Is being in a cult illegal?"

"No, but incest is."

"They haven't proven anything yet. She was arraigned on charges of receiving stolen property. Something about a diamond necklace."

"Not any old necklace," Shelly, the prison's only female correctional officer said. "The most expensive diamond necklace in the world. It cost almost fourteen million dollars, and it was Marie Antoinette's uncle who gave it to her."

"Or so they say. She denies it. Says she knew nothing about it."

"And the uncle?"

"That's the best part. Her uncle is Adam Habsburg, the fucking governor."

Their mouths dropped open and they laughed in amazement. I guess they'd missed the recent news headlines. "Okay, I call dibs," Larry said. "This one I gotta see for myself."

She processed in around ten. Paperwork, body cavity search, brown jumpsuit and rubber slippers, in that order. Larry walked her back to her cell, then came to my office to gossip.

"Well?" I said. Despite myself, I was curious.

"Well nothing," he said, clearly disappointed. "She's, like, totally normal. Quiet. Hardly said a word, except to answer direct questions. She has a weird tattoo on her chest. That's about it."

"How'd she seem?"

He thought for a moment. "Resolute? Like, not resigned, but accepting of what was happening all the same. I think I get why she's the queen."

"Let me guess: She expected you to wait on her hand and foot. Pulled a face at the uniform, nose in the air, all that."

"No. It was more like nothing fazed her. Like, she trusted she'd be okay because everything has always been okay for her."

"She did come from a cult. Lots of people crammed

together in a small space. A natural pecking order. Maybe prison reminds her of home."

"Maybe," Larry agreed. "Only . . . "

"What?"

"Well, it turns out she's been in that cult since she was fourteen. Maybe . . . maybe home, for her, *is* a prison."

I stared at him. Hard. "Larry, don't do it. Don't start empathizing with them. Once you start seeing them as people instead of prisoners, your job gets a helluva lot harder. Because then you let down your guard and let them in, and that's when you get hurt."

"Yeah, okay. Just saying. It's possible she's not the guilty one."

"Which is exactly the point of the justice system," I said. "She stays here until trial, in case she is guilty; and if she's not, she goes home no worse for the wear." Images of the last girl brawl flashed through my mind. Contrary to popular opinion, catfights aren't limited to hair-pulling and claws. Prison makes people more creative. "Well," I amended, remembering the shiv made from a shard of reinforced-chickenwire glass, "not too much worse for the wear."

THE WARDEN

Marie Antoinette was with us for several weeks before I made it to D Block to meet her. I knew who she was—she was all the officers talked about—but as she wasn't causing problems and the prison's annual budget was, I gave it and not her my full attention. I relied on staff reports instead of checking in on her myself, until Larry found her in a pool of blood. I heard him shout the code into his walkie-talkie, and then I ran. Because nothing fucks up a budget like an inmate death.

The obvious assumption was that she'd tried to kill herself. With what, though? She'd been given her own cell, and her contact with other inmates had been both limited and supervised. Then, we couldn't find a mark on her. The railroads of her wrists were undamaged. Her throat was untouched. Her ankles unmarked. So weak from blood loss that she required assistance to stand, it was only when three correctional officers pulled her to her feet that we realized where the blood was coming from.

But what tool had she used to perform the abortion?

The prison doctor took a look at her. Mary Toni swore up and down that she wasn't pregnant, had not been pregnant since Sophie, whoever that was. She didn't know why she was bleeding down there, either. "Though if I had to guess . . . " she told the physician.

"Yes?"

"Never mind." She wouldn't tell us what she'd been about to say. That was all she said that day, or the next, or the day after that. She bled through her clothes most days. The prison doctor couldn't figure out why. Nothing was obviously "wrong" with her. There were no signs of trauma. We gave her pads, and eventually adult diapers. It was like the period from hell.

THE INMATE

It was gross. Who just sits there slowly bleeding to death day in and day out? And in, like, the same expanding puddle for hours on end? They put me in the cell across from her and told me to watch her. *Was* she secretly hurting herself in some way?

Because I was bored, I reported that she was. "Hey!" I called to Larry, when he next walked by on rounds. "Hey! I just saw her! She has a piece of fence!"

Larry came as fast as his stubby little legs would carry him. He looked at her, but directed his questions to me. "Really? A piece of fence? Did you see what she did with it?"

Mary Toni, it should be noted, was at that moment

asleep on the bunk in her cell. They'd given her a mattress covered in plastic and taken all her sheets to cut down on bloody laundry. Also because there were fewer places to hide things then, were she in fact hiding something.

"Yeah, a piece of fence," I said to Larry. "Like, from a chain-link fence, you know, only straightened out so it's long and sharp at one end? I'm not sure where she stashed it just now."

"Habsburg-Auguste?" It was the only kind of command Larry knew how to give—more like a polite request. He wanted her to come to the door, so he could cuff her hands this side of the bars, then enter her cell to toss it.

"She's totally faking being asleep," I said.

He called her again. She stirred. Muttered. Raised her head to look at him.

"There's a witness saying you just tried to hurt yourself, Marie Antoinette. I gotta come in there, so I need you to come here. Can you stand?"

She rolled over and glanced self-consciously at the seat of her pants. A small stain blooming, but not a puddle yet. She got up and walked over to the bars.

"That's a good girl." He cuffed her wrists, unlocked her cell. "Now, where is it? Where's the piece of fence?" She didn't answer, so he flipped the plastic mattress over. Kicked the metal frame of her bunk for good measure, probably hoping the impact would loosen anything she might have hastily stuffed in a ledge. Larry even peered into her toilet. He sighed. "All right, what'd you do with it?"

A cramp struck Mary Toni then. She buckled, falling to her knees. Her arms stretched long above her in the cuffs. I saw Larry's hand go briefly to his nightstick. An unconscious reaction. He was scared! Unable to help myself, I let out a little giggle. He glared at me, realizing what I'd done. Embarrassed and mad, Larry decided to punish us both. No dinner for me that night—and Mary Toni, he kept chained to the bars.

She stayed in that position for hours. Kneeling, sitting

back on her feet, her hands for all the world like she was praying. The only problem was that she was facing my cell. There was nowhere for me to hide, and even though she kept her head bowed, I had the sense that she was watching me through her long, stringy white hair. I'd seen those eyes before. They were black.

It was sometime after lights out that Larry came back. He took the cuffs off gently, having calmed down again, and scared himself with the bruises they'd left on her wrists, which had hung at an odd angle from the cuffs for far too long. He knew I saw them, too, and that I could get him in trouble. "Say anything," he sneered, "and you won't eat for a week." I mimed zipping my lips.

After Larry went off to do only Larry knows what, I spoke to Mary Toni directly for the first time. "Hey. You okay?"

She was sitting on the bunk now, her back against the wall. She didn't turn her head or open her eyes, but she answered me. "Peachy," she said. Low and dry as the desert.

Suddenly, I felt bad. I owed this bitch nothing, but I didn't have to antagonize her, either. "Sorry," I said. "It was shitty of me to call Larry on you."

"Whatever," she said. "You're hardly the first person to turn on me for no reason lately."

A thought occurred to me. Something I'd overheard. "You're the one from the cult."

She smirked. "Is that what they're saying?"

"A sex cult. You slept with your uncle and you worship some obscure dude from the Bible."

"Mm." Neither confirming nor denying.

"So where's the necklace he gave you now?"

"Believe it or not, I've only ever seen the same picture as you. The one they keep flashing on the news. If the necklace does exist, I've never held it. And if I had, well, according to you I'm pretty good at making things disappear."

"If you're not doing it to yourself, why do you keep bleeding?"

"Some of the Sashes put a curse on me." Completely deadpan. It's the only reason I halfway believed her.

"They're the cult members? And what do you mean, 'curse'?"

"I made a mistake," she said. "Or, not even a mistake. Because that makes it sound unintentional. I made a choice. It fucked everyone over. And now they're getting back at me."

I nodded. Her situation sounded pretty similar to my own.

Later that night, when the blood between her legs woke her up and her rustling on that damn plastic mattress in turn roused me, I was moved to tear a wide strip of fabric from my sheet, ball it up, and toss it across the corridor into her cell. "It's clean," I said. "You can use it to sop up the blood."

She did, and we both fell back asleep. I awoke to the sounds of Mary Toni yelling, a nightstick striking D-Block bars. There were three of them in the cell with her, forcing her into a turtle suit.

"Why are you doing this?" Mary Toni protested. She wriggled and tried to break free of their grip. They held her tighter. One guard hit his baton against the bars again, like he was a judge calling for order in his court.

"You keep hurting yourself," he said.

"I do not!"

"The bleeding's one thing," he said. "Now we find you with bruises around your wrists and a contraband partial sheet. What were you trying to do? Suffocate your hands to death?"

"I'm not stupid," Mary Toni said. It sounded like she thought he was.

They hauled her off to solitary. A few weeks later, I saw her on TV.

THE LAWYER

I was under-qualified for the case, having not practiced law for almost a decade by the time Ennoia was arrested. On the other hand, I knew her better than any other lawyer could, as I'd spent the last decade not practicing law serving her. Which, in retrospect, maybe blinded me a little. Because I definitely thought she was innocent. And when you feel that strongly about a person or an ideal, you tend not to think so rationally at times. You get carried away by passion, by the power of your convictions. That's what faith is, right? At its best? So, yeah, I put in all the work. I read *Hampton v. State of Texas* and *People v. Koffel*, two recent cases in which the accused was charged with receipt of stolen property and found not guilty. I studied cases of purported incest, some with convictions, some that saw the charges overturned. I revisited Ruby Ridge and Waco and Buddhafield to see how juries had ruled in the past on cases featuring former cult members. I was prepared as I could be to go to bat for her.

But I never got the chance to.

THE MAID

The day that Ennoia came home on bail, no one was really sure how to act around her. Was she guilty? Did it matter? A label slapped on her by man's law had nothing to do with God's law. A guilty verdict could never change the fact that she was the mother of the heirs. What was important to determine, however, was that she was really Ennoia. Sure, God had spoken to King Louie more than two decades ago, told him that she was the one, gave him a little tickle in his crotch for a child. But now King Louie was doubting that revelation. Was wondering if he himself had been deceived. In which case, sleeping with her uncle and conceiving mongrel children could very well have been in Marie Antoinette's true nature. In which case, it was his fault, not hers, for fucking up.

He had to know for sure one way or another, 100%, through and through, no lingering questions in his heart. He could wait and hope for another sign from God. Or he could put her to the test. See just what his wife was made of.

TEZ

They wanted me to find out the truth. "Just touch her," they said. "It's easy. Then we'll know."

"It doesn't work like that," I reminded them, now fourteen myself—same as Mary Toni when she was taken. "I can't pick and choose what I see. The visions just come."

"You can try, anyway."

But I refused. Already I was the only one who knew about Fersen. I didn't want to know if my mother was also sleeping with my uncle.

Of course, because I wouldn't condemn her, I couldn't clear her name, either.

I was a selfish child, and Mary Toni died.

THE CHOREOGRAPHER

It wasn't so important to clear Adam's name. He'd served his purpose. People knew about Simon's Sorrow now. They knew about Simon. Instant converts and the curious alike were flocking from around the country to the branches closest to them. To worship. Learn more. To practice Restoration and prepare for the Second Coming.

It was time, therefore, to see Adam out, before he could do any real damage to the church's name. People knew he was a spokesperson, a celebrity face, for the church, and they believed that he'd slept with his niece, a church member. They did not all know that his niece was also Ennoia, the Holy Mother, the sacred chalice of the heirs. That he, and by extension she, had sullied the Simon's Sorrow brand, throwing human lust in the face of the divine. A story that would, if it got out, have been our total undoing.

So we cut the weak links from the chain.

King Louie invited Adam for a blessing ceremony: "A ritual," he promised, "that will clear the clouds surrounding you and let the truth be known." Adam still thought, at this point, that King Louie believed him, believed in his, Adam's, innocence—understood how politics were a game and politicians the pawns—that on this chess board the poles were reversed, the power was in the hands of the people—that they were the kings and queens, the knights and bishops moving in larger, more threatening swaths across the country—and what popular opinion dictated, he was obligated to act on, to take the fall for, even when it was in fact a bunch of non-kosher baloney. He thought King Louie, being the head of an organization himself, "got" it. What he didn't bank on was the church leader's more sophisticated understanding of sea changes. The notion that a leader serves by taking action . . . and the action he takes is never to serve anyone other than the Lord.

So the Chef prepared an artful charcuterie. The Sommelier, several bottles of Adam's favorite pinot. The Pharmacist spiked the pinot with ketamine. The Laundress brought a fresh pillow for his lolling head. The Nurse wiped the drool from his mouth. The Tailor supplied a hundred-foot parachute cord. The Fisherman tied the cord to a hook. The Butcher threaded the hook through Adam's back: around his spine and between his shoulder blades. The Contractor strung the cord from the rafters above the altar. The Groundskeepers latched onto the ends of the cord like a team. They leaned back in tandem and heaved.

Adam's body rose like Christ suspended from the cross, a body-raising if not a barn-raising, but just as symbolic. For they were building a new structure, an additional wing of the temple—a revision to, a re-envisioning of, the church, which henceforth would stand strong on its own reputation, its own emerging dominion as a global power.

Thus draped, Adam looked like he was flying. A flesh-and-blood version of the statue of Simon if ever there was one. His own body weight would eventually kill him, once his muscles ripped and tore away from his spine.

To complete the Biblical tableau, King Louie ordered strung up in adjacent fashion the Accountant to Adam's right and the PR Rep to Adam's left: two Sashes King Louie considered equally guilty. The Accountant had failed to catch the giant transfer of funds into one of the church's shell accounts, and the PR Rep was actively failing to contain, spin, or salvage anything positive about the public shit show at all. Ropes were knotted around their ankles and they were hoisted up feet-first. There they hung upside down, bound, gagged, and wriggling.

"In the Gospel of Luke," King Louie began, "we are told that during Our Blessed Lord's crucifixion, there were two other men condemned to the same death, one to either side of Him. The one to Christ's right has become known as the Penitent Thief, and the one to His left, the Impenitent Thief."

He strode to stand before Adam, and between the Accountant and the PR Rep. "While both men were suffering the same gruesome execution, and whereas both were in the presence of Christ, they reacted quite differently. The Impenitent Thief begged to come down from his cross. He *dared* Christ to save them and Himself."

King Louie glared at the three suspended bodies, two of which were still wiggling wildly and whimpering. "The Penitent Thief, on the other hand, asked to be taken up with Christ. 'Remember me when You come into Your Kingdom,' he said. And do you know how Christ responded?" King Louie looked at his congregation, waiting for a response that never came.

"Christ said, 'Amen, I say to you, today you will be with Me in Paradise.' That is the lesson of the martyr who accepts his cross. Who places his hope not in this world, but in the promise of the next."

On that note, King Louie exited the chapel. He left Adam, who was unconscious now, hanging from his spine, and he left the other two, who would not lose consciousness, hanging from their feet. The veins in the upper body cannot, like the legs, prevent the reflux of blood. Instead, the blood vessels rupture. Blood pools in the chest and the head. The contents of the stomach shake loose, get caught in the lungs. Eventually eyeballs burst from the immense pressure. It was a well-choreographed dance, only none of us stayed to watch it. The only thing worse than being martyred for your sins is when no one sticks around to watch you die.

THE HANDYMAN

Satisfying! Though I myself would have gone with something like Dante's version of hell. The third pit of Circle VIII in *The Inferno* is reserved for those guilty of simony, or using their positions in the church for personal monetary gain. That's what Adam did when he let Simon's Sorrow propel his political career, only to blow all that money on a necklace for a woman he never should have been with in the first place. Dante placed the simonists upside-down in round holes the size of baptismal fonts. The soles of their protruding feet he set on fire, an inverse baptism. Instead of being anointed with oil, they were doused in it.

MERCY

Adam's death, like his election, was a political decision.

THE JEWELER'S APPRENTICE

Mary Toni was next. We left Adam, the Accountant, and the PR Rep in the chapel and followed King Louie to the Icebox, where he'd kept Mary Toni imprisoned since bailing her out.

Somehow we knew, without being told, that we should walk side by side, forming two neat lines behind him. That this was a procession as much as a means of bi-locating; a journey and not just a field trip. We walked toward Mary Toni's doom, and we walked toward our own—for *if* King Louie found her wanting, and *if* the consequence was full Restoration, there'd be an all-out manhunt when she didn't show up in court for her trial. And would we really be able to hide anything then? Would we want to, given a chance to share our message with the world?

THE CHEF

And then she stood before us like she had on Day One. Stripped of her clothes as King Louie would have had her stripped of her dignity, but emboldened, too. Thirty-seven years old—more than twenty years the senior of the frightened teenager who'd once trembled on stage in the Great Hall, and later, acted upon the same. Her body was rounder. Her heavy breasts the trademark of the Madonna. She did not hunch her shoulders but squared them. Did not blush when commanded to submit her sex for inspection. She seemed, in all the ways that mattered, to have *become*. Fully Mary Toni and fully Ennoia. A mother who carried her children; a queen who carried her mantle;

a messiah who carried the key to another realm—formerly heaven, though now, it was assumed, hell.

Still, some things had not changed. Her dark eyes for one, which looked at nothing and no one but an invisible point in the distance. Unnaturally white hair that shrouded said eyes when she wanted it to, stealing their meaning.

FERSEN

It sucked. It sucked so hard seeing her up on that stage, made to stand there without any clothes while everyone judged the wonderful woman they'd claimed for so long to love. It was heartbreaking and took every last vestige of my own resolve and self-control not to run right up there, usher her off-stage with me, at the very least throw a goddamn blanket around her shivering shoulders. It confirmed for me that humankind has never evolved past its baser animal instincts; that is, self-preservation by means of aligning oneself with the dominant group, so as not to be cast aside and left to die the way the group was doing now to their former leader, their beautiful queen, Ennoia. The whole situation sickened me, and at the same time, planted a niggling little seed of excitement. Wonder at the possibility that, once left behind, she might not be missed; and if not missed, might she and I not escape—into each other's arms, in some other protected place, in some other country entirely? I could teach and she could raise our kids and we could start over. A new royal family, of the color and flavor I'd always believed ours should be. Free at last to love and be loved, without secrets, judgment, doubt. Oh, I lived whole lifetimes in the ten minutes she stood exposed onstage. I mapped alternate histories around her bare thighs, up the curve of one naked, perennially forbidden shoulder blade. Mary Toni was trying hard not to fall apart up there, and I, I was filled with hope! For the first time since I'd met her some thirty years before, the life

I'd dreamed of with her felt achievable. I'd only to reach out and grasp it, and taking her hand . . .

But not yet. I could not do anything to give myself away. To betray our relationship, thereby adding more fuel to the fire, meant that not only would Mary Toni most certainly have been punished immediately and extensively, but I would have been martyred right alongside Adam as well. Another soldier in the perpetual war who had served his purpose and run his course, and had no further choice but to retire and make room for the next in line.

THE TAILOR

She was brilliant up there. Impeccable. I would have challenged anyone in the room to find anything at fault with her bearing, her character, her body. Only persons of complete and utter integrity can stand that tall under fire and not buckle, for it is the strength of their convictions, their commitment to their values, that supports them even when the floor of the gallows gives way.

The whole time, too, she took their slander without retort. I remember her saying just one thing, and even that with her head held high: "Would contempt for their queen be cause for celebration, then let them, my Lord, eat cake."

THE GROUNDSKEEPER

She said no such thing.

THE CHEF

Still, after everyone had had their say, King Louie announced he needed more time to think. He remanded Mary Toni back to the Icebox, which was barely better than her cell at the prison on 969, except for the food. *That* we made sure was better. And we supplied her more pads and changed out her clothes more regularly, because she continued bleeding heavily from below. "Fibroids, most likely," the Doctor had said. "Or it could be uterine cancer." If the latter, then she was dying before us, might die before King Louie made up his mind. We couldn't have that. He needed time for God to speak to him, to reveal His true will. While he waited, he directed me in making all kinds of weird emetics and purges, as though by forcing it up and out the other end, he could somehow cure—at least forestall—the rotting taking place inside. It didn't work. Whatever properties those strange herbs and flowers had, that he'd coerced the Groundskeepers into gathering from the property's darker corners, made her vomit so intensely that soon she was puking up blood, too. And then, when not puking, coughing it up, like she'd somehow developed Joey's tuberculosis on top of it all. Though in those damp, imperfect conditions it was more likely the mold.

At any rate, one morning when I was delivering her breakfast, I found her sprawled in yet another puddle of her own blood. And while I'd hoped to give her a gift—her favorite breakfast, a tree-nut-based muesli with fresh yogurt (homemade!) and berries—she beat me to it. As I was sliding the tray beneath the cell door slot, she reached for my fingers. Caught one there, with her own. She meant me no harm—she didn't have the strength for it—only wanted to get my attention. Opening her mouth, caked at the corners with blood, she whispered, "The world, my dear Agnes, is a strange thing." I gasped and fell back where I was squatting, because no one in Simon's Sorrow knew my name. Rare was the Sash—King Louie, Madame DuBarry, Mercy, Savoy—who went by anything other than their title. But there she was, speaking to me like a sister, like she'd known who I was all along. And while it touched me, deeply, and something shifted in my heart toward her, I felt profoundly scared, too. There was simply no way she should have, could have, known. Unless this was Marie Antoinette's miracle, and God or Simon was speaking through her to me. But no, that thought was too much, so I pushed it aside and pushed her fingers away and stood up and ran back to the kitchen. To the familiar safety of carrots and milk, apples and cheese: everyday objects that didn't speak unless spoken to, and not even then.

THE BUTCHER

They gave her ergot for the bleeding. Same thing they'd given her mother. Predictably, it led to bigger problems. Blurry vision. Confusion. Convulsions. At one point, I swear I heard her say, "I always knew having kids was no good." As though pregnancy had caused the bleeding. Maybe it had. What do I know? But it seems a sorry thing for the mother of the heirs to say. Like she would put her life before her kids. Seems a sorry thing for any mother to say. She just wasn't who we thought she was.

FERSEN

When Mary Toni asked me to bring the kids to her, I didn't act immediately. She was in the cell of the Icebox. Guards were stationed outside it at all times. They'd been given explicit instructions not to let the mother interact with her children, and I knew that to try would only cause further problems. But also, I believed they'd soon have all the time in the world together. King Louie just needed a bit to come to his senses. As a result, it's my fault that Tez and Charlie didn't get to spend those final few weeks with their mom. I kept visiting, but I didn't give them that same opportunity. And I likewise deprived Mary Toni.

It wasn't until the morning of her death that I finally snuck the heirs down to see her. I knew the Sashes on guard duty well; they trusted me. I convinced them to take a break while I kept watch over the prisoner. As soon as they stepped out, I called Tez and Charlie downstairs from where they were hiding in the kitchen by banging a metal spoon on the concrete floor in a rhythm we'd worked out in advance. Tez was fifteen then and Charlie was almost seven. While I'd done my best to prepare them for the sight and smell of their wretched mother decomposing in captivity, they balked at the entrance to the Icebox. They were scared of the thing that looked a bit like their mother, but also like some bloody she-monster, and who certainly no longer smelled of lavender oil. Mary Toni lay on the floor with her face pressed up to the slot and one hand reaching her fingers out to touch them. Only they wouldn't, at first, get close enough.

"It's all right," I said to Tez and Charlie. "It's your mother. She won't bite. She wants to see you."

And from behind the door, Mary Toni started crying and pleading. "My babies. My beautiful ones. Please. I love you so much."

Then she collected herself enough to sing to them the song her father Frank had always sung to her. "You are my sunshine, my only sunshine," warbled out broken but beautiful from the small, dark slot and the boy heir, Charlie, broke into a run. He skidded to a stop outside her cell door and fell to the ground, where he grabbed her fingers and pressed his body up against the door trying in vain to get close to her. He was bawling and Mary Toni was somewhere between laughing and crying and while the scene broke my heart, I know it repaired hers. I wondered why I hadn't tried harder to get them together sooner, and I also knew that the minutes were ticking by. "Come on, Tez." I waved to her. "Hurry. We don't have much time." Reluctantly, she joined her brother, and then Mary Toni was asking them how they were and telling them not to worry, that they'd let her out soon and everything would be okay again.

I walked away to give them a moment together. And because from halfway up the stairs I'd be able to see when the Guards were on their way back. I cried then, for Mary Toni and her children, and for the devil I'd unwittingly become. She wasn't the monster; I was. I'd been so afraid for my own safety that I'd done nothing to advocate for hers. I was a coward, and no coward was worthy of Ennoia. I resolved to go straight to King Louie after tucking the children into bed for the night.

TEZ

She didn't look like my mother, or smell like my mother. But when she sang she sounded like her, and the sound rang true in my heart. Charlie and I crowded around the slot in the metal door and cried and asked her why she'd abandoned us, why she didn't come out and take care of us. And were the bad things people were saying about her true? Was Dad our dad? Were we the products of incest? What did incest even mean? We asked her so many questions she couldn't answer them all, and then she said, "Shh, shh, my children, there are things I must tell you. Please be quiet and listen, that I may say them while I have the time. For I don't think I will be of this world much longer."

Well, what did *that* mean and how could we possibly keep quiet when everything she said inspired a dozen more questions?

"My babies, no matter what happens, you must promise me one thing. Okay? Promise me just this one thing. You must forgive your father and the rest of the Sashes for what they have done to me. And you must forgive anyone else who would speak ill of me. Don't listen to the news. Don't let them fill your head with lies. This, here"—and she grabbed our arms as best she could through the slot—"this is what's real. This is who you are. You come from me and you come from God. You are children of God above all else. God is the only father you owe any allegiance to, for it was by His hand that you, my miracles, were delivered unto me."

I saw, then, her head on a platter. Like the head of John the Baptist, displayed on silver for the party. Shadow figures were gathering around the table, forks in hand and hungry mouths salivating. As though she, all along, had been the intended sacrifice—when the people she'd served would demand she herself be served to them.

The concrete of the floor was digging into my shoulder where I lay sideways upon it. I wanted to shift my weight, but then Mary Toni was squeezing our fingers so tightly it hurt and I didn't dare move. "And you were born pure, do you hear me?" she was saying. "Perfect and pure. No original sin for you. No such thing as original sin ever. You were conceived in love and born in love and it's how I would have you spend the rest of your days: mirroring that love to the world. Which means, first and foremost, letting go of the hate you might feel in your hearts before and even after this long nightmare is over. Forgive your transgressors. Live in love. And obey Fersen as though he is your second father."

Fersen called down the stairwell then. His voice was a hoarse, loud whisper, but I could hear the edge of panic in it. We didn't have much time.

"I love you," Mary Toni was saying, and Charlie and I were crying, because even though we were children yet we knew that this was bigger than us, and we'd be powerless in the way of all children to stop the things that happened to us and to those we loved.

"I promise to say goodbye if I can," she said. Then Fersen was scooping us up and tearing our grasping hands out of hers and I screamed and that was the last time I saw her.

THE ALTAR SERVER

Mid-morning, October 16, 2002, I went to see Ennoia in her cell. She was curled in a corner of the floor and shivering, and indeed it was cold there underground. I bade her good morning and asked if she needed anything, if there was anything within my limited scope of access that I could grant her.

"King Louie," she said. Her lips cracked and bled with the effort.

"I'm sorry," I said. "He's not available right now. He sent me to you in his place. Is there anything else?"

She was quiet for so long that I didn't think she was going to answer me. But then she did. "Pray with me," she said.

Formal prayers weren't part of the Simon's Sorrow orthodoxy. We broadly applied the term "prayer" to mean any intentional group activity, whether meditation or Restoration. It usually wasn't done by just two individuals at a time. But Jesus said, "Where two or three gather in my name, there am I," so I decided to humor her. "How should we begin?" I asked.

And she started reciting a poem I'd never heard before. About a queen, the Virgin Mary, and she a "banished child" of Eve. After, she was quiet again.

"I don't know that one," I admitted. "But it was nice."

"I learned it in Catholic school," she said. "Felt appropriate for the occasion."

Another beat passed. She recited the poem again. A third time. Each time she finished, she started over again, until it became the kind of rhythmic, whole-mind mantra that if you ask me, prayers were originally meant to be. The meanings of the words fell away and left just Mary Toni, banished daughter, in the valley of tears that was her cell. She wasn't weeping, but with everything she had left she was mourning—every conscious decision and happenstance event that had led to that moment in time.

What would become of Marie Antoinette Habsburg-Auguste? What of her children, the surviving heirs, Tez and Charlie?

Where would we, the Sashes, end up without our queen?

THE GROUNDSKEEPER

We were about to find out.

The final blow, the one that ultimately did Ennoia in, making King Louie's decision less a choice and more an eventuality, was Charlie's out-of-the-blue assertion that he'd been abused. And not by just anyone, but by his own mother—the queen and whitest light of them all, Marie Antoinette.

THE BUTCHER

It was an oddly cold day for mid-October. Charlie was in the chophouse with me—that's what I called the utility room off the kitchen where we cleaned the chickens and pigs—when I noticed the bruises on his wrist. There were several, in the long, slender shapes of what could only be fingers. Like a hand had grabbed him roughly and not let go. It could have been his older sister Tez. Part of a game, or even a fight they'd gotten into, maybe. But as naturally protective as adults are of children, we were extra protective of the heirs. Nothing caught our attention we didn't then excavate. We always dug down into the roots of the thing.

Myself a bigger, hairy man, I thought Charlie might feel more comfortable confiding in a woman. I looked around and spied the Chef in the kitchen. She was boiling eggs at the stove. Telling Charlie I needed another knife, I snuck in there and shared with the Chef my suspicions. "Maybe it's nothing," I said. "Or maybe someone's hurting him."

THE CHEF

I took it from there. Packed a picnic lunch for myself and the boy and we went out to the garden. As Charlie bit into an apple, his right hand holding the fruit to his mouth, the bruises on his right wrist clearly visible, I said brightly, "Oh! What happened there?" And pointed to his arm.

"What?" Charlie asked, turning his arm this way and that, like he'd find a ladybug crawling on it.

"There," I said, touching one of the marks. Charlie flinched. Clearly they hurt.

"Did you have an accident?"

Charlie shook his head, but didn't say anything.

"Did Tez do that?"

Another shake.

"Charlie?" I waited for him to look at me, to see what I could read in his eyes. "Did someone hurt you?"

He began picking blades of grass, ignoring me.

"You can tell me," I said. "It's okay. You're not in trouble."

"Let's play soccer," Charlie said, jumping up and changing the subject.

"Sure, but first I need to know if someone hurt you."

He sighed and fidgeted and wouldn't meet my eyes.

"Was it a man or a woman?" I asked. "Someone who lives here?"

He pursed his lips, now swinging his shoe over the grass.

"Does your mom know? Should we go see her?"

"No!" Charlie yelled, the fear in his suddenly saucer-like eyes unmistakable.

I felt sick and could barely ask the next question. "Charlie, was it your mom who hurt you?"

THE MAID

The boy came careening into the Great Hall so fast I thought for sure he was going to wipe out and crack his head on my wet floors.

"Charlie!" I reprimanded him. "I just mopped! Slow down!"

But he didn't. He kept right on running to his room.

The Chef came in straight after him. "Have you seen King Louie?" she asked, breathless and a little wide-eyed.

"The temple," I said, and she took off fast as the boy had. That afternoon, I found out why.

THE BUTCHER

It was worse than I ever could have imagined. The lying, cheating, stinking *whore* was not only cheating on her husband with her uncle; she was also diddling her son. How we ever held her up as Ennoia, I'm sure I don't know. Jesus wept, kid. Jesus wept.

TEZ

I tried to tell them it was an accident. Mary Toni had left the same dark marks on my arms when she'd grabbed at me through the slot of her cell. But mine had faded; they didn't look so clearly like hands. And yes, Charlie was scared of our mother, but only because she *was* scary down in the Icebox, her skin gone to gray and bleeding all the time.

But then Charlie started talking. Said how she'd once made him get naked in front of her when it wasn't bath time. She hadn't touched him, then, but she'd touched herself while watching him—and I cried because my brother couldn't have made that stuff up. He didn't know enough to. Had he dreamed it? Or had it happened?

I had to know. Against my better judgment, I took his hand. I saw things about my brother I'd never known. The secret hole where he hid his Hot Wheels cars. A private fear of pill bugs he didn't dare reveal. I saw the last time we'd played Mother, May I with Joey—an image so crystalline it at once broke my heart and made my heart burst with love—and I saw the truth about who had hurt Charlie.

Worse, I saw that it didn't matter. There was nothing I could say to clear Mary Toni's name. In the vision, I tried a hundred ways to get them to listen, and each time my words got twisted into a weapon they used against her. It was the most helpless I have ever felt.

Of small consolation was the knowledge that the guilty party, at least, had already gotten their due.

THE JEWELER'S APPRENTICE

There was no more deliberation, no further investigation. On the strength of his only surviving son's horrifying testimony, that evening King Louie privately decided to execute Marie Antoinette. It was to be a mercy killing, a kindness granted to save her immortal soul. Incest between consenting adults was one thing, but sexually abusing your own child? That level of atonement called for full Restoration.

TEZ

To be fair, Mary Toni had herself been a child bride, and even King Louie hadn't dared touch her. So I do get where he was coming from. Except that he was completely wrong.

MOTHER-EATING

Only a select few were invited to watch the ceremony; even fewer to participate.

FERSEN

Because who else could tell this part of the story, right? But the person who'd been there from the beginning?

It was midnight. I couldn't sleep, having been unable to locate King Louie and deliver my confession. Irritable, I wandered into the kitchen for a snack. The glow of the open refrigerator might have given me away except that I heard them before they saw me: a group of Sashes carrying out King Louie's orders. Acting on instinct—knowing only that *I did not want to be caught* (Caught doing what? Eating? Hardly a crime. Still.)—I shut the fridge door and pressed myself up against the walk-in pantry, hoping to blend in with the shadows. They passed by talking quietly among themselves. The Butcher. The Baker. Two Whores.

No one noticed me.

How could I have known what they were up to? And yet I had my suspicions. Once they'd gone downstairs, I tiptoed to the edge of the stairwell, listening. Voices. The grate and creak of dry metal. A shuffling, as people and prisoner gathered, stood, began walking again.

Long story short, Mary Toni didn't get to tell the children goodbye. Simon's Sorrow secreted their queen from her cell in the middle of the night. They bound her arms behind her and put a blindfold on her. Were they trying to obscure the Reaper's identity? Why bother—she knew who steered her by the shoulders. Or was it meant to be a tiny grace? If she could not see what cruel fate awaited her, perhaps she might fear it less. Might be oblivious to the hour of her death; and thereby more peaceful.

Thus blinded, she was taken to the chapel. Helped up

to the risers on which Adam had been martyred. Where stood a wooden guillotine.

THE TIGRESS

Except she didn't need help. Not really. She'd walked that stone floor with her eyes closed so many times as a teenager she could do it blindfolded. The stones were a little more worn down, maybe, but nothing else about the temple had changed.

FERSEN

Thinking of it now, I can't help but shake my head and laugh. Mary Toni lived with them for twenty-three years, and in the end, they didn't know her at all. Captivity and the endless hours it had afforded her to think had been one long practice in acceptance. The six-year-old who'd been terrified of death because it had robbed her of life *while she was still living* had come to more certain terms with the end than you or I ever will.

No, it was me who ran up to her shaking and emphatic that they let her go at once, that there'd been an egregious mistake. "It's me you want," I screamed, "not her. She's innocent. For fuck's sake, she's *Ennoia*. Let her go. Put me in her place if you must have blood, for blood there will be should you wrongly spill a drop of the holy mother's. Stop!" I said. "Stop!"

But a whole crowd of them were rushing to restrain me, and from the corner of my eye I could see King Louie. Did he know it was I who'd defiled his bride? Who'd passed my genes onto the children he'd then passed off as his own? I forgot about him just as promptly, though, when Mary Toni looked up from the block they'd kneeled her before, and, still blindfolded, called my name. I broke free of the Sashes restraining me and ran to her. Her head on the mantle of the elevated guillotine was level with my own.

I held her face, caressed it. Kissed her like I only ever had in the privacy of her bedroom, or before that, the seclusion of my fantasies. I told her I loved her, that the children loved her, that I was going to rescue her yet. "We were stupid," I said, "to stay for so long. It's my fault. I won't let them hurt you."

Then they were pulling me away and King Louie was shouting and I have only the untrustworthiness of my own two weeping eyes to back up what happened next. I saw, I swear I saw her mouth the words, "All things lead me to you. Fate may separate us but not disunite us."

Those words—they haunt me still. I looked them up once and found they mimicked something Julie says in Rousseau's novel of the same name. I have since read the book cover to cover fifteen times, wondering if she didn't mean to impart a further message to me through it. But while the letters contained therein are beautiful, they describe another relationship entirely.

Unless my experience of our love was really that different from my lover's.

The Guard and the Butcher held me immobile in a chair off to the side with a clear view of the nave. King Louie approached Ennoia to make his final sermon.

THE GUARD

Fersen was struggling so hard it took all of my attention to hold him still. I didn't wonder until later at the things he'd said to Mary Toni, or why he was fighting quite so adamantly for her innocence. When it became clear that he wasn't going to shut up long enough for King Louie to speak, I took the extra blindfold from my back pocket and tied it between his teeth like a gag. He jerked his head back and glared at me, but just because he was a fellow Sash never had, and did not then, warrant special treatment.

THE WHORE

I felt honored that King Louie had chosen little old me to help Restore Marie Antoinette. Sometimes wives need to be put in their place even when they're fulfilling God's prophecy. No bad deed and all that.

And it was exciting. Sneaking around in the wee hours, just a few of us clued in to what was happening. Beautiful, too. The Contractor had polished the gillo-whatsit with oil until it shone, and the blade up there was like another stained-glass window the way it caught and reflected the light. I'd felt cool, like I was 'in on the secret,' since joining Simon's Sorrow and the night the Tattooist had made it official. But this moment seemed extra privileged. For whatever happened, it would alter the course of the whole prophecy. And after, King Louie would tell us the new plan, as God would tell him.

But he was speaking just then, and had been for some time, pacing back and forth in front of the risers and rambling on and on. "Put to death, therefore," he said, quoting Colossians, "what is earthly in you." These he ticked off on his fingers: "Sexual immorality. Impurity. Passion. Evil desire. Covetousness." He turned to consider his wife. "Which is idolatry."

She looked so smug up there. Can you imagine? On the brink of having her head chopped off, and still she thought she was God's gift.

I wish we could have killed her multiple times. You know, brought her back to life just to kill her again. That's what she deserved for cheating on the family. For taking the fucking apple from the fucking tree.

THE NANNY

They didn't invite me to their middle-of-the-night murder.

I happened upon it completely by accident. Charlie had woken up thirsty, and with his mother in the Icebox (or so we thought), he'd come to me for a cup of water. I'd gone down to the kitchen for a glass, which took me past the chapel, and that's when I saw her. Marie, kneeled before a literal chopping block, the blade of a guillotine strung high above her head. For several seconds, my heart stopped beating. Then I laughed. *I must be dreaming*, I thought. I shook my head and walked on to the kitchen, convinced that even thirsty Charlie was a figment of the illusion. *King Louie wouldn't order his wife's death. And if he did, we'd all be there to witness it.* The Sashes were nothing if not a family. We did everything together. Praying. Eating. Fucking. Restoration. All of it, even the not-so-nice bits, were part of building God's kingdom on earth.

But then I got the glass of water, and I passed the chapel again, and everything was just as it had been before, so I still thought I was in the dream. I decided to stay and watch because why not? From the block, where Marie seemed not the least upset—in fact, she was *whistling*; another indicator it was a dream—she listened to King Louie finish his usual sermon. Then, as if I'd spoken my thoughts aloud (*her resolve is mistaken for disdain, her dignity for indifference*), she turned her head toward me and said, "I am calm, as people are whose conscience is clear."

And the blade dropped, and I squeezed my eyes shut and willed myself to wake up, because I didn't want to see that, and I didn't know why my brain was feeding me such gruesome images.

THE GROUNDSKEEPER

It was "Singing in the Rain." That's what she was whistling.

THE TUTOR

Still and always Alex DeLarge.

THE ARTIST

Watching the queen get beheaded felt like a Technicolor hallucination. Like watching Dorothy land in Oz and kill the witch. Only Ennoia was herself the witch, and her life was taken at that dead hour when humanity's resistance is at its lowest. 2:00 a.m.

THE RECEPTIONIST

Unfortunately, the cut wasn't clean. The blade lodged in the back of her neck nearly halfway through. Two guards leveraged their combined weight on the blade, grunting and shoving until the job was complete. Her separated head fell and banged down the steps of the riser. The blindfold came untied. On the last stair, her eyes flew back open. They appeared to look around. I swear Mary Toni could see.

I hope she could not feel.

THE BARBER

Blue blood? In name only. Blood spurted out like water from a fire hose, fast and strong and directional. But it was as red as any of ours.

One of the Whores actually stepped up, and, grabbing Ennoia's blindfold off the ground, saturated the thing in royal blood. "A keepsake!" she crowed. My upper lip curled in disgust. It wasn't the time.

It was never the time.

FERSEN

I strained so hard against the hands holding me back that I tore something in my shoulder. Finally I broke free, but it was too late. She'd been *sundered*. I didn't see her face; I couldn't bring myself to look at it. Nor could I tear my eyes from the jagged stump of her neck, which felt for self-evident reasons like something blasphemous. A scene, a piece, a part of the body that nobody is ever supposed to see. Muscle and bone and a gathering fog at the edges of my vision, a black cloud that my consciousness generated to shroud and protect her seeming nakedness. Her *inside-now-on-the-outside* exposure. As it settled, the gaping maw of her neck grew black, too. Until it became a black hole. The edges as imperfectly scribbled by the Guards as a child rendering a circle with a fat black crayon. Loops and loops of black wax drawn over and over on the same trajectory.

TEZ

A breaking bone. Air rushing out of a punctured balloon. And then the sound when sound stops, since after death there is no sound.

THE NANNY

Because I still believed I was dreaming, I cheered. It seemed a momentous occasion. The fulfillment of a prophecy we hadn't even known about—the fulfillment, therefore, of a destiny. Mary Toni became in that moment and for truly the first time, Ennoia. *The woman clothed with the sun.* Length of days was in her right hand; riches and honors in her left. She did not need a head because she shone with the light of a brilliant star: the brightest star in the galaxy. With her death, it was as though she'd conquered death forever. For Simon and for the Sashes.

For you and for me.

THE CHEF

It was the undoing of a system four decades in the making, revealed to King Louie as a young man, and made manifest in the communal body assembled from us, its organs and limbs. In an isolated system, everything would have worked out. We'd have raised the youngest heir to the age of reason; assumed body and soul beside Simon. Never mind that we'd sacrificed our queen. After all, lots of species practice matriphagy. Mother-eating. Several spiders. At least one kind of earwig. Even some vertebrates. You could say it's nature's way. The ultimate form of altruism. A leading example of purity.

In an isolated system.

But the nature of the church demanded it be public— be disseminated to and integrated with as many Outsiders as possible, for to welcome every soul who should, upon hearing truth spoken aloud, recognize it and seize upon it at once. As such, Simon's Sorrow could not conceal Mary Toni's death for long. Not when she was wanted for media appearances. Not when she was expected in court.

THE RECORD-KEEPER

Just when it seemed like the twenty-four-hour news cycle had forgotten us and moved on to other topics of national importance, an egg escaped. It was most unfortunate. We'd taken so many precautions over the years, trained on what to do in this very situation. And then when it finally happened, we totally fell apart.

Embarrassing.

Of course, we'd set ourselves up to fail from the beginning. With Madame DuBarry missing, the Tigress had assumed control. She sent a spunky little chick without much experience to fish for the next sacrifice. This Whore, she picked an equally spunky, equally petite elf-woman from a coffeeshop around the corner. Rule violation number one: hunting where we sleep and eat. It was too risky. But I guess that's what sparked their interaction. The barista recognized the Whore, or had "seen her around the neighborhood" at least, and a little flirtation naturally developed. Hoping she might get a little private play time with the barista before submitting her to the group, the Whore had dosed her extra. "I just wanted an hour alone with her," she protested when the barista's heart rate dropped dangerously low before we'd even gotten her into the Icebox.

Scared that she'd killed the egg outright (which would have been a grievous sin—killing, as opposed to sacrificing), the Whore had raised her head from the barista's pussy, where seconds before she'd been happily munching away, to notice the unnatural stillness of someone who's not just unconscious, but not breathing, either, and she'd run screaming for help from her room. The Doctor'd had to administer CPR, and the restarting of the barista's heart had shocked her back into a semi-drugged awareness, too. She was more aware, actually, than any of us realized. She watched as we carried her down to the Icebox, meaning she knew the way in. Meaning she knew the way out, too.

We left her there to sleep for a while, until the rest of the Sashes could assemble, and that's when the barista literally stood up and walked out like she was any other Sash, like she knew exactly what she was doing and where she was going and even as though she knew what she'd been brought there for. No doubt she remembered the spunky Whore, even felt how engorged her own clit was where the Whore had been working it for twenty delicious minutes, but we can assume these memories paled in comparison to the racks of whips, needles, hammers, and knives on the walls, because she left and went straight to the cops. On the way out, she even passed the freaking Receptionist, who could have stopped her but obviously didn't.

Like I said, embarrassing.

THE RECEPTIONIST

Yes, I saw the woman, the barista, and no, I didn't stop her. She just walked right past like she knew what she was doing, and she was exiting, not entering, so why would I try and stop her? Why would I greet someone on their way out? I assumed I'd missed her coming in, like maybe she'd made an appointment over my lunch break. Nothing about her marked her as an egg. It's not like eggs look egg-shaped, you know.

She had some interesting piercings. That's about all I remember.

THE CHEF

Whatever she told the cops was enough to convince them to drop by. Part of an "ongoing investigation," they said, since after Mary Toni had missed her court date, and despite receiving more than three thousand tips from do-gooders around the country who swore they'd seen a woman matching her description, the law had yet to catch a lukewarm break. Were we *sure* we didn't know where she was hiding? Did we understand it was illegal to *harbor a fugitive*? They interviewed us, one by one, trying to poke a hole in our story. Most of us didn't have to lie when we said we had no idea where she was. Only a few of us had been present for her death, had participated in her Restoration.

All of us except the Groundskeeper, who was a vegetarian, had helped to destroy the evidence at dinner. But only King Louie and I knew that.

THE RECORD-KEEPER

It's the kind of story they'll make movies about one day. How a woman from Austin, Texas sold her eighth-grade daughter to a cult in exchange for fifteen minutes of fame. And everything that happened after, and everything that's happened since.

THE NANNY

Charlie, having spent his entire life in captivity, was a difficult child—unnaturally anxious to please. The "miracles" he performed, if you want to call them that, were nothing more than a middle child's attempt to get his parents' attention. Some pretty skilled sleight of hand, I reckon, and some pretty strong powers of persuasion, too.

We warned the family who adopted him. Said, "Yes, he's six and handsome as cornsilk, but beware the fruit beneath the husk. It's infected with smut." It wasn't his fault. He didn't ask his mother to abuse him. So we understood that what made Charlie different was also what made him special.

If we just could have made it to his seventh birthday. Charlie, who held the keys to our deliverance. Maybe everything would have been different.

Alas. After King Louie was arrested and the children taken into protective custody, they were farmed out willy-nilly to whoever would have them—anyone, that was, except a former Sash. Without getting to know any of us, CPS wrote us all off in one fell swoop. Said we were "unfit" and would only reinforce the "dangerous ideas" Tez and

Charlie had learned beneath our roof. So away they went. And it seemed for a time that we'd lost the key to heaven.

Six months later, though, there was Charlie in the news. His very reactive adoptive father had caught him sneaking alcohol from the liquor cabinet. His very conservative adoptive mother had walked in on him masturbating. "Is this what they taught you at that church?" the woman had screeched, and scheming, manipulative Charlie said his mother and Savoy had taught him those tricks when they'd made him lie between them in bed. We'd almost gotten away with it—burying that particular story—but you can be sure Baptist Betty raised a stink on-air. After that, you could add child abuse to the list of Simon's Sorrow's public sins.

THE TUTOR

Tez, who'd laid low during the Simon's Sorrow fallout, briefly reappeared on the scene during this time. She appealed to her brother directly, begging him to "remember what had really happened," but Charlie either wouldn't or couldn't change his story. He stuck to his claim that his mother had sexually abused him, even when Tez finally went public to refute the story. "It was another woman in the church," she said in the only interview she gave as a teenager. "Eileen DuBarry." She went on to blame DuBarry for the Diamond Necklace Affair and Marie Antoinette's disappearance, but because Eileen DuBarry herself has never been found, Tez's claims cannot be substantiated.

THE JEWELER'S APPRENTICE

The Jeweler has never turned up, either.

THE PSYCHOLOGIST

Kids who are still kids when they bury their parents—it does something to them. Grief that deep operates at a cellular level. It mutates the body, and so rewritten into the genetic code, gets passed on during the fusing and dividing of the gametes. It *grows*, bigger and more insidious than we give it credit for, and inevitable as loss.

THE GUARD

The sins of his father poisoned Charlie, all right.

FERSEN

Only one person has ever come right out and asked me if I am Charlie's father. The Tailor said he'd "had a feeling" the night he'd seen me and Mary Toni talking backstage after her play; that he'd tried to dismiss it because of the preposterousness of the idea—really, what were the odds that someone who'd known Mary Toni Outside would join Simon's Sorrow? But that he'd started to wonder again the day he watched me pick wildflowers for Sophie's grave. He said I collapsed in a sobbing mess on her tiny mound, and while the death of any child was enough to make even the hardest heart shed a tear, my grief seemed peculiarly profound.

"Busted," I said with a smile, because although my heart was hammering madly at the prospect of being found out, my instinct was to play it off like a joke. Like I knew that he knew there was no way such a thing was possible, so let's all enjoy the absurdity of the proposition, ha ha ha. But the Tailor didn't smile. He kind of frowned. My pulse grew so rapid I feared I would faint. All it ever took was a seed. A single seed of dissension. A rumor! And it would have spread like wildfire through that group, and I would have been up there with my hands bound and my head next to Mary Toni's.

I wish to God it *had* happened that way. Because she wouldn't have been alone. And I wouldn't feel like I'm still alive for the simple sake of succumbing, over a longer and more agonized span of time than she, to the guilt I feel for ever having dared to *want*. Oblivious to the fact that what I took, she gave . . . until she'd given everything.

So I did what all expert negotiators do. I denied, and denied, and denied, and when by my denial my wrongdoing became only more obvious, I turned the tables and threatened him instead. Breathe so much as a word to anyone, I menaced, and I will publish your notebook for the world to read. He knew the one—where King Louie had recorded the Tailor's secret sexual shame. Which worked for a while. But now he's told you his secret, anyway, and I guess I have, too.

At least there's no more hiding.

THE BARBER

I always knew. The locket with the curl of Charlie's hair, that Mary Toni said was meant for his father? Of course I thought she meant King Louie, but later, I saw Fersen carrying it around like a pocket watch, chained to the inside of his vest. I didn't say anything because it wasn't my business. What is it that people say—their hairstylist is like their therapist? If I had a dollar for every secret someone let slip in my chair, well, let's just say I'd have more money than Simon's Sorrow. Especially today.

TEZ

There was a time I thought my visions came from God. That they were, as my father insisted, a gift of the Holy Spirit. But they aren't. When the visions come, whether bidden or unbidden (whether I am touched without consent, or I reach out to touch), they form like ice cubes. Beginning as a watery mass of competing stimuli. Slowly organizing themselves into a highly ordered state. There's a cold, removed clarity there. A kind of preordained neatness that's sterile. Were it of God—were there indeed a God—I think I'd feel Him like a more intentional presence. A warm and organic "shaping" of events as from the clay of possibility, rather than a chain reaction, which while impressive, is but the stuff of science. Something you read about in a textbook, not the Book of Simon.

So, I mourn Mary Toni, the cruel death she didn't deserve. I mourn King Louie, the father he couldn't actually be. I mourn my siblings, killed or screwed up and tainted by a cult that in its heyday did far more harm than good. I mourn the eggs, who were just people with a destiny they didn't see coming. I mourn the Sashes, who wasted their lives for no reason at all.

FERSEN

Life without Mary Toni . . . I mean, I still hardly know what to say. It's like the thing that got me out of bed every morning was sucked into a black hole, and when she went, so did my purpose. I didn't stay with Simon's Sorrow. Since I'd never believed in the prophecy, there was nothing to stay for. The state took my son and Tez, too. None of us were allowed contact with them. I could have fought for custody as Charlie's biological father, but all that admission would have achieved was further grinding Mary Toni's name into the mud, and persuading the rest of the Sashes that King

Louie's suspicion had been founded. As it is, of those who weren't in the chapel that night, at least half still believe she simply ran off; that she'd come to the church an innocent, and finally, in adulthood, found the ovaries to make off with what innocence remained. It's a fraction of those Sashes, plus several who believe in her guilt, who still carry a torch for the children. Who insist that, no matter the sins of the mother, the children are still the heirs, and at the appointed time, Simon will reveal Himself to them.

I no longer think she believed it, either. It was the note she left me, tucked among the petals of the carnations in her room. I told the Maid not to clean it—that we should leave the room as-was in memory of the queen—and that included the vase of white carnations on the window sill. I used to go in there, in the days and weeks following her death, wanting, I guess, to feel closer to her. When the water in the vase dried up and the carnations withered and turned brown, the note hidden there was revealed. *F— Our souls touch at all points. —M.* I kept the note, and I did not re-enter her room again.

She was a model for all women everywhere, yet we locked her up and saved her for ourselves. I will keep October 16 as a day of mourning for the rest of my life.

MERCY

The Lawyer told me King Louie descended into madness on death row. His fellow inmates wanted nothing to do with him. Before he was sentenced, when he was still in regular prison? They said a guard tried to beat him, and his billy club passed right through his body, like King Louie was made of smoke.

Maybe he was always mad. But at least he kept the presence of mind *not* to take the rest of us down with him.

At our last meeting, he gave me his bloodstone. Said, "I only part with this ring on my life."

Through him, I brought death to so many. But when life became more important, I couldn't protect him from it.

THE CHEF

I hereby swear that my testimony is true, and to the best of my knowledge, complete.

THE TAILOR

I hereby swear that my testimony is true, and to the best of my knowledge, complete.

THE MAID

I hereby swear that my testimony is true, and to the best of my knowledge, complete.

THE LAWYER

The Sashes all took plea bargains—a confession in exchange for a pardon.

Their sworn statements convicted King Louie. Mercy disappeared before he could be arraigned.

There's still an active reward being offered for information leading to his discovery and arrest. I wish I knew where he was. I could use that money myself.

MERCY

Remember the terms of our agreement: I give you this interview, and you won't give me up. You were lucky to find me the first time. You won't find me again.

THE RECORD-KEEPER

For years, Simon's Sorrow evaded paying taxes. Under the scrutiny of the national spotlight, however, it was determined that we owed millions in back taxes. To satisfy the debt, we sold everything. Furniture consoles with marble tops. Stools covered in damask, silk, and velvet. Glassware, china, and all of the Jeweler's trinkets.

The last thing to go were the clocks. Time now stands still at the deserted church.

THE GROUNDSKEEPER

Sometimes I set out walking across the university campus, no explicit destination in mind, I tell myself—just to "take in the evening." Invariably, but without consciously meaning to, I end up roaming west, toward Guadalupe and the Drag, where the broken stained-glass windows of Simon's Sorrow stare as blankly as the holes once did before the windows went in. When that happens—when I suddenly realize where I am—I take pains never to look at the building directly. The memory alone of the gardens . . . what they looked like then; what they must look like now . . . causes my chest to tighten. Makes it hard to breathe. Instead I watch the birds on the wire. Try to remember what it felt like to have a purpose, a family, a home. And when a bird takes off against the background of a crimson sky, my heart flies with it.

ACKNOWLEDGMENTS

At Christmas 2017, my mother-in-law gifted me a 23andMe DNA analysis kit. Per the kit's instructions, I dribbled some spit into a little plastic tube, mailed the tube to a lab somewhere, and a few weeks later I got back a report that detailed my genetic makeup. Buried among the lab's extensive findings was this inconspicuous one-liner: "You shared a common ancestor with Marie Antoinette."

Now, I'd always been a wee bit obsessed with the French queen's story, so to find out we were "sort of related" made my year. After sharing the news with my generous mother-in-law, she then sent me Antonia Fraser's *Marie Antoinette: The Journey*, a biography I promptly devoured. I went on to watch a bunch of documentaries about Marie Antoinette and listen to every podcast I could find, including *Queens Podcast* and *The History Chicks*, both of which have fantastic Marie Antoinette episodes. From these seeds, *Mother-Eating* was born. So, thank you, Pam, for that thoughtful gift!

Thanks are likewise owed to Kelli White, Chris Panatier, and Sara Kocek for their incisive early takes on the manuscript. Kelli offers freelance book editing at https://www.linkedin.com/in/kelliwhite/; check her out. The success of Chris's latest books, *Shitshow* and *The Redemption of Morgan Bright* explains why I wanted his feedback on my book. Sara owns Yellow Bird Editors in Austin, and I can't recommend her services highly enough.

Thomas Jung refined the archery scene. Most of the torture device details came from the Museum of Torture in Volterra, Italy. Visit it for a stomach-churning experience!

Max Booth III made many of the Sashes' arcs much better, and Lori Michelle Booth built the beautiful layout you're reading now. Thanks, Ghoulish Books!

Finally, a thank you from the bottom of my heart to Brandon, who supported this project every step of the way. Thanks for understanding why a writer needs to retreat from the rest of the world sometimes. After extended periods of solo writing and editing, I'm so lucky to have you to come home to.

ABOUT THE AUTHOR

Photo credit: Alicia Leigh Photography

Jess Hagemann's recent work has appeared or is forthcoming in *Beneath the Bluebonnets: Tales of Terror from Texas Women, Three Seasons of Winter,* and *Last Girls Club,* among others. Her debut novel *Headcheese* (2018) won an IPPY Award in Horror. Her sophomore novel *Mother-Eating* (2025) joins Marie Antoinette and cults. Jess received her MFA from the Jack Kerouac School, and has been awarded a teaching fellowship at McNeese State University as well as a writing residency at Dear Butte. She lives in Austin.

More at www.jesshagemann.com.

SCAN TO REVIEW THIS BOOK!

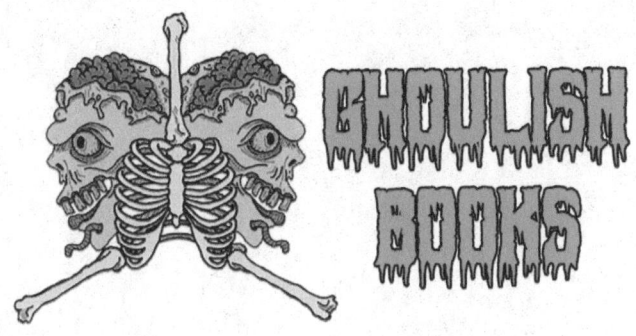

Patreon:
www.patreon.com/ghoulishbooks

Website:
www.Ghoulish.rip

Facebook:
www.facebook.com/GhoulishBooks

Twitter:
@GhoulishBooks

Instagram:
@GhoulishBookstore

Linktree:
linktr.ee/ghoulishbooks